AN EMBER IN THE ASHES

SABAA TAHIR

HARPER
Voyager

HarperVoyager
An imprint of HarperCollinsPublishers
1 London Bridge Street
London SE1 9GF

www.harpervoyagerbooks.co.uk

This paperback edition 2016
1

First published in Great Britain by HarperVoyager 2015

Published by arrangement with Razorbill, a member of Penguin Group (USA) LLC

Maps by Jonathan Roberts

Sabaa Tahir asserts the moral right to
be identified as the author of this work

A catalogue record for this book
is available from the British Library

UK ISBN: 978-0-00-810842-7
OM ISBN: 978-0-00-816443-0

Set in Electra LT Std by Palimpsest Book Production Limited,
Falkirk, Stirlingshire

Printed and bound in Great Britain by
Clays Ltd, St Ives plc

MIX
Paper from
responsible sources
FSC
www.fsc.org
FSC® C007454

For Kashi,
who taught me that my spirit
is stronger than my fear

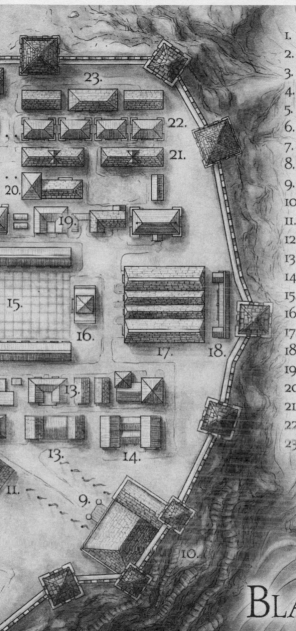

1. Entry Gate
2. Amphitheatre
3. Armoury
4. Stables
5. Main Training Field
6. Training Field 2
7. Training Field 3
8. 2nd Armoury
9. Commandant's House
10. Cliff Path
11. Centurion Quarters
12. Infirmary
13. Classrooms
14. Storage
15. Main Courtyard
16. Bell Tower/Drum Tower
17. Mess Hall
18. Slaves' Quarters
19. Training Rooms
20. Senior Skull Barracks
21. Skull Barracks
22. Cadet Barracks
23. Ycarling Barracks

BLACKCLIFF
ACADEMY

PART ONE

THE RAID

CHAPTER ONE

Laia

My big brother reaches home in the dark hours before dawn, when even ghosts take their rest. He smells of steel and coal and forge. He smells of the enemy.

He folds his scarecrow body through the window, bare feet silent on the rushes. A hot desert wind blows in after him, rustling the limp curtains. His sketchbook falls to the floor, and he nudges it under his bunk with a quick foot, as if it's a snake.

Where have you been, Darin? In my head, I have the courage to ask the question, and Darin trusts me enough to answer. *Why do you keep disappearing? Why, when Pop and Nan need you? When I need you?*

Every night for almost two years, I've wanted to ask. Every night, I've lacked the courage. I have one sibling left. I don't want him to shut me out like he has everyone else.

But tonight's different. I know what's in his sketchbook. I know what it means.

'You shouldn't be awake.' Darin's whisper jolts me from my thoughts. He has a cat's sense for traps – he got it from our mother.

3

I sit up on the bunk as he lights the lamp. No use pretending to be asleep.

'It's past curfew, and three patrols have gone by. I was worried.'

'I can avoid the soldiers, Laia. Lots of practice.' He rests his chin on my bunk and smiles Mother's sweet, crooked smile. A familiar look – the one he gives me if I wake from a nightmare or we run out of grain. *Everything will be fine*, the look says.

He picks up the book on my bed. '*Gather in the Night*,' he reads the title. 'Spooky. What's it about?'

'I just started it. It's about a jinn—' I stop. Clever. Very clever. He likes hearing stories as much as I like telling them. 'Forget that. Where were you? Pop had a dozen patients this morning.'

And I filled in for you because he can't do so much alone. Which left Nan to bottle the trader's jams by herself. Except she didn't finish. Now the trader won't pay us, and we'll starve this winter, and why in the skies don't you care?

I say these things in my head. The smile's already dropped off Darin's face.

'I'm not cut out for healing,' he says. 'Pop knows that.'

I want to back down, but I think of Pop's slumped shoulders this morning. I think of the sketchbook.

'Pop and Nan depend on you. At least talk to them. It's been months.'

I wait for him to tell me that I don't understand. That I should leave him be. But he just shakes his head, drops down into his bunk, and closes his eyes like he can't be bothered to reply.

'I saw your drawings.' The words tumble out in a rush, and Darin's up in an instant, his face stony. 'I wasn't spying,' I say. 'One of the pages was loose. I found it when I changed the rushes this morning.'

'Did you tell Nan and Pop? Did they see?'

'No, but—'

'Laia, listen.' Ten hells, I don't want to hear this. I don't want to hear his excuses. 'What you saw is dangerous,' he says. 'You can't tell anyone about it. Not ever. It's not just my life at risk. There are others—'

'Are you working for the Empire, Darin? Are you working for the Martials?'

He is silent. I think I see the answer in his eyes, and I feel ill. My brother is a traitor to his own people? My brother is siding with the Empire?

If he hoarded grain, or sold books, or taught children to read, I'd understand. I'd be proud of him for doing the things I'm not brave enough to do. The Empire raids, jails, and kills for such 'crimes', but teaching a six-year old her letters isn't evil – not in the minds of my people, the Scholar people.

But what Darin has done is sick. It's a betrayal.

'The Empire killed our parents,' I whisper. 'Our sister.'

I want to shout at him, but I choke on the words. The Martials conquered Scholar lands five hundred years ago, and since then, they've done nothing but oppress and enslave us. Once, the Scholar Empire was home to the finest universities and libraries in the world. Now, most of our people can't tell a school from an armoury.

'How could you side with the Martials? How, Darin?'

'It's not what you think, Laia. I'll explain everything, but—'

He pauses suddenly, his hand jerking up to silence me when I ask for the promised explanation. He cocks his head towards the window.

Through the thin walls, I hear Pop's snores, Nan shifting in her sleep, a mourning dove's croon. Familiar sounds. Home sounds.

Darin hears something else. The blood drains from his face, and dread flashes in his eyes. 'Laia,' he says. 'Raid.'

'But if you work for the Empire—' *Then why are the soldiers raiding us?*

'I'm not working for them.' He sounds calm. Calmer than I feel. 'Hide the sketchbook. That's what they want. That's what they're here for.'

Then he's out the door, and I'm alone. My bare legs move like cold molasses, my hands like wooden blocks. *Hurry, Laia!*

Usually, the Empire raids in the heat of the day. The soldiers want Scholar mothers and children to watch. They want fathers and brothers to see another man's family enslaved. As bad as those raids are, the night raids are worse. The night raids are for when the Empire doesn't want witnesses.

I wonder if this is real. If it's a nightmare. *It's real, Laia. Move.*

I drop the sketchbook out the window into a hedge. It's a poor hiding place, but I have no time. Nan hobbles into my room. Her hands, so steady when she stirs vats of jam or braids my hair, flutter like frantic birds, desperate for me to move faster.

She pulls me into the hallway. Darin stands with Pop at the back door. My grandfather's white hair is scattered as a haystack and his clothes are wrinkled, but there's no sleep in the deep grooves of his face. He murmurs something to my brother, then hands him Nan's largest kitchen knife. I don't know why he bothers. Against the Serric steel of a Martial blade, the knife will only shatter.

'You and Darin leave through the backyard,' Nan says, her eyes darting from window to window. 'They haven't surrounded the house yet.'

No. No. No. 'Nan,' I breathe her name, stumbling when she pushes me towards Pop.

Sabaa Tahir

'Hide in the east end of the Quarter—' Her sentence ends in a choke, her eyes on the front window. Through the ragged curtains, I catch a flash of a liquid silver face. My stomach clenches.

'A Mask,' Nan says. 'They've brought a Mask. Go, Laia. Before he gets inside.'

'What about you? What about Pop?'

'We'll hold them off.' Pop shoves me gently out the door. 'Keep your secrets close, love. Listen to Darin. He'll take care of you. Go.'

Darin's lean shadow falls over me, and he grabs my hand as the door closes behind us. He slouches to blend into the warm night, moving silently across the loose sand of the backyard with a confidence I wish I felt. Although I am seventeen and old enough to control my fear, I grip his hand like it's the only solid thing in this world.

I'm not working for them, Darin said. Then whom is he working for? Somehow, he got close enough to the forges of Serra to draw, in detail, the creation process of the Empire's most precious asset: the unbreakable, curved scims that can cut through three men at once.

Half a millennium ago, the Scholars crumbled beneath the Martial invasion because our blades broke against their superior steel. Since then, we have learned nothing of steelcraft. The Martials hoard their secrets the way a miser hoards gold. Anyone caught near our city's forges without good reason – Scholar or Martial – risks execution.

If Darin isn't with the Empire, how did he get near Serra's forges? How did the Martials find out about his sketchbook?

On the other side of the house, a fist pounds on the front door. Boots shuffle, steel clinks. I look around wildly, expecting to see

7

the silver armour and red capes of Empire legionnaires, but the backyard is still. The fresh night air does nothing to stop the sweat rolling down my neck. Distantly, I hear the thud of drums from Blackcliff, the Mask training school. The sound sharpens my fear into a hard point stabbing at my centre. The Empire doesn't send those silver-faced monsters on just any raid.

The pounding on the door sounds again.

'In the name of the Empire,' an irritated voice says, 'I demand you open this door.'

As one, Darin and I freeze.

'Doesn't sound like a Mask,' Darin whispers. Masks speak softly with words that cut through you like a scim. In the time it would take a legionnaire to knock and issue an order, a Mask would already be in the house, weapons slicing through anyone in his way.

Darin meets my eyes, and I know we're both thinking the same thing. If the Mask isn't with the rest of the soldiers at the front door, then where is he?

'Don't be afraid, Laia,' Darin says. 'I won't let anything happen to you.'

I want to believe him, but my fear is a tide tugging at my ankles, pulling me under. I think of the couple that lived next door: raided, imprisoned, and sold into slavery three weeks ago. *Book smugglers*, the Martials said. Five days after that, one of Pop's oldest patients, a ninety-three-year-old man who could barely walk, was executed in his own home, his throat slit from ear to ear. *Resistance collaborator.*

What will the soldiers do to Nan and Pop? Jail them? Enslave them?

Kill them?

We reach the back gate. Darin stands on his toes to unhook

the latch when a scrape in the alley beyond stops him short. A breeze sighs past, sending a cloud of dust into the air.

Darin pushes me behind him. His knuckles are white around the knife handle as the gate swings open with a moan. A finger of terror draws a trail up my spine. I peer over my brother's shoulder into the alley.

There is nothing out there but the quiet shifting of sand. Nothing but the occasional gust of wind and the shuttered windows of our sleeping neighbours.

I sigh in relief and step around Darin.

That's when the Mask emerges from the darkness and walks through the gate.

CHAPTER TWO

Elias

The deserter will be dead before dawn.

His tracks zigzag like a struck deer's in the dust of Serra's catacombs. The tunnels have done him in. The hot air is too heavy down here, the smells of death and rot too close.

The tracks are more than an hour old by the time I see them. The guards have his scent now, poor bastard. If he's lucky, he'll die in the chase. If not . . .

Don't think about it. Hide the backpack. Get out of here.

Skulls crunch as I shove a pack loaded with food and water into a wall crypt. Helene would give me hell if she could see how I'm treating the dead. But then, if Helene finds out why I'm down here in the first place, desecration will be the least of her complaints.

She won't find out. Not until it's too late. Guilt pricks at me, but I shove it away. Helene's the strongest person I know. She'll be fine without me.

For what feels like the hundredth time, I look over my shoulder. The tunnel is quiet. The deserter led the soldiers in the opposite

10

direction. But safety's an illusion I know never to trust. I work quickly, piling bones back in front of the crypt to cover my trail, my senses primed for anything out of the ordinary.

One more day of this. One more day of paranoia and hiding and lying. One day until graduation. Then I'll be free.

As I rearrange the crypt's skulls, the hot air shifts like a bear waking from hibernation. The smells of grass and snow cut through the fetid breath of the tunnel. Two seconds is all I have to step away from the crypt and kneel, examining the ground as if there might be tracks here. Then she is at my back.

'Elias? What are you doing down here?'

'Didn't you hear? There's a deserter loose.' I keep my attention fixed on the dusty floor. Beneath the silver mask that covers me from forehead to jaw, my face should be unreadable. But Helene Aquilla and I have been together nearly every day of the fourteen years we've been training at Blackcliff Military Academy; she can probably hear me thinking.

She comes around me silently, and I look up into her eyes, as blue and pale as the warm waters of the southern islands. My mask sits atop my face, separate and foreign, hiding my features as well as my emotions. But Hel's mask clings to her like a silvery second skin, and I can see the slight furrow in her brow as she looks down at me. *Relax, Elias*, I tell myself. *You're just looking for a deserter.*

'He didn't come this way,' Hel says. She runs a hand over her hair, braided, as always, into a tight, silver-blonde crown. 'Dex took an auxiliary company off the north watchtower and into the East Branch tunnel. You think they'll catch him?'

Aux soldiers, though not as highly trained as legionnaires and nothing compared to Masks, are still merciless hunters. 'Of course they'll catch him.' I fail to keep the bitterness out of my voice, and Helene gives me a hard look. 'The cowardly scum,' I add. 'Anyway, why are you awake? You weren't on watch this morning.' *I made sure of it.*

'Those bleeding drums.' Helene looks around the tunnel. 'Woke everyone up.'

The drums. Of course. *Deserter,* they'd thundered in the middle of the graveyard watch. *All active units to the walls.* Helene must have decided to join the hunt. Dex, my lieutenant, would have told her which direction I'd gone. He'd have thought nothing of it.

'I thought the deserter might have come this way.' I turn from my hidden pack to look down another tunnel. 'Guess I was wrong. I should catch up to Dex.'

'Much as I hate to admit it, you're not usually wrong.' Helene cocks her head and smiles at me. I feel that guilt again, wrenching as a fist to the gut. She'll be furious when she learns what I've done. She'll never forgive me. *Doesn't matter. You've decided. Can't turn back now.*

Hel traces the dust on the ground with a fair, practised hand. 'I've never even seen this tunnel before.'

A drop of sweat crawls down my neck. I ignore it.

'It's hot, and it reeks,' I say. 'Like everything else down here.' *Come on,* I want to add. But doing so would be like tattooing 'I am up to no good' on my forehead. I keep quiet and lean against the catacomb wall, arms crossed.

The field of battle is my temple. I mentally chant a saying my grandfather taught me the day he met me, when I was six. He insists it sharpens the mind the way a whetstone sharpens a blade. *The swordpoint is my priest. The dance of death is my prayer. The killing blow is my release.*

Helene peers at my blurred tracks, following them, somehow,

12

to the crypt where I stowed my pack, to the skulls piled there. She's suspicious, and the air between us is suddenly tense.

Damn it.

I need to distract her. As she looks between me and the crypt, I run my gaze lazily down her body. She stands two inches shy of six feet – a half-foot shorter than me. She's the only female student at Blackcliff; in the black, close-fitting fatigues all students wear, her strong, slender form has always drawn admiring glances. Just not mine. We've been friends too long for that.

Come on, notice. Notice me leering and get mad about it.

When I meet her eyes, brazen as a sailor fresh into port, she opens her mouth, as if to rip into me. Then she looks back at the crypt.

If she sees the pack and guesses what I'm up to, I'm done for. She might hate doing it, but Empire law would demand she report me, and Helene's never broken a law in her life.

'Elias—'

I prepare my lie. *Just wanted to get away for a couple of days, Hel. Needed some time to think. Didn't want to worry you.*

BOOM-BOOM-boom-BOOM.

The drums.

Without thought, I translate the disparate beats into the message they are meant to convey. *Deserter caught. All students report to central courtyard immediately.*

My stomach sinks. Some naïve part of me hoped the deserter would at least make it out of the city. 'That didn't take long,' I say. 'We should go.'

I make for the main tunnel. Helene follows, as I knew she would. She would stab herself in the eye before she disobeyed a direct order. Helene is a true Martial, more loyal to the Empire than to her own mother. Like any good Mask-in-training, she takes Blackcliff's motto to heart: *Duty first, unto death.*

I wonder what she would say if she knew what I'd really been doing in the tunnels.

I wonder how she'd feel about my hatred for the Empire.

I wonder what she would do if she found out her best friend is planning to desert.

CHAPTER THREE

Laia

The Mask saunters through the gate, big hands loose at his sides. The strange metal of his namesake clings to him from forehead to jaw like silver paint, revealing every feature of his face, from the thin eyebrows to the hard angles of his cheekbones. His copper-plated armour moulds to his muscles, emphasizing the power in his body.

A passing wind billows his black cape, and he looks around the backyard like he's arrived at a garden party. His pale eyes find me, slide up my form, and settle on my face with a reptile's flat regard.

'Aren't you a pretty one,' he says.

I yank at the ragged hem of my shift, wishing desperately for the shapeless, ankle-length skirt I wear during the day. The Mask doesn't even twitch. Nothing in his face tells me what he's thinking. But I can guess.

Darin steps in front of me and glances at the fence, as if gauging the time it will take to reach it.

'I'm alone, boy.' The Mask addresses Darin with all the emotion of a corpse. 'The rest of the men are in your house. You can run

15

if you like.' He moves away from the gate. 'But I insist you leave the girl.'

Darin raises the knife.

'Chivalrous of you,' the Mask says.

Then he strikes, a flash of copper and silver lightning out of an empty sky. In the time it takes me to gasp, the Mask has shoved my brother's face into the sandy ground and pinned his writhing body with a knee. Nan's knife falls to the dirt.

A scream erupts from me, lonely in the still summer night. Seconds later, a scimpoint pricks my throat. I didn't even see the Mask draw the weapon.

'Quiet,' he says. 'Arms up. Now get inside.'

The Mask uses one hand to yank Darin up by the neck and the other to prod me on with his scim. My brother limps, face bloodied, eyes dazed. When he struggles, a fish on a hook, the Mask tightens his grip.

The back door of the house opens, and a red-caped legionnaire comes out.

'The house is secure, Commander.'

The Mask shoves Darin at the soldier. 'Bind him up. He's strong.'

Then he grabs me by the hair, twisting until I cry out.

'Mmm.' He bends his head to my ear, and I cringe, my terror caught in my throat. 'I've always loved dark-haired girls.'

I wonder if he has a sister, a wife, a woman. But it wouldn't matter if he did. To him, I'm not someone's family. I'm just a thing to be subdued, used, and discarded. The Mask drags me down the hallway to the front room as casually as a hunter drags his kill. *Fight*, I tell myself. *Fight*. But as if he senses my pathetic attempts at bravery, his hand squeezes, and pain lances through my skull. I sag and let him pull me along.

Legionnaires stand shoulder-to-shoulder in the front room amid upturned furniture and broken bottles of jam. *Trader won't get anything now.* So many days spent over steaming kettles, my hair and skin smelling of apricot and cinnamon. So many jars, steamed and dried, filled and sealed. Useless. All useless.

The lamps are lit, and Nan and Pop kneel in the middle of the floor, their hands bound behind their backs. The soldier holding Darin shoves him to the ground beside them.

'Shall I tie up the girl, sir?' Another soldier fingers the rope at his belt, but the Mask leaves me between two burly legionnaires.

'She's not going to cause any trouble.' He stabs at me with those eyes. 'Are you?' I shake my head and shrink back, hating myself for being such a coward. I reach for my mother's tarnished armlet, wrapped around my bicep, and touch the familiar pattern for strength. I find none. Mother would have fought. She'd have died rather than face this humiliation. But I can't make myself move. My fear has ensnared me.

A legionnaire enters the room, his face more than a little nervous. 'It's not here, Commander.'

The Mask looks down at my brother. 'Where's the sketchbook?'

Darin stares straight ahead, silent. His breath is low and steady, and he doesn't seem dazed anymore. In fact, he's almost composed.

The Mask gestures, a small movement. One of the legionnaires lifts Nan by her neck and slams her frail body against a wall. Nan bites her lip, her eyes sparking blue. Darin tries to rise, but another soldier forces him down.

The Mask scoops up a shard of glass from one of the broken jars. His tongue flickers out like a snake's as he tastes the jam.

'Shame it's all gone to waste.' He caresses Nan's face with the edge of the shard. 'You must have been beautiful once. Such eyes.' He turns to Darin. 'Shall I carve them out of her?'

'It's outside the small bedroom window. In the hedge.' I can't manage more than a whisper, but the soldiers hear. The Mask nods, and one of the legionnaires disappears into the hallway. Darin doesn't look at me, but I feel his dismay. *Why did you tell me to hide it,* I want to cry out. *Why did you bring the cursed thing home?*

The legionnaire returns with the book. For unending seconds, the only sound in the room is the rustling of pages as the Mask flips through the sketches. If the rest of the book is anything like the page I found, I know what the Mask will see: Martial knives, swords, scabbards, forges, formulas, instructions – things no Scholar should know of, let alone re-create on paper.

'How did you get into the Weapons Quarter, boy?' The Mask looks up from the book. 'Has the Resistance been bribing some Plebeian drudge to sneak you in?'

I stifle a sob. Half of me is relieved Darin's no traitor. The other half wants to rage at him for being such a fool. Association with the Scholars' Resistance carries a death sentence.

'I got myself in,' my brother says. 'The Resistance had nothing to do with it.'

'You were seen entering the catacombs last night after curfew' – the Mask almost sounds bored – 'in the company of known Scholar rebels.'

'Last night, he was home well before curfew,' Pop speaks up, and it is strange to hear my grandfather lie. But it makes no difference. The Mask's eyes are for my brother alone. The man doesn't blink as he reads Darin's face the way I'd read a book.

'Those rebels were taken into custody today,' the Mask says. 'One of them gave up your name before he died. What were you doing with them?'

'They followed me.' Darin sounds so calm. Like he's done this before. Like he's not afraid at all. 'I'd never met them before.'

'And yet they knew of your book here. Told me all about it. How did they learn of it? What did they want from you?'

'I don't know.'

The Mask presses the shard of glass deep into the soft skin below Nan's eye, and her nostrils flare. A trickle of blood traces a wrinkle down her face.

Darin draws a sharp breath, the only sign of strain. 'They asked for my sketchbook,' he says. 'I said no. I swear it.'

'And their hideout?'

'I didn't see. They blindfolded me. We were in the catacombs.'

'*Where* in the catacombs?'

'I didn't see. They blindfolded me.'

The Mask eyes my brother for a long moment. I don't know how Darin can remain unruffled beneath that gaze.

'You're prepared for this.' The smallest bit of surprise creeps into the Mask's voice. 'Straight back. Deep breathing. Same answers to different questions. Who trained you, boy?'

When Darin doesn't answer, the Mask shrugs. 'A few weeks in prison will loosen your tongue.' Nan and I exchange a frightened glance. If Darin ends up in a Martial prison, we'll never see him again. He'll spend weeks in interrogation, and after that they'll either sell him as a slave or kill him.

'He's just a boy,' Pop speaks slowly, as if to an angry patient. 'Please—'

Steel flashes, and Pop drops like a stone. The Mask moves so swiftly that I don't understand what he has done. Not until Nan rushes forward. Not until she lets out a shrill keen, a shaft of pure pain that brings me to my knees.

Pop. Skies, not Pop. A dozen vows sear themselves into my mind. *I'll never disobey again, I'll never do anything wrong, I'll never complain about my work, if only Pop lives.*

But Nan tears her hair and screams, and if Pop was alive, he'd never let her go on like that. He wouldn't have been able to bear it. Darin's calm is sheared away as if by a scythe, his face blanched with a horror I feel down to my bones.

Nan stumbles to her feet and takes one tottering step towards the Mask. He reaches out to her, as if to put his hand on her shoulder. The last thing I see in my grandmother's eyes is terror. Then the Mask's gauntleted wrist flashes once, leaving a thin red line across Nan's throat, a line that grows wider and redder as she falls.

Her body hits the floor with a thud, her eyes still open and shining with tears as blood pours from her neck and into the rug we knotted together last winter.

'Sir,' one of the legionnaires says. 'An hour until dawn.'

'Get the boy out of here.' The Mask doesn't give Nan a second glance. 'And burn this place down.'

He turns to me then, and I wish I could fade like a shadow into the wall behind me. I wish for it harder than I've ever wished for anything, knowing all the while how foolish it is. The soldiers flanking me grin at each other as the Mask takes a slow step in my direction. He holds my gaze as if he can smell my fear, a cobra enthralling its prey.

No, please, no. Disappear, I want to disappear.

The Mask blinks, some foreign emotion flickering across his eyes – surprise or shock, I can't tell. It doesn't matter. Because in that moment, Darin leaps up from the floor. While I cowered, he loosened his bindings. His hands stretch out like claws as he lunges for the Mask's throat. His rage lends him a lion's strength, and for a second he is every inch our mother, honey hair glowing, eyes blazing, mouth twisted in a feral snarl.

The Mask backs into the blood pooled near Nan's head, and Darin is on him, knocking him to the ground, raining down blows.

The legionnaires stand frozen in disbelief and then come to their senses, surging forward, shouting and swearing. Darin pulls a dagger free from the Mask's belt before the legionnaires tackle him.

'Laia!' my brother shouts. 'Run—'

Don't run, Laia. Help him. Fight.

But I think of the Mask's cold regard, of the violence in his eyes. *I've always loved dark-haired girls.* He will rape me. Then he will kill me.

I shudder and back into the hallway. No one stops me. No one notices.

'Laia!' Darin cries out, sounding like I've never heard him. Frantic. Trapped. He told me to run, but if I screamed like that, he would come. He would never leave me. I stop.

Help him, Laia, a voice orders in my head. *Move.*

And another voice, more insistent, more powerful.

You can't save him. Do what he says. Run.

Flame flickers at the edge of my vision, and I smell smoke. One of the legionnaires has started torching the house. In minutes, fire will consume it.

'Bind him properly this time and get him into an interrogation cell.' The Mask removes himself from the fray, rubbing his jaw. When he sees me backing down the hallway, he goes strangely still. Reluctantly, I meet his eyes, and he tilts his head.

'Run, little girl,' he says.

My brother is still fighting, and his screams slice right through me. I know then that I will hear them over and over again, echoing in every hour of every day until I am dead or I make it right. I know it.

And still, I run.

*   *   *

The cramped streets and dusty markets of the Scholars' Quarter blur past me like the landscape of a nightmare. With each step, part of my brain shouts at me to turn around, to go back, to help Darin. With each step, it becomes less likely, until it isn't a possibility at all, until the only word I can think is *run*.

The soldiers come after me, but I've grown up among the squat, mud-brick houses of the Quarter, and I lose my pursuers quickly.

Dawn breaks, and my panicked run turns to a stumble as I wander from alley to alley. Where do I go? What do I do? I need a plan, but I don't know where to start. Who can offer me help or comfort? My neighbours will turn me away, fearing for their own lives. My family is dead or imprisoned. My best friend, Zara, disappeared in a raid last year, and my other friends have their own troubles.

I'm alone.

As the sun rises, I find myself in an empty building deep in the oldest part of the Quarter. The gutted structure crouches like a wounded animal amid a labyrinth of crumbling dwellings. The stench of refuse taints the air.

I huddle in the corner of the room. My hair has slipped free of its braid and lays in hopeless tangles. The red stitches along the hem of my shift are ripped, the bright yarn limp. Nan sewed those hems for my seventeenth year-fall, to brighten up my otherwise drab clothing. It was one of the few gifts she could afford.

Now she's dead. Like Pop. Like my parents and sister, long ago.

And Darin. Taken. Dragged to an interrogation cell where the Martials will do who-knows-what to him.

Life is made of so many moments that mean nothing. Then one day, a single moment comes along to define every second that comes after. The moment Darin called out – that was such a moment. It was a test of courage, of strength. And I failed it.

Laia! Run!

Why did I listen to him? I should have stayed. I should have done something. I moan and grasp my head. I keep hearing him. Where is he now? Have they begun the interrogation? He'll wonder what happened to me. He'll wonder how his sister could have left him.

A flicker of furtive movement in the shadows catches my attention, and the hair on my nape rises. A rat? A crow? The shadows shift, and within them, two malevolent eyes flash. More sets of eyes join the first, baleful and slitted.

Hallucinations, I hear Pop in my head, making a diagnosis. *A symptom of shock.*

Hallucinations or not, the shadows look real. Their eyes glow with the fire of miniature suns, and they circle me like hyenas, growing bolder with each pass.

'We *saw,*' they hiss. 'We *know your weakness. He'll die because of you.*'

'No,' I whisper. But they are right, these shadows. I left Darin. I abandoned him. The fact that he told me to go doesn't matter. How could I have been so cowardly?

I grasp my mother's armlet, but touching it makes me feel worse. Mother would have outfoxed the Mask. Somehow, she'd have saved Darin and Nan and Pop.

Even Nan was braver than me. Nan, with her frail body and burning eyes. Her backbone of steel. Mother inherited Nan's fire, and after her, Darin.

But not me.

Run, little girl.

The shadows inch closer, and I close my eyes against them, hoping they'll disappear. I grasp at the thoughts ricocheting through my mind, trying to corral them.

Distantly, I hear shouts and the thud of boots. If the soldiers are still looking for me, I'm not safe here.

Maybe I should let them find me and do what they will. I abandoned my blood. I deserve punishment.

But the same instinct that urged me to escape the Mask in the first place drives me to my feet. I head into the streets, losing myself in the thickening morning crowds. A few of my fellow Scholars look twice at me, some with wariness, others with sympathy. But most don't look at all. It makes me wonder how many times I walked right past someone in these streets who was running, someone who had just had their whole world ripped from them.

I stop to rest in an alley slick with sewage. Thick black smoke curls up from the other side of the Quarter, paling as it rises into the hot sky. My home, burning. Nan's jams, Pop's medicines, Darin's drawings, my books, gone. Everything I am. Gone.

Not everything, Laia. Not Darin.

A grate squats in the centre of the alley, just a few feet away from me. Like all grates in the Quarter, it leads down into the Serra's catacombs: home to skeletons, ghosts, rats, thieves . . . and possibly the Scholars' Resistance.

Had Darin been spying for them? Had the Resistance got him into the Weapons Quarter? Despite what my brother told the Mask, it's the only answer that makes sense. Rumour has it that the Resistance fighters have been getting bolder, recruiting not just Scholars, but Mariners, from the free country of Marinn, to the north, and Tribesmen, whose desert-territory is an Empire protectorate.

Pop and Nan never spoke of the Resistance in front of me. But late at night, I heard them murmuring of how the rebels freed Scholar prisoners while striking out at the Martials. Of how fighters raided the caravans of the Martial merchant class, the Mercators, and assassinated members of their upper class, the Illustrians. Only the rebels stand up to the Martials. Elusive as they are, they are the only weapon the Scholars have. If anyone can get near the forges, it's them.

The Resistance, I realize, might help me. My home was raided and burned to the ground, my family killed because two of the rebels gave Darin's name to the Empire. If I can find the Resistance and explain what happened, maybe they can help me break Darin free from prison – not just because they owe me, but because they live by *Izzat*, a code of honour as old as the Scholar people. The rebel leaders are the best of the Scholars, the bravest. My parents taught me that before the Empire killed them. If I ask for aid, the Resistance won't turn me away.

I step towards the grate.

I've never been in Serra's catacombs. They snake beneath the entire city, hundreds of miles of tunnels and caverns, some packed with centuries' worth of bones. No one uses the crypts for burial anymore, and even the Empire hasn't mapped out the catacombs entirely. If the Empire, with all its might, can't hunt out the rebels, then how will I find them?

You won't stop until you do. I lift the grate and stare into the black hole below. I have to go down there. I have to find the Resistance. Because if I don't, my brother doesn't stand a chance. If I don't find the fighters and get them to help, I'll never see Darin again.

CHAPTER FOUR

Elias

By the time Helene and I reach Blackcliff's belltower, nearly all of the school's three thousand students have formed up. Dawn's an hour away, but I don't see a single sleepy eye. Instead, an eager buzz runs through the crowd. The last time someone deserted, the courtyard was covered in frost.

Every student knows what's coming. I clench and unclench my fists. I don't want to watch this. Like all Blackcliff students, I came to the school at the age of six, and in the fourteen years since, I've witnessed punishments thousands of times. My own back is a map of the school's brutality. But deserters are always the worst.

My body is tight as a spring, but I flatten my gaze and keep my expression emotionless. Blackcliff's subject masters, the Centurions, will be watching. Drawing their ire when I'm so close to escaping would be unforgivably stupid.

Helene and I walk past the youngest students, four classes of maskless Yearlings, who will have the clearest view of the carnage. The smallest are barely seven. The biggest, nearly eleven.

The Yearlings look down as we pass; we are upperclassmen, and they are forbidden from even addressing us. They stand poker-straight, scims hanging at precise 45-degree angles on their backs, boots spit-shined, faces blank as stone. By now, even the youngest Yearlings have learned Blackcliff's most essential lessons: Obey, conform, and keep your mouth shut.

Behind the Yearlings sits an empty space in honour of Blackcliff's second tier of students, called Fivers because so many die in their fifth year. At age eleven, the Centurions throw us out of Blackcliff and into the wilds of the Empire without clothes, food, or weaponry, to survive as best as we can for four years. The remaining Fivers return to Blackcliff, receive their masks, and spend another four years as Cadets and then two more years as Skulls. Hel and I are Senior Skulls – just completing our last year of training.

The Centurions monitor us from beneath the arches that line the courtyard, hands on their whips as they await the arrival of Blackcliff's commandant. They stand as still as statues, their masks long since melded to their features, any semblance of emotion a distant memory.

I put a hand to my own mask, wishing I could rip it off, even for a minute. Like my classmates, I received the mask on my first day as a Cadet, when I was fourteen. Unlike the rest of the students – and much to Helene's dismay – the smooth liquid silver hasn't dissolved into my skin like it's supposed to. Probably because I take the damned thing off whenever I'm alone.

I've hated the mask since the day an Augur – an Empire holy man – handed it to me in a velvet-lined box. I hate the way it gloms on to me like some kind of parasite. I hate the way it presses into my face, moulding itself to my skin.

I'm the only student whose mask hasn't melded to him yet –

something my enemies enjoy pointing out. But lately, the mask has started fighting back, forcing the melding process by digging tiny filaments into the back of my neck. It makes my skin crawl, makes me feel like I'm not myself anymore. Like I'll never be myself again.

'Veturius.' Hel's lanky, sandy-haired platoon lieutenant, Demetrius, calls out to me as we take our spots with the other Senior Skulls. 'Who is it? Who's the deserter?'

'I don't know. Dex and the auxes brought him in.' I look around for my lieutenant, but he hasn't arrived yet.

'I hear it's a Yearling.' Demetrius stares at a hunk of wood poking out of the blood-browned cobbles at the base of the bell-tower. The whipping post. 'An older one. A fourth-year.'

Helene and I exchange a look. Demetrius's little brother also tried to desert in his fourth year at Blackcliff, when he was only ten. He lasted three hours outside the gates before the legion-naires brought him in to face the Commandant – longer than most.

'Maybe it was a Skull.' Helene scans the ranks of older students, trying to see if anyone is missing.

'Maybe it was Marcus,' Faris, a member of my battle platoon who towers over the rest of us, says, grinning, his blond hair popping up in an unruly cowlick. 'Or Zak.'

No such luck. Marcus, dark-skinned and yellow-eyed, stands at the front of our ranks with his twin, Zak: second-born, shorter and lighter, but just as evil. The Snake and the Toad, Hel calls them.

Zak's mask has yet to attach fully around his eyes, but Marcus's clings tightly, having joined with him so completely that all of his features – even the thick slant of his eyebrows – are clearly visible beneath it. If Marcus tried to remove his mask now, he'd take off half his face with it. Which would be an improvement.

As if he senses her glance, Marcus turns and looks Helene over with a predatory gaze of ownership that makes my hands itch to strangle him.

Nothing out of the ordinary, I remind myself. *Nothing to make you stand out.*

I force myself to look away. Attacking Marcus in front of the entire school would definitely qualify as out of the ordinary.

Helene notices Marcus's leer. Her hands ball into fists at her sides, but before she can teach the Snake a lesson, the sergeant-at-arms marches into the courtyard.

'ATTENTION.'

Three thousand bodies swing forward, three thousand pairs of boots snap together, three thousand backs jerk as if yanked straight by a puppeteer's hand. In the ensuing silence, you could hear a tear drop.

But we don't hear the Commandant of Blackcliff Military Academy approach; we feel her, the way you feel a storm coming. She moves silently, emerging from the arches like a fair-haired jungle cat from the underbrush. She wears all black, from her tight-fitting uniform jacket to her steel-toed boots. Her blonde hair is pulled, as always, into a still knot at her neck.

She's the only living female Mask – or will be until Helene graduates tomorrow. But unlike Helene, the Commandant exudes a deathly chill, as if her grey eyes and cut-glass features were carved from the underbelly of a glacier.

'Bring the accused,' she says.

A pair of legionnaires march out from behind the belltower, dragging a small, limp form. Beside me, Demetrius tenses. The rumours were right – the deserter's a Fourth-Yearling, no older than ten. Blood drips down his face, blending into the collar of his black fatigues. When the soldiers dump him before the Commandant, he doesn't move.

The Commandant's silver face reveals nothing as she looks down at the Yearling. But her hand strays towards the spiked riding crop at her belt, fashioned out of bruise-black ironwood. She doesn't remove it. Not yet.

'Fourth-Yearling Falconius Barrius.' Her voice carries, though it's soft, almost gentle. 'You abandoned your post at Blackcliff with no intention of returning. Explain yourself.'

'No explanation, Commandant, sir.' He mouths the words we've all said to the Commandant a hundred times, the only words you can say at Blackcliff when you've screwed up utterly.

It's a trial to keep my face blank, to drive emotion from my eyes. Barrius is about to be punished for the crime I'll be committing in less than thirty-six hours. It could be me up there in two days. Bloodied. Broken.

'Let us ask your peers their opinion.' The Commandant turns her gaze on us, and it's like being blasted by a frigid mountain wind. 'Is Yearling Barrius guilty of treason?'

'Yes, sir!' The shout shakes the flagstones, rabid in its ferocity.

'Legionnaires,' the Commandant says. 'Take him to the post.'

The resulting roar from the students jerks Barrius out of his stupor, and as the legionnaires tie him to the whipping post, he writhes and bucks.

His fellow Fourth-Yearlings, the same boys he fought and sweated and suffered with for years, thump the flagstones with their boots and pump their fists in the air. In the row of Senior Skulls in front of me, Marcus shouts his approval, his eyes lit with unholy joy. He stares at the Commandant with a reverence reserved for deities.

I feel eyes on me. To my left, one of the Centurions is watching. *Nothing out of the ordinary.* I lift my fist and cheer with the rest of them, hating myself.

The Commandant draws her crop, caressing it like a lover. Then she brings it whistling down onto Barrius's back. His gasp echoes through the courtyard, and every student falls silent, united in a shared, if brief, moment of pity. Blackcliff's rules are so numerous that it's impossible not to break them at least a few times. We've all been tied to that post before. We've all felt the bite of the Commandant's crop.

The quiet doesn't last. Barrius screams, and the students howl in response, flinging jeers at him. Marcus is loudest of all, leaning forward, practically spitting in excitement. Faris rumbles his approval. Even Demetrius manages a shout or two, his green eyes flat and distant as if he is somewhere else entirely. Beside me, Helene cheers, but there's no joy in her expression, only a stern sadness. The rules of Blackcliff demand that she voice her anger at the deserter's betrayal. So she does.

The Commandant seems indifferent to the clamour, fixated as she is on her work. Her arm rises and falls with a dancer's grace. She circles Barrius as his skinny limbs begin to seize, pausing between each lash, no doubt pondering how she can make the next one more painful than the last.

After twenty-five lashes, she takes him by his limp stalk of a neck and turns him around. 'Face them,' she says. 'Face the men you've betrayed.'

Barrius's eyes beseech the courtyard, seeking out anyone willing to offer him a shred of pity. He should have known better. His gaze collapses to the flagstones.

The cheers continue, and the crop comes down again. And again. Barrius falls to the white stones, the pool of blood around him spreading rapidly. His eyes flutter. I hope his mind is gone. I hope he can't feel it anymore.

I make myself watch. *This is why you're leaving, Elias. So you're never a part of this again.*

A gurgling moan trickles from Barrius's mouth. The Commandant drops her arm, and the courtyard is silent. I see the deserter breathing. In once. Out. And then nothing. No one cheers. Dawn breaks, the sun's rays tracing the sky above Blackcliff's ebony belltower like bloodied fingers, tingeing everyone in the courtyard a lurid red.

The Commandant wipes her crop on Barrius's fatigues before returning it to her belt. 'Take him to the dunes,' she orders the legionnaires. 'For the scavengers.' Then she surveys the rest of us.

'Duty first, unto death. If you betray the Empire, you will be caught, and you will pay. Dismissed.'

The lines of students dissolve. Dex, who brought the deserter in, slips away quietly, his darkly handsome face slightly sick. Faris lumbers after, no doubt to clap Dex on the back and suggest he forget his troubles at a brothel. Demetrius stalks off alone, and I know he's remembering that day two years ago when he was forced to watch his little brother die just like Barrius. He won't be fit to speak with for hours. The other students drain out of the courtyard quickly, still discussing the whipping.

'—only thirty lashes, what a weakling—'

'—did you hear him gasping, like a scared girl—'

'Elias.' Helene's voice is soft, as is the touch of her hand on my arm. 'Come on. The Commandant will see you.'

She's right. Everyone is walking away. I should too.

I can't do it.

No one looks at Barrius's bloody remains. He is a traitor. He is nothing. But someone should stay. Someone should mourn him, even if for a moment.

'Elias,' Helene says, urgent now. 'Move. She'll see you.'

'I need a minute,' I reply. 'You go on.'

She wants to argue with me, but her presence is conspicuous, and I'm not budging. She leaves with a last backward glance. When she's gone, I look up to see the Commandant watching me.

We lock eyes across the long courtyard, and I am struck for the hundredth time at how different we are. I have black hair, she has blonde. My skin glows golden brown, and hers is chalk-white. Her mouth is ever disapproving, while I look amused even when I'm not. I am broad-shouldered and well over six feet, while she is smaller than a Scholar woman, even, with a deceptively willowy form.

But anyone who sees us standing side by side can tell what she is to me. My mother gave me her high cheekbones and pale grey eyes. She gave me the ruthless instinct and speed that make me the best student Blackcliff has seen in two decades.

Mother. It's not the right word. *Mother* evokes warmth and love and sweetness. Not abandonment in the Tribal desert hours after birth. Not years of silence and implacable hatred.

She's taught me many things, this woman who bore me. Control is one of them. I tamp down my fury and disgust, emptying myself of all feeling. She frowns, a slight twist of her mouth, and raises a hand to her neck, her fingers following the whorls of a strange blue tattoo poking out of her collar.

I expect her to approach and demand to know why I'm still here, why I challenge her with my stare. She doesn't. Instead, she watches me for a moment longer before turning and disappearing beneath the arches.

The belltower tolls six, and the drums thud. *All students report to mess.* At the foot of the tower, the legionnaires heave up what's left of Barrius and carry him away.

The courtyard stands silent, empty except for me staring at a puddle of blood where a boy once stood, chilled by the knowledge that if I'm not careful, I'll end up just like him.

CHAPTER FIVE

Laia

The silence of the catacombs is as vast as a moonless night, and as eerie. Which isn't to say that the tunnels are empty; as soon as I drop through the grate, a rat skitters across my bare feet, and a clear, fist-sized spider descends on a thread inches from my face. I bite my hand so I don't scream.

Save Darin. Find the Resistance. Save Darin. Find the Resistance.

Sometimes I whisper the words. Mostly I chant them in my head. They keep me moving, a charm to ward off the fear nipping at my mind.

I'm not sure, really, what I should be looking for. A camp? A hideout? Any sign of life that isn't rodent in nature?

Since most of the Empire's garrisons are located east of the Scholars' Quarter, I head west. Even in this skies-forsaken place, I can point unfailingly to where the sun rises and where it sets, to the Empire's capital in the north, Antium, and to Navium, its main port due south. It's a sense I've had for as long as I can remember. When I was a child and Serra should have seemed vast to me, I was always able to find my way.

I take heart from it – at least I won't be wandering in circles.

For a time, sunshine trickles into the tunnels through the catacomb grates, weakly lighting the floor. I hug the crypt-pocked walls, swallowing my revulsion at the reek of rotting bones. A crypt is a good place to hide if a Martial patrol gets too close. *Bones are just bones*, I tell myself. *A patrol will kill you.*

In the daylight, it's easier to push away my doubts and convince myself that I'll find the Resistance. But I wander for hours, and eventually, the light fades and night falls, dropping like a curtain over my eyes. With it, fear comes rushing into my mind, a river that's broken a dam. Every thump is a murderous aux soldier, every scritch a horde of rats. The catacombs have swallowed me as a python swallows a mouse. I shudder, knowing that I have a mouse's chance of survival down here.

Save Darin. Find the Resistance.

Hunger gathers into a knot in my stomach, and thirst burns my throat. I spot a torch flickering in the distance, and feel a mothlike urge to head towards it. But the torches mark Empire territory, and the aux soldiers who get tunnel duty are probably Plebeians, the most lowborn of the Martials. If a group of Plebes catches me down here, I don't want to think of what they'll do.

I feel like a hunted, craven animal, which is exactly how the Empire sees me – how it sees all Scholars. The Emperor says that we are a free people who live under his benevolence. But that's a joke. We can't own property or attend schools, and even the mildest transgression results in enslavement.

No one else suffers such harshness. Tribesmen are protected under a treaty; during the invasion, they accepted Martial rule in exchange for free movement for their people. Mariners are protected by geography and the vast amounts of spices, meat, and iron they trade.

In the Empire, only Scholars are treated like trash.

Then defy the Empire, Laia, I hear Darin's voice. *Save me. Find the Resistance.*

The darkness slows my footsteps until I'm practically crawling. The tunnel I'm in narrows, the walls crowding closer. Sweat pours down my back, and my whole body quakes – I hate small spaces. My breath echoes raggedly. Somewhere ahead, water falls in a lonely drip. How many ghosts haunt this place? How many vengeful spirits roam these tunnels?

Stop, Laia. No such things as ghosts. As a child, I spent hours listening to Tribal tale-spinners weave their legends of the mythical fey: the Nightbringer and his fellow jinn; ghosts, efrits, wraiths, and wights.

Sometimes the tales spilled into my nightmares. When they did, it was Darin who calmed my fears. Unlike Tribesmen, Scholars are not superstitious, and Darin has always had a Scholar's healthy scepticism. *No ghosts here, Laia.* I hear his voice in my mind and close my eyes, pretending he's beside me, allowing myself to be reassured by his steady presence. *No wraiths either. There's no such thing.*

My hand goes to my armlet, as it always does when I need strength. It's nearly black with tarnish, but I prefer it that way; it draws less attention. I trace the pattern in the silver, a series of connecting lines that I know so well I see it in my dreams.

Mother gave me the armlet the last time I saw her, when I was five. It's one of the few clear memories I have of her – the cinnamon scent of her hair, the sparkle in her storm-sea eyes.

'*Keep it safe for me, little cricket. Just for a week. Just until I come back.*'

What would she say now, if she knew I'd kept the armlet safe but lost her only son? That I'd saved my own neck and sacrificed my brother's?

Set it right. Save Darin. Find the Resistance. I release the armlet and stumble on.

Soon after, I hear the first sounds behind me.

A whisper. The scrape of a boot on stone. If the crypts weren't silent, I doubt I'd have noticed, the sounds are so quiet. Too quiet for an aux soldier. Too furtive for the Resistance. A Mask?

My heart thumps, and I whirl, searching the tarry blackness. Masks can prowl through darkness like this as easily as if they are part wraith. I wait, frozen, but the catacombs fall silent again. I don't move. I don't breathe. I hear nothing.

Rat. It's just a rat. A *really big one, maybe* . . .

When I dare to take another step, I catch a whiff of leather and woodsmoke – human smells. I drop and search the floor with my hands for a weapon – a rock, a stick, a bone – anything to fight off whoever is stalking me. Then tinder hits flint, a hiss splits the air, and a moment later, a torch catches fire with a *whoosh*.

I stand, shielding my face with my hands, the impression of the flame pulsing behind my lids. When I force my eyes open, I make out a half-dozen hooded figures in a circle around me, all with loaded bows pointed at my heart.

'Who are you?' one of the figures says, stepping forward. Though his voice is cool and flat as a legionnaire's, he doesn't have the breadth and height of a Martial. His bare arms are hard with muscle, and he moves with fluid grace. A knife rests in one hand like it's an extension of his body, and he holds the torch in his other. I try to find his eyes, but they're hidden beneath the hood. 'Speak.'

'I—' After hours of silence, I can barely manage a croak. 'I'm looking for . . .'

Why didn't I think this through? I can't tell them I'm looking for the Resistance. No one with half a brain would admit to seeking out the rebels.

'Check her,' the man says when I don't go on.

Another of the figures, slight and womanly, slings her bow on her back. The torch sputters behind her, casting her face into deep shadow. She looks too small to be a Martial, and the skin of her hands doesn't have the dark hue of a Mariner's. She's probably either a Scholar or a Tribeswoman. Maybe I can reason with her.

'Please,' I say. 'Let me—'

'Shut it,' the man who'd spoken before says. 'Sana, anything?'

Sana. A Scholar name, short and simple. If she were Martial, her name would have been Agrippina Cassius or Chrysilla Aroman or something equally long and pompous.

But just because she's a Scholar doesn't mean I'm safe. I've heard rumours of Scholar thieves lurking in the catacombs, popping through grates to grab, raid, and usually kill whoever is nearby before dropping back into their lair.

Sana runs her hands over my legs and arms. 'An armlet,' she says. 'Might be silver. I can't tell.'

'You're not taking that!' I jerk away from her, and the thieves' bows, which had dropped a notch, come back up. 'Please, let me go. I'm a Scholar. I'm one of you.'

'Get it done,' the man says. Then he signals to the rest of his band, and they begin to slip back into the tunnels.

'Sorry about this.' Sana sighs, but she has a dagger in her hand now. I retreat a step.

'Don't. Please.' I knot my fingers together to hide their tremor. 'It was my mother's. It's the only thing I have left of my family.'

Sana lowers the knife, but then the leader of the thieves calls to her and, seeing her hesitation, stalks towards us. As he does, one of his men signals to him. 'Keenan, heads up. Aux patrol.'

39

'Pair and scatter.' Keenan lowers his torch. 'If they follow, lead them away from base, or you'll answer for it. Sana, get the girl's silver and let's go.'

'We can't leave her,' Sana says. 'They'll find her. You know what they'll do.'

'Not our problem.'

Sana doesn't move, and Keenan shoves the torch into her hands. When he takes me by the arm, Sana gets between us. 'We need silver, yes,' she says. 'But not from our own people. Leave her.'

The unmistakable, clipped cadence of Martial voices carries down the tunnel. They haven't seen the torchlight yet, but they will in just a few seconds.

'Damn it, Sana.' Keenan tries to go around the woman, but she shoves him away with surprising force, and her hood falls back. As the torchlight illuminates her face, I gasp. Not because she's older than I thought or because of her fierce animosity, but because on her neck, I see a tattoo of a closed fist raised high with a flame behind it. Beneath it, the word *Izzat*.

'You – you're—' I can't get the words out. Keenan's eyes fall on the tattoo, and he swears.

'Now you've done it,' he says to Sana. 'We can't leave her. If she tells them she saw us, they'll flood these tunnels until they find us.'

He puts out the torch with brute swiftness and grabs my arm, pulling me after him. When I stumble into his hard back, he jerks his head around, and for a second, I catch the angry shine of his eyes. His scent, sharp and smoky, wafts over me.

'I'm sorr—'

'Keep quiet and watch your step.' He's closer than I realized, his breath warm against my ear. 'Or I'll knock you senseless and leave you in one of the crypts. Now move.' I bite my lip and follow, trying to ignore his threat and instead focus on Sana's tattoo.

Izzat. It's Old Rei, the language spoken by Scholars before the Martials invaded and forced everyone to speak Serran. *Izzat* means many things. Strength, honour, pride. But in the past century, it's come to mean something specific: freedom.

This is no band of thieves. It's the Resistance.

CHAPTER SIX

Elias

Barrius's screams blister my brain for hours. I see his body fall, hear the rasp of his last breath, smell the taint of his blood on the flagstones.

Student deaths don't usually hit me this way. They shouldn't – the Reaper's an old friend. He's walked with all of us at Blackcliff at some point. But watching Barrius die was different. For the rest of the day, I'm short-tempered and distracted.

My odd mood doesn't go unnoticed. As I trudge to combat training with a group of other Senior Skulls, I realize Faris has just asked me a question for a third time.

'You look like your favourite whore's caught the pox,' he says when I mutter an apology. 'What the hell is wrong with you?'

'Nothing.' I realize too late how angry I sound, how unlike a Skull on the verge of Maskhood. I should be excited – bursting with anticipation.

Faris and Dex trade a sceptical glance, and I stifle a curse.

'You sure?' Dex asks. He's a rule-follower, Dex. Always has been. Every time he looks at me, I know he's wondering why my mask hasn't joined with me yet. *Piss off*, I want to say to him. Then I remind myself that he's not prying. He's my friend, and he's genuinely worried. 'This morning,' he says, 'at the whipping, you were—'

'Hey, leave the poor man be.' Helene strolls up behind us, flashing a smile at Dex and Faris and throwing a careless arm around my shoulders as we enter the armoury. She nods at a rack of scims. 'Go on, Elias, pick your weapon. I challenge you, best of three.'

She turns to the others and murmurs something as I walk away. I lift a blunted practice scim, checking its balance. A moment later, I feel her cool presence beside me.

'What did you tell them?' I ask her.

'That your grandfather's been hounding you.'

I nod. The best lies come from the truth. Grandfather is a Mask, and like most Masks, he's never satisfied with anything less than perfection.

'Thanks, Hel.'

'You're welcome. Repay me by pulling yourself together.' She crosses her arms at my frown. 'Dex is your platoon lieutenant, and you didn't commend him after he caught a deserter. He noticed. Your entire platoon noticed. And at the whipping, you weren't . . . with us.'

'If you're saying that I wasn't baying for the blood of a ten-year-old, you'd be right.'

Her eyes tighten, enough for me to know that some part of her sympathizes with me, even if she'll never admit it.

'Marcus saw you stay behind after the whipping. He and Zak are telling everyone that you thought the punishment was too harsh.'

I shrug. As if I care what the Snake and Toad say about me.

'Don't be an idiot. Marcus would love to sabotage the heir to Gens Veturia a day before graduation.' She refers to my familial house, one of the oldest and most respected in the Empire, by its formal title. 'He's all but accusing you of sedition.'

'He accuses me of sedition every other week.'

'But this time, you did something to earn it.'

My eyes jerk to hers, and for one tense moment, I think she knows everything. But there's no anger or judgment in her expression. Only concern.

She counts off my sins on her fingers. 'You're squad leader of the platoon on watch, yet you don't bring Barrius in yourself. Your lieutenant does it for you, and you don't commend him. You barely contain your disapproval when the deserter's punished. Not to mention the fact that it's the day before graduation, and your mask has only just begun to meld with you.'

She waits for a response, and when I give none, she sighs.

'Unless you're stupider than you look, even you can see how this appears, Elias. If Marcus reports you to the Black Guard, they might have enough evidence to pay you a visit.'

A prickle of unease creeps down my neck. The Black Guard is tasked with ensuring the loyalty of the military. They wear the emblem of a bird, and their leader, once picked, gives up his name and is known simply as the Blood Shrike. He's the right hand of the Emperor and the second most powerful man in the Empire. The current Blood Shrike has a habit of torturing first and asking questions later. A midnight visit from those black-armoured bastards will land me in the infirmary for weeks. My entire plan will be ruined.

I try not to glare at Helene. Must be nice to believe so fervently in what the Empire spoon-feeds us. Why can't I just be like her – like everyone else? Because my mother abandoned me? Because

I spent the first six years of my life with Tribesmen who taught me mercy and compassion instead of brutality and hatred? Because my playfellows were Tribeschildren, Mariners, and Scholars instead of other Illustrians?

Hel hands me a scim. 'Fall in,' she says. 'Please, Elias. Just for a day. Then we're free.'

Right. Free to report for duty as full-fledged servants of the Empire, after which we'll lead men to their deaths in the never-ending border wars with Wildmen and Barbarians. Those of us not ordered to the border will be given city commands, where we'll hunt down Resistance fighters or Mariner spies. We'll be free, all right. Free to laud the Emperor. Free to rape and kill.

Funny how that doesn't seem like freedom.

I keep quiet. Helene's right. I'm drawing too much attention to myself, and Blackcliff is the worst place to do so. Students here are like starving sharks when it comes to sedition. One whiff of it, and they swarm.

For the rest of the day, I do my best to act like a Mask on the verge of graduation – smug, brutish, violent. It's like covering myself in filth.

When I return to my cell-like quarters in the evening for a precious few minutes of free time, I tear off my mask and toss it on my cot, sighing when the liquid metal releases its hold.

At the sight of my reflection in the mask's polished surface, I grimace. Even with the thick black lashes that Faris and Dex love to mock, my eyes are so much my mother's that I hate seeing them. I don't know who my father is, and I no longer care, but for the hundredth time, I wish that he'd at least given me his eyes.

Once I escape the Empire, it won't matter. People will see my eyes and think *Martial* instead of *Commandant*. Plenty of Martials roam the south as merchants, mercenaries, and craftsmen. I'll be one among hundreds.

Outside, the belltower tolls eight. Twelve hours until graduation. Thirteen until the ceremony is done. Another hour for pleasantries. Gens Veturia is a distinguished house, and Grandfather will want me to shake dozens of hands. But eventually, I'll beg off and then . . .

Freedom. At last.

No student has ever deserted after graduating. Why would they? It's the hell of Blackcliff that drives its students to run. But after we're out, we get our own commands, our own missions. We get money, status, respect. Even the lowest-born Plebeian can marry high, if he becomes a Mask. No one with any sense would turn his back on that, especially after nearly a decade and a half of training.

Which is what makes tomorrow the perfect time to run. The two days after graduation are madness – parties, dinners, balls, banquets. If I disappear, no one will think to look for me for at least a day. They'll assume I've drunk myself into a stupor at a friend's house.

The passageway that leads from below my hearth into Serra's catacombs pulses at the edge of my vision. It took me three months to dig out that damn tunnel. Another two months to fortify and hide it from the prying eyes of aux patrols. And two more months to map out the route through the catacombs and out of the city.

Seven months of sleepless nights and peering over my shoulder and trying to act normal. If I escape, it will all have been worth it.

The drums beat, signalling the start of the graduation banquet. Seconds later, a knock comes at my door. *Ten hells.* I was supposed to meet Helene outside the barracks, and I'm not even dressed yet.

Helene knocks again. 'Elias, stop curling your eyelashes and get out here. We're late.'

'Hang on,' I say. As I pull off my fatigues, the door opens and Helene marches in. A blush blooms up her neck at my undressed state, and she looks away. I raise an eyebrow. Helene has seen me naked dozens of times – when wounded, or ill, or suffering through one of the Commandant's cruel strength-training exercises. By now, seeing me stripped shouldn't cause her to do anything more than roll her eyes and throw me a shirt.

'Hurry up, would you?' She fumbles to break the silence that's descended. I grab my dress uniform off a hook and button it on quickly, edgy at her awkwardness. 'The guys already went ahead. Said they'd save us seats.'

Helene rubs the Blackcliff tattoo on the back of her neck – a four-sided black diamond with curved sides that is inked into every student upon arrival at the school. Helene took it better than most of our class fellows, stoic and tearless while the rest of us whimpered.

The Augurs have never explained why they only choose one girl per generation for Blackcliff. Not even to Helene. Whatever the reason, it's clear they don't select at random. Helene might be the only girl here, but there's a reason she's ranked third in our class. It's the same reason that bullies learned early on to leave her alone. She's clever, swift, and ruthless.

Now, in her black uniform, with her shining braid encircling her head like a crown, she's as beautiful as winter's first snow. I watch her long fingers at her nape, watch her lick her lips. I wonder what it would be like to kiss that mouth, to push her to the window and press my body against hers, to pull out the pins in her hair, to feel its softness between my fingers.

'Uh . . . Elias?'

'Hmm . . .' I realize I've been staring and snap out of it. *Fantasizing about your best friend, Elias. Pathetic.* 'Sorry. Just . . . tired. Let's go.'

Hel gives me a strange look and nods at my mask, still sitting on the bed. 'You might need that.'

'Right.' Appearing without one's mask is a whipping offence. I haven't seen any Skull maskless since we were fourteen. Other than Hel, none of them have seen my face, either.

I put the mask on, trying not to shudder at the eagerness with which it attaches to me. *One day left.* Then I'll take it off forever.

The sunset drums thunder as we emerge from the barracks. The blue sky deepens to violet, and the searing desert air cools. Evening's shadows blend with the dark stones of Blackcliff, making the blockish buildings appear unnaturally large. My eyes rove the shadows, seeking out threats, a habit from my years as a Fiver. I feel, for an instant, as if the shadows are looking back at me. But then the sensation fades.

'Do you think the Augurs will attend graduation?' Hel asks.

No, I want to say. *Our holy men have better things to do, like locking themselves up in caves and reading sheep entrails.*

'Doubt it,' is all I say.

'I guess it would get tedious after five hundred years.' Helene says this without a trace of irony, and I wince at the sheer idiocy of the idea. How can someone as intelligent as Helene actually think the Augurs are immortal?

But then, she's not the only one. Martials believe that the Augurs' 'power' comes from being possessed by the spirits of the dead. Masks, in particular, revere the Augurs, for it is the Augurs who decide which Martial children will attend Blackcliff. It is the Augurs who give us our masks. And we're taught that it was the Augurs who raised Blackcliff in a single day, five centuries ago.

There are only fourteen of the red-eyed bastards, but on the rare occasions that they appear, everyone defers to them. Many of the Empire's leaders – generals, the Blood Shrike, even the Emperor – make a yearly pilgrimage to the Augurs' mountain lair, seeking counsel on matters of state. And though it's clear to anyone with an ounce of logic that they are a pack of charlatans, they're lionized throughout the Empire not just as immortal, but as oracles and mind-readers.

Most Blackcliff students only see the Augurs twice in our lives: when we're chosen for Blackcliff and when we're given our masks. But Helene has always had a particular fascination with the holy men – it's no surprise that she hoped they'd come to graduation.

I respect Helene, but on this, we don't agree. Martial myths are as believable as Tribal fables of jinn and the Nightbringer.

Grandfather is one of the few Masks who doesn't believe in Augur rubbish, and I repeat his mantra in my head. *The field of battle is my temple. The swordpoint is my priest. The dance of death is my prayer. The killing blow is my release.* The mantra is all I've ever needed.

It takes all my control to hold my tongue. Helene notices.

'Elias,' she says. 'I'm proud of you.' Her tone is strangely formal. 'I know you've struggled. Your mother . . .' She glances around and drops her voice. The Commandant has spies every where. 'Your mother's been harder on you than on any of the rest of us. But you showed her. You worked hard. You did every-thing right.'

Her voice is so sincere that for a moment, I waver. In two days, she won't think such things. In two days, she will hate me.

Remember Barrius. Remember what you'll be expected to do after graduation.

I jostle her shoulder. 'Are you turning sappy and girly on me?'

'Forget it, swine.' She punches me on the arm. 'I was just trying to be nice.'

My laugh is falsely hearty. *They'll send you to hunt me down when I run. You and the others, the men I call brothers.*

We reach the mess hall, and the cacophony within hits us like a wave – laughter and boasts and the raucous talk of three thousand young men on the verge of leave or graduation. It's never this loud when the Commandant is in attendance, and I relax marginally, glad to avoid her.

Hel pulls me to one of the dozens of long tables, where Faris is regaling the rest of our friends with a tale of his latest escapade at the riverside brothels. Even Demetrius, ever haunted by his dead brother, cracks a smile.

Faris leers, glancing between us suggestively. 'You two took your time.'

'Veturius was making himself pretty just for you.' Hel shoves Faris's boulder-like body over, and we sit. 'I had to drag him away from his mirror.'

The rest of the table hoots, and Leander, one of Hel's soldiers, calls for Faris to finish his story. Beside me, Dex is arguing with Hel's second lieutenant, Tristas. He's an earnest, dark-haired boy with a deceptively innocent look to his wide blue eyes, and his fiancée's name, *AELIA*, tattooed in block letters on his bicep.

Tristas leans forward. 'The Emperor's nearly seventy, and he has no male issue. This year might be *the* year. The year the Augurs choose a new Emperor. A new dynasty. I was talking to Aelia about it—'

'Every year, someone thinks it's the year.' Dex rolls his eyes. 'Every year, it's not. Elias, tell him. Tell Tristas he's an idiot.'

'Tristas, you're an idiot.'

'But the Augurs say—'

I snort quietly, and Helene gives me a sharp look. *Keep your doubts to yourself, Elias.* I busy myself with piling food on two plates and shove one toward her. 'Here,' I say. 'Have some slop.'

'What is it, anyway?' Hel pokes at the mash and takes a tentative sniff 'Cow dung?'

'No whining,' Faris says through a mouthful of food. 'Pity the Fivers. They have to come back to this after four years of happily robbing farmhouses.'

'Pity the Yearlings,' Demetrius counters. 'Can you imagine another twelve years? Thirteen?'

Across the hall, most of the Yearlings smile and laugh like everyone else. But some watch us, the way starving foxes might watch a lion – hungry for what we have.

I imagine half of them gone, half the laughter silenced, half the bodies cold. For that is what will happen in the years of deprivation and torment ahead of them. And they will face it either by living or dying, either by accepting or questioning. The ones who question are usually the ones who die.

'They don't seem to care much about Barrius.' The words are out of my mouth before I can help myself. Beside me, Helene's body stiffens like water freezing into ice. Dex frowns in disapproval, a comment dying on his lips, and silence falls across our table.

'Why would they be upset?' Marcus, sitting one table away with Zak and a knot of cronies, speaks up. 'That scum got what he deserved. I only wished he'd lasted longer so he could have suffered more.'

'No one asked what you think, Snake,' Helene says. 'Anyway, kid's dead now.'

'Lucky him.' Faris picks up a forkful of food and lets it plop unappetizingly back onto his steel plate. 'At least he doesn't have to eat this swill anymore.'

A low chuckle runs up and down the table, and conversation picks up again. But Marcus smells blood, and his malevolence taints the air. Zak turns his gaze to Helene and mutters something to his brother. Marcus ignores him, fixing his hyena eyes on me. 'You were damn broken up over that traitor this morning, Veturius. Was he a friend?'

'Piss off, Marcus.'

'Been spending a lot of time down in the catacombs too.'

'What is that supposed to mean?' Helene's hand is on her weapon, and Faris grabs her arm.

Marcus ignores her. 'You gonna do a runner, Veturius?'

My head comes up slowly. *It's a guess. He's guessing.* There's no way he could know. I've been careful, and *careful* at Blackcliff translates to *paranoid* for most people.

Silence falls at my table, at Marcus's. *Deny it, Elias. They're waiting.*

'You were squad leader on watch this morning, weren't you?' Marcus says. 'You should have been thrilled to see that traitor go down. You should have brought him in. Say he deserved it, Veturius. Say Barrius deserved what he got.'

It should be easy. I don't believe it, and that's what matters. But my mouth won't move. The words won't come. Barrius didn't deserve to be whipped to death. He was a child, a boy so afraid of staying at Blackcliff that he'd risked everything to escape it.

The silence spreads. A few Centurions look up from the head table. Marcus stands, and, quick as a flood, the mood of the hall changes, turning curious and expectant.

Son of a whore.

'Is this why your mask hasn't joined with you?' Marcus says. 'Because you're not one of us? Say it, Veturius. Say the traitor deserved his fate.'

'Elias,' Helene whispers. Her eyes plead. *Fall in. Just for one more day.*

'He—' *Say it, Elias. Doesn't change anything if you do.* 'He deserved it.'

I meet Marcus's eyes coolly, and he grins, like he knows how much the words cost.

'Was that so hard, bastard?'

I'm relieved when he insults me. It gives me the excuse I've wanted so badly. I spring toward him fists-first.

But my friends are expecting it. Faris, Demetrius, and Helene are on their feet, holding me back, an irritating wall of black and blond keeping me from beating that damn grin off Marcus's face.

'No, Elias,' Helene says. 'The Commandant will whip you for starting a fight. Marcus isn't worth that.'

'He's a bastard—'

'That'd be you, actually,' Marcus says. 'At least I know who my father is. *I* wasn't raised by a pack of camel-stroking Tribesmen.'

'You Plebeian trash—'

'Senior Skulls.' The Scim Centurion has made his way to the foot of the table. 'Is there a problem?'

'No, sir,' Helene says. 'Go, Elias,' she murmurs. 'Go get some air. I'll handle this.'

My blood still burning, I shove through the mess doors and find myself in the belltower courtyard before I even know where I'm going.

How the hell did Marcus figure out that I'm going to desert? How much does he know? Not too much, or I'd have been called to the Commandant's office by now. Damn him, I'm close. So close.

I pace the courtyard, trying to calm myself. The desert heat has faded, and a crescent moon hangs low on the horizon, thin and red as a cannibal's smile. Through the arches, Serra's lights glow dully, tens of thousands of oil lamps dwarfed by the vast darkness of the surrounding desert. To the south, a pall of smoke mutes the shine of the river. The smell of steel and forge wafts past, ever-present in a city known solely for its soldiers and weaponry.

I wish I could have seen Serra before all this, when it was capital of the Scholar Empire. Under the Scholars, the great buildings were libraries and universities instead of barracks and training halls. The Street of Storytellers was filled with stages and theatres instead of an arms market where the only stories told now are of war and death.

It's a stupid wish, like wanting to fly. For all their knowledge of astronomy and architecture and mathematics, the Scholars crumbled beneath the Empire's invasion. Serra's beauty is long gone. It's a Martial city now.

Above, the heavens glow, the sky pale with starlight. Some long-buried part of me understands that this is beauty, but I am unable to wonder at it, the way I did when I was a boy. Back then, I clambered up spiky Jack trees to get closer to the stars, sure that a few feet of height would help me see them better. Back then, my world had been sand and sky and the love of Tribe Saif, who saved me from exposure. Back then, everything was different.

'All things change, Elias Veturius. You are no boy now, but a man, with a man's burden upon your shoulders and a man's choice ahead of you.'

My knife is in my hands, though I don't remember drawing it, and I hold it to the throat of the hooded man beside me. Years of training keep my arm steady as a rock, but my mind races. Where had the man come from? I'd swear on the lives of everyone in my platoon that he hadn't been standing there a moment ago.

'Who the hell are you?'

He pulls down his hood, and I have my answer.

Augur.

CHAPTER SEVEN

Laia

We race through the catacombs, Keenan ahead of me, Sana at my heels. When Keenan is convinced we've left the aux patrol behind, he slows our pace and barks at Sana to blindfold me.

I flinch at the harshness in his tone. This is what's become of the Resistance? This band of thugs and thieves? How did it happen? Only twelve years ago, the rebels were at the height of their power, allying themselves with the Tribes and the king of Marinn. They'd lived their code – *Izzat* – fighting for freedom, protecting the innocent, elevating loyalty to their own people above all else.

Does the Resistance remember that code anymore? On the off chance that they do, will they help me? Can they help me?

You'll make them help you. Darin's voice again, confident and strong, like when he taught me to climb a tree, like when he taught me to read.

'We're here,' Sana whispers after what feels like hours. I hear a series of knocks and the scrape of a door opening.

Sana guides me forward, and a burst of cool air washes over me, fresh as spring after the stench of the catacombs. Light creeps through the edges of my blindfold. The rich green smell of tobacco curls up into my nose, and I think of my father, smoking a pipe as he drew pictures of efrits and wights for me. What would he say if he saw me now, in a Resistance hideout?

Voices mutter and murmur. Warm fingers tangle in my hair, and a moment later, my blindfold falls away. Keenan is right behind me.

'Sana,' he says. 'Give her some neem leaf and get her out of here.' He turns to another fighter, a girl a few years older than me who flushes when he speaks to her. 'Where's Mazen? Have Raj and Navid reported yet?'

'What's neem leaf?' I ask Sana when I'm sure Keenan can't hear. I've never heard of it, and I know most herbs from working with Pop.

'It's an opiate. It'll make you forget the last few hours.' At my widening eyes, she shakes her head. 'I won't give it to you. Not yet, anyway. Have a seat. You look a mess.'

The cavern we're in is so dark, it's hard to tell how big it is. Blue-fire lanterns, usually found in the finest Illustrian neighbourhoods, glow here and there, with pitch torches flickering between them. Clean night air flows through a constellation of gaps in the rock ceiling, and I can barely make out the stars. I must have been in the catacombs for nearly a day.

'It's draughty.' Sana pulls off her cloak, and her short, dark hair tufts out like a disgruntled bird's. 'But it's home.'

'Sana. You're back.' A stocky, brown-haired man approaches, looking at me curiously.

'Tariq,' Sana greets him. 'We ran into a patrol. Picked up someone on the way. Grab her some food, would you?' Tariq disappears, and Sana gestures for me to sit on a nearby bench, ignoring the stares coming our way from the dozens of people moving about the cavern.

There are an equal number of men and women here, most in dark, close-fitting clothing and nearly all dripping with knives and scims, as if expecting an Empire raid any moment. Some sharpen weapons, others watch over cook fires. A few older men smoke pipes. The bunks along the cavern wall are filled with sleeping bodies.

As I look around, I push a hank of hair out of my face. Sana's eyes narrow when she takes in my features. 'You look . . . familiar,' she says.

I allow my hair to fall forward again. Sana's old enough to have been in the Resistance for quite some time. Old enough to have known my parents.

'I used to sell Nan's jams at market.'

'Right.' She's still staring. 'You live in the Quarter? Why were you—'

'Why is she still here?' Keenan, who's been busy with a group of fighters in the corner, approaches, pulling back his hood. He's far younger than I expected, closer to my age than Sana's – which might explain why she bristles at his tone. Flame-red hair spills over his forehead and into his eyes, so dark at the roots it's almost black. He is only a few inches taller than me, but lean and strong, with a Scholar's even, fine features. A hint of ginger stubble shadows his jaw, and freckles spatter his nose. Like the other fighters, he wears nearly as many weapons as a Mask.

I realize I'm staring and glance away, heat rising in my cheeks. Suddenly, the looks he's been getting from the younger women in the cavern make sense.

'She can't stay,' he says. 'Get her out of here, Sana. Now.'

Tariq returns and, overhearing Keenan, slams a plate of food onto the table behind me. 'You don't tell her what to do. Sana's not some besotted recruit, she's the head of our faction, and you—'

'Tariq.' Sana puts a hand on the man's arm, but the look she gives Keenan could wither stone. 'I was giving the girl some food. I wanted to find out what she was doing in the tunnels.'

'I was looking for you,' I say. 'For the Resistance. I need your help. My brother was taken in a raid yesterday—'

'We can't help,' Keenan says. 'We're stretched thin as it is.'

'But—'

'We. Can't. Help.' He speaks slowly, as if I'm a child. Maybe before the raid, the chill in his eyes would have silenced me. But not now. Not when Darin needs me.

'You don't lead the Resistance,' I say.

'I'm second-in-command.'

He's higher up than I expected. But not high enough. I shake my hair out of my face and stand.

'Then it's not up to you, whether I stay or not. It's up to your leader.' I try to sound brave, although if Keenan disagrees, I don't know what I'll do. Start begging, maybe.

Sana's smile is sharp as a knife. 'Girl's got a point.'

Keenan moves towards me until he's standing uncomfortably close. He smells of lemon and wind and something smoky, like cedar. He takes me in from head to toe, and the look would be shameless if it wasn't for the slight puzzlement in his face, like he's seeing something he doesn't quite understand. His eyes are a dark secret, black or brown or blue – I can't tell. It feels as if they can see right through me to my weak, cowardly soul. I cross my arms and look away, embarrassed of my tattered shift, of the dirt, the cuts, the damage.

'That's an unusual armlet.' He reaches out a hand to touch it. The tip of his finger grazes my arm, sending a spark skittering across my skin, and I jerk away. He doesn't react. 'So tarnished, I might not have noticed it. It's silver, isn't it?'

'I didn't steal it, all right?' My body aches and my head spins, but I bunch my fists, afraid and angry all at once. 'And if you want it, you'll – you'll have to kill me to get it.'

He meets my eyes coolly, and I hope he doesn't call my bluff. He and I both know that killing me wouldn't be particularly difficult.

'I expect I would,' he says. 'What's your name?'

'Laia.' He doesn't ask for a family name – Scholars rarely take them.

Sana looks between us, bemused. 'I'll go get Maz—'

'No.' Keenan's already walking away. 'I'll find him.'

I sit back down, and Sana keeps glancing at my face, trying to puzzle out why I look familiar. If she'd seen Darin, she'd have known right away. He's the spitting image of our mother – and no one could forget Mother. Father was different – always in the background, drawing, planning, thinking. He gave me his unruly midnight hair and gold eyes, his high cheekbones and full, unsmiling lips.

In the Quarter, no one knew my parents. No one looked twice at Darin or me. But a Resistance camp is different. I should have realized that.

I find myself staring at Sana's tattoo, and my stomach lurches at the sight of the fist and flame. Mother had one just like it, above her heart. Father spent months perfecting it before inking it into her skin.

Sana sees me staring. 'When I got this tattoo, the Resistance was different,' she explains without my asking. 'We were better. But things changed. Our leader, Mazen, told us we needed to be bolder, to go on the attack. Most of the young fighters, the ones Mazen trains, tend to agree with that philosophy.'

It's clear Sana's not happy about this. I'm waiting for her to say more when a door opens on the far side of the cavern to admit Keenan and a limping, silver-haired man.

'Laia,' Keenan says. 'This is Mazen, he's—'

'Leader of the Resistance.' I know his name because my parents spoke it often when I was a child. And I know his face because it's on wanted signs all over Serra.

'So, you're our orphan of the day.' The man comes to a stop before me, waving me back down when I rise to greet him. He has a pipe clenched in his teeth, and the smoke blurs his ravaged face. The Resistance tattoo, faded but still visible, is a blue-green shadow on the skin below his throat. 'What is it you want?'

'My brother Darin's been taken by a Mask.' I watch Mazen's face carefully to see if he recognizes my brother's name, but he gives nothing away. 'Last night, in a raid at our house. I need your help to get him back.'

'We don't rescue strays.' Mazen turns to Keenan. 'Don't waste my time again.'

I try to quash my desperation. 'Darin's no stray. He wouldn't have even been taken if it wasn't for your men.'

Mazen swings around. 'My men?'

'Two of your fighters were interrogated by the Martials. They gave Darin's name to the Empire before they died.'

When Mazen looks at Keenan for confirmation, the younger man fidgets.

'Raj and Navid,' he says after a pause. 'New recruits. Said they were working on something big. Eran found their bodies in the west end of the Scholars' Quarter this morning. I heard a few minutes ago.'

Mazen swears and turns back to me. 'Why would my men give the Empire your brother's name? How do they know him?'

If Mazen doesn't know about the sketchbook, I'm not about to tell him. I don't understand what it means myself. 'I don't know,' I say. 'Maybe they wanted him to join. Maybe they were friends. Whatever the reason, they led the Empire to us. The Mask who killed them came for Darin last night. He —' My voice fails, but I clear my throat and force myself to keep talking. 'He killed my grandparents. He took Darin to jail. Because of *your* men.'

Mazen takes a long draw on his pipe, contemplating me, before shaking his head. 'I'm sorry for your loss. Truly. But we can't help you.'

'You – you owe me a blood debt. Your men gave up Darin—'

'And paid for it with their lives. You can't ask for more than that.' The little interest Mazen took in me disappears. 'If we helped every Scholar taken by the Martials, there'd be nothing left of the Resistance. Maybe if you were one of our own . . .' He shrugs. 'But you're not.'

'What about *Izzat*?' I grab his arm, and he pulls away, anger flashing in his eyes. 'You're bound to the code. Bound to aid any who—'

'The code applies to our own. Members of the Resistance. Their families. Those who have given everything for our survival. Keenan, give her the leaf.'

Keenan takes one of my arms, holding on tightly even when I try to throw him off.

'Wait,' I say. 'You can't do this.' Another fighter comes to restrain me. 'You don't understand. If I don't get him out of prison, they'll torture him – they'll sell him or kill him. He's all I have – he's the only one left!'

Mazen keeps walking.

CHAPTER EIGHT

Elias

The whites of the Augur's eyes are demon-red, vivid against his jet irises. His skin stretches across the bones of his face like a tortured body on the rack. Other than his eyes, he has no more colour to him than the translucent spiders that lurk in Serra's catacombs.

'Nervous, Elias?' The Augur pushes my knife away from his throat. 'Why? You needn't fear me. I'm only a cave-dwelling charlatan. A reader of sheep's entrails, yes?'

Burning, bleeding skies. How does he know I'd thought such things? What else does he know? Why is he even here?

'That was a joke,' I say hastily. 'A stupid, stupid joke—'

'Your plan to desert. Is that a joke also?'

My throat tightens. All I can think is *how does he – who told him – I'll kill them—*

'The ghosts of our misdeeds seek vengeance,' the Augur says. 'But the cost will be high.'

'The cost . . .' It takes me a second to understand. He's going to make me pay for what I was planning to do. The night air is

63

colder suddenly, and I remember the din and stench of Kauf Prison, where the Empire sends defectors to suffer at the hands of its most ruthless interrogators. I remember the Commandant's whip and Barrius's blood staining the courtyard stones. My adrenaline surges, my training kicking in, telling me to attack the Augur, to rid myself of this threat. But common sense overrules instinct. The Augurs are so highly respected that killing one isn't an option. Grovelling, however, might not hurt.

'I understand,' I say. 'I will humbly accept any punishment you deem—'

'I am not here to punish you. In any case, your future is punishment enough. Tell me, Elias. Why are you here? Why are you at Blackcliff?'

'To carry out the will of the Emperor.' I know these words better than my own name, I've said them so many times. 'To keep away threats, internal and external. To protect the Empire.'

The Augur turns to the diamond-patterned belltower. The words emblazoned in the tower's bricks are so familiar I hardly notice them anymore.

From among the battle-hardened youth there shall rise the Foretold, the Greatest Emperor, scourge of our enemies, commander of a host most devastating. And the Empire shall be made whole.

'The foretelling, Elias,' the Augur says. 'The future given to the Augurs in visions. That is the reason we built this school. That is the reason you are here. Do you know the story?'

The story of Blackcliff's origin was the first thing I learned as a Yearling: Five hundred years ago, a warrior brute named Taius united the fractured Martial clans and swept down from the north, crushing the Scholar Empire and taking over most of the continent. He named himself Emperor and established his dynasty.

He was called the Masked One, for the unearthly silver mask he wore to scare the hell out of his enemies.

But the Augurs, considered holy even then, saw in their visions that Taius's line would one day fail. When that day came, the Augurs would choose a new Emperor through a series of physical and mental tests: the Trials. For obvious reasons, Taius didn't appreciate this prediction, but the Augurs must have threatened to strangle him with sheep gut, because he didn't make a peep when they raised Blackcliff and began training students here.

And here we all are, five centuries later, masked just like Taius the First, waiting for the old devil's line to fail so one of us can become the shiny new Emperor.

I'm not holding my breath. Generations of Masks have trained and served and died without a whisper of the Trials. Blackcliff may have started out as a place to prepare the future Emperor, but now it's just a training ground for the Empire's deadliest asset.

'I know the story,' I say in response to the Augur's question. *But I don't believe a word of it, since it's mythical horse dung.*

'Neither mythical nor horse dung, I'm afraid,' the Augur says soberly.

It becomes harder to breathe suddenly. I haven't felt fear in so long that it takes me a second to recognize it. 'You *can* read minds.'

'A simplistic statement for a complex endeavour. But, yes. We can.'

Then you know everything. My plan to escape, my hopes, my hates. Everything. No one turned me in to the Augur. I turned myself in.

'It's a good plan, Elias,' the Augur confirms. 'Nearly foolproof. If you wish to carry it out, I will not stop you.'

TRICK! my mind screams. But I look into the Augur's eyes and see no lie there. What game is he playing? How long have the Augurs known that I want to desert?

'We've known for months. But it wasn't until you hid your supplies in the tunnel this morning that we understood you had committed yourself. We knew then we had to speak with you.' The Augur nods to the path that leads to the eastern watchtower. 'Walk with me.'

I'm too numb to do anything but follow. If the Augur isn't trying to keep me from deserting, then what does he want? What did he mean when he said my future would be punishment enough? Is he telling me I'll be caught?

We reach the watchtower, and the sentries stationed there turn and walk away, as if following a silent order. The Augur and I are alone, looking out over darkened sand dunes that stretch all the way to the Serran Mountain Range.

'When I hear your thoughts, I'm reminded of Taius the First,' the Augur says. 'Like you, soldiering was in his blood. And like you, he struggled with his destiny.' The Augur smiles at my stare of disbelief. 'Oh, yes. I knew Taius. I knew his forefathers. My kindred and I have walked this land for a thousand years, Elias. We chose Taius to create the Empire, just as we chose you, five hundred years later, to serve it.'

Impossible, my logical mind insists.

Shut it, logical mind. If this man can read minds, then immortality seems like the next reasonable step. Does this mean all that drivel about the Augurs being possessed by spirits of the dead is true? If only Helene could see me. How she'd gloat.

I watch the Augur out of the corner of my eye. As I take in his profile, I find that it's suddenly, oddly familiar.

'My name is Cain, Elias. I brought you to Blackcliff. I chose you.'

Condemned me, more like. I try not to think of the dark morning the Empire claimed me, but it haunts my dreams still. The soldiers surrounding the Saif caravan, dragging me from my bed. Mamie Rila, my foster mother, shrieking at them until her brothers pulled her back. My foster brother, Shan, rubbing the sleep from his eyes, bewildered, asking when I would return. And this man, this thing, pulling me to a waiting horse with the barest explanation. *You've been chosen. You will come with me.*

In my terrified child's mind, the Augur seemed larger, more menacing. Now, he comes to my shoulder and looks as if a stiff wind could knock him into the grave.

'I imagine you've chosen thousands of children over the years.' I take care to keep my tone respectful. 'That's your job, isn't it?'

'But you are the one I remember best. For the Augurs dream the future: all outcomes, all possibilities. And you are woven through every dream. A thread of silver in a tapestry of night.'

'And here I thought you drew my name out of a hat.'

'Hear me, Elias Veturius.' The Augur ignores my barb, and though his voice is no louder than it was a moment ago, his words are wrapped in iron, weighted down in certainty. 'The Foretelling is truth. A truth you will soon face. You seek to run. You seek to abandon your duty. But you cannot escape your destiny.'

'Destiny?' I laugh, a bitter thing. 'What destiny?'

Everything here is blood and violence. After I graduate tomorrow, nothing will change. The missions, the rote viciousness, will wear me down until there's nothing left of the boy the Augurs stole fourteen years ago. Maybe that's a type of destiny. But it's not one I'd choose for myself.

'This life is not always what we think it will be,' Cain says. 'You are an ember in the ashes, Elias Veturius. You will spark and burn, ravage and destroy. You cannot change it. You cannot stop it.'

'I don't want—'

'What you want doesn't matter. Tomorrow you must make a choice. Between deserting and doing your duty. Between running from your destiny and facing it. If you desert, the Augurs will not stop you. You will escape. You will leave the Empire. You will live. But you will find no solace in doing so. Your enemies will hunt you. Shadows will bloom in your heart, and you will become everything you hate – evil, merciless, cruel. You will be chained to the darkness within yourself as surely as if chained to the walls of a prison cell.'

He moves towards me, his black eyes pitiless. 'But if you stay, if you do your duty, you have a chance to break the bonds between you and the Empire forever. You have a chance at greatness you cannot conceive. You have a chance at true freedom – of body and of soul.'

'What do you mean, if I stay and do my duty? What duty?'

'You'll know when the time comes, Elias. You must trust me.'

'How can I trust you when you won't explain what you mean? What duty? My first mission? My second? How many Scholars will I have to torment? How much evil will I commit before I'm free?'

Cain's eyes are fixed on my face as he takes one step away from me and then another.

'When can I leave the Empire? In a month? A year? Cain!'

He fades as quickly as a star into the dawn. I reach out to grab him, to force him to stay and answer me. But my hand finds only air.

CHAPTER NINE

Laia

Keenan pulls me to a cavern door, and I hang limp, my breath gone from my body. His mouth moves, but I can't hear what he's saying. All I can hear are Darin's screams echoing in my ears.

I'll never see my brother again. The Martials will sell him if he's lucky and kill him if he's not. Either way, there's nothing I can do about it.

Tell them, Laia. Darin whispers in my head. *Tell them who you are.*

They might kill me, I argue back. *I don't know if I can trust them.*

If you don't tell them, I'll die, Darin's voice says. *Don't let me die, Laia.*

'The tattoo on your neck,' I shout at Mazen's retreating back. 'The fist and flame. My father put it there. You were the second person he tattooed, after my mother.'

Mazen stops.

'His name was Jahan. You called him Lieutenant. My sister's name was Lis. You called her the Little Lioness. My—' For a second, I falter, and Mazen turns around, a muscle in his jaw jumping. *Speak, Laia. He's actually listening.* 'My mother's name was Mirra. But you – everyone – called her the Lioness. Leader. Head of the Resistance.'

Keenan releases me as quickly as if my skin has turned to ice. Sana's gasp echoes in the sudden silence of the cavern. She'll know now why she'd found me familiar.

I glance around at the shocked faces uneasily. My parents were betrayed from within the Resistance. Nan and Pop never learned who it was.

Mazen says nothing.

Please don't let him be the traitor. Let him be one of the good ones.

If Nan could see me, she'd throttle me. I've kept the secret of my parents' identities all my life. Telling it makes me feel hollow inside. And what happens now? All of these rebels, many of whom fought alongside my parents, suddenly know whose child I am. They'll want me to be fearless and charismatic, like Mother. They'll want me to be brilliant and serene, like Father.

But I'm not any of those things.

'You served with my parents for twenty years,' I say to Mazen. 'In Marinn and then here, in Serra. You joined up the same time as my mother. You rose to the top with her and my father. You were third-in-command.'

Keenan's eyes flash between Mazen and me, the rest of his face still. Work in the cavern halts, and fighters whisper to each other as they gather around us.

'Mirra and Jahan had one child.' Mazen limps towards me. His eyes go from my hair to my eyes to my lips as he remembers, compares. 'She died when they did.'

'No.' I've held this in for so long that it feels wrong to speak of it. But I have to. It is the only thing I can say that might make a difference.

'My parents left the Resistance when Lis was four. They were expecting Darin. They wanted a normal life for their children. They disappeared. No trace. No trail.

'Darin was born. Then, two years later, I arrived. But the Empire was coming down hard on the Resistance. Everything my parents worked for was crumbling. They couldn't sit by and watch. They wanted to fight. Lis was old enough to stay with them. But Darin and I were too young. They left us with Mother's parents. Darin was six. I was four. They died a year later.'

'You tell a good tale, girl,' Mazen says. 'But Mirra didn't have parents. She was an orphan, like me. Like Jahan.'

'I'm not telling tales.' I pitch my voice low so it doesn't shake. 'Mother left home when she was sixteen. Nan and Pop didn't want her to go. After she left, she cut off all contact. They didn't even know she was alive until she knocked on their door asking them to take us in.'

'You're nothing like her.'

He might as well have slapped me. *I know I'm not like her*, I want to say. *I cried and cringed instead of standing and fighting. I abandoned Darin instead of dying for him. I'm weak in a way she never was.*

'Mazen,' Sana whispers, like I'll disappear if she speaks too loudly. 'Look at her. She has Jahan's eyes, his hair. Ten hells, she has his face.'

'I swear it's true. This armlet—' I lift my hand, and it glints in the cavern's light. 'It was hers. She gave it to me a week before the Empire caught her.'

'I'd wondered what she'd done with it.' The stiffness in Mazen's face dissolves, and the light of an old memory flares in his eyes.

71

'Jahan gave it to her when they got married. I never saw her without it. Why didn't you come to us before? Why didn't your grandparents contact us? We'd have trained you up the way Mirra would have wanted.'

The answer dawns on his face before I can say it.

'The traitor,' he says.

'My grandparents didn't know who to trust. They decided not to trust anyone.'

'And now they're dead, your brother is in jail, and you want our help.' Mazen brings his pipe back to his mouth.

'We must give her aid.' Sana is beside me, her hand on my shoulder. 'It's our duty. She's, as you say, *one of our own*.'

Tariq stands behind her, and I notice that the fighters have divided into two groups. The ones backing Mazen are closer to Keenan's age. The rebels clustered behind Sana are older. *She's the head of our faction*, Tariq had said. Now I realize what he meant: the Resistance is divided. Sana leads the older fighters. And, as she'd hinted at before, Mazen leads the younger ones – and serves as overall leader.

Many of the older fighters stare at me, perhaps searching my face for evidence of Mother and Father. I don't blame them. My parents were the greatest leaders in the Resistance's five-hundred-year history.

Then they'd been betrayed by one of their own. Caught. Tortured. Executed along with my sister, Lis. The Resistance collapsed and never recovered.

'If the Lioness's son is in trouble, we owe it to her to help,' Sana says to those gathered behind her. 'How many times did she save your life, Mazen? How many times did she save all of us?'

Suddenly, everyone is talking.

'Mirra and I set fire to an Empire garrison—'

'She could cut right to your soul with her eyes, the Lioness—'

'Saw her fend off a dozen auxes once – not a bit of fear in her—'

I have stories of my own. *She wanted to leave us. She wanted to abandon her children for the Resistance, but Father wouldn't let her. When they fought, Lis took me and Darin into the forest and sang so we wouldn't hear them. That's my first memory – Lis singing me a song while the Lioness raged a few yards away.*

After my parents left us with Nan and Pop, it took weeks for me to stop feeling jumpy, to get used to living with two people who actually seemed to love each other.

I say none of this, instead knotting my fingers together as the fighters tell their stories. I know they want me to be brave and charming, like Mother. They want me to listen, really listen, like Father.

If they learn what I truly am, they'll throw me out of here without a thought. The Resistance doesn't tolerate weaklings.

'Laia.' Mazen speaks over them, and they quiet down. 'We don't have the manpower to break into a Martial prison. We'd risk too much.'

I don't get the chance to protest because Sana's speaking for me.

'The Lioness would have done it for you without a second thought.'

'We have to bring down the Empire,' a blond man behind Mazen says. 'Not waste our time saving some boy.'

'We don't abandon our own!'

'We'll be the ones doing all the fighting,' another of Mazen's men calls from the back of the crowd, 'while you old-timers sit around taking all the credit.'

Tariq shoves past Sana, his face dark. 'You mean while we plan and prepare to make sure you young fools don't get ambushed—'

'Enough. Enough!' Mazen raises his hands. Sana pulls Tariq back, and the other fighters fall silent. 'We won't solve this by shouting at each other. Keenan, find Haider and bring him to my chambers. Sana, get Eran and join us. We'll decide this privately.'

Sana hurries away but Keenan doesn't move. I flush beneath his stare, not sure what to say. His eyes are almost black in the cavern's dim light.

'I see it now,' he murmurs, as if to himself. 'I can't believe I almost missed it.'

He can't have known my parents. He doesn't look much older than me. I wonder how long he's been in the Resistance, but before I can ask, he disappears into the tunnels, leaving me to stare after him.

Hours later, after I've forced food down my throat and pretended to sleep on a rock-hard bunk, after the stars have faded and the sun has risen, one of the cavern doors swings open.

Mazen enters, followed by Keenan, Sana, and two younger men. The Resistance leader limps to a table where Tariq is sitting and gestures me over. I try to read Sana's face as I join them, but her expression is carefully neutral. The other fighters gather around, as interested as I am to see what my fate will be.

'Laia,' Mazen says. 'Keenan here thinks we should keep you in camp. Safe.' Mazen infuses the word with scorn. Beside me, Tariq looks askance at Keenan.

'She'll cause less trouble here.' The red-haired fighter's eyes flash. 'Breaking her brother out will cost men – good men—' He stops at a look from Mazen and clamps his mouth shut. And though I hardly know Keenan, I'm stung at how violently he's opposing me. What have I ever done to him?

'It *will* cost good men,' Mazen says. 'Which is why I've decided that if Laia wants our help, she has to be willing to give us something in return.' Fighters from both factions eye their leader warily. Mazen turns to me. 'We'll help you, if you help us.'

'What could I possibly do for the Resistance?'

'You can cook, yes?' Mazen asks. 'And clean? Dress hair, press clothing—'

'Make soap, wash dishes, barter – yes. You've just described every freewoman in the Scholars' Quarter.'

'You can read too,' Mazen says. When I begin to deny the charge, he shakes his head. 'Empire rules be damned. You forget I knew your parents.'

'What does any of that have to do with helping the Resistance?'

'We'll break your brother out of prison if you spy for us.'

For a moment, I don't speak, though I feel a tug of curiosity. This is the last thing I expected. 'Who do you want me to spy on?'

'The Commandant of Blackcliff Military Academy.'

CHAPTER TEN

Elias

The morning after the Augur's visit, I stumble to the mess hall like a Cadet suffering his first hangover, cursing the overly bright sun. What little sleep I got was sabotaged by a familiar nightmare, one in which I wander through a stinking, body-strewn battlefield. In the dream, screams rend the air and somehow I know that the pain and suffering are my fault, that the dead have fallen by my hand.

Not the best way to start a day. Especially graduation day.

I run into Helene as she, Dex, Faris, and Tristas leave mess. She stuffs a rock-hard biscuit into my hand, ignoring my protests, and pulls me away from the hall.

'We're late.' I barely hear her over the ceaseless beating of the drums, which are ordering all graduates to the armoury to pick up our ceremonials – the armour of a full Mask. 'Demetrius and Leander already left.'

Helene chatters about how thrilling it will be to put on our ceremonials. Dimly, I listen to her and the others, nodding at appropriate times, exclaiming when necessary. All the while, I'm thinking of what Cain said to me last night. *You will escape. You will leave the Empire. You will live. But you will find no solace in doing so.*

Do I trust the Augur? He could be trying to trap me here, hoping I'll stay a Mask long enough to decide that a soldier's life is better than an exile's. I think of how the Commandant's eyes shine when she whips a student, how Grandfather boasts of his body count. They are my kin; their blood is my blood. What if their lusts for war and glory and power are mine too and I just don't know it? Could I learn to revel in being a Mask? The Augur read my thoughts. Does he see something evil inside me that I'm too blind to face?

But then, Cain seemed convinced that I'd meet the same fate if I deserted. *Shadows will bloom in your heart, and you will become everything you hate.*

So my choices are to stay and be evil or to run and be evil. Wonderful.

When we are halfway to the armoury, Hel finally notices my silence, taking in the rumpled clothing, the bloodshot eyes.

'You all right?' she asks.

'Fine.'

'You look like hell.'

'Rough night.'

'What happ—'

Faris, walking ahead with Dex and Tristas, drops back. 'Leave him alone, Aquilla. The man's tuckered out. Snuck down to the docks to celebrate a bit early, eh, Veturius?' He claps me on the shoulder with a big hand and laughs. 'Could have invited a fellow along.'

'Don't be disgusting,' Helene says.

'Don't be a prude,' Faris retorts.

A full-scale argument ensues, during which Helene's disapproval of prostitutes is vehemently shouted down by Faris while Dex argues that leaving school grounds to visit a brothel isn't strictly forbidden. Tristas points to the tattoo of his fiancée's name and declares neutrality.

Amid the swiftly flung insults, Helene's gaze slides to me repeatedly. She knows I don't frequent the docks. I avoid her eyes. She wants an explanation, but where would I even begin? *Well, you see, Hel, I wanted to desert today, but this damned Augur showed up and now . . .*

When we arrive at the armoury, students spill out the front doors, and Faris and Dex disappear into the crush. I've never seen the Senior Skulls so . . . happy. With liberation just a few minutes away, everyone is smiling. Skulls I barely ever speak to greet me, clap me on the back, joke with me.

'Elias, Helene.' Leander, his nose crooked from the time Helene broke it, calls us over. Demetrius stands beside him, grim as always. I wonder if he feels any joy today. Maybe he's just relieved to leave the place where he watched his brother die.

When he sees Helene, Leander self-consciously runs his hand over his curly hair – which sticks up all over the place no matter how short he cuts it. I try not to smile. He's liked her for ages, though he pretends not to. 'Armourer already called your names.' Leander nods to two stacks of armour and weaponry behind him. 'We grabbed your ceremonials for you.'

Helene goes for hers like a jewel thief for rubies, holding the bracers to the light, exclaiming at how Blackcliff's diamond symbol is seamlessly hammered into the shield. The close-fitting armour is forged by the Teluman smithy – one of the oldest in the Empire – and is strong enough to turn away all but the finest blades. Blackcliff's final gift to us.

Once the armour is on, I strap on my weaponry: scims and daggers of Serric steel, razor-sharp and graceful, especially compared to the dull, utilitarian weapons we've used until now. The last piece is a black cape held in place by a chain. When I'm done, I look up to see Helene staring at me.

'What?' I say. Her expression is so intent that I glance down, assuming I've put my chest plate on backwards. But everything is where it should be. When I look back up, she's standing before me, adjusting my cape, her long fingers brushing my neck.

'It wasn't straight.' She dons her helmet. 'How do I look?'

If the Augurs made my armour to accentuate my body's power, they made Hel's to accentuate her beauty.

'You look . . .' *Like a warrior goddess. Like a jinni of air come to bring us all to our knees. Skies, what the hell is wrong with me?* 'Like a Mask,' I say.

She laughs, girlish and preposterously alluring, drawing the attention of other students: Leander, who jerks his gaze away and rubs his crooked nose guiltily when I catch him looking, Faris, who grins and mutters something to an appraising Dex. Across the room, Zak stares too, the expression on his face something between longing and puzzlement. Then I see Marcus beside Zak, watching his brother as his brother watches Hel.

'Look, boys,' Marcus says. 'A bitch in armour.'

My scim is half-drawn when Hel puts a hand on my arm, her eyes flashing fire at me. *My fight. Not yours.*

'Go to hell, Marcus.' Helene finds her cape a few feet away and dons it. The Snake ambles over, his eyes creeping down her body, leaving no doubt as to what he's thinking.

'Armour doesn't suit you, Aquilla,' he says. 'I'd prefer you in a dress. Or nothing at all.' He lifts a hand to her hair, wrapping a loose tendril gently around his finger before yanking it hard, pulling her face towards his.

It takes me a second to recognize the snarl that splits the air as my own. I'm a foot from Marcus, my fists hungry for his flesh, when two of his toadies, Thaddius and Julius, grab me from behind, wrenching my arms back. Demetrius is beside me in a second, his sharp elbow jutting into Thaddius's face, but Julius aims a kick at Demetrius's back, and he goes down.

Then, in a flash of silver, Helene's holding one knife to Marcus's neck and the other to his groin.

'Let go of my hair,' she says. 'Or I'll relieve you of your manhood.'

Marcus releases the ice-blonde curl and whispers something in Helene's ear. And just like that, her confident air dissolves, the knife at Marcus's throat falters, and he grabs her face in his hands and kisses her.

I'm so disgusted that for a moment all I can do is gape and try not to vomit. Then a muffled scream erupts from Helene, and I tear my arms from Thaddius and Julius. In a second, I'm past them both, shoving Marcus away from Helene, landing blow after satisfying blow on his face.

Between my punches, Marcus is laughing, and Helene is wiping at her mouth frenziedly. Leander pulls at my shoulders, rabidly demanding a turn at the Snake.

Behind me, Demetrius is back on his feet trading punches with Julius, who overpowers him, shoving his pale head to the ground. Faris comes hurtling out of the crowd, his giant body thudding into Julius and knocking him down, a bull ramming through a fence. I spot Tristas's tattoo and Dex's dark skin, and all hell breaks loose.

Then someone hisses 'Commandant!' Faris and Julius lurch to their feet, I shove away from Marcus, and Helene stops clawing at her face. The Snake staggers up slowly, his eyes darkening into twin pools of bruise.

My mother cuts through the Skulls, coming straight for Helene and me.

'Veturius. Aquilla.' She spits our names like fruit gone bad. 'Explain.'

'No explanation, Commandant, sir,' Helene and I say at the same time.

I look past her, into the distance as I've been trained to, and her cold glare bores into me with the delicacy of a blunt knife. From his spot behind the Commandant, Marcus smirks, and I clench my jaw. If Helene is whipped because of his depravity, I'll hold off on deserting just so I can kill him.

'Eighth bell is minutes away.' The Commandant turns her gaze to the rest of the armoury. 'You will compose yourselves and report to the amphitheatre. Any more incidents like this and those involved will be shipped to Kauf, forthwith. Understood?'

'Yes, sir!'

The Skulls file out quietly. As Fivers, we all did six months' guard duty at Kauf Prison, far to the north. None of us would risk being sent there for something as stupid as a graduation-day brawl.

'Are you all right?' I ask Hel when the Commandant's out of earshot.

'I want to rip my face off and replace it with one that's never been touched by that swine.'

'You need someone else to kiss you is all,' I say, before realizing how that sounds. 'Not . . . uh . . . not that I'm volunteering. I mean—'

'Yeah, I got it.' Helene rolls her eyes. Her jaw goes tight, and I wish I'd kept my mouth shut about the kissing. 'Thanks, by the way,' she says. 'For punching him.'

'I'd have killed him if the Commandant hadn't shown up.'

Her eyes are warm when she looks at me, and I'm about to ask her what Marcus whispered in her ear when Zak passes us. He fiddles with his brown hair and slows, as if he wants to say something. But I look at him with murder in my eyes, and after a few seconds, he turns away.

Minutes later, Helene and I join the Senior Skulls lining up outside the amphitheatre's entrance, and the armoury brawl is forgotten. We march into the amphitheatre to the applause of family, students, city officials, the Emperor's emissaries, and an honour guard of nearly two hundred legionnaires.

I meet Helene's eyes and see my own astonishment mirrored there. It is surreal to be here on the field instead of watching enviously from the stands. The sky above burns brilliant and clean without a single cloud from horizon to horizon. Flags festoon the theatre's heights, the red-and-gold pennant of Gens Taia snapping in the wind beside the black, diamond-emblazoned standard of Blackcliff.

My grandfather, General Quin Veturius, head of Gens Veturia, sits in a shaded box in the front row. About fifty of his closest relatives – brothers, sisters, nieces, nephews – are arrayed around him. I don't have to see his eyes to know he's taking my measure, checking the angle of my scim, scrutinizing the fit of my armour.

After I was chosen for Blackcliff, Grandfather took one look at my eyes and recognized his daughter in them. He brought me into his home when Mother refused to bring me into hers. No doubt she was enraged that I had survived when she assumed she was rid of me.

I spent every leave training with Grandfather, enduring beatings and harsh discipline but gaining, in return, a distinct edge over my classmates. He knew I would need that edge. Few of Blackcliff's students have uncertain parentage, and none had ever been raised among the Tribes. Both facts made me an object of curiosity – and ridicule. But if anyone dared treat me poorly because of my background, Grandfather put them in their place, usually with the point of his sword – and quickly taught me to do the same. He can be as heartless as his daughter, but he's the only relative I have who treats me like family.

Though it's not regulation, I lift my hand in salute as I pass him, gratified when he nods in return.

After a series of formation drills, the graduates march to the wooden benches at the centre of the field and draw scims, holding them high. A low rumble starts up, growing until it sounds like a thunderstorm has been unleashed in the amphitheatre. It's the other Blackcliff students, pounding on their stone seats and roaring with a mix of pride and envy. Beside me, Helene and Leander both fail to suppress grins.

Amid the noise, silence descends in my head. It's a strange silence, infinitely small, infinitely large, and I'm locked inside it, pacing, circling the question. *Do I run? Do I desert?* Far away, like a voice heard underwater, the Commandant orders us to return scims and sit. She delivers a terse speech from a raised dais, and when it comes time to take our oaths to the Empire, I only know to stand because everyone around me does.

Stay or run? I ask myself. *Stay or run?*

I think my mouth moves along with everyone else's as they vow their blood and bodies to the Empire. The Commandant graduates us, and the cheer that erupts out of the new Masks, raw and relieved, is what wrenches me from my thoughts. Faris rips off his school tags and throws them into the sky, followed by the rest of us. They fly into the air, catching the sun like a flock of silver birds.

Families chant their graduates' names. Helene's parents and sisters call out *Aquilla!* Faris's family calls out *Candelan!* I hear *Vissan! Tullius! Galerius!* And then I hear a voice rising above all the rest. *Veturius! Veturius!* Grandfather stands in his box, backed by the rest of the family, reminding everyone here that one of the Empire's most powerful gens has seen a son graduate today.

I find his eyes, and for once, there's no criticism there, only a fierce pride. He grins at me, wolfish and white against the silver of his mask, and I find myself smiling back before confusion floods me and I look away. He won't be smiling if I desert.

'Elias!' Helene throws her arms around me, eyes shining. 'We did it! We—'

We spot the Augurs in the same moment, and her arms fall away. I've never seen all fourteen at once, and my stomach dips. Why are they here? Their hoods are thrown back, revealing their unsettlingly stark features, and, led by Cain, they ghost across the grass and form a half circle around the Commandant's dais.

The cheers of the audience fade into a questioning hum. My mother watches, her hand idle on her scim hilt. When Cain mounts the dais, she steps aside as if she expected him.

Cain raises his hand for silence, and in seconds, the crowd goes mute. From where I sit on the field, he's a bizarre spectre, so frail and ashen. But when he speaks, his voice rings out across the amphitheatre with a force that makes everyone sit up.

'From among the battle-hardened youth there shall rise the Foretold,' he says. 'The Greatest Emperor, scourge of our enemies, commander of a host most devastating. And the Empire shall be made whole.

'So the Augurs foretold five hundred years ago as we drew the stones of this school from the shuddering earth. And so the fore-telling shall come to pass. The line of Emperor Taius XXI *will* fail.'

A near-mutinous buzz rolls through the crowd. If anyone but an Augur had questioned the Emperor's line, he'd have already been struck down. The legionnaires of the honour guard bristle, hands on their weapons, but at one look from Cain, they settle back, a pack of barely cowed dogs.

'Taius XXI shall have no direct male issue,' Cain says. 'Upon his death, the Empire will fall unless a new Warrior Emperor is chosen.

'Taius the First, Father of our Empire and Pater of Gens Taia, was the finest fighter of his time. He was tested, tempered, and tried before he was deemed fit to rule. The people of the Empire expect no less of their new leader.'

Bleeding, burning skies. Behind me, Tristas elbows an openmouthed Dex triumphantly. We all know what Cain will say next. But I still don't believe what I'm hearing.

'Thus, the time for the Trials has come.'

The amphitheatre explodes. Or at least it sounds like it's exploded because I've never heard anything so loud. Tristas bellows, 'I told you!' at Dex, who looks as if someone's smashed him over the head with a hammer. Leander shouts, 'Who? Who?' Marcus laughs, a smug cackle that makes me yearn to stab him. Helene has a hand clapped over her mouth, her eyes comically wide as she grasps for words.

Cain's hand comes up again, and again, the crowd falls deathly silent.

'The Trials are upon us,' he says. 'To ensure the future of the Empire, the new Emperor must be at the peak of his strength, as Taius was when he took the throne. Thus do we turn to our battle-hardened youth, our newest Masks. But not all shall vie for this great honour. Only the greatest of our graduates are worthy, the strongest. Only four. Of these four Aspirants, one will be named the Foretold. One will swear fealty and serve as the Blood Shrike. The others will be lost, as leaves on the wind. This, too, we have seen.'

My blood begins to pound in my ears.

'Elias Veturius, Marcus Farrar, Helene Aquilla, Zacharias Farrar.' He calls our names in the order we're ranked. 'Rise and come forward.'

The amphitheatre is dead quiet. Numbly, I stand, shutting out the searching looks of my classmates, the glee on Marcus's face, the indecision on Zak's. *The field of battle is my temple. The swordpoint is my priest* . . .

Helene's back is ramrod straight, but she looks to me, to Cain, to the Commandant. At first, I think she's frightened. Then I notice the shine in her eyes, the spring in her step.

When Hel and I were Fivers, a Barbarian raiding party took us prisoner. I was trussed like a festival-day goat, but they tied Helene's hands in front of her with twine and propped her on the back of a pony, assuming she was harmless. That night, she used the twine to garrotte three of our jailers and broke the necks of the other three with her bare hands.

'*They always underestimate me*,' she said afterwards, sounding puzzled. She was right, of course. It's a mistake even I make. Hel's not frightened, I realize. She's euphoric. She wants this.

The walk to the stage takes too little time. In seconds, I'm standing in front of Cain with the others.

'To be chosen as an Aspirant for the Trials is to be granted the greatest honour the Empire has to offer.' Cain looks at each one of us, but it seems like his gaze lingers longest on me. 'In exchange for this great gift, the Augurs require an oath: that as Aspirants, you will see the Trials through until the Emperor is named. The penalty for breaking this oath is death.

'You must not undertake this oath lightly,' Cain says. 'If you wish, you may turn and leave this podium. You will remain a Mask, with all the respect and honour accorded to those of that title. Another will be chosen in your place. It is, in the end, your choice.'

Your choice. Those two words shake me to my marrow. *Tomorrow you will have to make a choice. Between deserting and doing your duty. Between running from your destiny and facing it.*

Cain doesn't mean doing my duty as a Mask. He wants me to choose between taking the Trials and deserting.

You devious, red-eyed devil. I want to be free of the Empire. But how can I find freedom if I take the Trials? If I win and become Emperor, I'll be tied to the Empire for life. And if I swear fealty, I'll be chained to the Emperor as the second-in-command – the Blood Shrike.

Or I'll be a leaf lost in the wind, which is just a fancy Augur way of saying *dead.*

Reject him, Elias. Run. By this time tomorrow, you'll be miles away.

Cain watches Marcus, and the Augur's head is tilted as if he's listening to something beyond our ken.

'Marcus Farrar. You are ready.' It's not a question. Marcus kneels and draws his sword, offering it up to the Augur, his eyes glinting with a strangely exultant zeal, as if he's already been named Emperor.

'Repeat after me,' Cain says. 'I, Marcus Farrar, swear by blood and by bone, by my honour and the honour of Gens Farrar, that I will dedicate myself to the Trials, that I will see them through until the Emperor is named or my body lies cold.'

Marcus repeats the vow, his voice echoing in the breathless silence of the amphitheatre. Cain closes Marcus's hands over his blade, pressing until blood drips from his palms. A moment later, Helene kneels, offering her sword, repeating the vow, her voice singing out across the field as clearly as a bell at dawn.

The Augur turns to Zak, who looks at his brother for a long moment before nodding and taking the oath. Suddenly, I'm the only one of the four Aspirants still standing, and Cain is before me, awaiting my decision.

Like Zak, I hesitate. Cain's words come back to me: *You are woven through our dreams. A thread of silver in a tapestry of night.* Is becoming Emperor my destiny, then? How can such a destiny lead to freedom? I have no desire to rule – the very idea of doing so is repellent to me.

But then my future as a deserter is no more appealing. *You will become everything you hate – evil, merciless, cruel.*

Do I trust Cain when he says I will find freedom if I take the Trials? At Blackcliff we learn to classify people: civilian, combatant, enemy, ally, informer, defector. Based on that, we decide our next steps. But I have no understanding of the Augur. I don't know his motivations, his desires. The only thing I have is my instinct, which tells me that in this matter, at least, Cain wasn't lying. Whether his prediction is true or not, he trusts that it is. And since my gut tells me to trust him, albeit grudgingly, there's only one decision that makes sense.

My eyes never leaving Cain's, I drop to my knees, draw my sword, and run the blade across my palm. My blood falls to the dais in a rapid drip.

'I, Elias Veturius, swear, by blood and by bone . . .'

CHAPTER ELEVEN

Laia

The Commandant of Blackcliff Military Academy.

My curiosity for the spy mission withers. The Empire trains the Masks at Blackcliff – Masks like the one who murdered my family and stole my brother. The school sprawls atop Serra's eastern cliffs like a colossal vulture, a jumble of austere buildings enclosed by a black granite wall. No one knows what happens behind that wall, how the Masks train, how many there are, how they are chosen. Every year, a new class of Masks leaves Blackcliff, young, savage, and deadly. For a Scholar – especially a girl – Blackcliff is the most dangerous place in the city.

Mazen goes on. 'She lost her personal slave—'

'The girl threw herself off the cliffs a week ago,' Keenan retorts, defying Mazen's glare. 'She's the third slave to die in the Commandant's service this year.'

'Quiet,' Mazen says. 'I won't lie to you, Laia. The woman's unpleasant—'

'She's insane,' Keenan says. 'They call her the Bitch of Blackcliff. You won't survive the Commandant. The mission will fail.'

Mazen's fist comes down on the table. Keenan doesn't flinch.

'If you can't keep your mouth shut,' the Resistance leader growls, 'then leave.'

Tariq's jaw drops as he looks between the two men. Sana, meanwhile, watches Keenan with a thoughtful expression. Others in the cavern stare too, and I get the feeling that Keenan and Mazen don't disagree very often. Keenan scrapes his chair back and leaves the table, disappearing into the muttering crowd behind Mazen.

'You're perfect for the job, Laia,' Mazen says. 'You have all the skills the Commandant would expect from a house slave. She'll assume you're illiterate. And we have the means to get you in.'

'What happens if I'm caught?'

'You're dead.' Mazen looks me straight in the eye, and I feel a bitter appreciation for his honesty. 'Every spy we've sent to Blackcliff has been discovered and killed. This isn't a mission for the fainthearted.'

I almost want to laugh. He couldn't have picked a worse person for it. 'You're not doing a very good job selling it.'

'I don't have to sell it,' Mazen says. 'We can find your brother and break him out. You can be our eyes and ears in Blackcliff. A simple exchange.'

'You trust me to do this?' I ask. 'You hardly know me.'

'I knew your parents. That's enough for me.'

'Mazen.' Tariq speaks up. 'She's just a girl. Surely we don't need to—'

'She invoked *Izzat*,' Mazen says. 'But *Izzat* means more than freedom. It means more than honour. It means courage. It means proving yourself.'

'He's right,' I say. If the Resistance is going to help me, I can't have the fighters thinking I'm weak. A glimmer of red catches my eye, and I look across the cavern to where Keenan leans against a bunk watching me, his hair like fire in the torchlight. He doesn't want me to take this mission because he doesn't want to risk the men to save Darin. I put a hand to my armlet. *Be brave, Laia.*

I turn to Mazen. 'If I do this, you'll find Darin? You'll break him out of jail?'

'You have my word. It won't be hard to locate him. He's not a Resistance leader, so it's not as if they'll send him to Kauf.' Mazen snorts, but mention of the infamous northern prison sends a chill across my skin. Kauf's interrogators have one goal: to make inmates suffer as much as possible before they die.

My parents died in Kauf. My sister, only twelve at the time, died there too.

'By the time you make your first report,' Mazen says, 'I'll be able to tell you where Darin is. When your mission is complete, we'll break him out.'

'And after?'

'We prise your slaves' cuffs off and pull you out of the school. We can make it look like a suicide, so you're not hunted. You can join us, if you like. Or we can arrange passage to Marinn for you both.'

Marinn. The free lands. What I wouldn't give to escape there with my brother, to live in a place with no Martials, no Masks, no Empire.

But first I have to survive a spy mission. I have to survive Blackcliff.

Across the cavern, Keenan shakes his head. But the fighters around me nod. *This is Izzat,* they seem to say. I fall silent, as if considering, but my decision is made the second I realize that going to Blackcliff is the only way to get Darin back.

'I'll do it.'

'Good.' Mazen doesn't sound surprised, and I wonder if he knew all along that I would say yes. He raises his voice so it carries. 'Keenan will be your handler.'

At this, the younger man's face goes, if possible, even darker. He presses his lips together as if to keep from speaking.

'Her hands and feet are cut up,' Mazen says. 'See to her injuries, Keenan, and tell her what she needs to know. She leaves for Blackcliff tonight.'

Mazen leaves, trailed by members of his faction, while Tariq claps me on the shoulder and wishes me luck. His allies pepper me with advice: *Never go looking for your handler. Don't trust anyone.* They only wish to help, but it's overwhelming, and when Keenan cuts through the crowd to retrieve me, I'm almost relieved.

Almost. He jerks his head to a table in the corner of the cavern and walks off without waiting for me.

A glint of light near the table turns out to be a small spring. Keenan fills two tubs with water and a powder I recognize as tanroot. He sets one tub on the table and one on the floor.

I scrub my hands and feet clean, wincing as the tanroot sinks into the scrapes I picked up in the catacombs. Keenan watches silently. Beneath his scrutiny, I am ashamed at how quickly the water turns black with muck – and then angry at myself for being ashamed.

When I'm done, Keenan sits at the table across from me and takes my hands. I'm expecting him to be brusque, but his hands are – not gentle, exactly, but not callous, either. As he examines my cuts, I think of a dozen questions I could ask him, none of which will make him think that I'm strong and capable instead of childish and petty. *Why do you seem to hate me? What did I do to you?*

'You shouldn't be doing this.' He rubs a numbing ointment on one of the deeper cuts, keeping his attention fixed on my wounds. 'This mission.'

You've made that clear, you jackass. 'I won't let Mazen down. I'll do what I have to.'

'You'll try, I'm sure.' I'm stung at his bluntness, though by now it should be clear that he has no faith in me. 'The woman's a savage. The last person we sent in—'

'Do you think I want to spy on her?' I burst out. He looks up, surprise in his eyes. 'I don't have a choice. Not if I want to save the only family I have left. So just—' *Shut it,* I want to say. 'Just don't make this harder.'

Something like embarrassment crosses his face, and he regards me with a tiny bit less scorn. 'I'm . . . sorry.' His words are reluctant, but a reluctant apology is better than none at all. I nod jerkily and realize that his eyes are not blue or green but a deep chestnut brown. *You're noticing his eyes, Laia. Which means you're staring into them. Which means you need to stop.* The smell of the salve stings my nostrils, and I wrinkle my nose.

'Are you using twin-thistle in this salve?' I ask. At his shrug, I pull the bottle from him and take another sniff. 'Try rilberry next time. It doesn't smell like goat dung, at least.'

Keenan raises a fiery eyebrow and wraps one of my hands with gauze. 'You know your remedies. Useful skill. Your grandparents were healers?'

'My grandfather.' It hurts to speak of Pop, and I pause a long while before going on. 'He started training me formally a year and a half ago. I mixed his remedies before that.'

'Do you like it? Healing?'

'It's a trade.' Most Scholars who aren't enslaved work menial jobs – as farmhands or cleaners or stevedores – backbreaking labour for which they're paid next to nothing. 'I'm lucky to have one. Though, when I was little, I wanted to be a *Kehanni*.'

Keenan's mouth curves into the barest smile. It is a small thing, but it transforms his entire face and lightens the weight on my chest.

'A Tribal tale-spinner?' he says. 'Don't tell me you believe in myths of jinn and efrits and wraiths that kidnap children in the night?'

'No.' I think of the raid. Of the Mask. My lightness melts away. 'I don't need to believe in the supernatural. Not when there's worse that roams the night.'

He goes still, a sudden stillness that draws my eyes up and into his. My breath hitches at what I see laid bare in his gaze: a wrenching knowledge, a bitter understanding of pain that I know well. Here's someone who has walked paths as dark as mine. Darker, maybe.

Then coldness descends over his face, and his hands are moving again.

'Right,' he says. 'Listen carefully. Today was graduation day at Blackcliff. But we've just learned that this year's ceremony was different. Special.'

He tells me of the Trials and the four Aspirants. Then he gives me my mission.

'We need three pieces of information. We need to know what each Trial is, where it's taking place, and when. And we need to know this before each Trial begins, not after.'

I have a dozen questions, but I don't ask, knowing he'll just think me more foolish.

'How long will I be in the school?'

Keenan shrugs and finishes bandaging my hands. 'We know

next to nothing about the Trials,' he says. 'But I can't imagine it will take more than a few weeks – a month, at most.'

'Do you – do you think Darin will last that long?'

Keenan doesn't answer.

* * *

Hours later, in the early evening, I find myself in a house in the Foreign Quarter with Keenan and Sana, standing before an elderly Tribesman. He's clad in the loose robes of his people and looks more like a kindly old uncle than a Resistance operative.

When Sana explains what she wants of him, he takes one look at me and folds his arms across his chest.

'Absolutely not,' he says in heavily accented Serran. 'The Commandant will eat her alive.'

Keenan throws Sana a pointed look, as if to say, *What did you expect?*

'With respect,' Sana says to the Tribesman, 'can we . . .' She gestures to a lattice-screen doorway leading to another room. They disappear behind the lattice. Sana's speaking too softly for me to hear, but whatever she's saying must not be working, because even through the screen, I can see the Tribesman shaking his head.

'He won't do it,' I say.

Beside me, Keenan leans against the wall, unconcerned. 'Sana can convince him. She's not leader of her faction for nothing.'

'I wish I could do something.'

'Try looking a little braver.'

'What, like you?' I arrange my face so it's blank as slate, slump against the wall, and look off into the distance. Keenan actually smiles for a fraction of a second. It takes years off his face.

I rub a bare foot across the hypnotic swirls of the thick Tribal rug on the floor. Pillows embroidered with tiny mirrors are strewn across it, and lamps of coloured glass hang from the roof, catching the last rays of sunlight.

'Darin and I came to a house like this to sell Nan's jams once.' I reach up to touch one of the lamps. 'I asked him why Tribesmen have mirrors everywhere, and he said—' The memory is clear and sharp in my mind, and an ache for my brother, for my grandparents, pulses in my chest with such violence that I clamp my mouth shut.

Tribesmen think the mirrors ward off evil, Darin said that day. He took out his sketchbook while we waited for the Tribal trader and started drawing, capturing the intricacy of the lattice screens and lanterns with small, quick strokes of charcoal. *Jinn and wraiths can't stand the sight of themselves, apparently.*

After that, he'd answered a dozen more of my questions with his usual quiet confidence. At the time, I'd wondered how he knew so much. Only now do I understand – Darin always listened more than he spoke, watching, learning. In that way, he was like Pop.

The ache in my chest expands, and my eyes are suddenly hot.

'It will get better,' Keenan says. I look up to see sadness flicker across his face, almost instantly replaced by that now-familiar chill. 'You'll never forget them, not even after years. But one day, you'll go a whole minute without feeling the pain. Then an hour. A day. That's all you can ask for, really.' His voice drops. 'You'll heal. I promise.'

He looks away, distant again, but I'm grateful to him anyway, because for the first time since the raid, I feel less alone. A second later, Sana and the Tribesman come around the screen.

'You're sure this is what you want?' the Tribesman asks me.

I nod, not trusting my voice.

He sighs. 'Very well.' He turns to Sana and Keenan. 'Say your goodbyes. If I take her now, I can still get her into the school by dark.'

'You'll be all right.' Sana hugs me tightly, and I wonder if she's trying to convince me or herself. 'You're the Lioness's daughter. And the Lioness was a survivor.'

Until she wasn't. I lower my gaze so Sana doesn't see my doubt. She heads out the door, and then Keenan is before me. I cross my arms, not wanting him to think I need a hug from him too.

But he doesn't touch me. Just cocks his head and lifts his fist to his heart – the Resistance salute.

'Death before tyranny,' he says. Then he, too, is gone.

* * *

A half hour later, dusk drops over the city of Serra, and I am following the Tribesman swiftly through the Mercator Quarter, home to the wealthiest members of the Martial merchant class. We stop before the ornate iron gate of a slaver's home, and the Tribesman checks my manacles, his tan robes swishing softly as he moves around me. I clasp my bandaged hands together to stop them from shaking, but the Tribesman gently prises my fingers apart.

'Slavers catch lies the way spiders catch flies,' he says. 'Your fear is good. It makes your story real. Remember: do not speak.'

I nod vigorously. Even if I wanted to say something, I'm too frightened. *The slaver is Blackcliff's sole supplier,* Keenan had explained while walking me to the Tribesman's house. *It's taken months for our operative to gain his trust. If he doesn't pick you for the Commandant, your mission's dead before it begins.*

We're escorted through the gates, and moments later, the slaver is circling me, sweating in the heat. He's as tall as the Tribesman but twice as broad, with a paunch that strains the buttons of his gold brocade shirt.

'Not bad.' The slaver snaps his fingers, and a slave-girl appears from the recesses of his mansion bearing a tray of drinks. The slaver slurps one down, pointedly not offering anything to the Tribesman. 'The brothels will pay well for her.'

'As a whore, she won't fetch more than a hundred marks,' the Tribesman says in his hypnotic lilt. 'I need two hundred.'

The slaver snorts, and I want to strangle him for it. The shaded streets of his neighbourhood are littered with sparkling fountains and bow-backed Scholar slaves. The man's house is a bloated hodgepodge of arches and columns and courtyards. Two hundred silvers is a drop in the bucket for him. He probably paid more for the plaster lions flanking his front door.

'I hoped to sell her as a house slave,' the Tribesman continues. 'I heard you were looking for one.'

'I am,' the slaver admits. 'Commandant's been on my back for days. Hag keeps killing off her girls. Temper like a viper.' The slaver eyes me the way a rancher eyes a heifer, and I hold my breath. Then he shakes his head.

'She's too small, too young, too pretty. She won't last a week in Blackcliff, and I don't want the bother of replacing her. I'll give you one hundred for her and sell her to Madam Moh over dockside.'

A bead of sweat trickles down the Tribesman's otherwise serene face. Mazen ordered him to do whatever it took to get me into Blackcliff. But if he drops his price suddenly, the slaver will be suspicious. If he sells me as a whore, the Resistance will have to get me out – and there is no guarantee they can do so quickly. If he doesn't sell me at all, my attempt to save Darin will fail.

Do something, Laia. Darin again, fanning my courage. *Or I'm dead.*

'I press clothes well, Master.' The words are out before I can reconsider. The Tribesman's mouth drops open, and the slaver regards me as if I'm a rat who has begun juggling.

'And, um . . . I can cook. And clean and dress hair,' I trail off into a whisper. 'I'd – I'd make a good maid.'

The slaver stares me down, and I wish I'd kept my mouth shut. Then his eyes grow shrewd, almost amused.

'Afraid of whoring, girl? Don't see why, it's an honest enough trade.' He circles me again, then jerks my chin up until I am looking into his reptilian green eyes. 'You said you can dress hair and press clothes? Can you barter and handle yourself in the market?'

'Yes, sir.'

'You can't read, of course. Can you count?'

Of course I can count. And I can read too, you double-chinned pig.
'Yes, sir. I can count.'

'She'll have to learn to keep her mouth shut,' the slaver says. 'I've got to eat the cost of cleanup. Can't send her to Blackcliff looking like a chimney sweep.' He considers. 'I'll take her for one hundred and fifty silver marks.'

'I can always take her to one of the Illustian houses,' the Tribesman suggests. 'Underneath all that dirt, she's a fine-looking girl. I'm sure they'd pay well for her.'

The slaver narrows his eyes. I wonder if Mazen's man has erred, trying to bargain higher. *Come on, you miser,* I think at the slaver. *Cough up a little extra.*

The slaver pulls out a sack of coins. I fight to hide my relief.

'A hundred and eighty marks then. Not a copper more. Take off her chains.'

Less than an hour later, I'm locked inside a ghost wagon that is heading for Blackcliff. Wide silver bands that mark me as a slave adorn each wrist. A chain leads from the collar around my neck to a steel rail inside the wagon. My skin still smarts from the scrubbing I got from two slave-girls, and my head aches from the tight bun they tamed my hair into. My dress, black silk with a corset-tight bodice and diamond-patterned skirt, is the finest thing I've ever worn. I hate it on sight.

The minutes crawl by. The inside of the wagon is so dark that I feel as if I've gone blind. The Empire throws Scholar children into these wagons, some as young as two or three, ripped screaming from their parents. After that, who knows what happens to them. The ghost wagons are so named because those who disappear into them are never seen again.

Don't think of such things, Darin whispers to me. *Focus on the mission. On how you'll save me.*

As I go over Keenan's instructions again in my head, the wagon begins to climb, moving achingly slow. The heat seeps into me, and when I feel as if I'll faint from it, I think up a memory to distract myself – Pop sticking his finger in a fresh jam pot three days ago and laughing while Nan whacked him with a spoon.

Their absence is a wound in my chest. I miss Pop's growling laugh and Nan's stories. And Darin – how I miss my brother. His jokes and drawings and how he seems to know everything. Life without him isn't just empty, it's scary. He's been my guide, my protector, my best friend for so long that I don't know what to do without him. The thought of him suffering torments me. Is he in a cell right now? Is he being tortured?

In the corner of the ghost wagon, something flickers, dark and creeping.

I want it to be an animal – a mouse or, skies, even a rat. But then the creature's eyes are on me, bright and ravenous. It is one of the *things*. One of the shadows from the night of the raid. *I'm going crazy. Bleeding, bat crazy.*

I close my eyes, willing the thing to disappear. When it doesn't, I swat at it with trembling hands.

'Laia . . .'

'Go away. You're not real.'

The thing inches close. *Don't scream, Laia,* I tell myself, biting down hard on my lip. *Don't scream.*

'*Your brother suffers, Laia.*' Each of the creature's words is deliberate, as if it wants to make sure I don't miss a single one. '*The Martials pull pain from him slowly and with relish.*'

'No. You're in my head.'

The creature's laugh is like breaking glass. '*I'm real as death, little Laia. Real as shattered bones and traitorous sisters and hateful Masks.*'

'You're an illusion. You're my . . . my guilt.' I grab Mother's armlet.

The shadow flashes its predator's grin, and now it's only a foot away. But then the wagon comes to a stop, and the creature gives me a last malevolent look before disappearing with a dissatisfied hiss. Seconds later, the wagon door swings open, and the forbidding walls of Blackcliff are before me, their oppressive weight driving the hallucination from my mind.

'Eyes down.' The slaver unchains me from the rail, and I force my gaze to the cobbled street. 'Only speak to the Commandant if she speaks to you. Don't look her in the eyes – she's flogged slaves for less. When she gives you a task, carry it out quickly and well. She'll disfigure you in the first few weeks, but you'll thank her for it eventually – if the scarring's bad enough, it'll keep the older students from raping you too often.

'The last slave lasted two weeks,' the slaver continues, oblivious to my growing terror. 'Commandant wasn't happy about it. My fault, of course – I should have given the girl some fair warning. Went batty when the Commandant branded her, apparently. Threw herself off the cliffs. Don't you do the same.' He gives me a hard look, like a father warning an errant child not to wander off. 'Or the Commandant will think I'm supplying her with inferior goods.'

The slaver nods a greeting to the guards stationed at the gates and pulls my chain as if I'm a dog. I shuffle after him. *Rape . . . disfigurement . . . branding. I can't do it, Darin. I can't.*

A visceral urge to flee sweeps through me, so powerful that I slow, stop, pull away from the slaver. My stomach roils, and I think I'll be sick. But the slaver yanks the chain hard, and I stumble forward.

There's nowhere to run, I realize as we pass beneath Blackcliff's iron-spiked portcullis and into the fabled grounds. *There's nowhere to go. There's no other way to save Darin.*

I'm in now. And there is no going back.

CHAPTER TWELVE

Elias

Hours after I'm named an Aspirant, I dutifully stand beside Grandfather in his cavernous foyer to greet guests arriving for my graduation party. Though Quin Veturius is seventy-seven years old, women blush when he looks them in the eye, and men wince when he deigns to shake their hands. The lamplight paints his thick mane of white hair gold, and the way he towers over everyone else, the way he nods at those entering his home, makes me imagine a falcon watching the world from an updraught.

By eighth bell, the mansion is packed with the finest Illustrian families, along with a few of the wealthiest Mercators. The only Plebeians are the stable hands.

My mother wasn't invited.

'Congratulations, Aspirant Veturius,' a moustached man who might be a cousin says as he shakes my hand in both of his, using the title the Augurs bestowed on me during graduation. 'Or should I say, *your Imperial Majesty*.' The man dares to meet Grandfather's gaze with an obsequious grin. Grandfather ignores him.

It's been like this all night. People whose names I don't know are treating me as if I'm their long-lost son or brother or cousin. Half of them probably are related to me, but they've never bothered acknowledging my existence before this.

The bootlickers are interspersed with friends – Faris, Dex, Tristas, Leander – but the person I wait most impatiently for is Helene. After I took the oath, the families of the graduates flooded the field, and she was swept away in a tide of Gens Aquilla before I had a chance to speak to her.

What is she thinking about the Trials? Are we competing against each other for emperorship? Or will we work together, as we have since entering Blackcliff? My questions lead to more questions, most urgently how becoming the leader of an Empire I loathe can possibly result in my attaining 'true freedom – of body and of soul'.

One thing is certain: as much as I want to escape Blackcliff, the school isn't done with me yet. Instead of a month of leave, we only get two days. Then the Augurs have demanded that all students – even graduates – return to Blackcliff to serve as witnesses to the Trials.

When Helene finally arrives at Grandfather's house, parents and sisters in tow, I forget to greet her. I'm too busy staring. She salutes Grandfather, slender and shining in her ceremonials, her black cloak fluttering lightly. Her hair, silver in the candlelight, pours down her back like a river.

'Careful, Aquilla,' I say as she approaches. 'You almost look like a girl.'

'And you almost look like an Aspirant.' Her smile doesn't reach her eyes, and instantly, I know something's off. Her earlier elation has evaporated, and she's jittery, the way she is before a battle she thinks she won't win.

'What's wrong?' I ask. She tries to get past me, but I take her hand and pull her back. There's a storm in her eyes, but she forces a smile and gently untangles her fingers from mine. 'Nothing's wrong. Where's the food? I'm starving.'

'I'll come with you—'

'Aspirant Veturius,' Grandfather booms. 'Governor Leif Tanalius wishes a word.'

'Best not keep Quin waiting,' Helene says. 'He looks determined.' She slips away, and I grit my teeth as Grandfather coerces me into a stilted discussion with the governor. I repeat the same boring conversation with a dozen other Illustrian leaders over the next hour, until at long last, Grandfather steps away from the unending stream of guests and pulls me aside.

'You're distracted when you can ill afford to be,' he says. 'These men could be very helpful.'

'Can they take the Trials for me?'

'Don't be an idiot,' Grandfather says in disgust. 'An Emperor is not an island. It takes thousands to run the Empire effectively. The city governors will report to you, but they'll mislead and manipulate you at every step, so you'll need a spy network to keep them in check. The Scholars' Resistance, border raiders, and the more troublesome of the Tribes will see a change in dynasty as an opportunity to sow disorder. You'll need the full support of the military to put down any hint of rebellion. In short, you need these men – as advisers, ministers, diplomats, generals, spymasters.'

I nod distractedly. There's a Mercator girl in a tantalizingly flimsy dress eyeing me from the door leading to the crowded garden. She's pretty. Really pretty. I smile at her. Maybe after I find Helene . . .

Grandfather grabs my shoulder and steers me away from the garden, which I've been inching toward. 'Pay attention, boy,' he says. 'The drums carried news of the Trials to the Emperor this morning. My spies tell me he left the capital as soon as he heard. He and most of his house will be here in a matter of weeks – the Blood Shrike too, if he wants to keep his head.' At my look of surprise, Grandfather snorts. 'Did you think Gens Taia would go down without a fight?'

'But the Emperor practically worships the Augurs. He visits them every year.'

'Indeed. And now they've turned against him by threatening to usurp his dynasty. He'll fight – you can count on it.' Grandfather narrows his eyes. 'If you want to win this, you need to wake up. I've already wasted too much time cleaning up your messes. The Farrar brothers are telling anyone who will listen that you nearly let a deserter escape yesterday, that your mask not joining with you is a sign of disloyalty. You're lucky the Blood Shrike is in the north. He'd have had you in the stocks by now. As it is, the Black Guard chose not to investigate once I reminded them that the Farrars are lowborn Plebeian scum and you're from the finest house in the Empire. Are you listening to me?'

'Of course I am.' I act affronted, but since I'm half eyeing the Mercator girl and half looking into the garden for Helene, Grandfather isn't convinced. 'I wanted to find Hel—'

'Don't you dare get distracted by Aquilla,' Grandfather says. 'How she managed to be named Aspirant in the first place I don't understand. Women have no place in the military.'

'Aquilla's one of the best fighters at the school.' At my defence of her, Grandfather slams his hand on an antique entryway table so hard that a vase falls from it and shatters. The Mercator girl yelps and scurries away. Grandfather doesn't blink.

'Rubbish,' Grandfather says. 'Don't tell me you have feelings for the wench.'

'Grandfather—'

'She belongs to the Empire. Though I suppose if you were named Emperor, you could set her aside as Blood Shrike and marry her instead. She's an Illustrian of strong stock, so at least you'd have a pack of heirs—'

'Grandfather. Stop.' I am uncomfortably aware of the heat rising in my neck at the prospect of making heirs with Helene. 'I don't think of her like *that*. She's a – she's—'

Grandfather lifts a silver eyebrow as I stammer like a fool. I am full of it, of course. Students don't get much in the way of women at Blackcliff, unless they rape a slave or pay a whore, neither of which I've ever had any interest in. I've had plenty of diversions during leave – but leave comes once a year. Helene is a girl, a pretty girl, and I spend most of my time around her. Of course I've thought of her in *that* way. But it doesn't mean anything.

'She's a comrade-in-arms, Grandfather,' I say. 'Could you love a fellow soldier the way you loved Grandmother?'

'None of my fellows were tall blonde girls.'

'Am I done here? I'd like to celebrate my graduation.'

'One more thing.' Grandfather disappears, returning a few moments later with a long package wrapped in black silk. 'These are for you,' he says. 'I was planning to leave them to you when you became Pater of Gens Veturia. But they'll serve you better now.'

When I open the package, I nearly drop it.

'Ten burning hells.' I stare at the scims in my hands, a matched set with intricate black etchings that probably have no equal in the Empire. 'These are Teluman scims.'

'Made by the current Teluman's grandfather. Good man. Good friend.'

Gens Teluman has produced the most talented Empire smiths

for centuries. The current Teluman smith spends months fashioning the Masks' Serric steel armour every year. But a Teluman scim – a true Teluman scim, able to cut through five bodies at once – is forged every few years, at the most. 'I can't take these.'

I try to give the blades back, but Grandfather plucks my own scims from where I've slung them on my back and replaces them with the Teluman blades.

'They are a fitting gift for an Emperor,' he says. 'See that you earn them. *Always victorious.*'

'*Always victorious.*' I echo the Veturia motto, and Grandfather leaves to attend to his guests. Still reeling from the gift, I head to the food tent, hoping to find Helene. Every few feet, people stop to chat with me. Someone shoves a plate of spiced kabobs into my hand. Someone else, a drink. A pair of older Masks bemoan the fact that the Trials didn't take place in their time, while a group of Illustrian generals discuss Emperor Taius in hushed tones, as if his spies might be watching. No one speaks of the Augurs with anything less than reverence. No one would dare.

When I finally escape the crowd, Helene's nowhere in sight, though I spot her sisters, Hannah and Livia, eyeing a bored-looking Faris.

'Veturius,' Faris grunts at me, and I'm relieved that he doesn't treat me with the same fawning awe as everyone else. 'I need you to introduce me.' He looks pointedly at a knot of silk-clad, bejewelled Illustrian girls lurking near the edges of the tent, some of whom are watching me in a disturbingly predatory way. I know a few of the girls well – too well, actually, for all that whispering they're doing to come to any good.

'Faris, you're a Mask. You don't need an introduction. Just go talk to them. If you're that nervous, ask Dex or Demetrius to go with you. Have you seen Helene?'

He ignores my question. 'Demetrius didn't come. Probably because fun is against his moral code. And Dex is drunk. Loosening up for once in his life, thank the skies.'

'What about Trist—'

'Too busy drooling at his fiancée.' Faris nods to one of the tables, where Tristas sits with Aelia, pretty and black-haired. He looks happier than I've seen him all year. 'And Leander confessed his love to Helene—'

'Again?'

'Again. She told him to piss off before she broke his nose a second time, and he went looking for solace in the back garden with some redhead. You're my last hope.' Faris looks lasciviously at the Illustrian girls. 'If we remind them that you'll be Emperor, I bet we could get two each.'

'Now there's a thought.' I actually consider this for a moment before remembering Helene. 'But I have to find Aquilla.'

At that moment, she walks into the tent and past the knot of girls, stopping when one speaks to her. She glances at me before whispering something. The girl's jaw drops open, and Helene turns back around and leaves the tent.

'I've got to catch Helene,' I say to Faris, who has noticed Hannah and Livia and is smiling invitingly at them while smoothing back his cowlick. 'Don't get too drunk,' I advise. 'And unless you want to wake up without your manhood, stay away from those two. They're Hel's little sisters.'

The smile drops off Faris's face, and he moves determinedly out of the tent. I hurry after Helene, spotting a flash of blonde heading through Grandfather's vast gardens and towards a rickety shed at the back of the house. The light of the party tents doesn't reach this far, and I have only starlight by which to navigate. I keep my plate, toss my drink, and pull myself atop the shed one-handed before clambering onto the sloped roof of the house.

'You could have picked an easier spot to get to, Aquilla.'

'It's quiet up here,' she says from the darkness. 'Plus you can see all the way to the river. Did you bring any for me?'

'Piss off. You probably had two plates while I shook hands with all those stuffed shirts.'

'Mother says I'm too skinny.' She spears a pastry off my plate with a dagger. 'What took you so long to get up here, anyway? Paying court to your bevy of maidens?'

My awkward conversation with Grandfather comes sharply to mind, and a thorny silence descends. Helene and I don't discuss girls. She teases Faris and Dex and the others about their dalliances, but not me. Never me.

'I – uh —'

'Would you believe Lavinia Tanalia had the nerve to ask me if you'd ever spoken of her? I about shoved a kabob skewer through that bursting bodice of hers.' The barest frisson of tension tinges Helene's voice, and I clear my throat.

'What'd you say to her?'

'I told her you called out her name every time you visited the dock girls. Shut her right up.'

I burst into laughter, understanding now the horrified look on Lavinia's face. Helene smiles, but her eyes are sad. She seems lonely, suddenly. When I tilt my head to capture her gaze, she looks away. Whatever is wrong, she's not ready to tell me.

'What will you do if you become Empress?' I ask. 'What will you change?'

'You're going to win, Elias. And I'll be your Blood Shrike.' She speaks with such conviction that for a second, it's like she's speaking some old truth, like she is telling me the colour of the sky. But then she shrugs and looks away. 'But if I won, I'd change everything. Expand trade south, bring women into the army, open up relations with the Mariners. And I'd – I'd do something about the Scholars.'

'You mean the Resistance?'

'No. What happens in the Quarter. The raids. The killing. It's not . . .' I know she wants to say that it's not right. But that would be sedition. 'Things could be better,' she says. There's a challenge in her face when she looks at me, and I lift my eyebrows. Helene never struck me as a Scholar sympathizer. I like her more for it.

'What about you?' she asks. 'What would you do?'

'Same as you, I guess.' I can't tell her that I have no interest in ruling and never will. She won't understand. 'Maybe I'd just let you run things while I lounged in my harem.'

'Be serious.'

'I'm very serious.' I grin at her. 'The Emperor does have a harem, right? Because that's the only reason I took the oath—' She shoves me – practically off the roof – and I beg for mercy.

'It's not funny.' She sounds like a Centurion, and I try to arrange my face in an appropriately sober manner. 'Our lives are on the line here,' she says. 'Promise me you'll fight to win. Promise me you'll give the Trials everything you've got.' She grabs a strap on my armour. 'Promise!'

'All right, bleeding skies. It was just a joke. Of course I'll fight to win. I'm not planning to die, that's for sure. But what about you? Don't you want to become Empress?'

She shakes her head vehemently. 'I'm better suited to being Blood Shrike. And I don't want to compete with you, Elias. The moment we start working against each other is the moment we let Marcus and Zak win.'

'Hel . . .' I think to ask her what's wrong again, hoping that all this talk of sticking together will make her want to confide in me. She doesn't give me the chance.

'Veturius!' Her eyes widen when she catches sight of the scabbards on my back. 'Are those Teluman blades?'

I show her the scims, and she is appropriately envious. We are quiet for a while after, content to contemplate the stars above us, to find music in the distant sounds that drift up from the forges.

I take in her slim body, her lean profile. What would Helene have been if not a Mask? It's impossible to imagine her as a typical Illustrian girl, angling for a good match, attending fetes and allowing herself to be seduced by fittingly highborn men.

I guess it doesn't matter. Whatever we might have been – healers or politicians, jurists or builders – was trained out of us, spun up and away into the funnel of darkness that is Blackcliff.

'What's going on with you, Hel?' I say. 'Don't insult me by pretending you don't know what I'm talking about.'

'I'm just nervous about the Trials.' She doesn't pause or stutter. She looks right into my eyes, her blue irises clear and mild, her head tilted slightly. Anyone else would believe her without question. But I know Helene, and I know instantly, down in my bones, that she's lying. In another flash of insight, born of the awareness that only makes itself known deep in the night, when the mind opens strange doors, I realize something else. This is not a quiet lie. It is violent and shattering.

She sighs at my expression. 'Leave it alone, Elias.'

'So there *is* something—'

'Fine.' She cuts me off. 'I'll tell you what's bothering me if you tell me what you were really doing in the tunnels yesterday morning.'

The comment is so unexpected that I have to look away from her. 'I told you, I—'

'Yes. You said you were looking for the deserter. And I'm saying there's nothing wrong with me. Now it's all clear and in the open.' There is a bite to her voice I'm not used to. 'And there's nothing else to talk about.'

She meets my gaze, an unfamiliar wariness in her eyes. *What are you hiding, Elias?* her expression asks.

Hel's a master at ferreting out secrets. Something about the combination of her loyalty and patience creates an uncanny urge to confide. She knows, for instance, that I smuggle sheets to the Yearlings so they don't get whipped for wetting their beds. She knows I write to Mamie Rila and my foster brother, Shan, every month. She knows I once dumped a bucket of cow dung on Marcus's bed. She chuckled for days over that one.

But there's so much now that she doesn't know. My loathing of the Empire. How desperately I want to be free of it.

We aren't kids anymore, laughing over shared confidences. We never will be again.

In the end, I don't answer her question. She doesn't answer mine. Instead, we sit without words, watching the city, the river, the desert beyond, our secrets heavy between us.

CHAPTER THIRTEEN

Laia

Despite the slaver's warning to keep my head down, I gaze at the school with sick wonder. Night blends into the grey of the stone until I can't tell where the shadows end and the buildings of Blackcliff begin. Blue-fire lamps make even the bare, sand training fields of the school seem ghostly. In the distance, moonlight glimmers off the columns and arches of a dizzyingly high amphitheatre.

Blackcliff's students are on leave, and the scrape of my sandals is the only sound to break the sinister quiet of the place. Every hedge is squared as if by a plane, every path is neatly paved without a crack in sight. There are no flowers or blooming vines crawling up the buildings, no benches where students can relax.

'Face forward,' the slaver barks. 'Eyes down.'

We head for a structure crouching on the lip of the southern cliffs like a black toad. It's built of the same brooding granite as the rest of the school. The Commandant's house. A sea of sand dunes stretches below the cliffs, lifeless and unforgiving. Far beyond the dunes, the blue jags of the Serran Range cut into the horizon.

A diminutive slave-girl opens the front door of the house. The first thing I notice is her eyepatch. *She'll disfigure you in the first few weeks*, the slaver had said. Will the Commandant take my eye too?

Doesn't matter. I reach for my armlet. *It's for Darin. All for Darin.*

The inside of the house is as gloomy as a dungeon, the smattering of candles providing little illumination against the dark stone walls. I look around, glimpsing the simple, almost monkish furnishings of a dining room and sitting room before the slaver grabs a fistful of my hair and pulls on it so hard I think my neck will break. A knife appears in his hand, its tip caressing my eyelashes. The slave-girl winces.

'You look up one more time,' the slaver says, his hot breath foul in my face, 'I'll carve out your eyes. Understand?'

My eyes water, and at my rapid nod, he releases me.

'Stop blubbering,' he says as the slave leads us upstairs. 'Commandant would rather put a scim through you than deal with tears, and I didn't spend one hundred eighty marks just to throw your corpse to the vultures.'

The slave-girl leads us to a door at the end of a hallway, straightening her already perfectly pressed black dress before knocking softly. A voice orders us to enter.

As the slaver pushes the door open, I get a glimpse of a heavily curtained window, a desk, and a wall of hand-drawn faces. Then I remember the slaver's knife and pin my eyes to the floor.

'It took you long enough,' a soft voice greets us.

'Forgive me, Commandant,' the slaver says. 'My supplier—'

'Silence.'

The slaver swallows. His hands rasp like a snake's coils as he rubs them together. I stand perfectly still. Is the Commandant looking at me? Examining me? I try to look beaten and obedient, the way I know Martials like Scholars to look.

A second later, she is before me, and I jump, surprised at how silently she's come around her desk. She's smaller than I expect – shorter than me and reed-slim. Almost delicate. If not for the mask, I might mistake her for a child. Her uniform is pressed to perfection, and her trousers are tucked into mirror-bright black boots. Every button of her ebony shirt gleams with the shimmer of a serpent's eyes.

'Look at me,' she says. I force myself to obey, instantly paralysed as I meet her gaze. Looking into her face is like looking at the flat, smooth surface of a gravestone. There isn't a shred of humanity in her grey eyes, nor any evidence of kindness in the planes of her masked features. A spiral of faded blue ink curls up the left side of her neck – a tattoo of some kind.

'What is your name, girl?'

'Laia.'

My head is jerked to one side, my cheek on fire before I even realize she's struck me. Tears spring to my eyes at the sharpness of the slap, and I dig my nails into my thigh to keep from running.

'Wrong,' the Commandant informs me. 'You have no name. No identity. You are a slave. That is all you are. That is all you will ever be.' She turns to the slaver to discuss payment. My face is still smarting when the slaver unhooks my collar. Before walking out, he pauses.

'May I offer you my congratulations, Commandant?'

'On what?'

'On the naming of the Aspirants. It's all over the city. Your son—'

'Get out,' the Commandant says. She turns her back on the startled slaver, who quickly retreats, and settles her gaze on me.

This *thing* actually spawned? What kind of demon had she whelped? I shudder, hoping I never find out.

The silence lengthens, and I remain still as a post, too afraid even to blink. Two minutes with the Commandant and she's already cowed me.

'Slave,' she says. 'Look behind me.'

I look up, and the peculiar impression of faces I'd got when I first walked in resolves itself. The wall behind the Commandant is covered with wood-framed posters of men and women, old and young. There are dozens, row after row.

WANTED·

REBEL SPY . . . SCHOLAR THIEVES . . . RESISTANCE
HENCHMAN . . .
REWARD: 250 MARKS . . . 1,000 MARKS.

'These are the faces of every Resistance fighter I've hunted down, every Scholar I've jailed and executed, most before my tenure as Commandant. Some after.'

A paper cemetery. The woman is sick. I look away.

'I will tell you the same thing I tell every slave brought into Blackcliff. The Resistance has tried to penetrate this school countless times. I have discovered it every time. If you are working with the Resistance, if you contact them, if you think of contacting them, I will know and I will destroy you. *Look.*'

I do as she asks, trying to ignore the faces and letting the images and words fade into a blur.

But then I see two faces that will not fade. Two faces that, however poorly rendered, I could never ignore. Shock courses through me slowly, as if my body is fighting it. As if I don't want to believe what I see.

MIRRA AND JAHAN OF SERRA

RESISTANCE LEADERS

TOP PRIORITY

DEAD OR ALIVE

REWARD: 10,000 MARKS

Nan and Pop never told me who destroyed my family. *A Mask*, they said. *Does it matter which one?* And here she is. This is the woman who crushed my parents under her steel-bottomed boot, who brought the Resistance to its knees by killing the greatest leaders it ever had.

How did she do it? How, when my parents were such masters of concealment that few knew what they looked like, let alone how to find them?

The traitor. Someone swore allegiance to the Commandant. Someone my parents trusted.

Did Mazen know he was sending me into the lair of my parents' murderer? He's a stern man, but he doesn't seem like a wilfully cruel one.

'If you cross me' – the Commandant holds my eyes relentlessly – 'you'll join the faces on that wall. Do you understand?'

Ripping my gaze from my parents, I nod, trembling in my struggle not to allow my body to betray my shock. My words are a strangled whisper.

'I understand.'

'Good.' She goes to the door and pulls on a cord. Moments later, the one-eyed girl appears to escort me downstairs. The Commandant closes the door behind me, and anger rises in me like a sickness. I want to turn around and attack the woman. I want to scream at her. *You killed my mother, who had a lion's heart, and my sister, who laughed like the rain, and my father, who captured truth with a few strokes of a pen. You took them from me. You took them from this world.*

But I don't turn back. Darin's voice comes to me again. *Save me, Laia. Remember why you're here. To spy.*

Skies. I didn't notice anything in the Commandant's office except for her wall of death. The next time I go in, I have to pay closer attention. She doesn't know I can read. I might learn something just by glancing at the papers on her desk.

My mind occupied, I barely hear the feather-light whisper of the girl as it drifts past my ear.

'Are you all right?'

Though she is only a few inches smaller than me, she seems tiny somehow, her stick-thin body swimming in her dress, her face pinched and frightened, like that of a starved mouse. A morbid part of me wants to ask her how she lost her eye.

'I'm fine,' I say. 'Don't think I got on her good side, though.'

'She doesn't have a good side.'

That's clear enough. 'What's your name?'

'I – I don't have a name,' the girl says. 'None of us do.'

Her hand strays to her eyepatch, and I suddenly feel sick. Is that what happened to this girl? She told someone her name and she had her eye gouged out?

'Be careful,' she says softly. 'The Commandant sees things. Knows things she shouldn't.' The girl hurries ahead of me, as if wishing to physically escape the words she's just spoken. 'Come, I'm supposed to take you to Cook.'

We make our way to the kitchen, and as soon as I walk in, I feel better. The space is wide, warm, and well lit, with a giant hearth and stove squatting in one corner and a wooden worktable sprawled in the centre. The roof drips with strings of shrivelled red peppers and paper-skinned onions. A spice-laden shelf runs along one wall, and the scent of lemon and cardamom permeates the air. If not for the largeness of the place, I could be back in Nan's kitchen.

A stack of dirty pots rises from a sink, and a kettle of water boils on the stove. Someone has laid out a tray with biscuits and jam. A small, white-haired woman in a diamond-patterned dress identical to mine stands at the worktable, chopping an onion with her back to us. Beyond her is a screened door that leads outside.

'Cook,' the girl says. 'This is—'

'Kitchen-Girl,' the woman addresses her without turning. Her voice is strange – raspy, as if she's ill. 'Didn't I ask you to wash those pots hours ago?' Kitchen-Girl doesn't get a chance to protest. 'Stop your dawdling and get to it,' the woman snaps. 'Or you'll be sleeping with an empty belly, and I'll not feel a shred of guilt.'

When the girl grabs her apron, Cook turns from her onion, and I stifle a gasp, trying not to gawp at the ruin of her face. Ropy, vivid red scars run from her forehead down across her cheeks, lips, and chin, all the way into the high neck of her black dress. It looks as though a wild animal clawed her to shreds and she had the misfortune of surviving. Only her eyes, a dark, agate blue, remain whole.

'Who—' She takes me in, standing unnaturally still. Then, without explanation, she turns and limps out the back door.

I look at Kitchen-Girl for aid. 'I didn't mean to stare.'

'Cook?' Kitchen-Girl moves timidly to the door, opening it a crack. 'Cook?'

When no response comes, Kitchen-Girl glances between me and the door. The kettle on the stove whistles shrilly.

'It's nearly ninth bell.' She twists her hands together. 'That's when the Commandant has evening tea. You're to take it up, but if you're late . . . the Commandant . . . she'll—'

'She'll what?'

'She – she'll be angry.' Terror – true, animal terror – fills the girl's face.

'Right,' I say. Kitchen-Girl's fear is contagious, and I hurriedly pour water from the kettle into the mug on the tray. 'How does she take it? Sugar? Cream?'

'She takes cream.' The girl rushes to a cupboard and pulls out a covered pail, spilling some of the milk. 'Oh!'

'Here.' I take the pail from her and spoon out the cream, trying to stay calm. 'See? All done, I'll just clean up—'

'There's no time.' The girl shoves the tray into my arms and pushes me towards the hall. 'Please – hurry. It's almost—'

The bells begin to toll.

'Go,' the girl says. 'Get up there before the last bell!'

The stairs are steep, and I'm walking too fast. The tray lists, and I barely have a chance to grab the cream pot before the teaspoon clatters to the ground. The bell tolls for a ninth time and falls silent.

Calm down, Laia. This is ridiculous. The Commandant probably won't even notice if I'm five seconds late, but she will notice if the tray is in disarray. I balance the tray in one hand and sweep up the spoon, taking a moment to neaten the crockery before approaching the door.

It swings open as I raise my hand to knock. The tray is out of my arms, the cup of hot tea sailing past my head and exploding against the wall behind me.

I'm still gaping when the Commandant pulls me into her office. 'Turn around.'

My whole body shakes as I turn to face the closed door. I don't register the zing of wood cutting through the air until the Commandant's riding crop slices into my back. The shock of it drops me to my knees. It comes down thrice more before I feel her hands in my hair. I yelp as she brings my face close to hers, the silver of her mask nearly touching my cheeks. I clench my teeth shut against the pain, forcing back tears as I think of the slaver's words. *The Commandant would rather put a scim in you than deal with tears.*

'I don't tolerate tardiness,' she says, her eyes eerily calm. 'It won't happen again.'

'Y-yes, Commandant.' My whisper is no louder than Kitchen-Girl's had been. It hurts too much to speak any louder. The woman releases me.

'Clean up the mess in the hall. Report to me tomorrow morning at sixth bell.'

The Commandant steps around me, and moments later, the front door slams shut.

The silverware rattles as I pick up the tray. Only four lashes and I feel as if my skin has been torn open and drenched in salt. Blood drips down the back of my shirt.

I want to be logical, practical, the way Pop taught me to be when dealing with injuries. *Cut the shirt off, my girl. Clean the wounds with witch hazel and pack them with turmeric. Then bandage them and change the dressings twice a day.*

But where will I get a new shirt? Witch hazel? How will I bandage the wounds with no one to help me?

For Darin. For Darin. For Darin.

But what if he's dead? a voice whispers in my head. *What if the Resistance doesn't find him? What if I'm about to put myself through hell for nothing?*

No. If I let myself go down that path, I won't make it through the night, let alone survive weeks of spying on the Commandant.

As I pile shards of ceramic on the tray, I hear a rustle on the landing. I look up, cringing, terrified the Commandant has returned. But it's only Kitchen-Girl. She kneels beside me and silently mops up the spilled tea with a cloth.

When I thank her, her head jerks up like a startled deer's. She finishes mopping and scurries down the stairs.

Back in the empty kitchen, I place the tray in the sink and collapse at the worktable, letting my head fall into my hands. I'm too numb for tears. It occurs to me then that the Commandant's office door is probably still open, her papers strewn about, visible to anyone with the courage to look.

Commandant's gone, Laia. Go up there and see what you can find. Darin would do it. He'd see this as the perfect chance to gather information for the Resistance.

But I'm not Darin. And in this moment, I can't think about the mission, or the fact that I'm a spy, not a slave. All I can think about is the throbbing in my back and the blood soaking my shirt.

You won't survive the Commandant, Keenan had said. *The mission will fail.*

I lower my head to the table, closing my eyes against the pain. He was right. Skies, he was right.

PART TWO

THE TRIALS

CHAPTER FOURTEEN

Elias

The rest of leave disappears, and in no time, Grandfather is pelting me with advice as we roll towards Blackcliff in his ebony carriage. He spent half of my leave introducing me to the heads of powerful houses and the other half railing at me for not solidifying as many alliances as possible. When I told him I wanted to visit Helene, he'd gone apoplectic.

'The girl's befuddling your senses,' he'd raged. 'Can't you spot a siren when you see one?' I choke back a laugh remembering this now, imagining Helene's face if she knew she was being referred to as a siren.

Part of me feels sorry for Grandfather. He is a legend, a general who has won so many battles that no one counts them anymore. The men in his legions worshipped him not only for his courage and cunning but for his uncanny ability to evade death even when facing appalling odds.

But at seventy-seven, he's long since ceased leading men into border wars. Which probably explains his fixation on the Trials.

Regardless of his reasoning, his advice is sound. I do need to prepare for the Trials, and the best way to do that is to get more information about them. I'd hoped the Augurs had, at some point in time, expanded on their original prophecy – perhaps even described what the Aspirants should expect. But despite combing through Grandfather's extensive library, I've found nothing.

'Damn you, listen to me.' Grandfather kicks me with a steel-toed boot, and I grab the seat of the carriage, pain shooting through my leg. 'Have you heard a word I've said?'

'The Trials are a test of my mettle. I might not know what's in store, but I must be prepared anyway. I must conquer my weaknesses and exploit competitors' weaknesses. Above all, I must remember that a Veturius is—'

'*Always victorious.*' We say it together, and Grandfather nods approvingly while I try not to betray my impatience.

More battles. More violence. All I want is to escape the Empire. Yet here I am. *True freedom – of body and soul.* That's what I'm fighting for, I remind myself. Not rulership. Not power. Freedom.

'I wonder where your mother stands on all this,' Grandfather muses.

'She won't favour me, that's for sure.'

'No, she won't,' Grandfather says. 'But she knows you have the best odds of winning. Keris gains much if she backs the right Aspirant. And loses much if she backs the wrong one.' Grandfather looks broodingly out the carriage window. 'I've heard strange rumours about my daughter. Things I might have once laughed at. She'll do everything she can to keep you from winning this. Don't expect anything less.'

When we arrive at Blackcliff amid dozens of other carriages, Grandfather crushes my hand in his grip.

'You will not disappoint Gens Veturia,' he informs me. 'You will not disappoint *me.*' I wince at his handshake, wondering if my own will ever be as intimidating.

Helene finds me after Grandfather drives away. 'Since everyone's back to witness the Trials, there won't be a new crop of Yearlings until the contest is over.' She waves to Demetrius, emerging from his father's carriage a few yards away. 'We're still in our old barracks. And we'll keep the same class schedule as before, except instead of Rhetoric and History, we have extra watches on the wall.'

'Even though we're full Masks?'

'I don't make the rules,' Helene says. 'Come on, we're late for scim training.'

We push through the throng of students towards Blackcliff's front gate. 'Did you find anything on the Trials?' I ask Hel. Someone taps my shoulder, but I ignore them. Probably an earnest Cadet trying to make class on time.

'Nothing,' Hel says. 'Stayed up all night in Father's library too.'

'Same here.' Damn. Pater Aquillus is a jurist, and his library is filled with everything from obscure law books to ancient Scholar tomes on mathematics. Between him and Grandfather, we have most relevant books in the Empire covered. There's nowhere else to search. 'We should check the— What, damn it?'

The tapping grows insistent, and I turn, intending to tell off the Cadet. Instead, I'm faced with a slave-girl looking up at me through impossibly long eyelashes. A heated, visceral shock flares through me at the clarity of her dark gold eyes. For a second, I forget my name.

I've never seen her before, because if I had, I'd remember. Despite the heavy silver cuffs and high, painful-looking bun that mark all of Blackcliff's drudges, nothing about her says *slave*. Her black dress fits her like a glove, sliding over every curve in a way that makes more than one head turn. Her full lips and fine, straight nose would be the envy of most girls,

129

Scholar or not. I stare at her, realize I'm staring, tell myself to stop staring, and then keep staring. My breath falters, and my body, traitor that it is, tugs me forward until there are only inches between us.

'Asp-aspirant Veturius.'

It's the way she says my name – like it's something to fear – that brings me back to myself. *Pull it together, Veturius.* I step away, appalled at myself when I see the terror in her eyes.

'What is it?' I ask calmly.

'The – the Commandant has requested you and Aspirant Aquilla to report to her office at – at sixth bell.'

'Sixth bell?' Helene shoves past the gate guards towards the Commandant's house, apologizing to a group of Yearlings when she knocks two of them over. 'We're late. Why didn't you summon us sooner?'

The girl trails us, too frightened to get closer. 'There were so many people – I couldn't find you.'

Helene waves off the girl's explanation. 'She's going to kill us. It must be about the Trials, Elias. Maybe the Augurs told her something.' Helene hurries ahead, clearly still hoping to make it to my mother's office on time.

'Are the Trials starting?' The girl claps her hands over her mouth. 'I'm sorry,' she whispers. 'I—'

'It's all right.' I don't smile at her. It will only scare her. For a female slave, a smile from a Mask is not usually a good thing. 'I'm actually wondering the same thing. What's your name?'

'S-slave-Girl.'

Of course. My mother would already have scourged her name out of existence.

'Right. You work for the Commandant?'

I want her to say no. I want her to say that my mother roped her into this. I want her to say she's assigned to the kitchens or the infirmary, where slaves aren't scarred or missing body parts.

But the girl nods in response to my question. *Don't let my mother break you*, I think. The girl meets my eyes, and there is that feeling again, low and hot and consuming. *Don't be weak. Fight. Escape.*

A gust of wind whips a strand free from her bun and across her cheekbone. Defiance flashes across her face as she holds my gaze, and for a second, I see my own desire for freedom mirrored, intensified in her eyes. It's something I've never detected in the eyes of a fellow student, let alone a Scholar slave. For one strange moment, I feel less alone.

But then she looks down, and I wonder at my own naivety. She can't fight. She can't escape. Not from Blackcliff. I smile joylessly; in this, at least, the slave and I are more similar than she'll ever know.

'When did you start here?' I ask her.

'Three days ago. Sir. Aspirant. Um—' She wrings her hands.

'Veturius is fine.'

She walks carefully, gingerly – the Commandant must have whipped her recently. And yet she doesn't hunch or shuffle like the other slaves. The straight-backed grace with which she moves tells her story better than words. She'd been a freewoman before this – I'd bet my scims on it. And she has no idea how pretty she is – or what kind of problems her beauty will cause for her at a place like Blackcliff. The wind pulls at her hair again, and I catch her scent – like fruit and sugar.

'Can I give you some advice?'

Her head flies up like a scared animal's. At least she's wary. 'Right now you . . .' *Will grab the attention of every male in a square mile.* 'Stand out,' I finish. 'It's hot, but you should wear a hood or a cloak – something to help you blend in.'

She nods, but her eyes are suspicious. She wraps her arms around herself and drops back a little. I don't speak to her again.

When we arrive at my mother's office, Marcus and Zak are already seated, clad in full battle armour. They fall silent as we enter, and it's obvious they've been talking about us.

The Commandant ignores Helene and me and turns from her window, where she's been staring out at the dunes. She motions the slave-girl close, then backhands her so hard that blood flies from her mouth.

'I said sixth bell.'

Anger floods me, and the Commandant senses it. 'Yes, Veturius?' Her lips purse, and she tilts her head as if to say, *Do you wish to interfere and bring my wrath down upon yourself?*

Helene elbows me, and, fuming, I keep quiet.

'Get out,' Mother says to the trembling girl. 'Aquilla, Veturius. Sit.'

Marcus watches the slave as she leaves. The lust on his face makes me want to push the girl out of the room faster while gouging the Snake's eyes out. Zak, meanwhile, ignores the girl and glances surreptitiously at Helene. His angular face is pale, and purple shadows darken his eyes. I wonder how he and Marcus spent their leave. Helping their Plebeian father with his smithing? Visiting family? Plotting ways to kill me and Helene?

'The Augurs are otherwise occupied' – a strange, smug smile creeps onto the Commandant's face – 'and have asked that in their stead, I give you the details of the Trials. Here.' The Commandant slides a piece of parchment across her desk, and we all lean forward to read it.

Four they are, and four traits we seek:
Courage to face their darkest fears

Cunning to outwit their foes
Strength of arms and mind and heart
Loyalty to break the soul.

'It is a foretelling You'll learn its meaning in the coming days.' The Commandant faces her window again, her hands behind her back. I watch her reflection, unnerved at the self-satisfaction oozing off her. 'The Augurs will plan and judge the Trials. But since this contest is meant to weed out the weak, I have proposed to our holy men that you remain at Blackcliff for the duration of the Trial. The Augurs agreed.'

I stifle a snort. Of course the Augurs agreed. They know this place is hell, and they'll want the Trials to be as difficult as possible.

'I have ordered the Centurions to intensify your training to reflect your status as Aspirants. I have no say in your conduct during the competition. However, outside the Trials, you are still subject to my rules. My punishments.' She begins to pace her office, and her eyes stab into me, warning of whippings and worse.

'If you win a Trial, you will receive a token from the Augurs – a prize, of sorts. If you pass a Trial but do not win, your reward is your life. If you fail a Trial, you will be executed.' She lets that pleasant fact sink in for a moment before going on.

'The Aspirant who wins two Trials first will be named victor. Whoever comes in second, with one win, will be named Blood Shrike. The others will die. There will be no tie. The Augurs wish me to stress that while the Trials are taking place, the accepted rules of sportsmanship apply. You will not engage in cheating, sabotage, or chicanery.'

I glance at Marcus. Telling him not to cheat is like telling him not to breathe.

'What about Emperor Taius?' Marcus says. 'The Blood Shrike? The Black Guard? Gens Taia isn't just going to disappear.'

'Taius will retaliate.' The Commandant passes behind me, and my neck prickles unpleasantly. 'He has left Antium with his gens and is heading south to disrupt the Trials. But the Augurs shared another foretelling: *Waiting vines circle and strangle the oak. The way is made clear, just before the end.*'

'What's that supposed to mean?' Marcus asks.

'It means that the Emperor's actions are not our concern. As for the Blood Shrike and Black Guard, their loyalty lies with the Empire – not Taius. They will be the first to pledge themselves to the new dynasty.'

'When do the Trials begin?' Helene asks.

'They may commence at any time.' My mother finally sits and steeples her fingers, her expression remote. 'And they may take any form. From the moment you leave this office, you must be prepared.'

'If they can take any form,' Zak speaks up for the first time, 'then how are we supposed to prepare? How will we know they've begun?'

'You'll know,' the Commandant says.

'But—'

'You'll know.' She stares directly at Zak, and he falls silent. 'Any other questions?' The Commandant doesn't wait for a response. 'Dismissed.'

We salute and file out. Not wanting to turn my back on the Snake and the Toad, I let them go ahead of me but immediately regret it. The slave-girl stands in the shadows near the stairs, and as Marcus passes her, he reaches out and yanks her close. She writhes in his grasp, trying to break his iron grip on her throat. He leans down and murmurs something to her. I reach for my scim, but Helene grabs my arm.

'Commandant,' she warns me. Behind us, my mother watches

from her study door, arms crossed. 'It's her slave,' Helene whispers. 'You'd be a fool to interfere.'

'Aren't you going to stop him?' I turn to the Commandant, keeping my voice low.

'She's a slave,' the Commandant says, as if that explains everything. 'She's to receive ten lashes for her incompetence. If you're intent on helping her, perhaps you wish to take on her punishment?'

'Of course not, Commandant.' Helene digs her nails into my arm and speaks for me, knowing that I'm on the verge of earning myself a whipping. She nudges me down the hall. 'Leave it,' she says. 'It's not worth it.'

She doesn't need to explain. The Empire doesn't chance the loyalty of its Masks. The Black Guard will be all over me if they hear I've taken a whipping for a Scholar drudge.

Ahead of me, Marcus laughs and releases the girl, then follows Zak down the stairs. The girl gulps down air, bruises blooming on her neck.

Help her, Elias. But I can't. Hel is right. The risk of punishment is too great.

Helene strides down the hall, giving me a pointed look. *Move.*

The girl pulls her feet back as we pass, trying to make herself small. Disgusted with myself, I spare her no more attention than I would a heap of trash. I feel heartless as I leave her there to face Mother's punishment. I feel like a Mask.

* * *

That night, my dreams are travels, filled with hisses and whispers. Wind circles my head like a vulture, and I flinch from hands burning with unnatural heat. I try to wake as discomfort turns into

135

nightmare, but I only slip deeper in, until eventually there is nothing but choking, burning light.

When I open my eyes, the first thing I notice is the hard, sandy ground beneath me. The second is that the ground is hot. Skin-shrivelling hot.

My hand shakes as I shield my eyes from the sun and scan the wasted landscape around me. A lone, gnarled Jack tree rises from the cracked land a few feet away. Miles to the west, a vast body of water lays shimmering like a mirage. The air reeks something horrible, a combination of carrion, rotting eggs, and Cadets' quarters in high summer. The land is so pale and desolate that I might be standing on a distant, dead moon.

My muscles ache, as if I've been lying in the same position for hours. The pain tells me that this is no dream. I stagger to my feet, a lonely silhouette in a vast emptiness.

The Trials, it seems, have begun.

CHAPTER FIFTEEN

Laia

Dawn is still a blue rumour on the horizon when I limp into the Commandant's chambers. She sits at her dressing table, observing her reflection in the mirror. Her bed looks untouched, as it does every morning. I wonder when she sleeps. If she sleeps.

She's clad in a loose black robe that softens the disdain on her masked face. It's the first time I've seen her out of uniform. The robe slips down her shoulder, and the unusual swirls of her tattoo are revealed to be part of an ornate A, the dark ink vivid against the chill paleness of her skin.

Ten days have passed since my mission began, and while I haven't learned anything that will help me save Darin, I *have* learned how to press a Blackcliff uniform in five minutes flat, how to carry a heavy tray up the stairs with half a dozen welts on my back, and how to remain so silent that I forget my own existence.

Keenan gave me only the barest details about this mission. I'm to gather information about the Trials, and then, when I leave Blackcliff for my errands, the Resistance will contact me. *Might take us three days,* Keenan said. *Or ten. Be prepared to report every time you go into the city. And never come looking for us.*

At the time, I'd suppressed the urge to ask him a dozen questions. Like how to get the information they want. Like how to keep the Commandant from catching me.

Now I'm paying for it. Now I don't want the Resistance to find me. I don't want them to learn what a terrible spy I am.

At the back of my mind, Darin's voice grows fainter: *Find something, Laia. Something that will save me. Hurry.*

No, another, louder part of me says. *Lay low. Don't risk spying until you're certain you won't get caught.*

Which voice do I listen to? The spy or the slave? The fighter or the coward? I thought the answers to such questions would be easy. That was before I learned what real fear was.

For now, I move around the Commandant quietly, setting down her breakfast tray, clearing her tea from the night before, laying out her uniform. *Don't look at me. Don't look at me.* My pleas seem to work. The Commandant acts as if I don't exist.

When I open the curtains, the first rays of morning illuminate the room. I stop to look at the emptiness beyond the Commandant's window, miles of whispering dunes, rippling like waves in the dawn wind. For a second, I lose myself in their beauty. Then Blackcliff's drums thud out, a wake-up call for the entire school and half the city.

'Slave-Girl.' The Commandant's impatience has me moving before she says another word. 'My hair.'

As I take a brush and pins from a table drawer, I catch a glimpse of myself in the mirror. The bruises from my run-in with Aspirant Marcus a week ago are fading, and the ten lashes I received afterwards have scabbed over. Other wounds have replaced them. Three lashes on my legs for a dust stain on my skirt. Four lashes on my wrists for not finishing her mending. A black eye from a Skull in a foul mood.

The Commandant opens a letter sitting on her dressing table. She keeps her head still as I pull back her hair, ignoring me entirely. For a second, I stand frozen, staring down at the parchment as she reads. She doesn't notice. Of course she doesn't. Scholars don't read – or so she assumes. I brush out her pale hair swiftly.

Look at it, Laia. Darin's voice. *Discover what it says.*

She will see. She will punish me.

She doesn't know you can read. She'll think you're an idiot Scholar gawping at pretty symbols.

I swallow. I should look. Ten days at Blackcliff with nothing to show for it but bruises and lashes is disastrous. When the Resistance demands a report, I won't have anything for them. What will happen to Darin then?

Again and again, I glance at the mirror to make sure the Commandant is enmeshed in her letter. When I'm sure, I risk a quick look down.

—too dangerous in the south, and the Commandant is not trustworthy. I advise that you return to Antium. If you must come south, travel with a small force—

The Commandant shifts, and I tear my eyes away, paranoid that I've been too obvious. But she reads on, and I risk another glance. By then, she's turned the parchment over.

—allies are deserting Gens Taia like rats fleeing a fire. I have learned that the Commandant is planning—

But I do not find out what the Commandant is planning, for at that moment, I look up. She is watching me in the mirror.

'The – the marks are beautiful,' I say in a choked whisper, dropping one of the hairpins. I bend to retrieve it, taking those precious seconds to hide my panic. I'll be whipped for reading something that doesn't even make any sense. Why did I let her see me? Why wasn't I more careful? 'I haven't seen much of words,' I add.

'No.' The woman's eyes flicker, and for a moment, I think she's mocking me. 'Your kind doesn't need to read.' She examines her hair. 'The right side's too low. Fix it.'

Though I feel like crying from relief, I keep my face carefully bland and slide another pin into her silken hair.

'How long have you been here, slave?'

'Ten days, sir.'

'Have you made any friends?'

This question is so preposterous coming from the Commandant that I almost laugh. Friends? At Blackcliff? Kitchen-Girl is too shy to talk to me, and Cook only speaks to give me orders. The rest of Blackcliff's slaves live and work on the main grounds. They are silent and distant – always alone, always wary.

'You're here for life, girl,' the Commandant says, inspecting her now-finished hair. 'Maybe you should get to know your fellows. Here.' She hands me two sealed letters. 'Take the one with the red seal to the couriers' office and the one with the black seal to Spiro Teluman. Don't leave him without a reply.'

Who Spiro Teluman is and how to find him I don't dare to ask. The Commandant punishes questions with pain. I take the letters and back out of the room to avoid any surprise attacks. A breath explodes out of me when I close the door. Thank the skies the woman is too arrogant to think her Scholar drudge can read. As I walk down the hall, I peek at the first letter and nearly drop it. It's addressed to Emperor Taius.

What would she be corresponding with Taius about? The Trials? I run an experimental finger near the seal. Still soft, it lifts cleanly.

There's a scrape behind me, and the letter falls from my

hand as I whip around. My mind screams *Commandant!* But the hall is empty. I pick up the letter and shove it into my pocket. It seems alive, like a snake or spider I've decided to keep as a pet. I touch the seal again before jerking my hand away. *Too dangerous.*

But I need something to give the Resistance. Every day when I leave Blackcliff to run the Commandant's errands, I fear Keenan will pull me aside and demand a report. Every day he doesn't is a reprieve. Eventually, I'll run out of time.

I have to get my cloak, so I head to the servants' quarters in the open-air hallway just outside the kitchen. My room, like Kitchen-Girl's and Cook's, is a dank hole with a low entrance and a ragged curtain that serves as a door. Inside, it's just wide enough to fit a rope pallet and a crate that serves as a side table.

From here, I can hear the low tones of Cook and Kitchen-Girl speaking. Kitchen-Girl, at least, has been slightly friendlier than Cook. She's helped me with my duties more than once, and at the end of my first day, when I thought I'd faint from the pain of the lashes I'd received, I saw her scuttle away from my quarters. When I went in, I found a healing salve and a mug of pain-numbing tea.

That's as far as her friendship extends. I've asked her and Cook questions, discussed the weather, complained about the Commandant. No response. I'm fairly certain that if I walked into the kitchen stark-naked and squawking like a chicken, I still wouldn't get a word out of them. I don't want to approach them again only to hit a wall of silence, but I need someone to tell me who Spiro Teluman is and how to find him.

I enter the kitchen to find them both sweating from the heat of the blazing hearth. Lunch is baking already. My mouth waters, and I long for Nan's food. We never had much, but whatever we did have was made with love, which I now know transforms simple fare into a feast. Here, we eat the Commandant's scraps, and no matter how hungry I am, they taste like sawdust.

Kitchen-Girl gives me a glance in greeting, and Cook ignores me. The older woman perches on a rickety stepstool to reach a string of garlic. She looks like she's about to fall, but when I offer a hand to brace her, she glares daggers at me.

I drop my hand and stand there awkwardly for a moment.

'Can – can you tell me where to find Spiro Teluman?'

Silence.

'Look,' I say. 'I know I'm new, but the Commandant told me to make friends. I thought—'

Ever so slowly, Cook turns to me. Her face is grey, as if she might be ill.

'Friends.' It's the first word she's said to me that isn't an order. The old woman shakes her head and takes her garlic to the counter. The anger in her strokes as she chops it is unmistakable. I don't know what I've done that's so terrible, but she won't help me now. I sigh and leave the kitchen. I'll have to ask someone else about Spiro Teluman.

'He's a swordsmith,' I hear a soft voice say. Kitchen-Girl has followed me out. She looks over her shoulder, worried Cook will hear her. 'You'll find him along the river, in the Weapons Quarter.' She quickly turns, ready to walk away, and it's this more than anything else that makes me speak to her. I haven't had a conversation with a normal person in ten days; I've barely said anything other than 'Yes, sir' and 'No, sir.'

'I'm Laia.'

Kitchen-Girl freezes. 'Laia.' She turns the word over in her mouth. 'I'm – I'm Izzi.'

For the first time since the raid, I smile. I'd nearly forgotten the sound of my own name. Izzi looks up towards the Commandant's room.

'The Commandant wants you to make friends so she can use them against you,' she whispers. 'That's why Cook is upset.'

I shake my head – I don't understand.

'It's how she controls us.' Izzi fingers her eyepatch. 'It's the reason Cook does whatever she asks. The reason why every slave in Blackcliff does what she asks. If you do something wrong, she won't always punish you. Sometimes, she'll punish the people you care about instead.' Izzi's so quiet I have to lean forward to hear her. 'If – if you want to have friends, make sure she doesn't know. Make sure it's secret.'

She slips back into the kitchen, quick as a cat in the night. I leave for the couriers' office, but I can't stop thinking about what she's told me. If the Commandant is sick enough to use the slaves' friendships against them, then it's no wonder Izzi and Cook keep their distance. Is that how Izzi lost her eye? Is that how Cook got her scars?

The Commandant hasn't punished me in any permanent way – yet. But it's only a matter of time. The Emperor's letter in my pocket seems suddenly heavier, and I close my hand over it. Do I dare? The faster I get information, the faster the Resistance can save Darin and the faster I can leave Blackcliff.

I debate with myself all the way to the school's gates. When I approach, the leather-armoured auxes, who usually delight in tormenting slaves, barely notice me. They're intent on two horsemen making their way up to the school. I use the distraction to slip quietly past.

Though it's still early morning, the desert heat has set in, and I fidget under the itchy weight of the cloak I've taken to wearing. Every time I put it on, I think of Aspirant Veturius, of that unabashed fire that burned in him when he first turned to me, of his smell when he stepped close, distractingly clean and masculine. I think of his words, spoken almost thoughtfully. *Can I give you some advice?*

I don't know what I expected of the Commandant's son. Someone like Marcus Farrar, who left me with a collar of bruises that ached for days? Someone like Helene Aquilla, who spoke to me as if I was less than dirt?

At the very least, I thought he'd look like his mother – blonde and wan and cold to the bone. But he is black-haired and gold-skinned and though his eyes are the same pale grey as the Commandant's, there is no trace there of the gimlet flatness that defines most Masks. Instead, when he'd met my gaze for a jolting moment, I'd seen life bursting through, chaotic and alluring beneath the shadow of the mask. I'd seen fire and desire, and my heart had thumped faster.

And his mask. So strange that it sits atop his face like a thing apart. Is it a sign of weakness? It can't be – I keep hearing he's Blackcliff's finest soldier.

Stop, Laia. Stop thinking of him. If he's thoughtful, then there's devilry behind it. If there's fire in his eyes, it's a lust for violence. He's a Mask. They're all the same.

I wind my way down from Blackcliff, out of the Illustrian Quarter and into Execution Square, home to the city's largest open-air market as well as one of only two couriers' offices. The gallows that give the square its name sit empty. But then, the day's just begun.

Darin once drew the Execution Square gallows, complete with bodies hanging from the gibbet. Nan saw the image and shuddered. *Burn it*, she'd said. Darin nodded, but later that night, I caught him working on it in our room.

'It's a reminder, Laia,' he'd said in his quiet way. 'It would be wrong to destroy it.'

The crowds move through the square sluggishly, wilted by the heat. I have to push and elbow to make any headway, eliciting grumbles from irritated merchants and a shove from a hatchet-faced slaver. As I dart under a palanquin marked with the symbol of an Illustrian house, I spot the couriers' office a dozen yards away. I slow, my fingers straying towards the letter to the Emperor. Once I hand it over, there's no getting it back.

'Bags, purses, and satchels! Silk-stitched!'

I need to open the note. I need to have something for the Resistance. But where can I do it without anyone noticing? Behind one of the stalls? In the shadows between two tents?

'We use the finest leather and hardware!'

The seal will lift cleanly enough, but I can't be jostled. If the letter tears or the seal is smudged, the Commandant will probably cut off my hand. Or my head.

'Bags, purses, and satchels! Silk-stitched!'

The bag-seller is right behind me, and I've a mind to tell him off. Then I smell cedarwood and glance over my shoulder to see a shirtless Scholar man, his muscled torso tanned and sweating. His hair, flaming red, glows below a black cap. Shock and recognition jolt my stomach. It's Keenan.

His brown eyes meet mine, and as he continues to yell out his wares, he tilts his head ever so slightly towards a side alley leading out of the square. My hands sweat in uneasy anticipation, and I make my way to the alley. What will I say to him? I have nothing – no leads, no information. Keenan doubted me from the beginning, and I am about to prove him right.

Dust-coated brick houses rise four storeys on either side of the alley, and the noises of the market fade. Keenan is nowhere to be seen, but a woman draped in rags detaches herself from a wall and approaches me. I eye her warily until she lifts her head. Through the filthy tangle of dark hair, I recognize Sana.

Follow, she mouths.

I want to ask her about Darin, but she's already hurrying away. She leads me through alley after alley, not stopping until we're close to Cobbler Row, nearly a mile from Execution Square. The air is dense with the chattering of shoemakers and the gamy scents of leather and tannin and dye. I think we're going to enter the row, but Sana turns instead into the narrow space between two buildings. She heads down a set of basement stairs so grimy that they look like the inside of a chimney.

Keenan opens the door at the base of the stairs before Sana can knock. He's replaced the leather bags with the black shirt and brace of knives he was wearing the first time I met him. A lock of red hair falls into his face, and he looks me over, his gaze lingering on my bruises.

'Thought she might have a tail,' Sana says as she pulls off the cloak and wig. 'But she didn't.'

'Mazen's waiting.' Keenan puts a hand on my back to nudge me forward into the narrow hallway. I wince and recoil – my lashes are still painful.

His eyes cut sharply to me and I think he's going to say something, but instead he drops his hand awkwardly, brow slightly furrowed, and leads us down the hallway and through a door. Mazen sits at a table in the room beyond, his scarred face lit by a lone candle.

'Well, Laia.' He lifts his grey eyebrows. 'What do you have for me?'

'Can you tell me about Darin first?' I ask, finally able to voice the question that has plagued me for a week and a half. 'Is he all right?'

'Your brother's alive, Laia.'

A sigh gusts out of me, and I feel like I can breathe again.

'But I can't tell you any more until you tell me what you have. We did make a deal.'

'Let her at least sit.' Sana pulls out a chair for me, and almost before I'm in it, Mazen leans forward.

'We have little time.' he says. 'Whatever you've got, we need.'

'The Trials started about – about a week ago.' I scramble to connect the few scraps of information I do have. I'm not ready to give him the letter – not yet. If he breaks the seal or tears it, I'm done for. 'That's when the Aspirants disappeared. There are four of them. Their names—'

'We know all that.' Mazen dismisses my words with the wave of a hand. 'Where were they taken? When does the Trial end? What's the next one?'

'We've heard that two of the Aspirants returned today,' Keenan says. 'Not long ago, in fact. Maybe half an hour.'

I think of the guards talking excitedly at Blackcliff's gate as two horsemen came up the road. *Laia, you fool.* If I'd paid closer attention to the auxes' gossip, I might have learned which Aspirants had survived the Trial. I might have had something useful to tell Mazen.

'I don't know. It's been so – so hard,' I say. Even as I speak, I hear how pathetic I sound and hate myself for it. 'The Commandant killed my parents. She has this wall with posters of every rebel she's caught. My parents were up there – their faces—'

Sana's eyes widen, and even Keenan looks slightly sick, his aloofness falling away for a moment. I wonder why I'm telling Mazen this. Perhaps because some part of me wonders if he knew the Commandant killed my parents – if he knew and sent me to Blackcliff anyway.

'I didn't know,' Mazen says, sensing my unasked question. 'But it's all the more reason that this mission must succeed.'

'I want to succeed more than anyone, but I can't get into her office. She never has visitors, so I can't eavesdrop on her—'

Mazen holds up a hand to stop me. 'What *do* you know, exactly?'

For one frantic moment I consider lying. I've read a hundred tales of heroes and the trials they face – what harm if I invent one and pass it off as truth? But I can't bring myself to do it. Not when the Resistance is placing their trust in me.

'I . . . nothing.' I stare at the floor, ashamed at the incredulity on Mazen's face. I reach for the letter but don't pull it out. *Too risky. Maybe he'll give you another chance, Laia. Maybe you can try again.*

'What, exactly, have you been doing all this time?'

'Surviving, from the looks of it,' Keenan says. His dark eyes flash to mine, and I can't tell if he's defending or insulting me.

'I was loyal to the Lioness,' Mazen says. 'But I can't waste my time helping someone who won't help me.'

'Mazen, for skies' sake.' Sana sounds aghast. 'Look at the poor girl—'

'Yes.' Mazen eyes the bruises on my neck. 'Look at her. She's a mess. The mission's too difficult. I made a mistake, Laia. I thought you'd take risks. I thought you were more like your mother.'

The insult levels me faster than a blow from the Commandant. Of course he's right. I'm nothing like my mother. She'd have never been in this position to begin with.

'We'll see about getting you out.' Mazen shrugs and stands. 'We're done here.'

'Wait . . .' Mazen can't abandon me now. Darin is lost if he does. Reluctantly, I take out the Commandant's letter. 'I have this. It's from the Commandant to the Emperor. I thought you could look at it.'

'Why didn't you say that to begin with?' He takes the envelope, and I want to tell him to be careful. But Sana beats me to it, and Mazen gives her a brief, annoyed look before gently lifting the seal.

Seconds later, my heart sinks again. Mazen tosses the letter to the table. 'Useless,' he says. 'Look.'

> *Your Imperial Majesty,*
> *I will make the arrangements.*
> *Ever your servant,*
> *Commandant Keris Veturia*

'Don't give up on me,' I say when Mazen shakes his head in disgust. 'Darin doesn't have anyone else. You were close to my parents. Think of them – please. They wouldn't want their only son to die because you refused to help.'

'I'm trying to help.' Mazen is unrelenting, and something about the set of his shoulders and the iron in his eyes reminds me of my mother. I understand now why he's leader of the Resistance. 'But you have to help me. This rescue mission will cost more than just lives. We'll be putting the Resistance itself on the line. If our fighters are caught, we risk them giving up information under interrogation. I'm gambling everything to help you, Laia.' He crosses his arms. 'Make it worth my while.'

'I will. I promise I will. One more chance.'

He stares stonily at me for a moment longer before looking to Sana, who nods, and Keenan, who offers a shrug that could mean any number of things.

'One chance,' Mazen says. 'Fail me again and we're done. Keenan, see her out.'

CHAPTER SIXTEEN

Elias

SEVEN DAYS EARLIER
The Great Wastes. That's where the Augurs have left me, in this salt-white flatness that stretches for hundreds of miles, marked by nothing but angry black cracks and the occasional gnarled Jack tree.

The pale outline of the moon sits above me like something forgotten. It's more than half-full, as it had been yesterday – which means that somehow the Augurs have moved me three hundred miles from Serra in one night. At this time yesterday, I was in Grandfather's carriage, on my way to Blackcliff.

My dagger is driven through a limp piece of parchment and into the scorched ground beside the tree. I tuck the weapon into my belt – it's the difference between life and death out here. The parchment is written in an unfamiliar hand.

The Trial of Courage:
The belltower. Sunset on the seventh day.

That's clear enough. If today counts as the first day, I have six full days to reach the belltower or the Augurs will kill me for failing the Trial.

The air's so dry that breathing burns my nostrils. I lick my lips, already thirsty, and hunch beneath the paltry shade of the Jack tree to consider my predicament.

The stink in the air tells me that the glittering patch of blue to the west of me is Lake Vitan. Its sulphurous stench is legendary, and it's the only source of water in this wasteland. It's also pure salt and so completely useless to me. In any case, my path lies east through the Serran Mountain Range.

Two days to get to the mountains. Two more to get to Walker's Gap, the only way through. A day to get through the Gap and a day to get down to Serra. Six full days exactly, if everything goes as planned.

It's too easy.

I think back to the foretelling I read in the Commandant's office. *Courage to face their darkest fears.* Some people might fear the desert. I'm not one of them.

Which means there's something else out here. Something that hasn't revealed itself.

I tear strips of cloth off my shirt and wrap my feet. I have only what I fell asleep with – my fatigues and my dagger. I'm suddenly, fervently grateful that I was too exhausted from combat training to strip before sleeping. Travelling the Great Wastes naked – that would be its own special sort of hell.

Soon the sun sinks into the wild sky of the west, and I stand in the rapidly cooling air. Time to run. I set out at a steady jog, my eyes roving ahead. After a mile, a breeze meanders past, and for a second, I think I smell smoke and death. The smell fades, but it leaves me uneasy.

What are my fears? I rack my brain, but I can't think of anything. Most of Blackcliff's students fear something, though never for long. When we were Yearlings, the Commandant ordered Helene to rappel down the cliffs again and again until she could drop with nothing but a clenched jaw to betray her terror. That same year, the Commandant forced Faris to keep a bird-eating desert tarantula as a pet, telling him that if the spider died, he would too.

There must be something I fear. Enclosed spaces? The dark? If I don't know my fears, I won't be prepared for them.

Midnight comes and goes, and still the desert around me is quiet and empty. I've travelled nearly twenty miles, and my throat is dry as dirt. I lick at the sweat on my arms, knowing that my need for salt will be as great as my need for water. The moisture helps, but only for a moment. I force myself to focus on the ache in my feet and legs. Pain I can handle. But thirst can drive a man insane.

Soon after, I crest a rise and spot something strange ahead: glimmers of light, like moonlight shining down on a lake. Only there's no lake around here. Dagger in hand, I slow to a walk.

Then I hear it. A voice.

It starts quietly enough, a whisper I can pass off as the wind, a scrape that sounds like the echo of my footsteps on the cracked ground. But the voice gets closer, clearer.

Eliassss.

Eliassss.

A low hill rises before me, and when I reach the top, the night breeze curdles, bringing with it the unmistakable smells of war – blood and dung and rot. Below me sits a battlefield – a killing field, actually, for no battle rages here. Everyone's dead. Moonlight glints off the armour of fallen men. This is what I saw earlier, from the rise.

It's a strange battlefield, unlike any I've encountered. No one moans or pleads for aid. Barbarians from the borderlands lay beside Martial soldiers. I spot what looks like a Tribal trader and beside him, smaller bodies – his family. What is this place? Why would a Tribesman battle against Martials and Barbarians out in the middle of nowhere?

'Elias.'

I practically leap from my skin at the sound of my name spoken in such silence, and my dagger is at the throat of the speaker before I can think. He is a Barbarian boy, no more than thirteen. His face is painted with blue woad, and his body is dark with the geometric tattoos unique to his people. Even in the light of the half-moon, I know him. I'd know him anywhere.

He is my first kill.

My eyes drop to the gaping wound in his stomach, a wound I put there nine years ago. A wound he doesn't seem to notice.

I drop my arm and back away. *Impossible.*

The boy's dead. Which means that all this – the battlefield, the smell, the Wastes – must be a nightmare. I pinch my arm to wake myself up. The boy tilts his head. I pinch myself again. I take my dagger and cut my hand with it. Blood drips to the ground.

The boy doesn't budge. I can't wake up.

Courage to face their darkest fears.

'My mother screamed and tore at her hair for three days after I died,' my first kill says. 'She didn't speak again for five years.' He talks quietly in the just-deepened voice of a teenaged boy. 'I was her only child,' he adds, as if in explanation.

'I'm – I'm sorry—'

The boy shrugs and walks away, gesturing for me to follow him onto the battlefield. I don't want to go, but he clamps a chill hand on my arm and pulls me behind him with surprising force. As we wind through the first of the bodies, I look down. A sick feeling seeps through me.

I recognize these faces. I killed every one of these people.

As I pass them, their voices murmur secrets in my head—

My wife was pregnant—

I was sure I'd kill you first—

My father swore revenge, but died before taking it—

I clap my hands over my ears. But the boy sees, and his clammy fingers pull mine away from my head with inexorable force.

'Come,' he says. 'There are more.'

I shake my head. I know exactly how many people I've killed, when they died, how, where. There are far more than twenty-one men on this battlefield. I can't have killed them all.

But we keep walking, and now there are faces I don't know. And it's a kind of relief, because these faces must be someone else's sins, someone else's darkness.

'Your kills,' the boy interrupts my thoughts. 'They're all yours. The past. The future. All here. All by your hand.'

My hands sweat, and I feel lightheaded. 'I – I don't—' There are scores of people on this battlefield. Well over five hundred. How could I be responsible for the deaths of so many? I look down. There's a lanky, fair-haired Mask on my left, and my stomach sinks because I know this Mask. Demetrius.

'No.' I bend down to shake him. 'Demetrius. Wake up. Get up.'

'He can't hear you,' my first kill says. 'He's gone.'

Beside Demetrius lies Leander, blood staining his halo of curly hair, trickling down his crooked nose and off his chin. And a few feet away, Ennis – another member of Helene's battle platoon. Further ahead, I spot a mane of white hair, a powerful body. Grandfather?

154

'No. No.' There isn't another word for what I'm seeing, because something so terrible shouldn't be allowed to exist. I bend next to another body – the gold-eyed slave-girl I've only just met. A raw red line cuts across her throat. Her hair is a mess, snaking out every which way. Her eyes are open, their brilliant gold faded to the colour of a dead sun. I think of her intoxicating smell, like fruit and sugar and warmth. I turn on my first kill.

'These are my friends, my family. People I know. I wouldn't hurt them.'

'Your kills,' the boy insists, and the terror inside me grows at the sureness with which he speaks. Is this what I will be? A mass murderer?

Wake up, Elias. Wake up. But I cannot wake, because I'm not asleep. The Augurs have somehow brought my nightmare to life, unrolled it before my eyes.

'How do I make it stop? I have to make it stop.'

'It's already done,' the boy says. 'This is your destiny – it is written.'

'No.' I push past him. The battlefield has to end eventually. I'll get by it, keep going through the desert, get out of here.

But when I reach the edge of the carnage, the ground lurches and the battlefield stretches out ahead of me again in its entirety. Beyond the battlefield, the landscape has changed – I'm still moving east through the desert.

'You can keep walking,' the disembodied whisper of my first kill brushes across my ear, and I start violently. 'You may even reach the mountains. But until you conquer your fear, the dead will remain with you.'

This is an illusion, Elias. Augur sorcery. Keep walking until you find your way out.

I force myself towards the shadow of the Serran Range, but

every time I reach the end of the battlefield, I feel the lurch and see the bodies spread out before me yet again. Every time it happens, it gets harder to ignore the carnage at my feet. My pace slows, and I struggle to stumble on. I pass by the same people over and over, until their faces are burned into my memory.

The sky lightens and dawn breaks. *Second day*, I think. *Go east, Elias.*

The battlefield grows hot and fetid. Clouds of flies and scavengers descend. I shout and attack them with my dagger, but I can't keep them away. I want to die of thirst or hunger, but I feel neither in this place. I count 539 bodies.

I won't kill so many. I tell myself. *I won't.* An insidious voice in my head chuckles when I try to convince myself of this. *You're a Mask*, the voice says. *Of course you'll kill so many. You'll kill more.* I run from the thought, willing with my entire mind to break free of the battlefield. But I cannot.

The sky darkens, the moon rises. I cannot leave. Daylight again. *It's the third day.* The thought appears in my head, but I hardly know what it means. I was supposed to do something by now. Be somewhere. I look to my right, at the mountains. *There. I'm supposed to go there.* I force my body to turn.

Sometimes, I talk to those I've killed. In my head, I hear them whisper back – not accusations, but their hopes, their wants. I wish they would curse me instead. It's worse, somehow, to hear all that would have been had I not killed them.

East. Elias, go east. It's the only logical thing I can think. But sometimes, lost in the horror of my future, I forget about going east. Instead, I wander from body to body, begging those I've killed for forgiveness.

Darkness. Daylight. *The fourth day.* And soon after, the fifth. But why am I counting the days? The days don't matter. I'm in hell. A hell I've made myself, because I am evil. As evil as my mother. As evil as any Mask who spends a lifetime relishing the blood and tears of his victims.

To the mountains, Elias, a faint voice whispers in my head, the last shred of sanity I have. *To the mountains.*

My feet bleed, and my face cracks from the wind. The sky is below me. The ground above. Old memories flit through my head – Mamie Rila teaching me to write my tribal name; the pain of a Centurion's whip tearing into my back that first time; sitting with Helene in the wilds of the north, watching as the sky swirled with impossible ribbons of light.

I trip over a body and crash to the ground. The impact shakes something loose in my mind.

Mountains. East. Trial. This is a Trial.

Thinking those words is like pulling myself from a pool of quicksand. This is a Trial, and I must survive it. Most of the people on the battlefield aren't dead yet – I just saw them. This is a test – of my mettle, my strength – which means there must be something specific I'm supposed to do to get out of here.

'Until you conquer your fear, the dead will remain with you.'

I hear a sound. The first sound I've heard in days, it feels like. There, shimmering like a mirage at the edge of the battlefield, is a figure. My first kill again? I stagger towards him but fall to my knees when I'm just a few feet away. Because it is not my first kill. It's Helene, and she is covered in blood and scratches, her silver hair tangled as she gazes at me with empty eyes.

'No,' I rasp. 'Not Helene. Not Helene. Not Helene.'

I chant it like a madman with only two words left in his mind. Helene's ghost comes closer.

'Elias.' Skies, her voice. Cracked and haunted. *So real.* 'Elias, it's me. It's Helene.'

157

Helene, on my nightmare battlefield? Helene, another victim?

No. I will not kill my oldest, best friend. This is a fact, not a wish. I will not kill her.

I realize in that moment that I cannot be afraid of something if there's no chance it could ever occur. The knowledge releases me, finally, from the fear that has consumed me for days.

'I won't kill you,' I say. 'I swear it. By blood and by bone, I swear it. And I won't kill any of the others, either. I won't.'

The battlefield fades, the smell fades, the dead fade, as if they had never been real. As if they had only ever been in my mind. Ahead, close enough to touch, sit the mountains I've been staggering towards for five days, their rocky trails curving and swooping like Tribal calligraphy.

'Elias?'

Helene's ghost is still here.

For a moment, I don't understand. She reaches for my face, and I flinch from her, expecting the cold caress of a spirit.

But her skin is warm.

'Helene?'

Then she's pulling me close, cradling my head, whispering that I'm alive, that she is alive, that we are both all right, that she's found me. I wrap my arms around her waist and bury my face in her stomach. And for the first time in nine years, I start to cry.

*　　*　　*

'We only have two days to get back.' These are the first words Hel's spoken since she half-dragged me out of the foothills and into a mountain cave.

I say nothing. I'm not ready for words yet. A fox roasts over a fire, and my mouth waters at the smell. Night has fallen, and outside the cave, thunder reverberates. Black clouds roll out from the Wastes, and the heavens break open, rain cascading through lightning-edged cracks in the sky.

'I saw you around noon.' She adds a few more branches to the fire. 'But it took me a couple of hours to come down the mountain to you. Thought you were an animal at first. Then the sun hit your mask.' She stares out at the sheeting rain. 'You looked bad.'

'How did you know I wasn't Marcus?' I croak. My throat is dry, and I take another sip of water from the reed canteen she's made. 'Or Zak?'

'I can tell the difference between you and a couple of reptiles. Besides, Marcus fears water. The Augurs wouldn't leave him in a desert. And Zak hates tight spaces, so he's probably underground somewhere. Here. Eat.'

I eat slowly, watching Helene all the while. Her usually sleek hair is matted, its silver sheen faded. She's covered in scratches and dried blood.

'What did you see, Elias? You were coming for the mountains, but you kept falling, clawing at the air. You talked about . . . about killing me.'

I shake my head. The Trial's not over, and I have to forget what I saw if I want to survive the rest of it.

'Where did they leave you?' I ask.

She wraps her arms around herself and hunches down, her eyes barely visible. 'Northwest. In the mountains. In a spire vulture's nest.'

I put down my fox. Spire vultures are massive birds with five-inch talons and wingspans that clear twenty feet. Their eggs are the size of a man's head, their hatchlings notoriously bloodthirsty.

But worst of all for Helene, the vultures build their nests above the clouds, atop the most unassailable peaks.

She doesn't have to explain the catch in her voice. She used to shake for hours after the Commandant made her scale the cliffs. The Augurs know all this, of course. They've picked it from her mind the way a thief picks a plum off a tree.

'How did you get down?'

'Luck. The mother vulture was gone, and the hatchlings were just breaking through their shells. But they were dangerous enough, even half-hatched.'

She pulls up her shirt to expose the pale, taut skin of her stomach, marred by a tangle of gouges.

'I jumped over the side of the nest and landed on a ledge ten feet down. I didn't – I didn't realize how high I was. But that wasn't the worst of it. I kept seeing . . .' She stops, and I realize that the Augurs must have forced her to face some foul hallucination, something equal to my nightmare battlefield. What darkness had she borne, thousands of feet up, with nothing between her and death but a few inches of rock?

'The Augurs are sick,' I say. 'I can't believe they'd—'

'They're doing what they have to, Elias. They're making us face our fears. They need to find the strongest, remember? The bravest. We have to trust them.'

She closes her eyes, shivering. I cross the space between us and put my hands on her arms to still her. When she lifts her lashes, I realize I can feel the heat of her body, that mere inches separate our faces. She has beautiful lips, I notice distractedly, the top one fuller than the bottom. I meet her gaze for one intimate, infinite moment. She leans towards me, those lips parting. A violent throb of desire tugs at me, followed by a frantic alarm bell. *Bad idea. Terrible idea. She's your best friend. Stop.*

I drop my arms and back away hastily, trying not to notice the flush on her neck. Helene's eyes flash – anger or embarrassment, I can't tell.

'Anyway,' she says. 'I got down last night and figured I'd take the rim trail to Walker's Gap. Fastest way back. There's a guard station at the other end. We can get a boat to cross the river and supplies – clothes and boots, at least.' She gestures to her ragged, bloodstained fatigues. 'Not that I'm complaining.'

She looks up at me, a question in her eyes. 'They left you in the Wastes, but . . .' *But you don't fear the desert. You grew up there.*

'No use thinking about it,' I say.

After that, we are silent, and when the fire burns down, Helene tells me she's turning in. But though she rolls over into a pile of leaves, I know sleep won't come to her. She's still clinging to the side of her mountain, just like I'm still wandering lost in my battlefield.

* * *

Helene and I are bleary-eyed and exhausted the next morning, but we start out well before dawn. We need to reach Walker's Gap today if we want to get back to Blackcliff by sunset tomorrow.

We don't speak – we don't have to. Travelling with Helene is like pulling on a favourite shirt. We spent all of our time as Fivers together, and we fall instinctively back into the pattern of those days, with me taking point and Helene the rear guard.

The storm rolls away north to reveal a blue sky and a land clean and glistening. But the crisp beauty conceals fallen trees and washed-out trails, hillsides treacherous with mud and debris.

There's an unmistakable tension in the air. Just like before, I have the sense that something lies in wait. Something unknown.

Helene and I don't stop to rest. Our eyes are peeled for bears, lynxes, wayward hunters – any creature that might call the mountains home.

In the afternoon, we climb the rise that leads to the Gap, a fifteen-mile-long river of forest amid the blue-speckled peaks of the Serran Range. The Gap appears almost gentle, carpeted with trees, rolling hills, and the occasional gold burst of a wildflower meadow. Helene and I exchange a glance. We both feel it. Whatever's coming, it's going to be soon.

As we move into the forest, the sense of danger increases, and I catch sight of a furtive movement at the edge of my vision. Helene looks back at me. She's seen it too.

We alter our route frequently and stay off the trails, which slows our pace but makes an ambush more difficult. As dusk approaches, we haven't made it out of the pass and are forced to move back to the trail so we can pick our way forward by moonlight.

The sun has just set when the forest falls silent. I shout Helene a warning and have barely enough time to bring my knife up before a dark shape hurtles out of the trees.

I don't know what I'm expecting. An army of those I killed, coming for revenge? A nightmare creature conjured by the Augurs?

Something that will strike fear into my very bones. Something to test my courage.

I don't expect the mask. I don't expect the cold, flat eyes of Zak glaring out at me.

Behind me, Helene screams, and I hear the crash of two bodies hitting the ground. I turn to see Marcus attacking her. Her face is frozen in terror at the sight of him, and she makes no move to defend herself as he pins down her arms, laughing like he did when he kissed her.

'Helene!' At my shout, she snaps out of her daze and strikes out at Marcus, twisting away from him.

Then Zak is on me, raining blows down on my head, my neck. He fights recklessly, almost frenziedly, and I easily evade his assault. I come around behind him, sweeping my dagger in an arc. He spins back to dodge the attack and lunges at me, teeth bared like a dog's. I duck beneath his arm and sink my dagger into his side. Hot blood sprays across my hand. I wrench the dagger out, and Zak groans and staggers back. Hand on his side, he stumbles into the trees, shouting for his twin.

Marcus, serpent that he is, darts into the forest after Zak. Blood shines on Marcus's thigh, and I feel a burst of satisfaction. Hel marked him. I give chase, the battle rage rising, blinding me to anything else. Distantly, Helene calls my name. Ahead of me, the Snake's shadow joins with Zak's, and they barrel ahead, unaware of how close I am.

'Ten burning hells, Zak!' Marcus says. 'The Commandant told us to finish them off before they left the Gap, and you go running into the woods like a scared little girl—'

'He stabbed me, all right?' Zak's voice is breathless. 'And she didn't tell us we'd be dealing with both of them at once, did she?'

'Elias!'

Helene's shout barely registers. Marcus and Zak's conversation leaves me dumbstruck. It's no surprise that my mother's in league with the Snake and Toad. What I don't understand is how she knew that Hel and I would be coming through the Gap.

'We have to finish them.' Marcus's shadow turns, and I bring my dagger up. Then Zak grabs him.

'We have to get out of here,' he says. 'Or we won't make it back on time. Leave them. Come on.'

Part of me wants to chase after Marcus and Zak and take the answers to my questions out of their hides. But Helene cries out again, her voice faint. She might be hurt.

When I get back to the clearing, Hel is slumped on the ground, her head tilted to the side. One arm is splayed out uselessly while she paws at her shoulder with the other, trying to staunch the sluggish pulse of blood draining out of her.

I close the distance between us in two strides, tearing off what remains of my shirt, wadding it and pressing down on the wound. She bucks her head, her knotted blonde hair whipping at her back as she cries out, a keening, animal wail.

'It's all right, Hel,' I say. My hands shake, and a voice in my head screams that it's not all right, that my best friend is going to die. I keep talking. 'You're going to be fine. I'm going to fix you right up.' I grab the canteen. I need to clean the wound and bind it. 'Talk to me. Tell me what happened.'

'Surprised me. Couldn't move. I – I saw him on the mountain. He was – he and I—' She shudders, and I understand now. In the desert, I saw images of war and death. Helene saw Marcus. 'His hands – everywhere.' She squeezes her eyes shut and draws her legs up protectively.

I'll kill him, I think calmly, making the decision as easily as I'd choose my boots in the morning. *If she dies – so will he.*

'Can't let them win. If they win . . .' Helene's words spill from her mouth. 'Fight, Elias. You have to fight. You have to win.'

I cut open her shirt with my dagger, jolted for a moment by the delicacy of her skin. Dark has settled in, and I can barely see the wound, but I can feel the warmth of the blood as it oozes into my hand.

Helene grabs my arm with her good hand as I pour water over the injury. I bind her up using what's left of my shirt and some strips from her fatigues. After a few moments, her hand goes slack – she's fallen unconscious.

My body aches in exhaustion, but I begin pulling vines down from the trees to make a sling. Hel can't walk, so I'll have to carry her to Blackcliff. As I work, my mind whirls. The Farrars ambushed us on the Commandant's orders. No wonder she couldn't contain her smugness before the Trials began. She was planning this attack. But how did she learn where we'd be?

It wouldn't take a genius, I suppose. If she knew the Augurs would leave me in the Great Wastes and Helene in spire vulture territory, she would also know the only way for us to get back to Serra was through the Gap. But if she told Marcus and Zak, then that means they cheated and sabotaged us, which the Augurs pointedly forbade.

The Augurs must know what happened. Why haven't they done anything about it?

When the sling is finished, I carefully load Helene into it. Her skin is blanched bone-white, and she shakes with cold. She feels light. Too light.

Again, the Augurs have preyed on the unexpected fear, the one I didn't realize I had. Helene is dying. I didn't know how terrifying it would be because she's never come so close to it before.

My doubts crowd in – I won't make it back to Blackcliff by sunset; the physician won't be able to save her; she'll die before I get to the school. *Stop, Elias. Move.*

After years of the Commandant's forced marches through the desert, carrying Helene is no burden. Though it's deep night, I move quickly. I still have to hike out of the mountains, get a boat from the river guardhouse, and row to Serra. I've already lost hours making the sling, and Marcus and Zak will be well ahead of me. Even if I don't stop from here until Serra, I'll be hard-pressed to reach the belltower before sunset.

The sky pales, casting the jagged peaks of the mountains around me in shadow. The day is well under way when I emerge from the Gap. The Rei River stretches out below, slow and curving like a well-sated python. Barges and boats dot the water, and just beyond the eastern banks sits the city of Serra, its dun-coloured walls imposing even from a distance of miles.

Smoke taints the air. A column of black rises into the sky, and though I can't see the guardhouse from this spot on the trail, I know with sinking certainty that the Farrars got there before me. That they burned it along with the boathouse attached to it.

I sprint down the mountain, but by the time I reach the guardhouse, it's nothing but a stinking, sooty hulk. The attached boathouse is a pile of smouldering logs, and the legionnaires manning it have cleared out – probably under orders from the Farrars.

I unlash Helene from my back. The jarring trip down the mountain has reopened her wound. My back is coated in her blood.

'Helene?' I sink to my knees and pat her face softly. 'Helene!' Not even a flick of the eyelids. She is lost inside herself, and the skin around her wound is red and fevered. She's getting an infection.

I stare flintily at the guard shack, willing a boat to appear. Any boat. A raft. A dinghy. A bleeding, hollowed-out log, I don't care. Anything. But of course, there's nothing. Sunset is, at most, an hour away. If I don't get us across this river, we're dead.

Strangely, it's my mother's voice I hear in my head, cold and pitiless. *Nothing is impossible.* It's something she's said to her students a hundred times – when we were exhausted from back-to-back training battles or we hadn't slept in days. She always demanded more. More than we thought we had to give. *Either find a way to complete the tasks I have set before you*, she would tell us, *or die in the attempt. Your choice.*

Exhaustion is temporary. Pain is temporary. But Helene dying because I didn't find a way to get her back on time – that's permanent.

I spot a smoking wooden beam half in the water, half out. It will do. I kick, shove, and roll the blasted thing to the river, where it bobs beneath the water threateningly before floating to the surface. Carefully, I lay Helene on the beam and lash her into place. Then I sling an arm around it and make for the closest boat as if all the jinn of air and sea are on my tail.

The river's waters run freely at this time, mostly empty of the barges and canoes that choke it in the morning. I angle towards a Mercator craft bobbing mid-river, its oars at rest. The sailors don't notice me approaching, and when I'm right alongside the rope ladder leading to the boat's deck, I cut Hel from the beam. She sinks into the water almost immediately. I grab the slick rope with one hand and Helene with the other, eventually working her body over my shoulder and clambering up the ladder to the deck.

A silver-haired Martial with a soldier's build – the captain, I assume – is overseeing a group of Plebeians and Scholar slaves stacking boxes of cargo.

'I am Aspirant Elias Veturius of Blackcliff.' I level my voice until it is as flat as the deck I stand on. 'And I am commandeering this vessel.'

The man blinks, taking in the sight before him: two Masks, one so covered in blood it appears that she's been tortured, and the other practically naked with a week's worth of beard, wild hair, and a mad look in his eyes.

But the merchant has clearly done his time in the Martial army because after only a moment, he nods.

'I am at your disposal, Lord Veturius.'

'Get this boat docked in Serra. Now.'

The captain shouts orders at his men, a whip much in evidence. In under a minute, the boat is chugging towards Serra's docks. I look balefully at the sinking sun, willing it to at least slow down. I have no more than a half hour left, and I still have to get through the dock traffic and up to Blackcliff.

I'm cutting it close. Too close.

Helene moans, and I place her on the deck gently. She is sweating despite the cool river air, and her skin is deathly pale. She opens her eyes for a moment.

'Do I look that bad?' she whispers, seeing the expression on my face.

'Actually, it's an improvement. The filthy woodswoman thing suits you.'

She smiles, a rare, sweet smile, but it fades quickly.

'Elias – you can't let me die. If I die, then you—'

'Don't talk, Hel. Rest.'

'Can't die. Augur said – he said if I lived, then—'

'Shhh . . .'

Her eyes flutter closed, and impatiently, I eye Serra's docks, still a half mile away and crowded with sailors, soldiers, horses, and wagons. I want to urge the boat faster, but the slaves are already rowing furiously, the captain's whip at their backs.

Before the boat docks, the captain lowers the gangplank, hails a legionnaire patrolling nearby, and relieves him of his horse. For once, I'm thankful for the severity of Martial discipline.

'Luck to you, Lord Veturius,' the captain says. I thank him and load Hel onto the waiting horse. She sags forward, but I don't have time to adjust her. I vault onto the beast and put heel to flank, my eyes on the sun hovering just above the horizon.

The city passes in a blur of gaping Plebeians, muttering auxes, and a riot of merchants and their stalls. I race past all of them, down Serra's main thoroughfare, through the dwindling crowds of Execution Square, and up the cobbled streets of the Illustrian Quarter. The horse surges on recklessly, and I'm too crazed to even feel guilty when I knock over a pedlar and his cart. Helene's head bobs back and forth like a slack marionette's.

'Hang on, Helene,' I whisper. 'Almost there.'

We enter an Illustrian market, scattering slaves in our wake before turning a corner. Blackcliff looms before us as suddenly as if it has sprung fully formed from the earth. The faces of the gate guards blur as we gallop past them.

The sun sinks lower. *Not yet*, I tell it. *Not yet*.

'Come on.' I dig my heels in deeper. 'Faster!'

Then we are across the training field, up the hill, and inside the central courtyard. The belltower rises in front of me, a few precious yards away. I jerk the horse to a halt and leap off it.

The Commandant stands at the base of the tower, her face stiff – from anger or nerves, I can't tell. Beside her, Cain waits with two other Augurs, both women. They look at me with mute interest, as if I am a mildly entertaining side act at a circus.

A scream tears through the air. The courtyard is lined with hundreds of people: students, Centurions, and families – including Helene's. Her mother falls to her knees, hysterical at the sight of her blood-covered daughter. Hel's sisters, Hannah and Livia, drop beside her as Pater Aquillus remains stone-faced.

Next to him, Grandfather stands in full battle dress. He looks like a bull about to charge, and his grey eyes blaze with pride.

I pull Helene into my arms and stride to the belltower. It's never seemed so long, this courtyard, not even when I've run a hundred sprints across it in the dead of summer.

My body drags. All I want is to collapse onto the ground and sleep for a week. But I take those last few steps, laying Helene down against the tower and reaching out a hand to touch the stone. A moment after my skin meets the rock, the sunset drums boom out.

The crowd erupts. I'm not sure who starts the cheer. Faris? Dex? Maybe even Grandfather. The whole square echoes with it. They must hear it down in the city.

'*Veturius! Veturius! Veturius!*'

'Get the physician,' I roar at a nearby Cadet who cheers with all the others. His hands freeze mid-clap, and he gapes at me. 'Now! Move!'

'Helene,' I whisper. 'Hold on.'

She's as waxen as a doll. I put a hand against her cold cheek, rubbing a circle over the skin with my thumb. She doesn't move. She doesn't draw breath. And when I put my fingers to her throat, to where her pulse should be, I feel nothing.

CHAPTER SEVENTEEN

Laia

Sana and Mazen disappear up an interior staircase as Keenan walks me out of the basement. I expect him to beg off as quickly as possible. Instead, he beckons me to follow him to a weed-choked backstreet nearby. The street is empty but for a band of urchins crouching over some small treasure, and they scatter at our approach.

I sidle a glance at the red-haired fighter, to find his attention fixed on me with an intensity that sends an unexpected flutter through my chest.

'They've been hunting you.'

'I'm fine,' I say. I won't let him think I'm weak. I'm on thin ice as it is. 'Darin's all that matters. The rest is just . . .' I shrug. Keenan cocks his head and brushes a thumb across the now-faint bruises on my neck. Then he takes my wrist and turns it over to reveal the angry welts the Commandant left there. His hands are slow and gentle as candle flame, and the warmth in my chest spreads up through my collarbone and down to my fingertips. My pulse skitters, and I shake his hand away, unnerved at my own reaction.

'Was it all the Commandant?'

'It's nothing to worry about,' I say more sharply than I intend. His eyes go cold at the bite in my voice, and I soften. 'I can do this, all right? It's Darin's life at stake here. I just wish I knew . . .' *If he is nearby. If he is all right. If he is in pain.*

'Darin's still in Serra. I heard the spy who gave the report.' Keenan walks me further down the street. 'But he's not . . . well. They've been at him.'

A punch to the stomach would have been gentler. I don't have to ask who 'they' are, I already know. *Interrogators. Masks.*

'Look,' Keenan says. 'You don't know the first thing about spying. That's clear. Here are some basics: Gossip with the other slaves – you'll be surprised at what you learn. Keep your hands busy – sewing, scrubbing, fetching. The busier you are, the less likely it is that anyone will question your presence, wherever you might be. If you see a chance to get your hands on real information, take it. But always have an exit plan. The cloak you're wearing is good – it helps you blend in. But you walk and act like a free-woman. If I noticed it, others will too. Shuffle, hunch. Act beaten. Act broken.'

'Why are you trying to help me?' I ask. 'You didn't want to risk the men to save my brother.'

He is suddenly very interested in the mouldering bricks of a nearby building. 'My parents are dead too,' he says. 'My whole family, actually. A long time ago now.' He gives me a quick, almost angry glance, and for a second, I see them in his eyes, this lost family, flashes of fiery hair and freckles. Did he have brothers? Sisters? Was he the oldest? The youngest? I want to ask, but his face is shuttered.

'I still think the mission is a terrible idea,' he says. 'But that doesn't mean I don't understand why you're doing it. And it doesn't mean I want you to fail.' He touches his fist to his heart and holds out his hand to me. 'Death before tyranny,' he murmurs.

'Death before tyranny.' I take his hand, aware of every muscle in his fingers.

No one has touched me for the past ten days except to hurt me. How I miss being touched – Nan stroking my hair, Darin arm-wrestling me and pretending to lose, Pop squeezing my shoulder good night.

I don't want Keenan to let go. As if he understands, he holds on a moment longer. But then he turns and walks away, leaving me alone on an empty street with fingers still tingling.

* * *

After delivering the Commandant's first letter to the couriers' office, I head to the smoke-choked streets near the river docks. Serran summers are always blistering, but the heat in the Weapons Quarter takes on an animal esurience.

The district is a hive of movement and sound, busier on a regular day than most markets are on festival days. Sparks fly from hammers as big as my head, forge fires glow a red deeper than blood, and cottony plumes of steam erupt every few feet from freshly quenched swords. Blacksmiths shout orders as apprentices jostle to follow them. And above it all, the strain and pump of hundreds of bellows, creaking like a fleet of ships in a storm.

Within seconds of entering the district, I am stopped by a platoon of legionnaires demanding to know my business. I offer them the Commandant's remaining letter only to find myself arguing with them over its authenticity for ten minutes. Finally, grudgingly, they send me on my way.

It makes me wonder yet again how Darin managed to get into the district not just once, but day after day.

They've been at him, Keenan said. How long can Darin hold out against his torturers? Longer than me, certainly. When Darin was fifteen, he fell from a tree while trying to draw Scholars working a Martial orchard. He arrived home with bone jutting out of his wrist, and I screamed and nearly fainted at the sight. *It's all right*, he said to me. *Pop will set it. Find him and then go back for my sketchbook. I dropped it, and I don't want someone to take it.*

My brother has Mother's iron will. If anyone can survive a Martial interrogation, it's him.

As I walk, I feel a tug on my skirt and glance down, expecting to find it caught beneath someone's boot. Instead, I catch a glimpse of a slit-eyed shadow slipping quickly across the cobbles. A tingle runs up my spine at the sight, and I hear a low, cruel cackle. My skin prickles – that laugh was directed at me. I'm certain of it.

Unsettled, I quicken my pace, eventually persuading an elderly Plebeian man to direct me to Teluman's forge. I find it just off the main street, marked only by an ornate iron *T* hammered into the door.

Unlike the other forges, this one is utterly silent. I knock, but no one answers. Now what? Do I open the door and risk angering the smith by barging in, or do I go back to the Commandant without a response when she specifically demanded one?

It's not a difficult choice.

The front door opens to an antechamber. A dust-coated counter splits the room, backed by dozens of glass display cases and another, narrower door. The forge itself sits in a larger room to my right, cold and empty, its bellows still. A hammer lies on an anvil, but the other tools hang neatly from pegs on the walls. Something strikes me about the room. It reminds me of another I've seen, but I can't place it.

Light filters in weakly through a bank of high windows, illuminating the dust I kicked up when entering. The place has an abandoned feel to it, and I feel my frustration building. How am I supposed to take back a response if the smith isn't here?

Sunlight glints off the row of glass cases, and my gaze is drawn to the weapons within. They are gracefully wrought, each one worked with the same intricate, almost obsessive detail, from hilt to crossbar to minutely etched blade. Intrigued by their beauty, I move closer. The blades remind me of something, as the whole shop does – something important, something I should be able to put my finger on.

And then I understand. The Commandant's letter falls from my suddenly numb hand, and I *know*. Darin drew *these* weapons. He drew *this* forge. He drew that hammer and that anvil. I've spent so much time trying to figure out how to save my brother that I'd nearly forgotten the drawings that had got him into trouble in the first place. And here is their source, before my eyes.

'Something the matter, girl?'

A Martial man comes through the narrow back door, looking more like a river pirate than a blacksmith. His head is shaved, and he drips with piercings – six through each ear, one in his nose, his eyebrows, his lips. Multicoloured tattoos – of eight-pointed stars, lush-leafed vines, a hammer and anvil, a bird, a woman's eyes, scales – run from his wrists up his arms and into a black leather jerkin. He can't be more than fifteen years older than me. Like most Martials, he's tall and muscled, but lanky, without the brawn I'd expect of a blacksmith.

Is *this* the man Darin was spying on?

'Who are you?' I'm so thrown off that I forget he's a Martial.

The man lifts his eyebrows as if to say, *Me? Who in the ten hells are you?* 'This is my shop,' he says. 'I'm Spiro Teluman.'

Of course he is, Laia, you idiot. I scramble for the note from the Commandant, hoping the smith thinks my comment is the result of being a dim-witted Scholar rat. He reads the note but says nothing.

'She – she requested a response. Sir.'

'Not interested.' He looks up. 'Tell her I'm not interested.' Then he returns to the back room.

I stare after Teluman uncertainly. Does he know my brother was taken to prison for spying on his shop? Has the smith seen what Darin drew? Is his shop always abandoned? Is that how Darin got so close? I'm still trying to piece it all together when an unsettling feeling creeps up my neck, like the greedy touch of a ghost's fingers.

'*Laia.*'

A clump of shadows is gathered at the foot of the door, black as spilled ink. The shadows take shape, eyes glinting, and I begin to sweat. *Why here? Why now?* How can creatures of my own mind not be controllable by me? Why can I not will them away?

'*Laia.*' The shadows rise, morphing into a manlike shape. They take on form and colour, and the voice is as familiar and true as if my brother is standing in front of me.

'*Why did you leave me, Laia?*'

'Darin?' I forget that this is a hallucination, that I'm in a Martial forge with a murderous-looking blacksmith yards away.

The simulacrum tilts its head, just like Darin used to. '*They're hurting me, Laia.*'

It's not Darin. My mind is slipping. This is guilt, fear. The voice changes, twisting and layering as if there are three Darins all talking at once. The light in the fake-Darin's eyes goes out as quickly as a sun in a storm, and his irises darken into black pits, as if his entire body is filled with shadow.

'I won't survive it, Laia. It hurts.'

The simulacrum's hand shoots out to grab my arm, and a bone-deep cold jolts through me. I scream before I can stop myself, and a second later, the creature's hand drops away. I feel a presence behind me and turn to find Spiro Teluman wielding the most beautiful scim I've ever seen. He pushes me casually to the side, holding the scim to the simulacrum.

As if he can see the creatures. As if he can hear them.

'Begone,' he says.

The simulacrum swells, titters, and then falls into a pile of laughing shadows, their cackles falling against my ears like slivers of ice.

'We have the boy now. Our brothers gnaw at his soul. Soon he will be mad and ripe. Then we shall feast.'

Spiro brings the scim down. The shadows scream, and the sound is like nails on wood. They squeeze under the door, a mass of rats escaping a flood. Seconds later, they're gone.

'You – you can see them,' I say. 'I thought they were all in my head. I thought I was going mad.'

'They're called ghuls,' Teluman says.

'But . . .' Seventeen years of Scholar pragmatism protest the existence of creatures that are supposed to be nothing but legend. 'But ghuls aren't real.'

'They are as real as you or I. They left our world for a time. But they've returned. Not everyone can see them. They feed off sorrow and sadness and the stink of blood.' He looks around his forge. 'They like this place.'

His pale green eyes meet mine, careful and wary. 'I've changed my mind. Tell the Commandant I'll consider her request. Tell her to send me some specs. Tell her to send them with you.'

* * *

My mind whirls with questions when I leave the smithy. Why did Darin draw Teluman's shop? How did he get in? Why can Teluman see the ghuls? Did he see the shadow-Darin too? Is Darin dying? If ghuls are real, then are jinn real too?

When I arrive back at Blackcliff, I attack my tasks with a single-minded focus, losing myself in the polishing of floors and scrubbing of baths so that I might escape the cyclone of thoughts in my head.

By late evening, the Commandant still has not returned. I head to the kitchen smelling of polish, my head aching with the indecipherable echo of Blackcliff's drums, which have been pounding all day.

Izzi risks a glance in my direction while she folds a stack of towels. When I smile, she offers a tentative twitch of her lips in return. Cook wipes down the counters for the night, ignoring me, as usual. I think back to Keenan's advice: to gossip, to keep myself busy. Quietly, I take up a basket of mending and sit at the worktable. As I watch Cook and Izzi, I suddenly wonder if they are related. They tilt their heads in the same way, they are both small and fair-haired. And there's a quiet companionship between them that makes my heart ache for Nan.

Eventually, Cook turns in for the night, and silence fills the kitchen. Somewhere in the city, my brother suffers in a Martial prison. *You have to get information, Laia. You have to get the Resistance something. Get Izzi to talk.*

'The legionnaires were in an uproar outside,' I say without looking up from my mending. Izzi makes a polite sound.

'And the students too. I wonder why.' When she doesn't respond, I shift my sitting position, and she glances over her shoulder at me.

'It's the Trials.' She stops her folding for a moment. 'The Farrar brothers came back this morning. Aquilla and Veturius barely made it on time. They'd have been killed if they'd showed up even seconds later.'

This is the most she's said to me at once, and I have to remind myself not to stare. 'How do you know all this?' I ask.

'The entire school's talking about it.' Izzi lowers her voice, and I inch closer. 'Even the slaves. Not much else to talk about around here, unless you want to sit around comparing bruises.'

I chuckle, and it feels strange, almost wrong, like making a joke at a funeral. But Izzi smiles, and I don't feel as bad. The drums start up again, and though Izzi doesn't halt her work, I can tell she's listening.

'You understand the drums.'

'They mostly give orders. *Blue Platoon report for watch. All Cadets to the armoury.* That sort of thing. Right now they're ordering a sweep of the eastern tunnels.' She looks down at the neat stack of towels. A strand of blonde hair falls into her face, making her appear especially young. 'When you've been here for a while, you'll learn to understand them.'

As I take in that disturbing fact, the front door slams shut. Izzi and I both jump.

'Slave-Girl.' It's the Commandant. 'Upstairs.'

Izzi and I exchange a glance, and I'm surprised to find my heart thudding uncomfortably fast. A slow dread sinks into my bones with every step up the stairs. I don't know why. The

Commandant calls me up every evening to take her clothes for washing and braid her hair for the night. *It's no different today, Laia.*

When I enter her room, she stands at her dresser, idly passing a dagger through a candle flame.

'Did you bring back an answer from the swordsmith?'

I relay Teluman's reply, and the Commandant turns to regard me with cool interest. It's the most emotion I've seen from her.

'Spiro hasn't accepted a new commission in years. He must have taken a liking to you.' The way she says it makes my skin crawl. She tests the edge of her knife on her forefinger, then wipes away the drop of blood that beads there.

'Why did you open it?'

'Sir?'

'The letter,' she says. 'You opened it. Why?' She stands before me, and if running would have done me any good, I'd have been out the door in a heartbeat. I twist the cloth of my shirt in my hands. The Commandant tilts her head, awaiting my answer as if genuinely curious, as if I might somehow say something that will satisfy her.

'It was an accident. My hand slipped and . . . and broke the seal.'

'You can't read,' she says. 'So I don't see why you would bother to open it purposefully. Unless you're a spy planning to give over my secrets to the Resistance.' Her mouth twists into what might be a smile if it didn't appear so joyless.

'I'm not – I'm . . .' How did she find out about the letter? I think of the scrape I heard in the hallway after I left her rooms this morning. Did she see me tamper with it? Had the couriers' office noticed a flaw in the seal? It doesn't matter. I think of Izzi's warning when I first got here. *The Commandant sees things. Knows things she shouldn't.*

A knock comes at the door, and on the Commandant's command, two legionnaires enter and salute.

'Hold her down,' the Commandant says.

The legionnaires grab me, and the presence of the Commandant's knife is suddenly, sickeningly clear. 'No – please, no—'

'Silence.' She draws the word out softly, like the name of a lover. The soldiers pin me to a chair, their armoured hands as heavy as manacles around my arms, their knees coming down on my feet. Their faces give nothing away.

'Normally, I'd take an eye for such insolence,' the Commandant muses. 'Or a hand. But I don't think Spiro Teluman will be so interested in you if you're marred. You're lucky I want a Teluman blade, girl. You're lucky he wants a taste of you.'

Her eyes fall on my chest, on the smooth skin above my heart. 'Please,' I say. 'It was a mistake.'

She leans in close, her lips inches from mine, those dead eyes lit, for just a moment, with terrifying fury.

'Stupid girl,' she whispers. 'Haven't you learned? I don't abide mistakes.'

She shoves a gag in my mouth, and then the knife is burning, searing, carving a path through my skin. She works slowly, so slowly. The smell of singed flesh fills my nostrils, and I hear myself begging for mercy, then sobbing, then screaming.

Darin. Darin. Think of Darin.

But I can't think of my brother. Lost in the pain, I can't even remember his face.

CHAPTER EIGHTEEN

Elias

Helene's not dead. She can't be. She survived initiation, the wilds, border skirmishes, whippings. That she'd die now, at the hands of someone as vile as Marcus, is unthinkable. The part of me that is still a child, the part of me that I didn't know still existed until this moment, howls in rage.

The crowd in the courtyard pushes forward. Students crane their necks, trying to get a look at Helene. My mother's ice-chiselled face disappears from view.

'Wake up, Helene,' I yell at her, ignoring the pressing crowd. 'Come on.'

She's gone. It was too much for her. For a second that never seems to end, I hold her, numb as the realization sinks in. *She's dead.*

'Out of the way, damn you.' Grandfather's voice seems far away, but a second later, he's beside me. I stare at him, shaken. Only a few days ago, I saw him dead on the nightmare battlefield. But here he is, alive and well. He lays a hand against Helene's throat. 'Still alive,' he says. 'Barely. Clear the way.' His scim is out, and the crowd backs away. 'Get the physician! Find a litter! Move!'

'Augur,' I choke out. 'Where's the Augur?' As if my thoughts summon him, Cain appears. I thrust Helene at Grandfather, struggling not to wrap my hands around the Augur's neck for what he's put us through.

'You have the power to heal,' I say through gritted teeth. 'Save her. While she's still alive.'

'I understand your anger, Elias. You feel pain, sorro—' His words fall upon my ears like the incessant caws of a crow.

'Your rules – no cheating.' *Calm, Elias. Don't lose it. Not now.* 'But the Farrars cheated. They knew we were coming through the Gap. They ambushed us.'

'The Augurs' minds are linked. If one of us aided Marcus and Zak, the rest would know. Your whereabouts were concealed from all others.'

'Even my mother?'

Cain pauses for a telling moment. 'Even her.'

'You've read her mind?' Grandfather speaks up from beside me. 'You're absolutely certain she didn't know where Elias was?'

'Reading thoughts isn't like reading a book, General. It requires study—'

'Can you read her or not?'

'Keris Veturia walks dark paths. The darkness cloaks her, hiding her from our sight.'

'That's a no, then,' Grandfather says dryly.

'If you can't read her,' I say, 'how do you know she didn't help Marcus and Zak cheat? Did you read them?'

'We do not feel the need—'

'Reconsider.' My temper surges. 'My best friend is dying because those sons of a whore pulled the wool over your eyes.'

'Cyrena,' Cain says to one of the other Augurs, 'stabilize Aquilla and isolate the Farrars. No one is to see them.' The Augur turns back to me. 'If what you say is true, then the balance is upset, and we must restore it. We will heal her. But if we cannot prove that Marcus and Zacharias cheated, then we must leave Aspirant Aquilla to her fate.'

I nod tersely, but in my head, I'm screaming at Cain. *You idiot. You stupid, repulsive demon. You're letting those cretins win. You're letting them get away with murder.*

Grandfather, unusually silent, walks with me to the infirmary. When we reach the infirmary doors, they open, and the Commandant emerges.

'Giving your lackeys warning, Keris?' Grandfather towers over his daughter, his lip curling.

'I don't know what you mean.'

'You're a traitor to your gens, girl,' Grandfather says, the only man in the Empire brave enough to refer to my mother as a girl. 'Don't think I'll forget it.'

'You picked your favourite, General.' Mother's eyes slide to me, and I spot a flash of unhinged rage. 'And I've picked mine.'

She leaves us at the infirmary door. Grandfather watches her go, and I wish I knew what he was thinking. What does he see when he looks at her? The little girl she was? The soulless creature she is now? Does he know why she became like this? Did he watch it happen?

'Don't underestimate her, Elias,' he says. 'She's not used to losing.'

CHAPTER NINETEEN

Laia

When I open my eyes, the low roof of my quarters looms over me. I don't remember losing consciousness. Perhaps I've been out for minutes, perhaps hours. Through the curtain strung across my doorway, I catch a glimpse of a sky that looks as if it's still undecided as to whether it's night or morning. I push myself to my elbows, stifling a moan. The pain is all consuming, so pervasive it feels as if I've never been without it.

I don't look at the wound. I don't need to. I watched the Commandant as she carved it into me, a thick-lined, precise K stretching from my collarbone to the skin over my heart. She's branded me. Marked me as her property. It's a scar I'll carry to the grave.

Clean it. Bandage it. Get back to work. Don't give her an excuse to hurt you again.

The curtain shifts. Izzi slips in and sits at the end of my pallet, small enough that she doesn't need to stoop to avoid hitting her head.

'It's nearly dawn.' Her hand drifts to her eyepatch, but, catching herself, she knots her fingers into her shirt. 'The legionnaires brought you down last night.'

'It's so ugly.' I hate myself for saying it. *Weak, Laia. You're so weak.* Mother had a six-inch scar on her hip from a legionnaire who nearly got the best of her. Father had lash marks on his back – he never said how he got them. They both wore their scars proudly – proof of their ability to survive. *Be strong like them, Laia. Be brave.*

But I'm not strong. I'm weak, and I'm sick of pretending I'm not.

'Could be worse.' Izzi raises a hand to her missing eye. 'This was my first punishment.'

'How – when—' Skies, there's no delicate way to ask about this. I fall silent.

'A month after we arrived here, Cook tried to poison the Commandant.' Izzi toys with her eyepatch. 'I was five, I think. It was more than ten years ago now. The Commandant smelled the poison – Masks are trained in such things. She didn't lay a finger on Cook – just came at me with a hot poker and made Cook watch. Right before, I remember wishing for someone. My mother? My father? Someone to stop her. Someone to take me away. After, I remember wanting to die.'

Five years old. For the first time, it sinks in that Izzi has been a slave nearly her whole life. What I've gone through for eleven days she has suffered for years.

'Cook kept me alive, after. She's good at remedies. She wanted to bandage you up last night, but . . . well, you wouldn't let either of us near you.'

I remember, then, the legionnaires throwing my numb body into the kitchen. Gentle hands, soft voices. I fought them with whatever I had left, thinking they meant me harm.

Our silence is broken by the echo of the dawn drums. A moment later, Cook's raspy voice echoes down the corridor, asking Izzi if I'm up yet.

'The Commandant wants you to bring her sand from the dunes for a scrub,' Izzi says. 'Then she wants you to take a file to Spiro Teluman. But you should let Cook tend to you first.'

'No.' My vehemence startles Izzi to her feet. I lower my voice. So many years around the Commandant would make me jumpy too. 'The Commandant will want the scrub for her morning bath. I don't want to be punished for being late.'

Izzi nods, then offers me a basket for the sand and hurries away. When I stand, my vision swoops. I wrap a scarf around my neck to cover the K and lurch from my room.

Every step is pain, every ounce of weight pulls at the wound, making me lightheaded and nauseous. Unwillingly, my mind flashes back to the single-minded concentration on the Commandant's face as she cut into me. She is a connoisseur of pain the way others are connoisseurs of wine. She took her time with me – and that made it so much worse.

I move to the back of the house with excruciating slowness. By the time I reach the cliff path that leads down to the dunes, my whole body shakes. Hopelessness steals over me. How can I help Darin if I can't even walk? How can I spy if my every attempt is punished like this?

You can't save him because you won't survive the Commandant much longer. My doubts rise insidiously from the soil of my mind like creeping, choking vines. *That will be the end of you and your family. Crushed from existence like so many others.*

The trail twists and turns back on itself, treacherous as the shifting dunes. A hot wind blows into my face, forcing tears from my eyes before I can stop them, until I can hardly see where I am going. At the base of the cliffs, I fall to the sand. My sobs echo in this empty place, but I don't care. There is no one to hear me.

My life in the Scholars' Quarter was never easy – sometimes it was horrible, like when my friend Zara was taken, or when Darin and I rose and slept with the ache of hunger in our bellies. Like all Scholars, I learned to lower my eyes before the Martials, but at least I never had to bow and scrape before them. At least my life was free of this torment, this waiting, always, for more pain. I had Nan and Pop, who protected me from far more than I ever realized. I had Darin, who loomed so large in my life that I thought him immortal as the stars.

Gone now. All of them. Lis with her laughing eyes, so vivid in my mind that it seems impossible that she's been dead twelve years. My parents, who wanted so badly to free the Scholars but who only managed to get themselves killed. Gone, like everyone else. Leaving me here, alone.

Shadows emerge from the sand, circling me. Ghuls. *They feed off sorrow and sadness and the stink of blood.*

One of them screams, startling me into dropping the basket. The sound is eerily familiar.

'*Mercy!*' They mock in a multilayered, high-pitched voice. '*Please, have mercy!*'

I clap my hands over my ears, recognizing my own voice in theirs, my pleas to the Commandant. How did they know? How did they hear?

The shadows titter and circle. One, braver than the rest, nips at my leg, teeth flashing. A chill pierces my skin, and I cry out.

'Stop!'

The ghuls cackle and parrot my plea. '*Stop! Stop!*'

If only I had a scim, a knife – something to scare them off, the way Spiro Teluman did. But I have nothing, so I try instead to stagger away, only to run straight into a wall.

At least that's what it feels like. It takes me a moment to realize that it's not a wall, but a person. A tall person, broad-shouldered and muscled like a mountain cat.

I flinch back, losing my balance, and two big hands steady me. I look up and freeze when I find myself staring into familiar, pale grey eyes.

CHAPTER TWENTY

Elias

The morning after the Trial, I wake before dawn, groggy from the sleeping draught I realize I've been dosed with. My face is shaven, I'm clean, and someone's changed me into fresh fatigues.

'Elias.' Cain emerges from the shadows of my room. His face is drawn, as if he's been up all night. He holds up his hand at my instant barrage of questions.

'Aspirant Aquilla is in the very capable hands of Blackcliff's physician,' he says. 'If she's meant to live, she will. The Augurs will not interfere, for we found nothing to indicate that the Farrars cheated. We have declared Marcus the winner of the First Trial. He has been given a prize of a dagger and—'

'*What?*'

'He returned first—'

'Because he *cheated*—'

The door opens, and Zak limps in. I reach for the blade Grandfather left at my bedside. Before I can fling it at the Toad, Cain is between us. I get up and quickly stuff my feet into my boots – I won't be caught lounging on a bed while this filth is within ten feet of me.

Cain steeples his bloodless fingers and examines Zak. 'You have something to say.'

'You should heal her.' Veins stand out in Zak's neck, and he shakes his head like a wet dog ridding itself of water. 'Stop it!' he says to the Augur. 'Stop trying to get in my head. Just heal her, all right?'

'Feeling guilty, you ass?' I try to shove past Cain, but the Augur blocks me with surprising swiftness.

'I'm not saying we cheated.' Zak looks quickly at Cain. 'I'm saying you should heal her. Here.'

Cain's whole body goes still as he fixates on Zak. The air shifts and grows heavy. The Augur is reading him. I can feel it.

'You and Marcus found each other.' Cain furrows his brow. 'You were . . . led to each other . . . but not by one of the Augurs. Nor by the Commandant.' The Augur closes his eyes, as if listening harder, before opening them.

'Well?' I ask. 'What did you see?'

'Enough to convince me that the Augurs must heal Aspirant Aquilla. But not enough to convince me that the Farrars committed sabotage.'

'Why can't you just look into Zak's mind like you do everyone else's and—'

'Our power is not without its limits. We cannot penetrate the minds of those who have learned to shield themselves.'

I give Zak an appraising look. How in the ten hells did he figure out how to keep the Augurs out of his head?

'You both have an hour to leave school grounds,' Cain says. 'I'll inform the Commandant that I've dismissed you from your duties for the day. Go for a walk, go to the market, go to a whorehouse.

I don't care. Don't return to the school until evening, and don't come back to the infirmary. Do you understand?'

Zak frowns. 'Why do we have to leave?'

'Because your thoughts, Zacharias, are a pit of agony. And yours, Veturius, echo with such deafening vengeance that I can hear nothing else. Neither will allow me to do what I must to heal Aspirant Aquilla. So you will leave. Now.'

Cain moves aside, and, reluctantly, Zak and I walk out the door. Zak tries to hurry away from me, but I've got questions that need answering and I'm not about to let him worm his way out of them. I catch up to him.

'How did you figure out where we were? How did the Commandant know?'

'She has ways.'

'What ways? What did you show Cain? How did you manage to keep him out of your head at will? Zak!' I pull his shoulder around so he faces me. He throws my hand off but doesn't walk away.

'All that Tribal rubbish about jinn and efrits, ghuls and wraiths – it's not rubbish, Veturius. It's not myth. The old creatures are real. They're coming for us. Protect her. It's the only thing you're good for.'

'What do you care about her? Your brother's tormented her for years, and you've never said a word to stop him.'

Zak regards the sand training fields, empty at this early hour.

'You know the worst thing about all this?' he says quietly. 'I was so close to leaving him behind forever. So close to being free of him.'

It's not what I expect to hear. Ever since we came to Blackcliff, there has been no Marcus without Zak. The younger Farrar is closer to his brother than Marcus's own shadow.

'If you want to be free of him, then why go along with his every whim? Why not stand up to him?'

'We've been together for so long.' Zak shakes his head. His face is unreadable where the mask hasn't yet melded. 'I don't know who I am without him.'

When he walks to the front gates, I don't follow. I need to clear my head. I make for the eastern watchtower, where I strap myself into a harness and rappel down to the dunes.

Sand swirls around me. My thoughts are confused. I trudge along the base of the cliffs, watching the horizon pale as the sun rises. The wind grows stronger, hot and insistent. As I walk, it seems like shapes appear in the sands, figures spinning and dancing, feeding off the wind's ferocity. Whispers ride the air, and I think I hear the piercing staccato of wild laughter.

The old creatures are real. They're coming for us. Is Zak trying to tell me something about the next Trial? Is he saying that my mother is consorting with demons? Is that how she sabotaged me and Hel? I tell myself that these thoughts are ridiculous. Believing in the Augurs' power is one thing. But jinn of fire and vengeance? Efrits bound to elements like wind, sea, or sand? Maybe Zak's just cracked from the strain of the First Trial.

Mamie Rila used to tell stories of the fey. She was our Tribe's *Kehanni*, our tale-spinner, and she wove whole worlds with her voice, with the flick of a hand or the tilt of her head. Some of those legends stuck in my head for years – the Nightbringer and his hatred for Scholars. The efrits' skill at awakening latent magic in humans. Soul-hungry ghuls who feed on pain like vultures on carrion.

But those are just stories.

The wind carries the haunting sound of sobbing to my ears. At first, I think I'm imagining it and chide myself for letting Zak's talk of the fey get to me. But then it gets louder. Ahead of me, at the foot of the twisting path that leads up to the Commandant's house, sits a small crumpled figure.

It's the slave-girl with the gold eyes. The one Marcus nearly choked to death. The one I saw lifeless on the nightmare battlefield.

She holds her head with one hand and bats at the empty air with the other, muttering through her sobs. She staggers, falls to the ground, then rises laboriously. It's clear she's not well, that she needs help. I slow, thinking to turn away. My mind roves back to the battlefield and my first kill's assertion: that everyone on that field will die by my hand.

Stay away from her, Elias, a cautious voice urges. *Have nothing to do with her.*

But why stay away? The battlefield was the Augurs' vision of my future. Maybe I should show the bastards that I'm going to fight that future. That I won't just accept it.

I stood by like a fool once before with this girl. I watched and did nothing as Marcus left bruises all over her. She needed help, and I refused to give it. I won't make the same mistake again. Without any more hesitation, I walk towards her.

CHAPTER TWENTY-ONE

Laia

It's the Commandant's son. Veturius.

Where did he come from? I push at him violently, then immediately regret doing so. A normal Blackcliff student would beat
me for touching him without permission – and this is no student,
but an Aspirant and the Commandant's spawn. I have to get out
of here. I have to get back to the house. But the weakness that
has plagued me all morning takes firm hold, and I fall to the sand
a few feet away, sweating and nauseous.

Infection. I know the signs. I should have let Cook dress the
wound last night.

'Who were you talking to?' Veturius asks.

'N-no-no one, Aspirant, sir.' *Not everyone can see them,* Teluman
had said of the ghuls. It's clear Veturius can't.

'You look terrible,' he says. 'Come into the shade.'

'The sand. I have to take it up or she'll – she'll—'

'Sit.' It's not a request. He picks up my basket and takes my
hand, leading me to the shade of the cliffs and setting me down
on a small boulder.

When I chance a look at him, he is gazing out at the horizon, his mask catching the dawn light like water catching the sun. Even at a distance of a few feet, everything about him screams violence, from the short black hair to the big hands to the fact that each muscle is honed to deadly perfection. The bandages that encircle his forearms and the scratches that mar his hands and face only make him look more vicious.

He has just one weapon, a dagger at his belt. But then, he's a Mask. He doesn't need weapons because he is one, particularly when faced with a slave who barely comes up to his shoulder. I try to scoot away further, but my body is too heavy.

'What's your name? You never said.' He fills my basket with sand, not looking at me.

I think of when the Commandant asked me this question and the blow I received for answering honestly. 'S-Slave-Girl.'

He is quiet for a moment. 'Tell me your real name.'

Though calmly spoken, the words are a command. 'Laia.'

'Laia,' he says. 'What did she do to you?'

How strange, that a Mask can sound so kind, that the deep thrum of his baritone can offer comfort. I could close my eyes and not know I was speaking to a Mask at all.

But I can't trust his voice. He's *her* son. If he is showing concern, there is a reason for it – and not one that favours me.

Slowly, I push back my scarf. When he sees the K, his eyes go hard behind the mask, and for a moment, sadness and fury burn in his gaze. I'm startled when he speaks again.

'May I?' He lifts a hand, and I barely feel it when his fingers brush the skin near my wound.

'Your skin's hot.' He lifts the basket of sand. 'The wound is bad. It needs attention.'

'I know that,' I say. 'Commandant wanted sand, and I didn't

have time to – to—' Veturius's face swims for a moment, and I feel strangely weightless. He's close then, close enough for me to feel the heat of his body. The scent of cloves and rain drifts over me. I close my eyes to stop everything from lurching, but it doesn't help. His arms are around me, hard and gentle all at once, and he lifts me up.

'Let me go!' My strength peaks, and I shove at his chest. What is he doing? Where is he taking me?

'How else do you plan to get back up the cliffs?' he asks. His broad strides carry us easily up the winding switchbacks. 'You can barely stand.'

Does he actually think I'm stupid enough to accept his 'help'? This is a trick he's plotted with his mother. Some further punishment awaits. I have to escape him.

But as he walks, another wave of dizziness hits me, and I clutch his neck until it passes. If I hold on tight enough, he won't be able to throw me to the dunes. Not without getting dragged down himself.

My eyes fall on his bandaged arms, and I remember that the First Trial ended yesterday.

Veturius catches me looking. 'Just scratches,' he says. 'Augurs left me in the middle of the Great Wastes for the First Trial. After a few days without water, I started falling down a lot.'

'They left you in the Wastes?' I shudder. Everyone's heard of that place. It makes the Tribal lands look almost habitable. 'And you survived? Did they at least warn you?'

'They like surprises.'

Even through my sickness, the impact of what he's said isn't lost on me. If the Aspirants don't know what will happen in the Trials, how can I possibly find out?

'Doesn't the Commandant know what you'll be up against?'

Why am I asking him so many questions? It's not my place. My head must be addled from the wound. But if my curiosity bothers Veturius, he doesn't say so.

'She might. Doesn't matter. Even if she knows, she wouldn't tell me.'

His mother doesn't want him to win? Part of me wonders at their bizarre relationship. But then I remind myself that they're Martials. Martials are different.

Veturius crests the cliff and ducks beneath the clothes fluttering on the line, heading down the slaves' corridor. When he carries me into the kitchen and sets me down on a bench beside the worktable, Izzi, scrubbing the floor, drops her brush and stares open-mouthed. Cook's glance falls to my wound, and she shakes her head.

'Kitchen-Girl,' Cook says. 'Take the sand upstairs. If the Commandant asks about Slave-Girl, tell her she's taken ill and that I'm tending to her so she can get back to work.'

Izzi picks up the basket of sand without a sound and disappears. A wave of nausea breaks over me, and I'm forced to drop my head between my legs for a few moments.

'Laia's wound's infected,' Veturius says when Izzi leaves. 'Do you have bloodroot serum?'

If Cook is surprised that the Commandant's son is using my given name, she doesn't show it. 'Bloodroot's too valuable for the likes of us. I've tanroot and wildwood tea.'

Veturius frowns and gives Cook the same instructions Pop would have. Wildwood tea three times a day, tanroot to clean the wound, and no bandage. He turns to me. 'I'll find some bloodroot and bring it to you tomorrow. I promise. You'll be all right. Cook knows her remedies.'

I nod, unsure if I should thank him, still waiting for him to reveal his true purpose for helping me. But he doesn't say anything else, apparently satisfied with my response. He stuffs his hands in his pockets and walks out the back door.

Cook rustles around the cabinets, and a few minutes later, a mug of steaming tea is in my hands. After I drink it down, she sits in front of me, her scars inches from my face. I gaze at them, but they no longer seem grotesque. Is it because I've got used to seeing them? Or because I have a disfigurement of my own?

'Who's Darin?' Cook asks. Her sapphire eyes glint, and for a moment, they are hauntingly familiar. 'You called for him in the night.'

The tea takes the edge off my dizziness, and I sit up. 'He's my brother.'

'I see.' Cook drips tanroot oil on a square of gauze and dabs it onto the wound. I wince in pain and grip the seat. 'And is he in the Resistance too?'

'How could you—' *How could you know that?* I almost say, but then I recover my wits and press my lips together.

Cook catches the slip and pounces. 'It's not hard to tell. I've seen a hundred slaves come and go. Resistance fighters are always different. Never broken. At least not when they first arrive. They have . . . hope.' She curls her lip, as if she's speaking of a colony of diseased criminals instead of her own people.

'I'm not with the rebels.' I wish I hadn't spoken. Darin says my voice goes high when I lie, and Cook seems like the type to notice. Sure enough, her eyes narrow.

'I'm not a fool, girl. Do you have any idea what you're doing? The Commandant will find you out. She'll torture you, kill you. Then she'll punish anyone she thinks you were friends with. That means Iz – Kitchen-Girl.'

'I'm not doing anything wro—'

'There was a woman once,' she interrupts me abruptly. 'Joined the Resistance. Learned to mix powders and potions so that the very air would turn to fire and stones to sand. But she got in over her head. Did things for the rebels – horrible things – that she never dreamt she'd do. Commandant caught her like she'd caught so many others. Carved her up good and ruined her face. Made her swallow hot coals and ruined her voice. Then she made the woman a slave in her house. But not before killing everyone the woman knew. Everyone she loved.'

Oh no. The source of Cook's scars becomes sickeningly clear. She nods, grimly acknowledging the dawning horror on my face.

'I lost everything – my family, my freedom – all for a cause that never had any hope to begin with.'

'But—'

'Before you came here, the Resistance sent a boy. Zain. He was supposed to be a gardener. Did they tell you about him?'

I almost shake my head but stop, crossing my arms instead. She doesn't acknowledge my silence. She's not guessing about me. She knows.

'It was two years ago. Commandant caught him. Tortured him in the school's dungeon for days. Some nights we could hear him. Screaming. When she was done with Zain, she gathered every last slave in Blackcliff. She wanted to know who'd been friends with him. Wanted to teach us a lesson for not turning in a traitor.' Cook's eyes are fixed on me, unrelenting. 'Killed three slaves before she was satisfied that the message had sunk in. Lucky I'd warned Izzi away from the boy. Lucky she listened.'

Cook gathers her supplies and shoves them back into a cabinet. She picks up a cleaver and hacks at a bloody slab of meat waiting on the worktable.

'I don't know why you ran away from your family to join those rebel bastards.' She flings the words at me like stones. 'I don't care. Tell them you quit. Ask for another mission, somewhere where you won't hurt anyone. Because if you don't, you'll die, and skies only knows what will happen to the rest of us.' She points the cleaver at me, and I shift back in my chair, watching the knife. 'Is that what you want?' she says. 'Death? Izzi tortured?' She leans forward, spittle flying from her mouth. The knife is inches from my face. 'Is it?'

'I didn't run away,' I burst out. Pop's body, Nan's glazed irises, Darin's flailing limbs all flash before my eyes. 'I didn't even want to join. My grandparents – a Mask came—'

I bite my tongue. *Shut it, Laia.* I scowl at the old woman, unsurprised to see her glaring back.

'Tell me the truth about why you joined the rebels,' she says, 'and I'll keep my mouth shut about your dirty little secret. Ignore me, and I'll tell that ice-hearted vulture upstairs exactly what you are.' She drives the cleaver into the worktable and drops into the seat next to me, waiting.

Damn her. If I tell her about the raid and what came after, she might still rat me out. But if I say nothing, I've no doubt that she'll march to the Commandant's room this instant. She's just insane enough to do it.

I have no choice.

As I speak of what happened that night, she remains silent and unmoved. When I finish, my eyes are swollen, but Cook's mangled face reveals nothing.

I wipe my face on my sleeve. 'Darin's stuck in prison. It's only a matter of time before they torture him to death or sell him as a slave. I have to get him out before then. But I can't do it alone. The rebels said if I spied for them, they'd help me.' I stand shakily. 'You could threaten to turn my soul over to the

Nightbringer himself. Doesn't matter. Darin's my only family. I have to save him.'

Cook says nothing, and after a minute passes, I assume she's chosen to ignore me. Then, as I move to the door, she speaks.

'Your mother. Mirra.' At the sound of Mother's name, I jerk my head around. Cook is examining me. 'You don't look like her.'

I'm so surprised I don't bother to deny it. Cook has to be in her seventies. She'd have been in her sixties when my parents controlled the Resistance. What was her real name? What had her role been? 'You knew my mother?'

'Knew her? Yes, I knew her. Always liked y-y-your father better.' She clears her throat and shakes her head in irritation. Strange. I've never heard her stutter. 'Kind man. Sm-smart man. Not – not like your m-m-mother.'

'My mother was the Lioness—'

'Your mother – isn't – worth your words.' Cook's voice drops into a snarl. 'Never – never listened to anything but her own selfishness. The *Lioness*.' Her mouth twists around the name. 'She's the reason – the reason – I'm here.' Her breath heaves now, as if she's having some sort of fit, but she barrels on, determined to get out whatever it is she wishes to say. 'The Lioness, the Resistance, and their grand plans. Traitors. Liars. F-fools.' She stands and reaches for her cleaver. 'Don't trust them.'

'I don't have a choice,' I say. 'I have to.'

'They'll use you.' Her hands shake, and she grips the counter. She gasps out the last few words. 'They take – take – take. And then – then – they'll throw you to the wolves. I warned you. Remember. I warned you.'

CHAPTER TWENTY-TWO

Elias

At exactly midnight, I return to Blackcliff in full battle armour, dripping with weaponry. After the Trial of Courage, I'm not about to be caught shoeless with only a dagger for defence.

Though I'm desperate to know if Hel is all right, I resist the urge to go to the infirmary. Cain's orders to stay away didn't leave room for argument.

As I stalk past the gate guards, I fervently hope not to run into my mother. I think I'd snap at the sight of her, especially knowing that her scheming nearly killed Helene. And especially after seeing what she'd done to the slave-girl this morning.

When I'd seen the K carved into the girl – *Laia* – I'd flexed my fists, imagining, for one glorious moment, the feel of inflicting such pain on the Commandant. *See how she likes it, the hag.* At the same time, I wanted to back away from Laia in shame. Because the woman who'd done such evil shares my blood. She is half of me. My own reaction – that ravenous lust for violence – is proof. *I'm not like her.*

Or am I? I think back to the nightmare battlefield. Five hundred and thirty-nine bodies. Even the Commandant would be hard-pressed to take so many lives. If the Augurs are right, I'm not like my mother. I'm worse.

You will become everything you hate, Cain had said when I'd considered deserting. But how could leaving my mask behind make me any worse of a person than the one I saw on that battle-field?

Lost in my thoughts, I don't notice anything unusual about Skulls' quarters when I arrive at my room. But after a moment, it sinks in. Leander's not snoring, and Demetrius isn't mumbling his brother's name. Faris's door isn't open, as it almost always is.

The barracks are abandoned.

I draw my scims. The only sound is the occasional pop of the oil lamps flickering against the black brick.

Then, one by one, the lamps go out. Grey smoke seeps beneath the door at one end of the hall, expanding like a roiling bank of storm cloud. In an instant, I realize what's happening.

The Second Trial, the Trial of Cunning, has begun.

'Watch out!' a voice shouts from behind me. Helene – *alive* – shoves through the doors at my back, fully armed and without a hair out of place. I want to tackle her in a hug, but instead I drop to the floor as a volley of razor-edged throwing stars hurtles through the space where my neck was.

The stars are followed by a trio of attackers who spring from the smoke like coiled snakes. They are lithe and quick, their bodies and faces wrapped in funereal strips of black cloth. Almost before I'm on my feet, one of the assassins has a scim at my throat. I spin back and kick his feet out from under him, but my leg meets only air.

Strange, he was there – just now—

At my side, Helene's scim flashes swift as quicksilver as an assassin presses her towards the smoke. 'Evening, Elias,' she calls over the clash of scims. She catches my eye, an irrepressible grin spreading across her face. 'Miss me?'

I don't have the breath to answer. The other two assassins come at me fast, and though I fight with both scims, I can't get the upper hand. My left scim finally hits its mark, sinking into the chest of my opponent. Bloodthirsty triumph surges through me.

Then the attacker flickers and disappears.

I freeze, doubting what I've seen. The other assassin takes advantage of my hesitation and shoves me back into the smoke.

It's as if I've been dropped into the darkest, blackest cave in the Empire. I try to feel my way forward, but my limbs are leaden, and in moments I slip to the floor, my body a deadweight. A throwing star cuts through the air, and I barely register the fact that it has grazed my arm. My scims hit the stone of the hallway, and Helene screams. The sounds are muted, as if I'm hearing them through water.

Poison. The word brings me out of my senselessness. *The smoke is poisonous.*

With my last shreds of consciousness, I scour the ground for my scims and crawl out of the darkness. A few breaths of clean air help me reclaim my wits, and I notice that Helene has disappeared. As I search the smoke for any sign of her, an assassin emerges.

I duck beneath his scim, intending to wrap my arms around his chest and slam him to the floor. But when my skin meets his, cold lances through me, and I gasp and jerk away. It feels as if I've dipped my arm into a bucket of snow. The assassin flickers and disappears, reappearing a few yards away.

They're not human, I realize. Zak's warning echoes in my head. *The old creatures are real. They're coming for us.* Ten burning hells.

And I thought he had cracked. How is it possible? How could the Augurs have—

The assassin circles me, and I shelve my questions. How this thing got here doesn't matter. How to kill it – that's a question worth answering.

A flash of silver catches my eye – Helene's gauntleted hand, clawing the floor as she tries to pull herself out of the smoke. I drag her out, but she's too bleary to stand, so I throw her over my shoulder and flee down the hall. When I'm well away, I dump her to the ground and turn to face the enemy.

The three of them are on me at once, moving too fast for me to counter. Within half a minute, I have nicks all over my face and a gash in my left arm.

'Aquilla!' I holler. She staggers to her feet. 'A little help, yeah?'

She draws her scim and plunges into the fight, forcing two of the attackers to engage.

'They're wraiths, Elias,' she shouts. 'Bleeding, burning wraiths.'

Ten hells. Masks train with scims and staffs and our bare hands, on horses and boats, blindfolded and chained, with no sleep, with no food. But we've never trained against something that isn't supposed to exist.

What did that damn foretelling say? *Cunning to outwit their foes*. There's a way to kill these things. They must have a weakness. I just have to figure out what it is.

Lemokles offence. Grandfather created the offence himself. A *series of full-body attacks allowing one to identify a combatant's deficiencies*.

I attack head, then legs, arms, and torso. A dagger I fling at the wraith's chest goes right through him, falling to the floor with a clatter. But he doesn't try to block the dagger. Instead, his hand flashes up to protect his throat.

Behind me, Helene shouts for aid as the other two wraiths press the attack. One lifts a dagger high above her heart, but before it comes down, I whip my scim around and through his neck.

The wraith's head plunges to the ground, and I grimace as an unearthly scream echoes in the hall. Seconds later, the head – and the body it goes with – disappears.

'Watch your left,' Hel shouts. I sweep my scim in an arc to my left without looking. A hand closes on my wrist, and piercing cold numbs my arm to the shoulder. But then my scim strikes home, the hand is gone, and another eldritch scream pierces the air.

The assault slows as the last wraith circles us.

'You really should run,' Helene says to the creature. 'You're just going to die.'

The wraith looks between us and sets upon Helene. *They always underestimate me.* Even wraiths, apparently. She ducks beneath his arm, light-footed as a dancer, and takes off his head with one clean stroke. The wraith vanishes, the smoke dissipates, and the barracks go still, as if the last fifteen minutes never happened.

'Well, that was—' Helene's eyes go wide, and I lunge to one side without needing to be told, turning just in time to see a knife hurtling through the air. It misses me – barely – and Helene is past me in a blur of blonde and silver.

'Marcus,' she says. 'I'm on him.'

'Wait, you idiot! It might be a trap!'

But the door is already swinging shut behind her, and I hear the crash of scim striking scim, followed by the crunch of bone beneath fist.

I burst from the barracks to see Helene advancing on Marcus, who has a hand to his bloodied nose. Helene's eyes are ferocious slits, and for the first time, I see her as others must – deadly, remorseless. A Mask.

Though I want to help her, I hold back, scanning the darkened grounds around us. If Marcus is here, Zak won't be far.

'All healed up, Aquilla?' Marcus feints left with his scim, and when Helene counters, he grins. 'You and I have some unfinished business.' His eyes inch over her form. 'You know what I've always wondered? If raping you will be like fighting you. All those lean muscles, that pent-up energy—'

Helene delivers a roundhouse that leaves Marcus on his back with blood pouring from his mouth. She stamps on his sword arm and presses her scimpoint to his throat.

'You filthy son of a whore,' she spits at him. 'Just because you got one lucky swipe in the forest doesn't mean I can't still gut you with my eyes closed.'

But Marcus gives her a vicious smile, unfazed by the steel digging into his throat. 'You're mine, Aquilla. You belong to me, and we both know it. The Augurs told me. Save yourself the trouble and join me now.'

The blood drains from Helene's face. There's black, hopeless rage in her eyes, the type of anger you feel when your hands are tied and there's a knife at your jugular.

Only Helene is the one holding the blade. What in the skies is wrong with her?

'Never.' The tone of her voice doesn't match the strength of the scim in her fist, and, as if she knows it, her hand shakes. 'Never, Marcus.'

A flicker in the shadows beyond the barracks catches my eyes. I'm halfway there when I see Zak's light brown hair and the flash of an arrow cutting through the air.

'Drop, Hel!'

She plunges to the ground, the arrow sailing harmlessly over her shoulder. I know instantly that she was never in any danger, at least not from Zak. Not even a one-eyed Yearling with a lame arm would miss a shot that easy.

The brief distraction is all Marcus needs. I expect him to attack Hel, but he rolls away and flees into the night, still grinning, Zak close behind.

'What the hell was that?' I bellow at Helene. 'You could have cut him open and you *choke*? What was that rubbish he was spouting—'

'Now's not the time.' Helene's voice is tight. 'We need to get out of the open. The Augurs are trying to kill us.'

'Tell me something I don't know—'

'No, *that's* the Second Trial, Elias, them actively trying to assassinate us. Cain told me after he healed me. The Trial will last until dawn. We have to be clever enough to avoid our murderers – whoever or whatever they might be.'

'Then we need a base,' I say. 'Out here, anyone can pick us off with an arrow. There's no visibility in the catacombs, and the barracks are too cramped.'

'There.' Hel points to the eastern watchtower, which overlooks the dunes. 'The legionnaires manning it can set a guard at the entrance, and it's a good fighting space.'

We make for the tower, sticking close to the walls and the shadows. At this hour, there isn't a single student or Centurion out. Silence hangs over Blackcliff, and my voice seems inordinately loud. I lower it to a whisper. 'I'm glad you're all right.'

'Worried, were you?'

'Of course I was worried. I thought you were dead. If something had happened to you . . .' It doesn't bear thinking about. I look Helene square in the face, but she only meets my gaze for a second before flicking her eyes away.

'Yes, well, you should have been worried. I heard you dragged me to the belltower covered in blood.'

'I did. Wasn't pleasant. You stank, for one.'

'I owe you, Veturius.' Her eyes soften, and the steely, Blackcliff-trained part of me shakes its head. She can't turn into a girl on me now. 'Cain told me everything you did for me, from the second Marcus attacked. And I want you to know—'

'You'd have done the same.' I cut her off gruffly, satisfied by the stiffening of her body, the ice in her eyes. *Better ice than warmth. Better strength than weakness.*

Unspoken things have arisen between Helene and me, things that have to do with how I feel when I see her bare skin and her awkwardness when I tell her I worry for her. After so many years of straightforward friendship, I don't know what these things mean. But I do know that now's not the time to think about them. Not if we want to survive the Second Trial.

She must get it; she gestures for me to take point, and we don't speak as we head to the watchtower. When we reach its base, I allow myself to relax for a second. The tower sits at the edge of the cliffs and overlooks the dunes to the east and the school to the west. Blackcliff's watch wall extends north and south. Once we're at the top, we'll see any threat long before it reaches us.

But when we're halfway up the tower's inner stairs, Helene slows behind me.

'Elias.' The warning in her voice has me drawing both of my scims – the only thing that saves me. A shout sounds from below us, another from above, and suddenly the stairwell echoes with the ping of arrows and the shuffle of boots. A squad of legionnaires pours down the stairs, and for a second, I'm confused. Then they're on me.

'Legionnaires,' Helene shouts. 'Stand down – stand—'

I want to tell her to save her breath. No doubt the Augurs told the legionnaires that for this night, we are enemies and they are to kill us on sight. Damn it. *Cunning to outwit their foes.* We should have realized that anyone – everyone – could be an enemy.

'Back-to-back, Hel!'

Her back is to mine in an instant. I cross scims with the soldiers coming down from the top of the tower while she battles those heading up from the base. My battle rage surges, but I rein it in, fighting to wound, not kill. I know some of these men. I can't just butcher them.

'Damn it, Elias!' Hel screams. One of the legionnaires I've slashed pushes down past me and marks Hel's sword arm. *'Fight! They're Martials, not turn-tail Barbarian rabble!'*

Hel's fighting off three soldiers below her and two above, with more coming. I have to clear the stairs so we can make it to the top of the tower. It's the only way we'll avoid death-by-skewering.

I let the battle rage take me and surge up the stairs, scims flying. One cuts into the gut of a legionnaire, the other slides across a throat. The stairwell isn't wide enough for two scims, so I sheathe one and pull out my dagger, driving it into the kidney of a third soldier and the heart of a fourth. In seconds, the way above is clear, and Helene and I race up the stairs. We get to the top of the watchtower only to find more soldiers waiting.

Are you going to kill them all, Elias? How many added to your tally? Four already – ten more? Fifteen? Just like your mother. Fast as her. Ruthless as her.

My body freezes as it never has in battle, my foolish heart taking control. Helene shouts, spins, kills, defends, while I stand there. Then it's too late to fight, because a jut-jawed brute with arms like tree trunks tackles me.

'Veturius!' Helene says. 'More soldiers coming from the north!'

'Mrffggg.' The big aux has my face smashed against the side of the watchtower, his hand so tight around my skull that I'm sure

211

he means to crush it. He uses his knee to pin me, and I can't budge an inch.

For a moment, I admire his technique. He recognizes that he can't counter my fighting skills and has instead used surprise and his colossal bulk to best me.

My admiration fizzles as stars burst before my eyes. *Cunning! You have to use cunning!* But the time for cunning is past. I shouldn't have got distracted. I should have run a scim through the aux's chest before he ever got to me.

Helene darts away from her attackers to help me, pulling on my belt as if to yank me away from the giant soldier, but he pushes her away.

The aux slides me along the wall to a niche in the battlements and shoves me through, holding me by my neck above the dunes like a child with a rag doll. Six hundred feet of hungry air grasps at my legs. Behind my captor, a sea of legionnaires tries to pull Helene down, barely keeping a hold on her as she twists and spits, a cat in a net.

Always victorious. Grandfather's voice echoes in my head. *Always victorious.* I dig my fingers into the tendons of the brute's arms, trying to work myself free.

'I bet ten marks on you.' The aux appears genuinely pained. 'But orders are orders.'

Then he opens his hand and lets me fall.

The fall lasts an eternity and no time at all. My heart shoots into my throat, my stomach plunges, and then, with a jerk that rattles my skull, I'm not falling anymore. But I'm not dead, either. My body dangles, tethered by a rope hooked to my belt.

Helene had yanked on my belt – she must have attached the rope then. Which means she is on the other end. Which means if the soldiers throw her over and I'm still dangling like a comatose spider, we'll both fall hard and fast to the hereafter.

I swing towards the cliff face and scrabble for a handhold. The rope is thirty feet long, and this close to the base of the watchtower, the cliffs aren't as sheer. A granite shelf juts out from a fissure a few feet away. I wedge myself in tightly and only just in time.

A shriek echoes from above me followed by a tumble of blonde and silver. I brace my legs and pull in the rope as fast as I can, but I am still nearly yanked off the rock shelf by the force of Helene's weight.

'I've got you, Hel,' I shout, knowing how terrified she must be hanging hundreds of feet in the air like this. 'Hold on.'

When I pull her into the fissure, she is wild-eyed and shaking. There is hardly room for both of us on the shelf, and she grabs my shoulders to anchor herself.

'It's all right, Hel.' I tap the ledge with a boot. 'See? Solid rock beneath us.' She nods into my shoulder, clinging to me in a most un-Helene-like way.

Even through our armour, I feel her curves, and my stomach leaps strangely. She fidgets, which really doesn't help things, seemingly as aware as I of the closeness of our bodies. My face grows hot at the sudden tension between us. *Focus, Elias.*

I pull away from her as an arrow thunks into the rock beside us – we've been spotted.

'We're easy pickings on this ledge,' I say. 'Here.' I unknot the cord from my belt and hers, and stuff it into her hands. 'Tie this to an arrow. Make it tight.'

She does as I ask while I grab a bow from my back and scan the cliffs for a harness. One dangles fifteen feet away. It's a shot I could make with my eyes closed – except that the legionnaires are hauling the harness back up the cliff face and into the tower.

Helene hands me the arrow, and before more missiles come hurtling from above, I lift my bow, notch the arrow, shoot.

And miss.

'Damn it!' The legionnaires pull the harness just out of range. They yank up the other harnesses along the cliff, strap themselves in, and begin rappelling down.

'Elias—' Helene nearly flings herself off the ledge trying to avoid an arrow, grabbing on to my arm. 'We have to get out of here.'

'I figured that out, thanks.' I barely dodge an arrow myself. 'If you've got a genius plan, I'm open to ideas.'

Helene grabs the bow from me, takes aim with the corded arrow, and a second later, one of the legionnaires rappelling down goes limp. She pulls the body over and unbuckles him from the harness. I try to ignore the distant thump of the soldier's body hitting the dunes. Hel frees the cord while I grab the harness and strap myself in – I'll have to carry her down.

'Elias,' she whispers when she realizes what we have to do. 'I – I can't—'

'You can. I won't let you fall. I promise.'

I test the harness anchor with a sharp yank, hoping it will hold the weight of two fully armed Masks.

'Climb onto my back.' I take her chin and force her to meet my eyes. 'Rope us together like before. Wrap your legs around my waist. Don't let go until we hit the sand.'

She does as I ask and ducks her head into my neck as I leap off the edge, her breath coming short and fast.

'Don't fall, don't fall,' I hear her muttering. 'Don't fall, don't—'

Arrows streak towards us from the tower, and the legionnaires have dropped level now. They draw scims and glide across the cliff face. My hand itches towards a weapon, but I resist – I have to keep hold of the ropes so we don't plummet to the desert floor.

'Keep them off me, Hel.'

Her legs tighten around my hips and her bow twangs as she launches arrow after arrow into our pursuers.

Thwunk. Thwunk. Thwunk.

One howl of agony is joined by another and another as Helene draws and shoots, fast as lightning striking. The arrows from the tower thin as we drop, clattering off our armour uselessly. Every muscle in my arms strains to keep us dropping steadily. *Almost there . . . almost . . .*

Then a searing pain shoots through my left thigh. We slide fifty feet as I lose control of the descender. Helene grabs me as her head snaps back, and she screams, a girlish shriek I know I should never, ever mention.

'Damn it, Veturius!'

'Sorry,' I grind out when I get hold of the ropes. 'I'm hit. They still coming?'

'No.' Helene cranes her neck back and stares up the sheer cliff face. 'They're going back up.'

The hairs on the back of my neck rise in warning. There's no reason for the soldiers to stop the attack. Not unless they think someone else will take over for them. I peer down at the dunes, still two hundred feet below us. I can't tell if there's anyone down there.

A gust of wind blows out of the desert, knocking us hard against the cliff face, and I almost lose control of the ropes again. Helene yelps, her arm tense around me. My leg burns with pain, but I ignore it – it's just a flesh wound.

For a second, I think I hear a peal of deep, mocking laughter.

'Elias.' Helene looks out at the desert, and I know what she's going to say before she says it. 'There's something—'

The wind steals the words from her mouth, sweeping out of the dunes with unnatural fury. I release the descender, and we drop. But not fast enough.

A violent gust rips my hands from the ropes, halting our descent. Sand from the dunes rises in a funnel around us. Before my disbelieving eyes, the particles weave together, coalescing into large, manlike shapes with grasping hands and holes for eyes.

'What are they?' Helene slashes the air uselessly with her scim, her strokes increasingly uncontrolled.

Not human and not friendly. The Augurs have already unleashed one supernatural terror on us. It isn't much of a stretch to assume that they'd trot out another.

I reach for the ropes, now hopelessly tangled. The pain in my thigh explodes, and I look down to see the arrow being slowly pulled through my flesh by a sandy hand. The laughter echoes again as I hurriedly break off the arrowhead – I'll be crippled for life if it's dragged through my leg.

Sand buffets my face, biting at my skin before solidifying into another creature. This one looms over us, a miniature mountain, and although his features are poorly defined, I can still make out his wolf's smile.

I smother my disbelief and try to think back to Mamie Rila's stories. We've already dealt with wraiths, and this thing is big – not like a wight or a ghul. Efrits are supposed to be shy, but jinn are vicious and cunning . . .

'It's a jinn!' I shout over the wind. The sand creature laughs as delightedly as if I'm juggling and pulling faces.

'Jinn are dead, little Aspirant.' His screams are like a wind out of the north. Then he swoops in close, eyes narrowing. His other brethren form up behind him, dancing and somersaulting with the zeal of acrobats at a carnival. *'Destroyed by your kind long ago,*

in a great war. I am Rowan Goldgale, king of the sand efrits. I will claim your souls as mine.'

'Why would a king of efrits concern himself with mere humans?' Helene plays for time as I frantically untangle the ropes and straighten the descender.

'Mere humans!' The efrits behind the king hoot with laughter. *'You are Aspirants. Your footsteps echo in the sand and the stars. To own souls such as yours is a great honour. You will serve me well.'*

'What's he talking about?' Helene asks me in an undertone.

'No idea,' I say. 'Keep him distracted.'

'Why enslave us?' Helene asks. 'When we would – ah – serve you willingly?'

'Stupid girl! In these sacks of flesh, your souls are useless. I must awaken and tame them. Only then can you serve me. Only then—'

His voice is lost in a whoosh of wind as we drop away. The efrits shriek and streak after us, surrounding and blinding us, tearing my hands from the ropes once more.

'Take them,' Rowan bays at his cohort. Helene's grip on me loosens as an efrit works his way between us. Another prises the scim from her hand and the bow from her back, shrieking in elation as the weapons drop to the dunes.

Yet another efrit saws at our rope with a sharp rock. I draw my scim and shove it through the creature, twisting, hoping steel will kill the thing. The efrit howls – in pain or anger, I can't tell. I try to take off its head, but it flits up out of reach, cackling nastily.

Think, Elias! The shadow-assassins had a weakness. The efrits must too. Mamie Rila told tales about them, I know she did. But I can't bleeding remember any of them.

'Ahhhh!' Helene's arms jerk free of me, and she holds on with only her legs. The efrits ululate, doubling their efforts to pull her away. Rowan puts his hands on either side of her face and squeezes, imbuing her with an otherworldly gold light.

'*Mine!*' the efrit says. '*Mine. Mine. Mine.*'

The rope frays. Blood pours from the wound on my thigh. The efrits rip Helene away, and as they do, I spot a niche in the cliff that runs all the way down to the desert floor. Mamie Rila's face appears in my head, illuminated by the campfire as she chants:

Efrit, efrit of the wind, kill him with a star-steel pin.

Efrit, efrit of the sea, light a fire to make him flee.

Efrit, efrit of the sand, a song is more than he can stand.

I hurl my scim up at the efrit sawing at the ropes and swing forward, plucking Helene from the grip of the efrits and shoving her into the niche, all the while ignoring her yell of surprise and the angry, tearing hands at my back.

'Sing, Hel! Sing!'

She opens her mouth, to shout or sing, I don't know, because the rope finally gives way and I plummet. Helene's pale face fades away above me. Then the world goes quiet and white, and I know no more.

CHAPTER TWENTY-THREE

Laia

Izzi finds me after I leave the kitchen, still shaken by Cook's warning. The girl offers me a sheaf of papers – the Commandant's specs for Teluman.

'I offered to take them,' she says. 'But she – she didn't like that idea.'

No one pays me heed as I make my way through Serra to Teluman's forge. No one can see the raw, bloody *K* beneath the cloak I wear. As I stumble along, it's clear I'm not the only injured slave. Some Scholar slaves have bruises. Some have whip marks. Others walk as if injured inside, hunched and limping.

While still in the Illustrian Quarter, I pass a large glass display of saddles and bridles and stop short, startled at my own reflection, at the haunted, hollow-eyed creature looking back at me. Sweat soaks my skin, half from fever, half from the unabating heat. My dress clings to my body, my skirt bunching and tangling around my legs.

It's for Darin. I keep walking. *Whatever you're suffering, he's suffering worse.*

As I near the Weapons Quarter, my feet slow. I remember the Commandant's words from last night. *You're lucky I want a Teluman blade, girl. You're lucky he wants a taste of you.* I loiter near the smithy door for long minutes before entering. Surely Teluman won't want to come near me when my skin is the colour of whey and I'm sweating buckets.

The shop is as quiet as it was the first time I visited, but the smith is here. I know it. Sure enough, within seconds of me opening the door, I hear the whisper of footsteps, and Teluman appears from the back room.

He takes one look at me and disappears, returning seconds later with a dripping glass of cool water and a chair. I drop into the seat and drain the water, not stopping to consider if it might be poisoned.

The forge is cool, the water cooler, and for a second, my fevered shaking slows. Then Spiro Teluman slips past me to the forge door.

He locks it.

Slowly, I stand, holding the glass out like an offering, like a trade, like I'll give him his glass back and he'll unlock the door and let me go without hurting me. He takes it from my hand, and I wish then that I'd kept it, broken it to use as a weapon.

He looks into the glass. 'Who did you see when the ghuls came?'

The question is so unexpected that I'm startled into the truth. 'I saw my brother.'

The smith scrutinizes my face, his brow furrowed as if he's considering something, making a decision. 'You're his sister then,' he says. 'Laia. Darin spoke of you often.'

'He – he spoke—' Why would Darin speak to this man about me? Why would he speak to this man at all?

'Strangest thing.' Teluman leans back against the counter. 'The

Empire tried forcing apprentices on me for years, but I didn't find one until I caught Darin spying on me from up there.' The shutters on the high bank of windows are open, revealing the crate-littered balcony of the building next door. 'Dragged him down. Thought I'd haul him to the auxes. Then I saw his sketchbook.' He shakes his head, not needing to explain. Darin put so much life into his drawings that it seemed if you just reached out, you could pull them from the page.

'He wasn't just drawing the inside of my forge. He was designing the weapons themselves. Such things I'd only seen in dreams. I offered him the apprentice spot there and then, thinking he'd run, that I'd never see him again.'

'But he didn't run,' I whisper. He wouldn't run – not Darin.

'No. He came into the forge, looked around. Cautious, yes. Not afraid. I never saw your brother afraid. He felt fear – I'm sure he did. But he never seemed to focus on what could turn out wrong. He only ever thought about how things could turn out right.'

'The Empire thought he was Resistance,' I say. 'All this time, he was working for the Martials? If that's true, why is he still in jail? Why haven't you got him out?'

'Do you think the Empire would allow a Scholar to learn their secrets? He wasn't working for the Empire. He was working for me. And I parted ways with the Empire a long time ago. I do enough for them to keep them off my back. Armour, mostly. Until Darin came, I hadn't made a true Teluman scim for seven years.'

'But . . . his sketchbook had pictures of swords—'

'That damn sketchbook.' Spiro snorts. 'I told him to keep it here, but he wouldn't listen. Now the Empire has it, and there's no getting it back.'

'He wrote down formulas in it,' I say. 'Instructions. Things — things he shouldn't have known—'

'He was my apprentice. I taught him to make weapons. Fine weapons. Teluman weapons. But *not* for the Empire.'

I swallow nervously as the implications of his words sink in. No matter how clever Scholar uprisings have been, in the end it comes down to steel against steel, and in that battle, the Martials always win.

'You wanted him to make weapons for the Scholars?' *That would be treason.* When Spiro nods, I can't believe him. This is a trick, like with Veturius this morning. It's something Teluman's planned with the Commandant to test my loyalty.

'If you'd really been working with my brother, someone would have seen. Other people must work here. Slaves, assistants—'

'I'm the Teluman smith. Other than my apprentice, I work alone, as my forefathers did. It's the reason your brother and I were never caught. I *want* to help Darin. But I can't. The Mask who took Darin recognized my work in his sketches. I've been questioned about it twice already. If the Empire learns I took your brother as my apprentice, they'll kill him. Then they'll kill me, and right now I'm the only chance the Scholars have at casting off their chains.'

'Were you working with the Resistance?'

'No,' Spiro says. 'Darin didn't trust them. He tried to stay away from the fighters. But he used the tunnels to get here, and a few weeks ago, two rebels spotted him leaving the Weapons Quarter. Thought he was a Martial collaborator. He had to show them his sketchbook to keep them from killing him.' Spiro sighs. 'Then, of course, they wanted him to join up. Wouldn't leave him alone. Lucky, in the end. That connection to the Resistance is the only reason either of us is still alive. As long as the Empire thinks he's holding rebel secrets, they'll keep him in prison.'

'But he told them he wasn't with the Resistance,' I say. 'When the Mask raided us.'

'Stock answer. Empire expects real rebels to deny membership for days – weeks, even – before giving in. We prepared for this. I taught him how to survive interrogation and prison. As long as he stays here in Serra and out of Kauf, he should be fine.'

For how long, I wonder.

I'm afraid to cut Teluman off, but I'm more afraid not to. If he's telling the truth, then the more of this I listen to, the more danger I'm in. 'The Commandant's expecting a reply. She'll send me back for it in a few days. Here.'

'Laia – wait—'

But I shove the papers in his hands, dart to the door, and unlock it. He can easily come after me, but he doesn't. Instead, he watches as I hurry down the alley. When I turn the corner, I think I hear him curse.

* * *

At night, I toss restlessly in the tiny box that is my room, the rope of my pallet digging into my back, the roof and walls so close that I can't breathe. My wound burns, and my mind echoes with Teluman's words.

Serric steel is the heart of the Empire's strength. No Martial would give up its secrets to a Scholar. And yet something about Teluman's claims rings true. When he spoke of Darin, he captured my brother perfectly – his drawings, the way he thinks. And Darin, like Spiro, told me he wasn't with the Martials or the Resistance. It all aligns.

Except the Darin I knew wasn't interested in rebellion.

Or was he? Memories cascade through my head: Darin's silence when Pop told us of how he set the bones of a child beaten by auxes. Darin excusing himself when Nan and Pop discussed the most recent Martial raids, fists clenched. Darin ignoring us to draw Scholar women flinching from Masks and children fighting over a rotted apple in the gutter.

I thought my brother's silence meant he was pulling away from us. But maybe silence was his solace. Maybe it was the only way he could fight his outrage at what was happening to his people.

When I do fall asleep, Cook's warning about the Resistance burrows its way into my dreams. I see the Commandant cut me over and over. Each time, her face changes from Mazen's to Keenan's to Teluman's to Cook's.

I wake to choking darkness and gasp for breath, trying to push away the walls of my quarters. I scramble out of my bed, through the open-air corridor, and into the back courtyard, guzzling the cool night breezes.

It's past midnight, and clouds scud over a nearly full moon. In a few days, it will be time for the Moon Festival, the Scholars' midsummer celebration of the largest moon of the year. Nan and I were supposed to hand out cakes and pastries this year. Darin was supposed to dance until his feet fell off.

In the moonlight, the forbidding buildings of Blackcliff are almost beautiful, the sable granite softened to blue. The school is, as always, eerily hushed. I never feared the night, not even as a child, but Blackcliff's night is different, heavy with a silence that makes you look over your shoulder, a silence that feels like a living thing.

I look up at the stars hanging low in a sky that makes me think I'm seeing the infinite. But beneath their cold gaze, I feel small. All the beauty of the stars means nothing when life here on earth is so ugly.

I didn't used to think so. Darin and I spent countless nights on the roof of our grandparents' house tracing the path of the Great River, the Archer, the Swordsman. We'd watch for falling stars, and whoever saw one first would issue a dare. Since Darin's eyes were sharp as a cat's, I was always the one stuck stealing apricots from the neighbours, or pouring cold water down the back of Nan's shirt.

Darin can't see the stars now. He's stuck in a cellblock, lost in the labyrinth of Serra's prisons. He'll never see the stars again, unless I get the Resistance what they want.

A light flares in the Commandant's study, and I start, surprised she's still awake. Her curtains flutter, and voices drift down through the open window. She's not alone.

Teluman's words come back to me. *I never saw your brother afraid. He never seemed to focus on what could turn out wrong. He only ever thought about how things could turn out right.*

A worn trellis runs up alongside the Commandant's window, covered in summer-dead vines. I give the trellis a shake – it's rickety, but not un-climbable.

She's probably not saying anything useful anyway. She's probably talking to a student.

But why would she meet a student at midnight? Why not during the day?

She'll whip you. My fear pleads with me. *She'll take an eye. A hand.*

But I've been whipped and beaten and strangled, and I've survived. I've been carved up with a hot knife, and I've survived.

Darin didn't let fear control him. If I want to save him, I can't let fear control me either.

Knowing my courage will diminish the longer I think about it, I grab the trellis and climb. Keenan's advice pops into my head. *Always have an exit plan.*

I grimace. Too late for that now.

Every scrape of my sandals sounds to me like a detonation. A loud creak makes my heart stutter, but after a minute of paralysis, I realize the sound is just the trellis groaning under my weight.

When I reach the top, I still can't hear the Commandant. The windowsill is a foot to my left. Three feet below the sill, a section of stone has crumbled, leaving a small foothold. I take a breath, grab the sill, and swing from the trellis to the window. My feet scrape against the sheer wall for a terrifying moment before I find the foothold.

Don't collapse, I beg the stone beneath my feet. *Don't break*.

My chest wound has opened again, and I try to ignore the blood dripping down my front. My head is even with the Commandant's window. If she leans out, I'm dead.

Forget that, Darin tells me. *Listen*. The clipped tones of the Commandant's voice float through the window, and I lean forward.

'—be arriving with his entire retinue, my Lord Nightbringer. Everyone – his councillors, the Blood Shrike, the Black Guard – as well as most of Gens Taia.' The subdued nature of the Commandant's voice is a revelation.

'Make sure of it, Keris. Taius must arrive after the Third Trial, or our plan is for naught.'

At the sound of the second voice, I gasp and nearly fall. The voice is deep and soft, not a sound so much as a feeling. It is storm and wind and leaves twisting in the night. It is roots sucking deep at the earth, and the pale, sightless creatures that live below the ground. But there's something wrong with this voice, something diseased at its core.

Though I've never heard the voice before, I find myself trembling, tempted for a second to drop to the ground just to get away from it.

Laia. I hear Darin. *Be brave.*

I risk a peek through the curtains and catch a glimpse of a figure standing in the corner of the room, swathed in darkness. He looks to be nothing more than a medium-sized man in a cloak. But I know in my bones that this is no normal man. Shadows pool near his feet, writhing, as if trying to get the figure's attention. Ghuls. When the thing turns towards the Commandant, I flinch, for the darkness beneath his hood has no place in the human world. His eyes glow, slitted suns filled with ancient malevolence.

The figure moves, and I jerk away from the window.

The Nightbringer, my mind screams. *She called him the Nightbringer.*

'We have a different problem, my lord,' the Commandant says. 'The Augurs suspect my interference. My . . . instruments are not as subtle as I'd hoped.'

'Let them suspect,' the creature says. 'As long as you shield your mind and we continue teaching the Farrars to shield theirs, the Augurs will remain ignorant. Though I do wonder if you've chosen the right Aspirants, Keris. They've just botched a second ambush, though I told them everything they needed to end Aquilla and Veturius.'

'The Farrars are the only choice. Veturius is too stubborn, and Aquilla too loyal to him.'

'Then Marcus must win, and I must be able to control him,' the shadow-man says.

'Even if it is one of the others.' The Commandant's voice is filled with a doubt I never imagined her capable of expressing. 'Veturius, for instance. You can kill him and take his form—'

'Changing form is no easy task. And I am not an assassin, Commandant, to be used to kill off those who are thorns in your side.'

'He's no thorn—'

'If you want your son dead, do it yourself. But do not let it interfere with the task I have given you. If you cannot perform that task, our partnership is at an end.'

'Two Trials remain, my Lord Nightbringer.' The Commandant's voice is low with suppressed rage. 'As both will take place here, I'm sure I can—'

'You have little time.'

'Thirteen days is plenty—'

'And if your attempts at sabotaging the Trial of Strength fail? The Fourth Trial is only a day later. In two weeks, Keris, you *will* have a new Emperor. See that it's the right one.'

'I will not fail you, my lord.'

'Of course not, Keris. You've never failed me before. As a token of my faith in you, I've brought you another gift.'

A rustle, a rip, and then a sharp intake of breath.

'Something to add to that tattoo,' the Commandant's guest says. 'Shall I?'

'No,' the Commandant breathes. 'No, this one's mine.'

'As you will. Come. See me to the gate.'

Seconds later, the window slams shut, nearly jarring me from my perch, and the lamps go out. I hear the distant thud of the door, and all falls silent.

My whole body shakes. Finally, *finally*, I have something useful for the Resistance. It's not everything they want to know. But it might be enough to sate Mazen, to buy more time. Half of me is jubilant, but the other half is still thinking about the creature the Commandant called the Nightbringer. What *was* that thing?

Scholars do not, on principle, believe in the supernatural. Scepticism is one of the few remnants of our bookish past, and most of us hold on to it tenaciously. Jinn, efrits, ghuls, wraiths – they belong in Tribal myth and legend. Shadows coming alive are a trick of the eye. A shadow-man with a voice out of hell – there should be an explanation for him too.

Except there is no explanation. He is real. Just like the ghuls are real.

A sudden wind sweeps in from the desert, shaking the trellis and threatening to rip me from my perch. Whatever that thing is, I decide, the less I know about it, the better. All that matters is that I've got the information I need.

I reach my foot out to the trellis but pull it back quickly when another gust of wind whips past. The trellis creaks, tips, and, before my horrified eyes, drops with a deafening clatter to the flagstones. *Bleeding hells.* I wince, waiting for Cook or Izzi to come out and discover me.

Seconds later, sandals rasp on the courtyard stone. Izzi emerges from the servants' hallway, a shawl wrapped tight around her shoulders. She looks down at the trellis and then up at the window. When she spots me, her mouth is an O of surprise, but she simply lifts the trellis and watches as I climb down.

When I turn to face her, I'm hastily composing a fleet of explanations, none of which make any sense. But she speaks first.

'I want you to know that I think what you're doing is brave. Really brave.' Her words come out in a torrent, as if she's been hoarding them all for this moment. 'I know about the raid and your family and the Resistance. I wasn't spying on you, I swear it. It's just, after I took up the sand this morning, I realized I left the irons in the oven to heat. When I came back to get them, you and Cook were talking, and I didn't want to interrupt. Anyway, I was thinking – I could help you. I know things, lots of things. I've been at Blackcliff forever.'

For a second, I'm speechless. Do I beg her not to tell anyone else? Do I get unfairly angry at her for eavesdropping? Do I just stare because I didn't think she had that many words in her? I have no idea, but I do know one thing: I can't accept her help. It's too risky.

Before I've said anything, she stuffs her hands under her shawl and shakes her head.

'Never mind.' She looks so lonely – a loneliness of years, of a whole life. 'It was a stupid idea. Sorry.'

'It's not stupid,' I say. 'Just dangerous. I don't want you getting hurt. If the Commandant finds out, she'll kill us both.'

'Might be better than how things are now. At least I'll die having done something useful.'

'I can't let you, Izzi.' My rejection hurts her, and I feel terrible for it. But I'm not so desperate that I'll put her life at risk. 'I'm sorry.'

'Right.' She's back in her shell now. 'Never mind. Just . . . forget it.'

I've made the right decision. I know it. But as Izzi walks away, lonely and miserable, I hate the fact that it's me who has made her feel that way.

* * *

Though I beg Cook to let me run errands for her so I can be out in the markets every day, I hear nothing from the Resistance.

Until finally, on the third day after overhearing the Commandant, I'm shoving my way past the crowds in the couriers' office, and a hand lands on my waist. I instinctively jab back with my elbow to knock the wind out of the fool who thinks he can take liberties. Another hand catches my arm.

'Laia.' A low voice murmurs into my ear. Keenan's voice.

My skin thrills at the familiar scent of him. He lets my arm go, but his hand tightens on my waist. I'm tempted to push him away and tell him off for touching me, but at the same time, the feel of his hand sends a jolt up my spine.

'Don't turn,' he says. 'Commandant's put a tail on you. He's trying to work his way through the crowd. We can't risk a meeting now. Do you have anything for us?'

I raise the Commandant's letter to my face and fan myself, hoping the movement will conceal the fact that I'm talking.

'I do.' I'm practically vibrating with excitement, but I sense only tension from Keenan. When I turn to look at him, he gives me a sharp squeeze of warning, but not before I see the grim cast of his face. My elation fades. Something is wrong.

'Is Darin okay?' I whisper. 'Is he—' I can't say the words. My fear stifles me into silence.

'He's in a death cell here in Serra, in Central Prison.' Keenan speaks softly, the way Pop used to when he gave patients the worst news. 'He's to be executed.'

All the air drains from my lungs. I can't hear the office clerks yelling, or feel the hands pushing me, or smell the sweat of the crowd.

Executed. Killed. Dead. Darin will be dead.

'We still have time.' To my surprise, Keenan sounds sincere. *My parents are dead too*, he said when I saw him last. *My whole family, actually.* He understands what Darin's execution will do to me. Perhaps he's the only one who does.

'The execution will happen after the new Emperor is named. That might not be for a while yet.'

Wrong, I think.

In two weeks, the shadow-man had said, *you will have a new Emperor.* My brother doesn't have a while. He has two weeks.

I need to tell Keenan this, but when I turn to do so, I see a legionnaire standing in the entryway of the couriers' office, watching me. The tail.

'Mazen won't be in the city tomorrow.' Keenan bends down, as if he's dropped something on the floor. Keenly aware of the Commandant's man, I continue looking straight ahead. 'But the next day, if you can get out and lose the tail—'

'No,' I mutter, fanning myself again. 'Tonight. I'll get out again tonight. When she's sleeping. She never leaves her room before dawn. I'll sneak out. I'll find you.'

'Too many patrols out tonight. It's the Moon Festival—'

'The patrols will be focused on groups of revellers,' I say. 'They won't notice one slave-girl. Please, Keenan. I have to talk to Mazen. I have information. If I can get it to him, he can get Darin out before he's executed.'

'Fine.' Keenan looks casually towards the tail. 'Make your way to the festival. I'll find you there.'

A moment later, he's gone. I deliver my letter to the couriers' desk and pay the fee. Seconds later, I'm outside, watching market-goers rush by. Will the information I have be enough to save my brother? Will it be enough to convince Mazen that he should spring Darin now instead of later?

It will be, I decide. It must be. I haven't come this far to watch my brother die. Tonight, I'll convince Mazen to get Darin out. I'll vow to stay a slave until I have the information he wants. I'll promise myself to the Resistance. I'll do whatever it takes.

But first things first. How am I going to sneak out of Blackcliff?

CHAPTER TWENTY-FOUR

Elias

The singing is a river that winds through my pain-infused dreams, quiet and sweet, drawing out memories of a life I've nearly forgotten, a life before Blackcliff. The silk-draped caravan trundling through the Tribal desert. My playfellows, running riot in the oasis, their laughter ringing like bells. Walking in the shade of the date trees with Mamie Rila, her voice as steady as the hum of life in the desert around us.

But when the singing stops, the dreams fade, and I descend into nightmares. The nightmares transform into a black pit of pain, and the pain stalks me like a vengeful twin. A door of clutching darkness opens behind me, and a hand snatches at my back, trying to drag me through.

Then the singing begins again, a thread of life in the infinite black, and I reach for it and hold on as tight as I can.

* * *

I come to consciousness light-headed, as if I've returned to my body after long years away. Though I expect soreness, my limbs move easily, and I sit up.

Outside, the evening lamps have just been lit. I know I'm in the infirmary because it's the only place in all of Blackcliff with white walls. The room is empty of everything but the bed in which I lie, a small table, and a plain wooden chair occupied by a dozing Helene. She looks terrible, her face covered in bruises and scratches.

'Elias!' Her eyes fly open when she hears me move. 'Thank the skies. You've been out for two days.'

'Remind me,' I croak, my throat dry, head aching. Something happened on the cliffs. Something strange . . .

Helene pours me a glass of water from a pitcher on the table. 'We were attacked by efrits during the Second Trial, on our way down the cliffs.'

'One of them cut the rope,' I say, remembering. 'But then—'

'You stuffed me in that niche but didn't have the sense to hold on to it yourself.' Helene glowers at me, but her hands shake as she gives me the water. 'Then you dropped like a lead weight. Smacked your head on the way down. You should have died, but that rope between us anchored you. I sang at the top of my lungs until every last efrit bolted. Then I got you to the desert floor and holed up in a little cave behind some tumbleweeds. Good little fort, actually. Easy to defend.'

'You had to fight? Again?'

'The Augurs tried to kill us four more times. The scorpions were obvious, but the viper almost got you. Then there were wights – evil little bastards, them, nothing like the stories. Pain in the arse to kill, too – you have to squash them like bugs. The legionnaires were the worst, though.' Helene goes pale, and the dark humour in her voice fades. 'They kept coming. I'd take down one or two, and four more would replace them. They'd have rushed me, but the opening to the cave was too narrow.'

'How many did you kill?'

'Too many. But it was them or us, so it's hard to feel guilty.'

Them or us. I think of the four soldiers I killed in the watchtower stairwell. I guess I should be thankful I didn't have to add to that tally.

'At dawn,' she continues, 'an Augur showed up. Ordered the legionnaires to haul you to the infirmary. She said Marcus and Zak were injured too, and that since I was the only one unmarked, I'd won the Trial. Then she gave me this.' She pulls back the neck of her tunic to reveal a shimmering, tight-fitting shirt.

'Why didn't you tell me you'd won?' Relief floods me. I'd have broken something if Marcus or Zak had taken the victory. 'And they gave you a . . . shirt?'

'Made of living metal,' Helene says. 'Augur-forged, like our masks. Turns away all blades, the Augur said – even Serric steel. Good thing, too. Skies only know what we'll face next.'

I shake my head. Wraiths and efrits and wights. Tribal tales come to life. I never dreamt it possible. 'The Augurs don't let up, do they?'

'What do you expect, Elias?' Helene asks quietly. 'They're choosing the next Emperor. That's no small thing. You – we – need to trust them.' She takes a breath, and her next words come out in a rush. 'When I saw you fall, I thought you were dead. And there were so many things I needed to say to you.' She brings her hand hesitantly to my face, her shy eyes speaking an unfamiliar language.

Not so unfamiliar, Elias. Lavinia Tanalia looked at you like that. And Ceres Coran. Right before you kissed them.

But this is different. This is Helene. *So what? You want to see what it's like – you know you do.* As soon as I think it, I'm disgusted at myself. Helene's not a quick tumble or a night's indiscretion. She's my best friend. She deserves better.

'Elias . . .' Her voice is slow as a summer breeze, and she bites her lip. *No. Don't let her.*

I pull my face away, and she snatches her hand back as if from a flame, her cheeks crimson.

'Helene—'

'Don't worry about it.' She shrugs, her tone falsely light. 'I guess I'm just happy to see you. Anyway, you never said – how do you feel?'

The speed with which she moves on startles me, but I'm so relieved to avoid an awkward conversation that I, too, pretend nothing has happened. 'My head hurts. I feel . . . fuzzy. There was this . . . this singing. Do you know . . .?'

'You were probably dreaming.' Helene looks away uncomfortably, and, groggy though I might be, I can tell she's hiding something. When the door opens to admit the physician, she jumps from her chair, seemingly relieved at the presence of someone else in the room.

'Ah, Veturius,' the physician says. 'Awake at last.' I've never liked him. He's a skeletal, pompous ass who delights in discussing his healing methods while patients writhe in pain. He bustles over and removes the bandage on my leg.

My mouth drops open. I expected a bloody wound. But there's nothing left of the injury except a scar that looks weeks old. It tingles when I touch it but is otherwise free of pain.

'A southern poultice,' the physician says, 'of my own making. I've used it many times, I confess, but with you, I've got the formula perfect.'

The physician removes the bandage from my head. It's not even bloodstained. A dull ache flares out from behind my ear, and I reach up to feel the ridge of a scar there. If what Helene said was true, this wound should have left me knocked out for weeks. And yet it has healed in days. Miraculous. I contemplate the physician. Too miraculous for this smug bag of bones to have done it on his own.

Helene, I note, is pointedly not looking at me.

'Did an Augur visit?' I ask the physician.

'Augur? No. Just myself and the apprentices. And Aquilla, of course.' He gives Hel an irritated glance. 'Sat in here singing lullabies every chance she got.'

The physician pulls a bottle from his pocket. 'Bloodroot serum for the pain,' he says. *Bloodroot serum.* The words trigger something in my mind, but it flits away.

'Your fatigues are in the closet,' the physician says. 'You're free to go, though I recommend you take it easy. I've told the Commandant you won't be fit for training or watch until tomorrow.'

The second the physician leaves, I turn on Helene. 'No poultice in the world could heal wounds like this. And yet I didn't get a visit from an Augur. Only you.'

'The wounds must not have been as bad as you thought.'

'Helene. Tell me about your singing.'

She opens her mouth, as if to speak, then breaks for the door faster than a whip. Unfortunately for her, I'm expecting it.

Her eyes flash when I grab her hand, and I see her weigh her options. *Do I fight him? Is it worth it?* I wait her out, and she relents, pulling her fingers from mine and sitting back down.

'It started in the cave,' she says. 'You kept twitching, like you were having a fit of some kind. When I sang to keep the efrits away, you calmed down. Your colour was better, your head wound stopped bleeding. So I – I kept singing. I got tired as I did it – weak, like I had a fever.' Her eyes are panicked. 'I don't know what it means. I'd never try to harness the spirits of the dead. I'm no witch, Elias, I swear—'

'I know that, Hel.' Skies, what would my mother make of this? The Black Guard? Nothing good. Martials believe that supernatural power comes from spirits of the dead and that only the Augurs are possessed by such spirits. Anyone else with even a touch of power would be accused of witchcraft and sentenced to death.

The evening's shadows dance across Hel's face, and it reminds me of how she looked when Rowan Goldgale grabbed her and lit her with that strange glow.

'Mamie Rila used to tell stories,' I say carefully, not wanting to spook Helene. 'She talked of humans with strange skills that were awoken by contact with the supernatural. Some could harness strength, others could change the weather. A few could even heal with their voices.'

'Not possible. Only the Augurs have true power—'

'Helene, we fought wraiths and efrits two nights ago. Who's to say what's possible and what isn't? Maybe when that efrit touched you, it woke something up inside you.'

'Something strange.' Helene hands me my fatigues. I've only unsettled her more. 'Something inhuman. Something—'

'Something that probably saved my life.'

Hel grabs my shoulder, her slim fingers digging into me. 'Promise you won't tell anyone, Elias. Let everyone think the physician is a miracle worker. Please. I have to – to understand this first. If the Commandant knows, she'll tell the Black Guard and—'

They'll try to purge it out of you. 'Our secret,' I say. She looks marginally relieved.

When we leave the infirmary, I'm greeted by a cheer – Faris, Dex, Tristas, Demetrius, Leander – hooting and banging me on the back.

'I knew the bastards wouldn't off you—'

'Cause for celebration, let's smuggle in a keg—'

'Back up,' Helene says. 'Let him breathe.' She's interrupted by the thudding of the drums.

All new graduates to training field one for combat practice immediately.

The message repeats, and groans and eye-rolling abound. 'Do us a favour, Elias,' Faris says. 'When you win and become grand overlord, get us out of here, will you?'

'Oi,' Helene says. 'What about me? What if I win?'

'If you win, then the docks get shut down and we'll never have any fun again,' Leander says, winking at me.

'You twit, Leander, I would not shut down the docks,' Helene fumes. 'Just because I don't like brothels—' Leander backs away, his hands protecting his nose.

'Forgive him, oh hallowed Aspirant,' Tristas intones, blue eyes sparkling. 'Do not strike him down. He is but a poor servant—'

'Oh, piss off, all of you,' Helene says.

'Half past ten, Elias,' Leander calls as he and the others walk away. 'My room. We'll have a proper celebration. Aquilla, you can come too, but only if you promise not to break my nose again.'

I tell him I won't miss it, and after he and the others leave, Hel hands me a vial. 'You almost forgot the bloodroot serum.'

'Laia!' I realize the source of the niggling feeling I had earlier. I'd promised the slave-girl bloodroot three days ago. She'll be in terrible pain from her wound. Has she been taking care of it? Has Cook been cleaning it? Has—

'Who's Laia?' Helene interrupts my thoughts, her voice danger-ously serene.

'She's . . . no one.' My promise to a Scholar slave isn't something Helene will understand. 'What else happened while I was at the infirmary? Anything interesting?'

Helene throws me a look that says she's allowing me to change the subject. 'Resistance ambushed a Mask – Daemon Cassius – in his house. Pretty gruesome, apparently. His wife found him this morning. No one heard a thing. The bastards are getting bolder. And . . . there's something else.' She drops her voice. 'My father's heard a rumour that the Blood Shrike's dead.'

I stare at her incredulously. 'The Resistance?'

Helene shakes her head. 'You know that the Emperor's a few weeks away from Serra – at the most. He's started to plan his attack on Blackcliff – on us, the Aspirants.'

Grandfather warned me about this. Still, it's unpleasant to hear.

'When the Blood Shrike heard about the attack plans, he tried to resign his post. So Taius had him executed.'

'You can't resign as Blood Shrike.' You serve until you die. Everyone knows that.

'Actually,' Helene says, 'the Blood Shrike *can* resign, but only if the Emperor agrees to release him from service. It's not commonly known – Father says it's some odd loophole in Empire law. Anyway, if the rumour is true, then the Blood Shrike was a fool to even ask. Taius isn't going to free his right-hand man right when Gens Taia is being shoved out of power.'

She looks up at me, expecting a response, but I just stare at her open-mouthed, because something huge has occurred to me, something I haven't understood until now.

If you do your duty, the Augur said, *you have a chance to break the bonds between you and the Empire forever.*

I know how to do it. I know how I'll find my freedom.

If I win the Trials, I become Emperor. Nothing but death can release the Emperor from his duty to the Empire. But that's not the case for the Blood Shrike. *The Blood Shrike can resign, but only if the Emperor agrees to release him from service.*

I'm not supposed to win the Trials. Helene is. Because if she wins and I become Blood Shrike, then she can set me free.

The revelation is like a punch to the gut and flying, all at once. The Augurs said whoever won two Trials first would become Emperor. Marcus and Helene are both up one. Which means I have to win the next Trial and Helene has to win the Fourth. And sometime between now and then, Marcus and Zak have to die.

'Elias?'

'Yes,' I say too loudly. 'Sorry.' Hel looks annoyed.

'Thinking of *Laia?*' The mention of the Scholar girl is so incongruous to my thoughts that for a second I'm stunned silent, and Helene stiffens.

'Well, don't mind me, then,' she says. 'Not like I just spent two days by your bedside singing you back to life or anything.'

For a second I don't know what to say. I don't know this Helene. She's acting like an actual girl. 'No, Hel, it's not like that. I'm just tired—'

'Forget it,' she says. 'I have to get to watch.'

'Aspirant Veturius.' A Yearling jogs towards me, a note in his hand. I take the note from him, all the while asking Helene to wait. But she ignores me and, even as I'm trying to explain, she walks away.

CHAPTER TWENTY-FIVE

Laia

Hours after telling Keenan I'd get out of Blackcliff to meet him, I feel like the world's biggest fool. Tenth bell has come and gone. The Commandant dismissed me and retreated to her room an hour ago. She shouldn't emerge until dawn, especially since I spiked her tea with kheb leaf – a scentless, tasteless herb Pop used to help patients rest. Cook and Izzi are asleep in their quarters. The house is silent as a mausoleum.

And still I sit in my room, trying to concoct a way out of this place.

I can't just walk past the gate guards so late at night. Bad things happen to slaves foolish enough to do so. Besides which, the risk that the Commandant will hear about my midnight wandering is too great.

But I can, I decide, create a distraction and *sneak* past the guards. I think back to the flames that consumed my house on the night of the raid. Nothing distracts better than fire.

So, armed with tinder, flint, and a striker, I slip out of my room. A loose black scarf obscures my face, and my dress, high-necked and long-sleeved, conceals both my slaves' cuffs and the Commandant's mark, still scabbed and painful.

The servants' corridor is empty. I move silently to the wooden gate leading to Blackcliff's grounds and ease it open.

It squeals louder than a gutted pig.

I grimace and scurry back to my quarters, waiting for someone to come to investigate the noise. When no one does, I creep out of my room—

'Laia? Where are you going?'

I jump and drop the flint and striker to the ground, barely keeping hold of the tinder.

'Bleeding skies, Izzi!'

'Sorry!' She picks up the flint and striker, brown eyes widening when she realizes what they are. 'You're trying to sneak out.'

'Am not,' I say, but she gives me a look that makes me fidget. 'Fine, I am, but—'

'I . . . could help you,' she whispers. 'I know a way out of the school that even the legionnaires don't patrol.'

'It's too dangerous, Izzi.'

'Right. Of course.' She retreats but then stops, small hands twisting together.

'If – if you were planning to set a fire and sneak through the front gate while the guards are distracted, it won't work. The legionnaires will send the auxes to deal with the fire. They never leave a gate unattended. Never.'

As soon as she says it, I know she's right. I should have realized that fact myself. 'Can you tell me about this way out?' I ask her.

'It's a hidden trail,' she says. 'A rock path and a scanty one at that. I'm sorry, but I'd have to show you – which means I'd have to come with you. I don't mind. It's what a – a friend would do.' She says the word *friend* like it's a secret she wishes she knew.

'I'm not saying that we're friends,' she continues in a rush. 'I mean – I don't know. I've never really had . . .'

A *friend*. She's about to say it, but she looks away, embarrassed.

'I'm to meet with my handler, Izzi. If you come and the Commandant catches you—'

'She'll punish me. Maybe kill me. I know. But she might do that anyway if I forget to dust her room or if I look her in the eye. Living with the Commandant is like living with the Reaper. And anyway, do you really have a choice? I mean' – she looks almost apologetic – 'how else are you planning to get out of here?'

Good point. I don't want her to get hurt. I lost Zara to the Martials a year ago. I can't bear the thought of another friend suffering at their hands.

But I don't want Darin to die either. Every second I waste is a second he is rotting in prison. And it's not as if I'm forcing her into this. Izzi *wants* to help. A host of what-ifs parade through my head. I silence them. *For Darin.*

'All right,' I say to Izzi. 'This hidden trail – where does it let out?'

'The docks. Is that where you're going?'

I shake my head. 'I have to get into the Scholars' Quarter for the Moon Festival. But I can make my way there from the docks.'

Izzi nods. 'This way, Laia.'

Please don't let her get hurt. She ducks into her room for a cloak, then takes my hand and pulls me to the back of the house.

CHAPTER TWENTY-SIX

Elias

Though the physician excused me from training and watch, my mother doesn't seem to care. Her note to me is an order to report to training field two for hand-to-hand combat. I pocket the bloodroot serum – it will have to wait – and spend the next two hours attempting to keep the Combat Centurion from beating me to a pulp.

By the time I change into fresh fatigues and leave the training field, tenth bell's come and gone, and I have a party to go to. The boys – and Helene – will be waiting. I shove my hands in my pockets as I walk. I hope Hel loosens up a little – at least enough to forget that she was so irritated with me earlier. If I want her to set me free from the Empire, making sure she doesn't hate me seems like a good first step.

My fingers brush up against the bottle of bloodroot in my pocket. *You told Laia you'd take it to her, Elias,* a voice chides me. *Days ago.*

But I also said I'd join Hel and the boys in the barracks. Hel's already mad at me. If she finds out I'm visiting Scholar slave-girls in the dead of night, she won't be pleased.

245

I stop and consider. If I'm quick about it, Hel will never know where I've been.

The Commandant's house is dark, but I stick to the shadows anyway. The slaves might be in bed, but if my mother's asleep, then I'm a swamp jinn. I prowl around to the servants' entrance, thinking to leave the oil in the kitchen. Then I hear voices.

'This hidden trail – where does it let out?' I recognize the speaker's murmur. Laia.

'The docks.' That's Izzi, the kitchen slave. 'Is that where you're going?'

After listening a moment longer, I realize that they're planning to take the treacherous hidden trail out of the school and into Serra. The trail isn't watched, solely because no one is stupid enough to risk sneaking out that way. Demetrius and I tried it without ropes on a dare six months ago and nearly broke our necks.

The girls will have a hell of a time making it across. And it will be doubly miraculous if they make it back. I start after them, thinking to tell them that the risk isn't worth it, not even for the legendary Moon Festival.

But then the air shifts and freezes me in my tracks. I smell grass and snow.

'So,' Helene says from behind me. 'That's who Laia is. A slave.' She shakes her head. 'I thought you were better than the others, Elias. I never imagined you would take a *slave* to your bed.'

'It's not like that.' I wince at how I sound: like a typical bumbling male, denying wrongdoing to his woman. Except Helene's not my woman. 'Laia's not—'

'Do you think I'm stupid? Or blind?' There is something dangerous in Helene's eyes. 'I saw how you looked at her. That day when she brought us to the Commandant's house before the

Trial of Courage. Like she was water and you were just dying of thirst.' Hel collects herself. 'Doesn't matter. I'm reporting her and her friend to the Commandant right now.'

'For what?' I'm astounded at Helene, at the depths of her anger.

'For sneaking out of Blackcliff.' Helene's practically gnashing her teeth. 'For defying their master, attempting to attend an illegal festival—'

'They're just girls, Hel.'

'They're *slaves*, Elias. Their only concern is pleasing their master, and in this case, I assure you, their master would not be pleased.'

'Calm down.' I look around, worried someone will hear us. 'Laia's a person, Helene. Someone's daughter or sister. If you or I had been born to different parents, we might be in her shoes instead of our own.'

'What are you saying? That I should feel sorry for the Scholars? That I should think of them as equals? We conquered them. We rule them now. It's the way of the world.'

'Not all conquered people are turned into slaves. In the Southern Lands, the Lake People conquered the Fens and brought them into the fold—'

'What is *wrong* with you?' Helene stares at me as if I've sprouted another head. 'The Empire has rightfully annexed this land. It's *our* land. We fought for it, died for it, and now we're tasked with keeping it. If doing so means we have to keep the Scholars enslaved, so be it. Have a care, Elias. If anyone heard you spouting this trash, the Black Guard would toss you into Kauf without a thought.'

'What happened to you wanting to change things?' Her righteousness is getting damn irritating. I thought she was better than this. 'That night after graduation, you said you'd improve things for the Scholars—'

'I meant better living conditions! Not setting them free! Elias, look at what the bastards have been doing. Raiding caravans, killing innocent Illustrians in their beds—'

'You're not actually referring to Daemon Cassius as *innocent*. He's a Mask—'

'The girl's a slave,' Helene snaps. 'And the Commandant deserves to know what her slaves are doing. Not telling her is tantamount to aiding and abetting the enemy. I'm turning them in.'

'No,' I say. 'You're not.' My mother's already made her mark on Laia. She's already gouged out Izzi's eye. I know what she'll do if she learns they sneaked out. There won't be enough left to feed the scavengers.

Helene crosses her arms in front of her. 'How do you plan to stop me?'

'That healing power of yours,' I say, hating myself for blackmailing her but knowing it's the only thing that will get her to back down. 'The Commandant would be mighty interested in that, don't you think?'

Helene goes still. In the light of the full moon, the shock and hurt on her masked face hit me like a blow to the chest. She backs away, as if worried that I'll spread my sedition. As if it's a plague.

'You're unbelievable,' she says. 'After – after everything.' She sputters, she's so angry, but then she draws herself up, pulling out the Mask that lives at her core. Her voice goes flat, her face expressionless.

'I want nothing to do with you,' she says. 'If you want to be a traitor, you're on your own. You stay away from me. In training. At watch. In the Trials. Just stay away.'

Damn it, Elias. I needed to make up with Helene tonight, not antagonize her further.

'Hel, come on.' I reach for her arm, but she wants none of it. She throws off my hand and stalks off into the night.

I gaze after her, poleaxed. *She doesn't mean it,* I tell myself. *She just needs to cool down.* By tomorrow, she'll be rational – I can explain why I didn't want to turn the girls in. *And apologize for blackmailing her with knowledge she trusted me to keep secret.* I grimace. Yes, I'll definitely wait until tomorrow. If I approach her now, she'll probably try to geld me.

But that still leaves Laia and Izzi.

I stand in the dark, considering. *Mind your own business, Elias,* part of me says. *Leave the girls to their fate. Go to Leander's party. Get drunk.*

Idiot, a second voice says. *Follow the girls and talk them out of this lunacy before they get caught and killed. Go. Now.*

I listen to the second voice. I follow.

CHAPTER TWENTY-SEVEN

Laia

Izzi and I sneak across the courtyard, our eyes flicking nervously to the windows of the Commandant's rooms. They're dark, which I hope means that for once, she's asleep.

'Tell me,' Izzi whispers. 'You ever climbed a tree?'

'Of course.'

'Then this will be a cinch for you. It's not much different, really.'

Ten minutes later, I teeter on a six-inch-wide ledge hundreds of feet above the dunes, glaring daggers at Izzi. She is skittering along ahead, swinging from rock to rock like a trim blonde monkey.

'This is not a cinch,' I hiss. 'This is nothing like climbing trees!'

Izzi peers down at the dunes speculatively. 'I hadn't realized how high it was.'

Above us, a heavy yellow moon dominates the star-strewn sky. It's a beautiful summer night, warm without a breath of wind. Since death lurks a misstep away, I can't bring myself to enjoy it. After taking a deep gulp of air, I move another few inches down the path, praying the stone won't crumble beneath my feet.

Izzi looks back at me. 'Not there. Not there – not—'

'Gaaaaa!' My foot slips, only to land on solid rock a few inches lower than I expect.

'Shut it!' Izzi flaps a hand at me. 'You'll wake half the school!'

The cliff is pocked with knobs of jutting rock, some of which deteriorate as soon as I touch them. There is a trail here, but it is more appropriate for squirrels than humans. My foot slips on a particularly crumbly bit of stone, and I hug the cliff face until the vertigo sweeps past. A minute later, I accidentally shove my finger into the home of some angry, sharp-pincered creature, and it scuttles over my hand and arm. I bite my lip to suppress a scream and shake my arm so vigorously that the scabs over my heart open. I hiss at the sudden, searing pain.

'Come on, Laia,' Izzi calls from ahead of me. 'Almost there.'

I force myself forward, trying to ignore the maw of grasping air at my back. When we finally reach a wide patch of solid ground, I nearly kiss the dirt in thankfulness. The river laps calmly at the nearby docks, the masts of dozens of small riverboats bobbing gently up and down like a forest of dancing spears.

'See?' Izzi says. 'That wasn't so bad.'

'We still have to go back.'

Izzi doesn't answer. Instead, she looks intently into the shadows behind me. I turn, searching them with her, listening for anything out of the ordinary. The only sound is of water slapping hull.

'Sorry.' She shakes her head. 'I thought . . . never mind. Lead the way.'

The docks crawl with laughing drunks and sailors stinking of sweat and salt. The ladies of the night beckon to anyone passing, their eyes like fading coals.

Izzi stops to stare, but I pull her after me. We stick to the shadows, trying our best to disappear into the darkness, to catch no one's eye.

Soon we leave the docks behind. The further we get into Serra, the more familiar the streets become, until we climb over a low section of mud-brick wall and into the Quarter.

Home.

I never appreciated the smell of the Quarter before: clay and earth and the warmth of animals living close together. I trace my finger through the air, marvelling at the whorls of dust dancing in the soft moonlight. Laughter tinkles from nearby, a door slams, a child shouts, and beneath it all, the low murmur of conversation thrums. So different from the silence that weighs on Blackcliff like a death shroud.

Home. I want it to be true. But this isn't home. Not anymore. My home was taken from me. My home was burned to the ground.

We make our way towards the square at the centre of the Quarter, where the Moon Festival is in full swing. I push back my scarf and undo my bun, letting my hair fall loose like all the other young women.

Beside me, Izzi's right eye is wide as she takes it all in. 'I've never seen anything like this,' she says. 'It's beautiful. It's . . .' I take the pins from her fair hair. She puts her hands to her head, blushing, but I pull them down.

'Just for tonight,' I say. 'Or we won't blend in. Come on.'

Smiles greet us as we make our way through the exuberant crowds. Drinks are offered, salutations exchanged, compliments murmured, sometimes shouted, to Izzi's embarrassment.

It is impossible not to think of Darin and how much he loved the festival. Two years ago, he dressed in his finest clothing and dragged us to the square early. That was when he and Nan still laughed together, when Pop's advice was law, when he had no secrets from me. He brought me stacks of moon cakes, round and yellow like the full moon. He admired the sky lanterns that lit the streets, strung so cleverly that they looked as if they were floating. When the fiddles warbled and the drums thumped, he grabbed Nan and paraded her around the dance stages until she was breathless with laughter.

This year's festival is packed, but remembering Darin, I feel wrenchingly alone. I've never thought about all the empty spaces at the Moon Festival, all the places where the disappeared, the dead, and the lost should be. What's happening to my brother in prison while I stand in this joyful crowd? How can I smile or laugh when I know he's suffering?

I glance at Izzi, at the wonder and joy on her face, and sigh, pushing away the dark thoughts for her sake. There must be other people here who feel as lonely as I do. Yet no one frowns, or cries, or sulks. They all find reason to smile and laugh. Reason to hope.

I spot one of Pop's former patients and make a sharp turn away from her, pulling my scarf back up to shadow my face. The crowd is thick, and it will be easy to lose anyone familiar in the throng, but it's better if I go unrecognized.

'Laia.' Izzi's voice is small, her touch light on my arm. 'Now what do we do?'

'Whatever we want,' I say. 'Someone is supposed to find me. Until he does, we watch, dance, eat. We blend in.' I eye a nearby cart, manned by a laughing couple and surrounded by a mob of outstretched hands.

'Izzi, have you ever tasted a moon cake?'

I cut through the crowd, emerging minutes later with two hot moon cakes dripping with chilled cream. Izzi takes a slow bite, closes her eye, and smiles. We wander to the dance stages, filled with pairs: husbands and wives, fathers and daughters, siblings, friends. I shed the slave's shuffle I've adopted and walk the way I used to, my head straight and my shoulders thrown back. Beneath my dress, my wound stings, but I ignore it.

Izzi finishes off her moon cake and stares at mine so intently that I hand it over. We find a bench and watch the dancers for a few minutes until Izzi nudges me.

'You have an admirer.' She gobbles up the last bite of cake. 'By the musicians.'

I look over, thinking it must be Keenan, but instead see a young man with a somewhat bemused expression on his face. He seems distantly familiar.

'Do you know him?' Izzi asks.

'No,' I say after considering for a few moments. 'I don't think so.'

The young man is tall as a Martial, with broad shoulders and sun-gold arms that gleam in the lantern-light. The hard lines of his stomach are visible beneath his hooded vest, even from this distance. The black strap of a pack cuts diagonally across his chest. Though his hood is up, shadowing much of his face, I see high cheekbones, a straight nose, and full lips. His features are arresting, almost Illustrian, but his clothes and the dark shine of his eyes mark him as a Tribesman.

Izzi watches the boy, studying him, almost. 'Are you sure you don't know him? Because he definitely seems to know you.'

'No, I've never seen him before.' The boy and I lock eyes, and when he smiles, blood rushes to my cheeks. I look away, but the draw of his stare is powerful, and a moment later, my gaze creeps back. He's still looking at me, arms folded across his chest.

A second later I feel a hand on my shoulder and smell cedar and wind.

'Laia.' The beautiful boy by the stage is forgotten as I turn to Keenan. I take in his dark eyes and red hair, not realizing that he's staring back until a few seconds have passed and he clears his throat.

Izzi slips a few feet away, eyeing Keenan with interest. I told her that when the Resistance showed up, she was to act like she didn't know me. Somehow, I don't think they will appreciate that a fellow slave knows all about my mission.

'Come on,' Keenan says, weaving past the dance stages and between two tents. I follow, and Izzi trails us, discreetly and at a distance.

'You found your way,' he adds.

'It was . . . simple enough.'

'I doubt that. But you managed it. Well done. You look . . .' His eyes search my face and then travel down my body. Such a look from another man would merit a slap, but from Keenan, it's more tribute than insult. There is something different about his usually aloof features – surprise? Admiration? When I smile tentatively at him, he gives his head a slight shake, as if clearing it.

'Is Sana here?' I ask.

'She's at base.' His shoulders are tense, and I can tell he's troubled. 'She wanted to see you herself, but Mazen didn't want her to come. They had quite a battle over it. Her faction's been pushing for Mazen to get Darin out. But Mazen . . .' He clears his throat and, as if he's said too much, nods tersely to a tent ahead of us. 'Let's head around back.'

A white-haired Tribal woman sits in front of the tent, peering into a crystal ball as two Scholar girls wait to hear what she'll say, their faces sceptical. On one side of her, a torch-juggler has amassed a large crowd, and on the other, a Tribal *Kehanni* spins her tales, her voice rising and swooping like a bird in flight.

'Hurry up.' Keenan's sudden brusqueness startles me. 'He's waiting.'

When I enter the tent, Mazen stops speaking to the two men flanking him. I recognize them from the cave. They are his other lieutenants, closer to Keenan's age than Mazen's and possessed of the younger man's taciturn coolness. I stand taller. I won't be intimidated.

'Still in one piece,' Mazen says. 'Impressive. What have you got for us?'

I tell him everything I know about the Trials and the Emperor's arrival. I don't reveal how I got the information, and Mazen doesn't ask. When I'm done, even Keenan looks stunned.

'The Martials will name the new Emperor in less than two weeks,' I say. 'That's why I told Keenan we had to meet tonight. It wasn't easy to get out of Blackcliff, you know. I only risked it because I knew I had to get you this information. It's not everything you wanted, but surely it's enough to convince you that I'll complete the mission. You can get Darin out now' – Mazen's brows furrow, and I rush on – 'and I'll stay at Blackcliff as long as you need me to.'

One of the lieutenants, a stocky, fair-haired man who I think is called Eran, whispers something in Mazen's ear. Irritation flashes briefly across the older man's eyes.

'The death cells aren't like the main prison block, girl,' he says. 'They're near impenetrable. I expected to have a few weeks to break your brother out, which is why I even agreed to do it. These things take time. Supplies and uniforms need procuring, guards need bribing. Less than two weeks . . . that's nothing.'

'It's possible,' Keenan speaks up from behind me. 'Tariq and I were discussing it—'

'If I want your opinion, or Tariq's,' Mazen says, 'I'll ask for it.'

Keenan's lips go thin, and I expect him to retort. But he just nods, and Mazen goes on.

'It's not enough time,' he muses. 'We'd need to take the whole damn prison. That's not something you can do unless . . .' He strokes his chin, deep in thought, before nodding. 'I have a new mission for you: find me a way into Blackcliff, a way no one else knows of. Do that and I'll be able to get your brother out.'

'I have a way!' Relief floods me. 'A hidden trail – it's how I came here.'

'No.' Mazen punctures my elation as quickly as it had ballooned. 'We need something . . . different.'

'More manoeuvrable,' Eran says. 'By a large group of men.'

'The catacombs run under Blackcliff,' Keenan says to Mazen. 'Some of those tunnels must lead to the school.'

'Perhaps.' Mazen clears his throat. 'We've searched down there before and found nothing of use. But you, Laia, will have an advantage, since you'll be looking from within Blackcliff itself.' He rests his fists on the table and leans towards me. 'We need something soon. A week, at most. I'll send Keenan to give you a specific date. Don't miss that meeting.'

'I'll find you an entrance,' I say. Izzi will know of something. One of the tunnels beneath Blackcliff must be unguarded. This, finally, is a task I know I can accomplish. 'But how will an entrance into Blackcliff help you break Darin out of the death cells?'

'A fair question,' Keenan says softly. He meets Mazen's gaze, and I'm surprised at the open hostility in the older man's face.

'I have a plan. That's all that any of you need to know.' Mazen nods at Keenan, who touches my arm and makes for the door of the tent, indicating I should follow.

For the first time since the raid, I feel light, as if just maybe I'll be able to accomplish what I set out to do. Outside the tent, the fire-thrower is midshow, and I spot Izzi in the crowd, clapping as the flame lights the night. I am almost giddy with hope until I see Keenan watching the dancers whirl, his brow furrowed.

'What's wrong?'

'Will you, uh . . .' He runs a hand through his hair, and I don't think I've ever seen him so agitated. 'Will you honour me with a dance?'

I'm not sure what I am expecting him to say, but it isn't that. I manage a nod, and then he's leading me to one of the dance stages. Across the stage, the tall Tribal boy from earlier is dancing with a dainty Tribeswoman who has a smile like lightning.

The fiddlers begin a swift, tempestuous tune, and Keenan takes my hip in one hand and my fingers in the other. At his touch, my skin comes alive as if warmed by the sun.

He's a little stiff, but he knows the steps well enough. 'You're not bad at this,' I say to him. Nan taught me all the old dances. I wonder who taught Keenan.

'That shocks you?'

I shrug. 'You don't strike me as the dancing type.'

'I'm not. Usually.' His dark gaze roams over me, as if he's trying to puzzle something out. 'I thought you'd be dead within a week, you know. You surprised me.' He finds my eyes. 'I'm not used to being surprised.'

The warmth of his body envelops me like a cocoon. I feel suddenly, deliciously breathless. But then he breaks eye contact, his fine features cold. The prickle of rejection tingles unpleasantly across my skin even as we continue to dance.

He's your handler, Laia. That's all. 'If it makes you feel any better, I thought I'd be dead within a week too.' I smile, and he gives me a quirk of his mouth in return. *He holds happiness at bay*, I realize. *He doesn't trust it.* 'Do you still think I'm going to fail?' I ask.

'I shouldn't have said that.' He glances down at me and then quickly away. 'But I didn't want to risk the men. Or – or you.' He mutters these words, and I lift my eyebrows in disbelief.

'Me?' I say. 'You threatened to shove me into a crypt five seconds after meeting me.'

Keenan's neck reddens, and he's still refusing to look at me. 'I'm sorry about that. I was a . . . a . . .'

'Jackass?' I offer helpfully.

He smiles in full this time, dazzling and all too brief. When he nods, it's almost shy, but moments later, he's serious again.

'When I said you would fail, I was trying to scare you. I didn't want you to go to Blackcliff.'

'Why?'

'Because I knew your father. No – that's not right.' He shakes his head. 'Because I *owe* your father.'

I stop mid-dance, only picking up again when someone jostles us.

Keenan takes that as his cue to continue. 'He picked me up off the streets when I was six. It was winter, and I was begging. Not very successfully, either. I was probably a few hours from dead. Your father brought me to camp, clothed me, fed me. He gave me a bed. A family. I'll never forget his face, or how he sounded when he asked me to come with him. Like I was doing him a favour instead of the other way around.'

I smile. That was my father, all right.

'The first time I saw your face in the light, you looked familiar. I couldn't place you, but I – I knew you. When you told us . . .' He shrugs.

'I don't agree with the old-timers about much,' he says, 'but I do agree that it's wrong to leave your brother in prison when we can help him – especially since it's our men who put him there, and especially since your parents did more for most of us than we can ever repay them for. But sending you to Blackcliff . . .' He scowls. 'That's poor repayment to your father. I know why Mazen did it. He needed to make both factions happy, and giving you a mission was the best way. But I still don't think it's right.'

Now I'm the one flushing, because this is the most he's ever spoken to me, and there's a vehemence in his face that's almost too much.

'I'm doing my best to survive,' I say lightly. 'Lest you waste away with guilt.'

'You *will* survive,' Keenan says. 'All of the rebels have lost someone. It's why they fight. But you and me? We're the ones who've lost everyone. Everything. We're alike, Laia. So you can trust me when I say that you're strong, whether you know it or not. You'll find that entrance. I know you will.'

They are the warmest words I've heard in so long. Our eyes lock again, but this time, Keenan doesn't look away. The rest of the world fades as we whirl. I say nothing, for the quiet between us is sweet and graceful and of our own choosing. And though he, too, doesn't speak, his dark eyes smoulder, telling me something I don't quite understand. Desire, low and dizzying, unfurls in my stomach. I want to hold this closeness to me as if it's a treasure. I don't want to release it. But then the music stops, and Keenan lets go of me.

'Get back safe.' His words are perfunctory, as if he's speaking to one of his fighters. I feel as if I've been doused with river water.

Without another word, he disappears into the crowd. The fiddlers begin a different tune, the dance picks up around me, and like a fool, I stare into the crush, knowing he won't come back but hoping anyway.

CHAPTER TWENTY-EIGHT

Elias

Sneaking into the Moon Festival is child's play.

I pocket my Mask – my face serves as my best disguise – and burgle riding clothes and a pack from a Tribal caravan. After that, I break into an apothecary for willadonna, a physician's staple that, when pressed into an oil, dilates the pupils wide enough for a Martial to pass as a Scholar or Tribesman for an hour or two.

Easy. Moments after putting the willadonna in, I'm swept into the heart of the festival with a tide of Scholars. I count twelve exits and identify twenty potential weapons before I realize what I'm doing and force myself to relax.

I pass food stalls and dance stages, jugglers and fire-eaters, acrobats, *Kehannis*, singers, and players. Musicians strum ouds and lyres, guided by the jubilant beat of drums.

I pull out of the crowds, suddenly disorientated. It's been so long since I've heard drums as music that I instinctively try to translate the beats into orders and find myself bewildered when I cannot.

When I finally am able to push the thudding to the back of my head, I'm bowled over by the colours and smells and unadulterated joy around me. Even as a Fiver, I never saw anything like this. Not in Marinn or the Tribal deserts, not even beyond the Empire, where woad-coated Barbarians danced beneath starlight for days, as if possessed.

A pleasant peacefulness steals over me. No one looks at me with loathing or fear. I don't have to watch my back or keep up the granite exterior.

I feel free.

For a few minutes I meander through the crowd, eventually making my way to the dance stages, where I've spotted Laia and Izzi. The two were surprisingly difficult to follow. While tracking them through the docks, I lost sight of Laia a few times altogether. But once in the Quarter, under the bright lights of the sky lanterns, I find the girls easily.

At first, I think to approach them, tell them who I am, and get them back to Blackcliff. But they look like I feel. Free. Happy. I can't bring myself to ruin it for them, not when their lives are ordinarily so dismal. So instead, I watch.

They both wear plain black silk dresses, which, while excellent for sneaking around and keeping slaves' cuffs hidden, don't blend so well into the rainbow plumage of the throng.

Izzi has let her blonde hair fall into her face, masking her eyepatch surprisingly well. She makes herself small, barely noticeable as she peeks out from the curtain of her hair.

Laia, on the other hand, would be noticeable pretty much anywhere. The high-necked dress she's wearing clings to her body in ways I find painfully unfair. Beneath the light of the sky lanterns, her skin glows the colour of warm honey. She holds her head high, the elegance of her neck heightened by the inky fall of her hair.

I want to touch that hair, smell it, run my hands through it, wrap it around my wrist and – *damn it, Veturius, get a hold of yourself. Stop staring.*

After I pull my eyes from her, I realize that I'm not the only one dumbstruck. Many of the young men around me sneak glances at her. She doesn't seem to notice, which, of course, makes her all the more intriguing.

And here you are, Elias, staring at her again. You twit. This time, my attention hasn't gone unobserved.

Izzi is watching me.

The girl might have only one eye, but I'm fairly certain she sees more than most. *Get out of here, Elias,* I tell myself. *Before she figures out why you look so damn familiar.*

Izzi leans over and whispers something into Laia's ear. I'm about to walk away when Laia looks up at me.

Her eyes are a dark jolt. I should look away. I should leave. She'll figure out who I am if she stares long enough. But I can't bring myself to move. For a heavy, heated moment, we are immobile, content to watch each other. *Skies, she's beautiful.* I smile at her, and the blush that rises on her face makes me feel oddly triumphant.

I want to ask her to dance. I want to touch her skin and talk to her and pretend that I'm just a normal Tribal boy and she's just a normal Scholar girl. *Stupid idea,* my mind warns. *She'll recognize you.*

So what? What would she do? Turn me in? She can't tell the Commandant she saw me here without incriminating herself too.

But while I'm still considering, a muscular, red haired boy comes up behind her. He touches her shoulder with a possessiveness in his eyes that I don't like. Laia, in return, stares at him as if no one else exists. Maybe she knew him before she became a slave. Maybe he's the reason she sneaked out. I scowl and look away. He's not bad-looking, I suppose, but he seems too grim to be any fun.

Also, he's shorter than me. Considerably shorter. Half a foot, at least.

Laia leaves with the redhead. Izzi gets up after a moment and follows.

'Looks like she's taken, lad.' A Tribal girl wearing a bright green dress covered in tiny circular mirrors sashays up to me, her dark hair done up in hundreds of braids. She speaks Sadhese, the Tribal tongue I grew up with. Against her dusky skin, her smile is a blinding flash of white, and I find myself returning it. 'I guess I'll have to do,' she says.

Without waiting for a reply, she pulls me to the dance floor, a remarkably bold thing for a Tribal girl to do. I look at her closely and realize that she's not a girl but a grown woman, perhaps a few years older than me. I eye her warily. Most Tribeswomen have a few children by their mid-twenties.

'Don't you have a husband who'll take off my head if he sees me dancing with you?' I respond in Sadhese.

'I don't. Why, are you interested in the position?' She runs a warm, slow finger down the skin of my chest and stomach, all the way to my belt. For the first time in a decade or so, I blush. Her wrist, I notice, is free of the Tribal braid tattoo that would mark her as married.

'What's your name and Tribe, lad?' she asks. She's a good dancer, and when I match her step for step, I can tell she's pleased.

'Ilyaas.' I haven't spoken my Tribal name in years. Grandfather Martialized it within about five minutes of meeting me. 'Ilyaas An-Saif.' As soon as I say it, I wonder if it's a mistake. The story of Mamie Rila's adopted son being taken to Blackcliff isn't well known – the Empire ordered Tribe Saif to keep it quiet. Still, Tribesmen love to talk.

But if the woman recognizes the name, she doesn't acknowledge it.

'I'm Afya Ara-Nur,' she says.

'Shadows and light,' I translate her first name and her Tribal name. 'Fascinating combination.'

'Mostly shadows, to be honest.' She leans towards me, and the smoulder in her brown eyes makes my heart beat a little faster. 'But keep that between us.'

I tilt my head as I look at her. I don't think I've ever met a Tribal woman with such sultry self-possession. Not even a *Kehanni*. Afya smiles a secret smile and asks me a few polite questions about Tribe Saif. How many weddings have we had in the past month? How many births? Will we journey to Nur for the Fall Gathering? Though the questions are suitable for a Tribal woman, I'm not fooled. Her simple words don't match the sharp intelligence of her eyes. Where is her family? Who is she, really?

As if sensing my suspicion, Afya tells me of her brothers: rugtraders based in Nur, here to sell their wares before bad weather closes off the mountain passes. As she speaks, I look around surreptitiously for these brothers of hers – Tribal men are notoriously protective of their unwed women, and I'm not looking for a fight. But though there are plenty of Tribesmen in the crowd, none of them so much as look at Afya.

We stay together for three dances. When the last is over, Afya curtsies and offers me a wooden coin with a sun on one side and clouds on the other.

'A gift,' she says. 'For honouring me with such fine dances, Ilyaas An Saif.'

'The honour is mine.' I'm surprised. Tribal tokens mark a favour owed – they're not offered lightly and are rarely given out by women.

As if she knows what I'm thinking, Afya stands on her tiptoes. She's so tiny, I have to stoop to hear her. 'If the heir of Gens Veturia should ever need a favour, *Ilyaas*, Tribe Nur will be honoured to be of service.' Immediately my body tenses, but she puts two fingers to her lips – the most binding of Tribal vows. 'Your secret is safe with Afya Ara-Nur.'

I raise an eyebrow. Whether she recognized the name Ilyaas or has seen me around Serra masked, I don't know. Whoever Afya Ara-Nur is, she's no simple Tribal woman. I nod in acknowledgment, and her white teeth flash.

'Ilyaas . . .' She drops down, no longer whispering. 'Your lady is free now – see.' I look over my shoulder. Laia has returned to the dance stage and is watching the redhead walk away from her. 'You must claim her for a dance,' Afya says. 'Go on!'

She gives me a small shove and disappears, the bells on her ankle tinkling. I stare after her for a moment, looking at the coin thoughtfully before pocketing it. Then I turn and make my way to Laia.

CHAPTER TWENTY-NINE

Laia

'May I?'

My mind is still on Keenan, and I am startled to find the Tribal boy standing beside me. For a moment I can only stare dumbly up at him.

'Would you like to dance?' he clarifies, offering a hand. The low hood shadows his eyes, but his lips curve into a smile.

'Um . . . I . . .' Now that I've given my report, Izzi and I should get back to Blackcliff. Dawn is still a few hours away, but I shouldn't risk getting caught.

'Ah.' The boy smiles. 'The redhead. Your . . . husband?'

'What? No!'

'Fiancé?'

'No. He's not—'

'Lover?' The boy lifts an eyebrow suggestively.

My face grows hot. 'He's my – my friend.'

'Then why worry?' The boy flashes a grin tinged with wickedness, and I find myself smiling in return. I glance over my shoulder at Izzi, talking to an earnest-looking Scholar. She laughs at something he says, her hands, for once, not straying to her eyepatch. When she catches me watching, she looks between the Tribal boy and me and waggles her eyebrows. My face goes hot again. One dance can't hurt; we can leave after.

The fiddlers are playing a lilting ballad, and at my nod, the boy takes my hands as confidently as if we've been friends for years. Despite his height and the width of his shoulders, he leads with a grace that is effortless and sensual all at once. When I peek at him, I find him staring down at me, a faint smile on his lips. My breath hitches, and I cast about for something to say.

'You don't sound like a Tribesman.' There. That's neutral enough. 'You've hardly got an accent.' Though his eyes are Scholar-dark, his face is all edges and hard lines. 'You don't really look like one either.'

'I can say something in Sadhese, if you like.' He drops his lips to my ear, and the spice of his breath sends a pleasant shiver through me. '*Menaya es poolan dila dekanala.*'

I sigh. No wonder Tribesmen can sell anything. His voice is warm and deep, like summer honey dripping off the comb.

'What—' My voice is hoarse, and I clear my throat. 'What does it mean?'

He gives me that smile again. 'I'd really have to show you.'

Up comes the blush. 'You're very bold.' I narrow my eyes. Where *have* I seen him before? 'Do you live around here? You seem familiar.'

'And you're calling me bold?'

I look away, realizing how my comment must sound. He chuckles in response, low and hot, and my breath catches again. I feel suddenly sorry for the girls in his tribe.

'I'm not from Serra,' he says. 'So. Who's the redhead?'

'Who's the brunette?' I challenge back.

'Ah, you were spying on me. That's very flattering.'

'I wasn't – I was – so were you!'

'It's all right,' he says reassuringly. 'I don't mind if you spy on me. The brunette is Afya of Tribe Nur. A new friend.'

'Just a friend? Looked to me like a bit more than that.'

'Maybe.' He shrugs. 'You never answered my question. About Red?'

'Red is a friend.' I mimic the boy's pensive tone. 'A new friend.'

The boy tosses his head back and laughs, a laugh that falls gentle and wild like desert rain. 'You live in the Quarter?' he asks.

I hesitate. I can't tell him I'm a slave. Slaves aren't allowed at the Moon Festival. Even a stranger to Serra will know that.

'Yes,' I say. 'I've lived in the Quarter for years with my grandparents And – and my brother. Our house isn't far from here.'

I don't know why I say it. Perhaps I think that by speaking the words, they will prove true, and I will turn to see Darin flirting with girls, Nan hawking her jams, and Pop dealing, ever gently, with overly worried patients.

The boy spins me around and then pulls me back into the circle of his arms, closer than before. His smell, spicy and heady and bizarrely familiar, makes me want to lean closer, to inhale. The hard planes of his muscles press into me, and when his hips brush mine, I nearly fumble my steps.

'And how do you fill your days?'

'Pop's a healer.' My voice falters at the lie, but since I can't very well tell him the truth, I rush on. 'My brother's his apprentice. Nan and I make jam. Mostly for the tribes.'

'Mmm. You strike me as a jam-maker.'

'Really? Why?'

He grins down at me. Up close, his eyes look almost black, especially shadowed as they are by long eyelashes. Right now, they shine with barely restrained mirth. 'Because you're so sweet,' he says in a mock-saccharine voice.

The mischief in his eyes makes me forget, for a too-brief second, that I am a slave and that my brother is in prison and that everyone else I love is dead. Laughter explodes out of me like a song, and my eyes blur and tear. A snort escapes, which sets my dance partner to laughing, which makes me laugh harder. Only Darin ever made me laugh like this. The release is foreign and familiar, like crying, but without the pain.

'What's your name?' I ask, as I wipe my face.

But instead of answering, he goes still, his head cocked as if he's listening for something. When I speak, he puts a finger to my lips. A moment later, his face hardens.

'We have to go,' he says. If he didn't look so dead serious, I'd think he was trying to get me to come with him to his camp. 'A raid – a Martial raid.'

Around us, dancers spin on obliviously. None of them has heard the boy. Drums thump, children scamper and giggle. All seems well.

Then he shouts it, loud enough that everyone can hear. 'Raid! Run!' His deep voice echoes across the dance stages, as commanding as a soldier's. The fiddlers stop mid-note, the drums cease. 'Martial raid! Get out! Go!'

A burst of light shatters the silence – one of the sky lamps has exploded – and another – and another. Arrows zing through the air – the Martials are shooting out the lights, hoping to leave the festival-goers in darkness so they can herd us easily.

'Laia!' Izzi is beside me, eye wide with panic. 'What's happening?'

'Some years the Martials let us have the festival. Other years they don't. We have to get out of here.' I grab Izzi's hand, wishing I'd never brought her, wishing I'd thought more of her safety.

Sabaa Tahir

'Follow me.' The boy doesn't wait for an answer, just pulls me to a nearby street, one that isn't yet flooded with people. He keeps to the walls, and I follow behind, holding tightly to Izzi and hoping it's not too late for us to escape.

When we reach the middle of the street, the Tribesman pulls us into a narrow, trash-strewn alley. Screams rend the air and steel flashes. Seconds later, festival-goers stream past, many falling out of sight, cut down as they run, like stalks of wheat beneath a sickle.

'We have to get out of the Quarter before they lock it down,' the Tribesman says. 'Anyone caught in the streets will be thrown into ghost wagons. You'll have to move fast. Can you do that?'

'We – we can't go with you.' I pull my hand from the boy's. He'll head for his caravan, but Izzi and I will find no safety there. Once his people see we're slaves, they'll turn us over to the Martials, who will turn us over to the Commandant. And then . . .

'We don't live in the Quarter. I'm sorry I lied.' I back away, pulling Izzi with me, knowing that the quicker we go our separate ways, the better it will be for all concerned. The Tribesman shoves back his hood to reveal a head of close-cropped black hair.

'I know that,' he says. And though his voice is the same, there's something subtly different about him. A menace, a power in his body that wasn't there before. Without thinking, I take another step back. 'You have to go to Blackcliff,' he says.

For a moment, his words don't register. When they do, my knees go weak. He's a spy. Did he see my slaves' cuffs? Did he overhear me talking to Mazen? Will he turn Izzi and me in?

Then Izzi gasps. 'A-aspirant Veturius?'

When Izzi says his name, it's like lamplight flooding a murky chamber. His features, his height, his easy grace – everything makes perfect sense – and yet no sense at all. What is an Aspirant doing at a Moon Festival? Why was he trying to pass as a Tribesman? Where's his damned mask?

'Your eyes . . .' *They were dark*, I think wildly. *I'm sure they were dark.*

'Willadonna,' he says. 'Broadens the pupils. Look, we should really—'

'You're spying on me for the Commandant,' I burst out. It's the only explanation. Keris Veturia ordered her son to follow me, to see what I know. But if that's the case, he probably overheard me talking to Mazen and Keenan. He has more than enough information to turn me in for treason. Why dance with me? Why laugh and joke with me? Why warn the festival-goers about the raid?

'I wouldn't spy for her if it meant my life.'

'Then why are you here? There's no possible reason—'

'There is, but it's not one I can explain right now.' Veturius looks to the streets, then adds, 'We can argue about it if you like. Or we can get the hell out of here.'

He's a Mask, and I should look away from him. I should show my subservience. But I can't stop staring. It's a jolt, his face. A few minutes ago, I thought he was beautiful. I thought his words in Sadhese were hypnotic. I danced with a Mask. A bleeding, burning Mask.

Veturius peers out of the alleyway and shakes his head. 'The legionnaires will have sealed off the Quarter by the time we get to one of the gates. We'll have to take the tunnels and hope they haven't sealed those off.' He moves confidently to a grate in the alleyway, as if he knows exactly where we are in the Quarter.

When I don't follow, he makes a sound of irritation. 'Look, I'm not in league with her,' he says. 'In fact, if she finds out I came here, she'll probably flay me. Slowly. But that's nothing compared to what she'll do to you if you're caught in this raid or if she discovers you missing from Blackcliff at dawn. If you want to live, you'll have to trust me. Now move.'

Izzi does as he says, and reluctantly, I follow, my whole body rebelling at the thought of putting my life in the hands of a Mask.

Almost as soon as we drop down into the tunnel, Veturius pulls fatigues and boots from the bag across his chest and begins tearing off his Tribal clothes. My face burns, and I turn away, but not before seeing the chilling map of silvery scars across his back.

Seconds later, he walks past us, masked once more and gesturing for us to follow. Izzi and I run to keep up with his long strides. He moves stealthily as a cat, silent but for a word of encouragement here and there.

We make our way north and east through the catacombs, stopping only to avoid passing Martial patrols. Veturius never falters. When we reach a pile of skulls blocking the passage ahead, he moves a few aside and helps us through the opening. When the tunnel we're in narrows to a locked grate, he plucks two pins from my hair and picks the lock in seconds. Izzi and I exchange a glance at that – his sheer competence is unnerving.

I've no idea how much time has passed. At least two hours. It must be nearly dawn. We won't make it back on time. The Commandant will catch us. Skies, I shouldn't have brought Izzi. I shouldn't have put her at risk.

My wound chafes against my dress until it's bleeding. It is only a few days old, and the infection has lingered. The pain combined with my fear makes me light-headed.

Veturius slows when he sees my face. 'We're almost there,' he says. 'Do you need me to carry you?'

I shake my head vehemently. I don't want to be close to him again. I don't want to breathe in his smell or feel the warmth of his skin.

Eventually, we stop. Low voices mutter from around a corner ahead of us, and a flickering torch deepens the shadows the light can't reach.

'All the underground entrances to Blackcliff are guarded,' Veturius whispers. 'This one has four guards. If they see you, they'll sound an alarm, and these tunnels will be swarming with soldiers.' He looks between Izzi and me to make sure we understand before going on. 'I'm going to draw them off. When I say *docks*, you'll have a minute to get around this corner, up the ladder, and out the grate. When I say *Madame Moh's*, it means you're nearly out of time. Shut the grate behind you. You'll be in Blackcliff's main cellar. Wait for me there.'

Veturius disappears into the gloom of a tunnel just behind us. A few minutes later, we hear what sounds like drunken singing. I peer around the corner to see the guards elbowing each other and grinning. Two leave to investigate. Veturius's voice is convincingly slurred, and there's a loud crash followed by a curse and burst of laughter. One of the soldiers who's gone to investigate calls to the other two. They disappear. I lean forward, preparing to run. *Come on. Come on.*

Finally, Veturius's voice drifts down the tunnels:

'—dow' by the docksh—'

Izzi and I bolt for the ladder, and in seconds, we've reached the grate. I'm congratulating myself on our speed when Izzi, perched above me, lets out a strangled cry.

'I can't get it open!'

I climb past her, grab the grate, and shove it upward. It doesn't budge.

The guards get closer. I hear another loud crash and then Veturius saying, 'The best girls are at Madame Moh's, they really know how to—'

'Laia!' Izzi looks frantically towards the fast-approaching torch-light. *Ten burning hells*. With a muffled grunt, I throw my whole body towards the grate, wincing at the pain lancing through my torso. The grate creaks open unwillingly, and I practically shove Izzi through before leaping up myself, shutting it just as the soldiers emerge into the tunnel below.

Izzi takes cover behind a barrel, and I join her. A few seconds later, Veturius climbs out of the grate, giggling drunkenly. Izzi and I exchange another glance, and as preposterous as it is, I find I'm suppressing my laughter.

'Thanksh, boys,' Veturius calls down into the tunnel. He slams the grate shut, spots us, and holds a finger to his lips. The soldiers can still hear us through the slats in the grate.

'Aspirant Veturius,' Izzi whispers. 'What will happen to you if the Commandant finds out you've helped us?'

'She won't find out,' Veturius says. 'Unless you plan on telling her, which I don't suggest. Come on, I'll take you back to your quarters.'

We slip up the cellar stairs and out to Blackcliff's funereally quiet grounds. I shiver, although the night's not cold. It's still dark, but the eastern sky pales, and Veturius speeds his gait. As we hurry across the grass, I stumble, and he is beside me, steadying me, his warmth seeping into my skin.

'All right?' he asks.

My feet ache, my head pounds, and the Commandant's mark burns like fire. But more powerful is the tingling enveloping my entire body at the Mask's closeness. *Danger!* My skin seems to scream. *He's dangerous!*

'Fine.' I jerk away from him. 'I'm fine.'

As we walk, I sneak glances at him. With his mask on and the walls of Blackcliff rising around him, Veturius is every inch the Martial soldier. Yet I can't reconcile the image before me with the handsome Tribesman I danced with. All that time, he knew who I was. He knew I was lying about my family. And though it's ridiculous to care what a Mask thinks, I feel suddenly ashamed of those lies.

We reach the servants' corridor, and Izzi breaks away from us.

'Thank you,' she says to Veturius. Guilt washes over me. She'll never forgive me, after what she's been through.

'Izzi.' I touch her arm. 'I'm sorry. If I'd known about the raid, I never—'

'Are you joking?' Izzi says. Her eye darts to Veturius standing behind me, and she smiles, a blaze of white that startles me with its beauty. 'I wouldn't have traded this for anything. Good night, Laia.'

I stare after her, open-mouthed, as she disappears down the hallway and into her room. Veturius clears his throat. He's watching me with a strange, almost apologetic expression in his eyes.

'I – uh – have something for you.' He pulls a bottle from his pocket. 'Sorry I didn't get it to you earlier. I was . . . indisposed.' I take the bottle, and when our fingers touch, I pull away quickly. It's the bloodroot serum. I'm surprised he remembered.

'I'll just—'

'Thank you,' I say at the same time. We both fall silent. Veturius rubs a hand through his hair, but a second later his entire body goes still, a deer that's heard the hunter.

'What—' I gasp when his arms come around me, sudden and hard. He pushes me to the wall, heat flaring from his hands and tingling across my skin, sending my heart into a feverish beat. My own reaction to him, confusion tumbled with head-spinning want, shocks me into silence. *What is wrong with you, Laia?* Then his hands tighten on my back, as if in warning, and he dips his head low to my ear, his breath a bare whisper.

'Do what I tell you, when I tell you. Or you're dead.'

I knew it. How could I have trusted him? Stupid. So stupid.

'Push me away,' he says. 'Fight me.'

I shove at him, not needing his encouragement.

'Get away from—'

'Don't be like that.' His voice is louder now, sleek and menacing and devoid of anything resembling decency. 'You didn't mind before—'

'Leave her, soldier,' a bored, wintery voice says.

My blood goes cold, and I twist away from Veturius. There, detaching from the kitchen door like a wraith, stands the Commandant. How long has she been watching us? Why is she even awake?

The Commandant steps into the corridor and surveys me dispassionately, ignoring Veturius.

'So that's where you'd got to.' Her pale hair is loose around her shoulders, her robe pulled tight. 'I just came down. Rang the bell for water five minutes ago.'

'I – I—'

'I suppose it was only a matter of time. You are a pretty thing.' She doesn't reach for her crop or threaten to kill me. She doesn't even seem angry. Just irritated.

'Soldier,' she says. 'Back to the barracks with you. You've had her for long enough.'

'Commandant, sir.' Veturius breaks away from me with seeming reluctance. I try to squirm away from him, but he keeps a proprietary arm slung around my hips 'You sent her to her quarters for the night. I assumed you were done with her.'

'Veturius?' The Commandant, I realize, hadn't recognized him in the dark. She hadn't cared enough to give him a second look. Her eyes shift to her son in disbelief. 'You? And a slave?'

'I was bored.' He shrugs. 'I've been stuck in the infirmary for days.'

My face goes hot. I understand, now, why he put his hands on me, why he told me to fight him. He is trying to protect me from the Commandant. He must have sensed her presence. She will have no way of proving I haven't spent the last few hours with Veturius. And since students rape slaves all the time, neither he nor I will be punished.

But it's still humiliating.

'You expect me to believe you?' The Commandant cocks her head. She senses the lie – she smells it. 'You've never touched a slave in your life.'

'With all due respect, sir, that's because the first thing you do when you get a new slave is take her eye out.' Veturius tangles his fingers in my hair, and I yelp. 'Or carve up her face. But *this* one' – he yanks my head towards his, a warning in his eyes when he glances down at me – 'is still intact. Mostly.'

'Please.' I drop my voice. If this is going to work, I need to play along, disgusting as it is. 'Tell him to leave me alone.'

'Get out, Veturius.' The Commandant's eyes glitter. 'Next time find a kitchen drudge to entertain you. The girl is mine.'

Veturius gives his mother a short salute before releasing me and sauntering through the gate without so much as a backward glance.

The Commandant looks me over, as if for signs of what she thinks just happened. She jerks my chin up. I pinch myself on the leg hard enough to draw blood, and my eyes fill with tears.

'Would it have been better if I'd cut your face like Cook's?' she murmurs. 'Beauty's a curse when one lives among men. You might have thanked me for it.'

She runs a fingernail across my cheek, and I shudder.

'Well. . . .' She lets me go and walks back to the kitchen door with a smile, a twist of her mouth that is all bitterness and no mirth. The spirals of her strange tattoo catch the moonlight. 'There's time yet for that.'

CHAPTER THIRTY

Elias

For three days after the Moon Festival, Helene avoids me. She ignores knocks on her door, leaves the mess hall when I appear, and begs off when I approach her head on. When we're paired together in training, she attacks me as if I'm Marcus. When I speak to her, she goes suddenly deaf.

I let it go at first, but by the third day, I'm sick of it. On my way to combat training, I'm concocting a plan to confront her – something involving a chair and rope and maybe a gag so she has no choice but to listen to me – when Cain appears beside me as suddenly as a ghost. My scim is half-drawn before I realize who it is.

'Skies, Cain. Don't do that.'

'Greetings, Aspirant Veturius. Wonderful weather.' The Augur looks up at the hot blue sky admiringly.

'Yeah, if you're not training with double scims under the baking sun,' I mutter. It's not even noon, and I'm so covered in sweat that I've given up and taken off my shirt. If Helene was speaking to me, she'd frown and say it's not regulation. I'm too hot to care.

'You are healed from the Second Trial?' Cain asks.

'No thanks to you.' The words are out before I can stop them, but I don't feel particularly regretful. Multiple attempts on my life have taken a toll on my manners.

'The Trials are not meant to be easy, Elias. That is why they are called the Trials.'

'I hadn't noticed.' I speed up, hoping Cain will piss off. He doesn't.

'I bring you a message,' he says. 'The next Trial will take place in seven days.'

At least we get some warning this time. 'What's it going to be?' I ask. 'Public flogging? A night locked in a trunk with a hundred vipers?'

'Combat against a formidable foe,' Cain says. 'Nothing you can't handle.'

'What foe? What's the catch?' No way the Augur will tell me what I'm up against without leaving something essential out. It's going to be a sea of wraiths we're fighting. Or jinn. Or some other beastie they've woken from the darkness.

'We haven't woken anything from the darkness that wasn't already awake,' Cain says.

I bite back a response. If he picks my mind again, I swear, I'll shove this blade through him, Augur or not.

'It wouldn't do any good, Elias.' He smiles, almost sadly, then nods to the field, where Hel is training. 'I ask that you pass the message along to Aspirant Aquilla.'

'As Aquilla isn't speaking with me, that might be a bit difficult.'

'I'm sure you'll find a way.'

He drifts off, leaving me more ill-tempered than before.

When Hel and I argue, we usually patch things up in a few hours – a day at most. Three days is a record for us. Worse, I've never seen her lose her temper the way she did three nights ago. Even in battle, she is always cool, controlled.

But she's been different the past few weeks. I've known it, though like a fool I've tried not to see it. But I can't ignore her behaviour anymore. It has to do with that spark between us, that attraction. Either we crush it or we do something about it. And I'm thinking that while the latter might be more enjoyable, it will create complications neither of us needs.

When did Helene change? She has always been in control of every emotion, every desire. She's never shown interest in any of her comrades, and, other than Leander, none of us is stupid enough to try to start anything with her.

So what happened between us that changed things? I think back to the first time I noticed her acting strange: the morning she found me in the catacombs. I'd tried to distract her by leering. I'd done it without thinking, hoping to keep her from finding my pack. I figured she'd just think it was me being male.

Is that what did it? That one look? Has she been acting so strangely because she thinks I want her, and so she feels like she has to want me back?

If that's the case, then I need to clear things up with her straightaway. I'll tell her that it was a fluke. That I didn't mean anything by it.

Will she accept my apology? *Only if you grovel enough.*

Fine. It will be worth it. If I want my freedom, I *have* to win the next Trial. In the first two, Hel and I depended on each other for survival. The third will probably be the same. I need her on my side.

I find Hel on the combat field sparring with Tristas while a Combat Centurion looks on. The boys and I tease Tristas for constantly mooning over his fiancée, but he's one of the finest swordsmen at Blackcliff, clever and cat-swift. He waits for Helene to slip up, taking note of the aggression in her strokes. But her defence is as impenetrable as the walls of Kauf. Minutes after I arrive at the field, she's thrown off Tristas's attack and jabbed his heart.

'Greetings, oh holy Aspirant,' Tristas calls out when he sees me. At Helene's stiffening shoulders, he glances between us and makes a quick departure. Along with Faris and Dex, Tristas has tried repeatedly to figure out what went wrong between Helene and me on the night of the party – which neither of us attended. But Hel's been as silent as I have, and they've given up, instead grunting to one another pointedly when she and I beat each other down on the battlefield.

'Aquilla,' I call to her as she sheathes her scims. 'I need to talk to you.'

Silence.

Fine, then. 'Cain said to tell you the next Trial is in seven days.'

I head to the armoury, unsurprised when I hear her footsteps trailing.

'Well, what is it?' She grabs my shoulder and pulls me around. 'What's the Trial?'

Her face is flushed, and her eyes flash. *Skies, she's pretty when she's angry.*

The thought surprises me, accompanied as it is by a pulse of fierce desire. *It's Helene, Elias. Helene.*

'Combat,' I say. 'We'll be up against a "formidable foe".'

'Right,' she says. 'Good.' But she doesn't move, only glares at me, unaware that the tendrils of hair that have escaped her braid make the glare much less intimidating than she'd like.

'Hel, look, I know you're mad, but—'

'Oh, go put on a shirt.' She stalks away, muttering about twits who flaunt regulation. I stifle an angry retort. Why is she so damn stubborn?

As I enter the armoury, I run straight into Marcus, who shoves me into the doorframe. For once, Zak's not with him.

'Your whore's still not talking to you?' he says. 'Not spending time with you either, is she? Avoiding you . . . avoiding the other boys . . . *alone* . . .' He looks speculatively at Helene's retreating back, and I go for my scim, but Marcus is already holding a dagger to my stomach.

'She belongs to me, you know. I dreamt it.' His calmness chills me more than any boasting could. 'One of these days, I'll find her, and you won't be around,' he says. 'And I'll make her mine.'

'You stay away from her. Anything happens to her, I'll slit you open from your neck to your sorry—'

'It's always threats with you,' Marcus says. 'You never actually *do* anything. Not surprising for a traitor whose mask hasn't even melded yet.' He leans forward. 'The mask knows you're weak, Elias. It knows you don't belong. That's why it's still not a part of you. That's why I should kill you.'

His dagger cuts into my stomach, releasing a trickle of blood. One thrust, one pull upward, and he could gut me like a fish. I shake with anger. I'm at his mercy, and I hate him for it.

'But the Centurions are watching.' Marcus's gaze flicks to our left, where the Combat Centurion is fast approaching. 'And I'd rather kill you slow.' He strolls away lazily, saluting the Combat Centurion as he passes.

Furious with myself, with Helene, with Marcus, I shove open the armoury door and go straight to the heavy weaponry rack, settling on a tri-flanged mace. I swing it through the air and pretend I'm taking off Marcus's head.

When I get back out to the field, the Combat Centurion pairs me with Helene. My rage spills out of me, tainting every move. Helene, on the other hand, channels her fury into a steely efficiency.

She sends my mace flying, and only a few minutes later, I'm forced to yield. Disgusted, she stalks away to battle her next opponent while I'm still scrambling to my feet.

From the other side of the field, I see Marcus watching – not me but her, his eyes gleaming, his fingers caressing a dagger.

Faris gives me a hand up, and I call Dex and Tristas over, grimacing at the bruises Helene's gifted me. 'Is Aquilla still avoiding you?'

Dex nods. 'Like the pox.'

'Keep an eye on her anyway,' I say. 'Even if she wants you to stay away. Marcus knows she's avoiding us. It's only a matter of time before he decides to attack.'

'You do know that she'll kill us if she catches us playing guard dog,' Faris says.

'Which do you prefer,' I say, 'angry Helene or beaten Helene?'

Faris goes pale, but he and Dex vow to keep an eye on her, glaring at Marcus as they leave the field.

'Elias.' Tristas lingers, looking alarmingly awkward. 'If you like, we can discuss . . . uh . . .' He scratches his tattoo. 'Well, it's just I've had some ups and downs with Aelia. So with Helene, if you want to talk about it . . .'

Ah. Right. 'Helene and I aren't – we're just friends.'

Tristas sighs. 'You know she's in love with you, right?'

'She's – not – no–' I can't seem to make my mouth work, so I just close it and look at him in mute appeal. Any second, he's going to grin and slap me on the back. He's going to say, 'Just kidding! Ha, Veturius, the look on your face . . .'

Any second.

'Trust me,' Tristas says. 'I have four older sisters. And I'm the only one of the guys who's been in a relationship that's lasted longer than a month. I can see it every time she looks at you. She's in love with you. She has been for a while.'

'But she's Helene,' I say stupidly. 'I mean – come on, we've all thought about Helene.' Tristas nods gamely. 'But she doesn't think of us. She's seen us at our worst.' I think of the Trial of Courage, of my sobs when I realized that she was real and not a hallucination. 'Why would she—'

'Who knows, Elias,' Tristas says. 'She can kill a man with a twist of her hand, she's a demon with a sword, and she can drink most of us under the table. And because of all that, maybe we've forgotten that she's a girl.'

'I have *not* forgotten that Helene's a girl.'

'I'm not talking about physically. I'm talking about in her head. Girls think about things like this differently than we do. She's in love with you. And whatever happened between you two is because of it. I promise you.'

It's not true, my head tells me with the zeal of denial. *Just lust. Not love.*

Shut it, head, my heart says. I know Helene like I know fighting, like I know killing. I know the smell of her fear and the rawness of blood against her skin. I know that she flares her nostrils very slightly when she lies and that she puts her hands between her knees when she sleeps. I know the beautiful parts. The ugly parts.

Her anger at me is from a deep place. A dark place. A place she doesn't admit she has. The day I looked at her so thoughtlessly, I made her think that maybe I had that place too. That maybe she wasn't alone in that place.

'She's my best friend,' I say to Tristas. 'I can't go down that road with her.'

'No, you can't.' There's sympathy in Tristas's eyes. He knows what she means to me. 'And that's the problem.'

CHAPTER THIRTY-ONE

Laia

My sleep is fitful and scanty, haunted by the Commandant's threat. *Time enough for that yet.* When I wake before dawn, scraps of nightmare stay with me: my face carved and branded; my brother hanging from the gallows, fair hair fluttering in the wind.

Think of something else. I close my eyes and see Keenan, remembering how he asked me to dance, so shy and unlike himself. That fire in his eyes as he spun me around – I thought it must mean something. But he left so abruptly. Is he all right? Did he escape the raid? Did he hear Veturius shout out the warning?

Veturius. I hear his laugh and smell the spice of his body, and I have to force those sensations away and replace them with the truth. He's a Mask. He's the enemy.

Why did he help me? He risked imprisonment by doing so – worse than that, if rumours about the Black Guard and their purges are true. I can't believe he did it solely for my benefit. A lark, then? Some sick Martial game I don't yet understand?

Don't stick around to find out, Laia, Darin whispers in my head. *Get me out of here.*

Footsteps shuffle in the kitchen – Cook making breakfast. If the old woman is up, Izzi won't be far behind. I dress quickly, hoping to get to her before Cook sets us to our daily drudgery. Izzi will know of a secret entrance to the school.

But Izzi, it turns out, left early on an errand for Cook.

'She won't be back until noon,' Cook informs me. 'Not that it's your concern.' The old woman points to a black folio on the table. 'Commandant says you're to take that folio to Spiro Teluman first thing, before attending to your other duties.'

I stifle a groan. I'll just have to wait to talk to Izzi.

When I get to Teluman's shop, I'm surprised to see the door open, the forge fire burning. Sweat streams down the smith's face and into his burn-scarred jerkin as he hammers at a glowing chunk of steel. Beside him stands a Tribal girl clad in sheer, rose-coloured robes, their hems embroidered with tiny round mirrors. The girl is murmuring something I can't hear over the ringing of the hammer. Teluman nods a greeting at me but continues his conversation with the girl.

As I watch them speak, I realize she's older than I first thought, perhaps in her mid-twenties. Her silky black hair, shot through with fiery red, is woven into thin, intricate braids, and her dainty face is vaguely familiar. Then I recognize her: she danced with Veturius at the Moon Festival.

She shakes Teluman's hand, offers him a sack of coins, and then makes her way out the forge's back door with an appraising glance in my direction. Her eyes linger on my slaves' cuffs, and I look away.

'Her name's Afya Ara-Nur,' Spiro Teluman says when the woman is gone. 'She's the only female chieftain among the Tribes. One of the most dangerous women you'll ever meet. Also one of the cleverest. Her tribe carries weapons to the Marinn branch of the Scholars' Resistance.'

288

'Why are you telling me this?' What's wrong with him? That's the type of knowledge that will get me killed.

Spiro shrugs. 'Your brother made most of the weapons she's taking. I thought you'd want to know where they're going.'

'No, I *don't* want to know.' Why doesn't he understand? 'I want nothing to do with . . . whatever it is you're doing. All I want is for things to go back to the way they were. Before you made my brother your apprentice. Before the Empire took him because of it.'

'You might as well wish away that scar.' Teluman nods to where my cloak has fallen open, revealing the Commandant's K. Hastily, I pull the garment closed.

'Things will never go back to the way they were.' He flips the metal he's shaping with a pair of tongs and continues hammering. 'If the Empire freed Darin tomorrow, he'd come here and start making weapons again. His destiny is to rise, to help his people overthrow their oppressors. And mine is to help him do it.'

I'm so angry at Teluman's presumption that I don't think before I speak. 'So now you're the saviour of the Scholars, after spending years creating the weapons that have destroyed us?'

'I live with my sins every day.' He throws down the tongs and turns to me 'I live with the guilt. But there are two kinds of guilt, girl: the kind that drowns you until you're useless, and the kind that fires your soul to purpose. The day I made my last weapon for the Empire, I drew a line in my mind. I'd never make a Martial blade again. I'd never have Scholar blood on my hands again. I won't cross that line. I'll die before I cross it.'

His hammer is clenched in his hand like a weapon, his hard-angled face lit with tightly controlled fervour. So this is why Darin agreed to be his apprentice. There's something of our mother in this man's ferocity, something of our father in the way he carries himself. His passion is true and contagious. When he speaks, I want to believe.

He opens his hand. 'You have a message?'

I give him the folio. 'You said you'd die before you crossed that line. And yet you're making a weapon for the Commandant.'

'No.' Spiro peruses the folio. 'I'm *pretending* to make a weapon for her so she'll keep sending you with messages. As long as she thinks my interest in you will get her a Teluman blade, she won't do you any irreparable harm. I might even be able to persuade her to sell you to me. Then I'll break those damned things off' – he nods to my cuffs – 'and set you free.' At my surprise, Spiro looks away, as if embarrassed. 'It's the least I can do for your brother.'

'He's going to be executed,' I whisper. 'In a week.'

'Executed?' Spiro says. 'Not possible. He'd still be in Central Prison if he was to be executed, and he was moved from there. Where, I don't yet know.' Teluman's eyes narrow. 'How did you learn he was to be executed? Who have you been talking to?'

I don't answer. Darin might have trusted the smith, but I can't bring myself to. Maybe Teluman really is a revolutionary. Or maybe he's a very convincing spy.

'I have to go,' I say. 'Cook's expecting me back.'

'Laia, wait—'

I don't hear the rest. I'm already out the door.

As I walk back to Blackcliff, I try to push his words from my head, but I can't. Darin's been moved? When? Where? Why didn't Mazen mention it?

How is my brother? Is he suffering? What if the Martials have broken his bones? Skies, his fingers? What if—

No more. Nan once said that there's hope in life. If Darin's alive, nothing else matters. If I can get him out, the rest can be fixed.

My path back takes me through Execution Square, where the gibbets are conspicuously empty. No one has been hung for days. Keenan said the Martials are saving the executions for the new Emperor. Marcus and his brother will enjoy such a spectacle. What if one of the others wins? Would Aquilla smile as innocent men and women twist at the end of a rope? Would Veturius?

Ahead of me, the crowd slows to a standstill as a Tribal caravan twenty wagons long ambles across the square. I turn to go around it, but everyone else has the same idea, resulting in a mess of swearing, shoving, mired bodies.

And then, amid the chaos: 'You're all right.'

I recognize his voice instantly. He wears a Tribal vest, but even with the hood up, his hair trickles out like a tongue of flame.

'After the raid,' Keenan says, 'I wasn't sure. I've been watching the square all day, hoping you'd come through.'

'You got out too.'

'All of us did. Just in time. The Martials took more than a hundred Scholars last night.' He cocks his head. 'Your friend escaped?'

'My . . . ah . . .' If I say Izzi's all right, I'm as good as admitting that I brought her with me to an information drop. Keenan regards me with his unflinching stare. He'll know a lie a mile away.

'Yes,' I say. 'She escaped.'

'She knows you're a spy.'

'She's helped me. I know I shouldn't have let her, but—'

'But it just happened. Your brother's life is at risk here, Laia. I understand.' A fight breaks out behind us, and Keenan rests a hand on my back, turning me so he's between me and the flying punches. 'Mazen's set a meeting eight days from now, in the morning. Tenth bell. Come here, to the square. If you need to meet before, wear a grey scarf over your hair and wait on the south side of the square. Someone will be watching for you.'

'Keenan.' I think of what Teluman said about Darin. 'Are you sure my brother's in Central Prison? That he's to be executed? I heard he's been moved—'

'Our spies are reliable,' Keenan says. 'Mazen would know if he'd been transferred.'

My neck prickles. Something's not right. 'What aren't you telling me?'

Keenan rubs the stubble on his face, and my unease swells. 'It's nothing you need to worry about, Laia.'

Ten hells. I turn his face towards me, forcing him to meet my eyes. 'If it affects Darin,' I say, 'I need to worry about it. Is it Mazen? Has he changed his mind?'

'No.' Keenan's tone does little to reassure me. 'I don't think so. But he's been . . . strange. Quiet about this mission. Hiding the spy reports.'

I try to justify this. Perhaps Mazen is worried the mission will be compromised. When I say as much, Keenan shakes his head.

'It's not just that,' he says. 'I can't confirm it, but I think he's planning something else. Something big. Something that doesn't involve Darin. But how can we save Darin and take on another mission? We don't have enough men.'

'Ask him,' I say. 'You're his second. He trusts you.'

'Ah.' Keenan grimaces. 'Not exactly.'

Has he fallen out of favour? I don't get a chance to ask. Ahead of us, the caravan lurches out of the way, and the pent-up crowd surges forward. In the crush, my cloak rips free. Keenan's eyes drop to the scar. It's so prominent, so red and hideous, I think miserably. How could he not look?

'Ten bleeding hells. What happened?'

'The Commandant punished me. A few days ago.'

'I didn't know, Laia.' All his aloofness dissolves as he stares at the scar. 'Why didn't you tell me?'

'Would you have cared?' His eyes jerk to mine, surprised. 'Anyway, it's nothing compared to what it could have been. She took Izzi's eye. And you should see what she did to Cook. Her entire face . . .' I shudder. 'I know it's ugly . . . horrible—'

'No.' He says the word like it's an order. 'Don't think that. It means you survived her. It means you're brave.'

The crowd moves around me, past me. People elbow and mutter at us. But then it all fades, because Keenan has taken my hand and is looking from my eyes to my lips and back up in a way that needs no translation. I notice a freckle, perfect and round, at the corner of his mouth. A slow warmth uncurls low in my body as he pulls me to him.

Then a leather-clad Mariner shoves past, breaking us apart, and Keenan's mouth twitches in a brief, rueful smile. He squeezes my hand once. 'I'll see you soon.'

He melts into the crowd, and I hurry back towards Blackcliff. If Izzi knows of an entrance, I still have time to see it for myself and head back here to pass along the information. The Resistance can get Darin out, and I'll be done with all of this. No more scars or whippings. No more terror and fear. *And maybe*, a quiet part of me whispers, *I'll get more than just a few moments with Keenan.*

I find Izzi in the back courtyard, scrubbing sheets beside the water pump.

'I only know of the hidden trail, Laia,' Izzi says to my question. 'And even that's not secret. Just so dangerous that most people don't use it.'

I vigorously crank water from the pump, using the squeal of metal to drown out our voices. Izzi's mistaken. She has to be.

'What about the tunnels? Or . . . do you think one of the other slaves will know something?'

'You saw how it was last night. We only got through the tunnels because of Veturius. As for the other slaves, it's risky. Some of them spy for the Commandant.'

No – no – no. What just minutes ago seemed like a wealth of time – eight whole days – is no time at all. Izzi hands me a freshly washed sheet, and I hang it on the line with impatient hands. 'A map, then. There must be a map to this place somewhere.'

At this, Izzi brightens. 'Maybe,' she says. 'In the Commandant's office—'

'The only place you'll find a map of Blackcliff,' a raspy voice intrudes, 'is in the Commandant's head. And I don't think you want to go rummaging around in there.'

I gape like a fish as Cook, as silent-footed as her mistress, materializes from behind the sheet I've just hung up.

Izzi jumps at Cook's sudden appearance, but then, to my shock, she stands and crosses her arms. 'There must be something,' she says to the old woman. 'How'd she get the map in her head? She must have a point of reference.'

'When she became Commandant,' Cook says, 'the Augurs gave her a map to memorize and burn. That's how it's always been done at Blackcliff.' At the surprise on my face, she snorts. 'When I was younger and even stupider than you, I kept my eyes and ears open. Now my head's filled with useless knowledge that does no one any good.'

'But it's not useless,' I say. 'You must know of a secret way into the school—'

'I don't.' The scars on Cook's face are livid against her skin. 'And if I did, I wouldn't tell you.'

'My brother's in Central's death cells. He's going to be executed in days, and if I don't find a secret way into Blackcliff—'

'Let me ask you a question, girl,' Cook says. 'It's the Resistance who says your brother's in prison, the Resistance who says he's going to be executed, right? But how do they *know*? And how do *you* know they're telling the truth? Your brother might be dead. Even if he is in Central's death cells, the Resistance will never get him out. A blind, deaf stone could tell you that.'

'If he was dead, they'd have told me.' Why can't she just help me? 'I trust them, all right? I *have* to trust them. Besides, Mazen says he has a plan—'

'Bah.' Cook sneers. 'The next time you see this Mazen, you ask him where, exactly, your brother is in Central. What cell? You ask him how he knows and who his spies are. Ask him how having an entrance to Blackcliff will help him break into the most fortified prison in the south. After he answers, we'll see if you still trust the bastard.'

'Cook—' Izzi speaks up, but the old woman whirls on her.

'Don't you start. You've got no idea what you're getting into. The only reason I haven't turned her in to the Commandant,' Cook practically spits at me, 'is because of you. As it is, I can't trust that Slave-Girl won't give up your name to make the Commandant go easy on her.'

'Izzi . . .' I look to my friend. 'No matter what the Commandant did, I would never—'

'You think that carving on your heart makes you an expert in pain?' Cook says. 'Ever been tortured, girl? Ever been tied to a table while hot coals burned into your throat? Ever had your face carved up with a dull knife while a Mask poured salt water into your wounds?'

I stare at her stonily. She knows the answer.

'You can't know if you'd betray Izzi,' Cook says, 'because you've never had your limits tested. The Commandant was trained at Kauf. If she interrogated you, you'd betray your own mother.'

'My mother's dead,' I say.

'And thank the skies for it. Who knows what d-d-damage she and her rebels would have caused if she still – still lived.'

I look at Cook askance. Again, the stutter. Again, when she's speaking of the Resistance.

'Cook.' Izzi stands eye-to-eye with the old woman, though she somehow seems taller. 'Please help her. I've never asked you for anything. I'm asking you now.'

'What's your stake in it?' Cook's mouth twists like she's tasted something sour. 'Did she promise to get you out? To save you? Stupid girl. Resistance never saves anyone they can leave behind.'

'She didn't promise me anything,' Izzi says. 'I want to help her because she's my – my friend.'

I'm your friend, Cook's dark eyes say. I wonder, for the hundredth time, who this woman is and what the Resistance – and my mother – did to her that she would hate and mistrust them so much.

'I just want to save Darin,' I say. 'I just want out of here.'

'Everyone wants out of here, girl. I want out. Izzi wants out. Even the damn students want out. If you want to leave so badly, I suggest you go to your precious Resistance and ask for another mission. Somewhere where you won't get yourself killed.'

She stalks away, and I should be angry, but instead I'm repeating what she said in my head. *Even the damn students want out. Even the damn students want out.*

'Izzi.' I turn to my friend. 'I think I know how to find a way out of Blackcliff.'

* * *

Hours later, as I crouch behind a hedge outside Blackcliff's barracks, I'm wondering if I've made a mistake. The curfew drums thud and fall silent. I've been sitting here for an hour with roots and rocks digging into my knees. Not a single student has emerged from the barracks.

But at some point, one will. As Cook said, even the students want out of Blackcliff. They must sneak out. How else would they manage their drinking and whoring? Some must bribe the gate guards or tunnel guards, but surely there's another way out of here.

I fidget and shift, exchanging one prickly branch for another. I can't lurk in the shadow of this squat shrub for much longer. Izzi is covering for me, but if the Commandant calls and I don't appear, I'll be punished. Worse, Izzi might be punished.

Did she promise to get you out? To save you?

I promised Izzi no such thing, but I should. Now that Cook's brought it up, I can't stop thinking about it. What will happen to Izzi when I'm gone? The Resistance said they'd make my sudden disappearance from Blackcliff look like suicide, but the Commandant will question Izzi anyway. The woman's not easily fooled.

I can't just leave Izzi here to face interrogation. She's the first true friend I've had since Zara. But how can I get the Resistance to shelter her? If it hadn't been for Sana, they wouldn't have even helped me.

There must be a way. I could bring Izzi with me when I leave this place. The Resistance wouldn't be so heartless as to send her back – not if they knew what would happen to her. As I consider, I set my sights back on the buildings before me, just in time to see two figures emerge from the Skulls' barracks. Light glints off the lighter hair of one, and I recognize the prowling gait of the other. Marcus and Zak.

The twins turn away from the front gates and pass by the tunnel grates closest to the barracks, instead heading for one of the training buildings.

I follow them, close enough to hear them speak but far enough that they won't notice me. Who knows what they'd do if they caught me trailing them?

'—can't stand this,' a voice drifts back to me. 'I feel like he's taking over my mind.'

'Stop being such a damned girl,' Marcus replies. 'He teaches us what we need to avoid the Augurs' mind-leeching. You should be grateful.'

I edge closer, interested despite myself. Could they be speaking of the creature from the Commandant's study?

'Every time I look into his eyes,' Zak says, 'I see my own death.'

'At least you'll be prepared.'

'No,' Zak says quietly. 'I don't think so.'

Marcus grunts in irritation. 'I don't like it any better than you do. But we have to win this thing. So man up.'

They enter the training building, and I grab the heavy oak door just before it shuts, watching them through the crack. Blue-fire lanterns dimly light the hall, and their footsteps echo between the pillars on either side. Just before the building curves, they disappear behind one of the columns. Stone grates against stone, and all goes silent.

I enter the building and listen. The hallway is quiet as a tomb, but that doesn't mean the Farrars are gone. I make my way to the pillar where they disappeared, expecting to see a training-room door.

But there's nothing there, only stone.

I move on to the next room. Empty. The next. Empty. Moonlight from the windows tinges every room a ghostly blue-white, and they are, all of them, empty. The Farrars have disappeared. But how?

A secret entrance. I'm certain of it. Giddy relief floods me. I found it, found what Mazen wants. *Not yet, Laia.* I still have to figure out how the twins are getting in and out.

The next night, at the same late hour, I position myself in the training building itself, across from the pillar where I saw the Masks disappear. The minutes pass. Half an hour. An hour. They don't appear.

Eventually, I make myself leave. I can't risk missing a summons from the Commandant. I feel like shouting in frustration. The Farrars might have disappeared into the secret entrance before I ever got to the building. Or they might arrive there when I'm already in my bed. Whatever the case, I need more time to watch.

'I'll go tomorrow,' Izzi says when she meets me in my quarters as the final peals of eleventh bell fade. 'The Commandant rang for water. Asked where you were when I took it to her. I told her Cook sent you on a late-night errand, but that excuse won't work twice.'

I don't want to let Izzi help, but I know I won't succeed without her. Every time she leaves for the training building, my resolve to get her out of Blackcliff grows stronger. I will not leave her here when I go. I cannot.

We alternate nights, risking all in the hopes that we'll spot the Farrars again. But maddeningly, we come up with nothing.

'If all else fails,' Izzi says the night before I'm to make my report, 'you can ask Cook to teach you how to blow a hole in the outer wall. She used to make explosives for the Resistance.'

'They want a *secret* entrance,' I say. But I smile, because the thought of a giant, smoking hole in Blackcliff's wall is a happy one.

Izzi heads out to watch for the Farrars, and I wait for the Commandant to summon me. But she doesn't, and instead I lay in my pallet, staring at the pitted stone of my roof, forcing myself not to imagine Darin suffering at the hands of the Martials, trying to figure out a way to explain my failure to Mazen.

Then, just before eleventh bell, Izzi bursts into my room.

'I found it, Laia! The tunnel the Farrars have been using. I found it!'

CHAPTER THIRTY-TWO

Elias

I start losing battles.

It's Tristas's fault. He planted the seed of Helene being in love with me in my head, and now it's sprouted like a misbegotten weed from hell.

At scim training, Zak comes at me with unusual sloppiness, but instead of obliterating him, I let him knock me on my ass because I've caught a glimpse of blonde across the field. What does that lurch in my stomach mean?

When the Hand-to-Hand Centurion screams at me for poor technique, I barely hear him, instead considering what will happen to Hel and me. Is our friendship ruined? If I don't love her back, will she hate me? How am I supposed to get her on my side for the Trials if I can't give her what she wants? So many bleeding, stupid questions. Do girls think like this all the time? No wonder they're so confusing.

The Third Trial, the Trial of Strength, is in two days. I know I have to focus, to ready my mind and my body. I *must* win.

But in addition to Helene, there's someone else crowding my thoughts: Laia.

I try for days not to think about her. In the end, I stop resisting. Life is hard enough without having to avoid entire rooms in my own head. I imagine the fall of her hair and the glow of her skin. I smile at how she laughed when we danced, with a freedom of spirit I found exhilarating in its possibility. I remember how her eyes closed when I spoke to her in Sadhese.

But at night, when my fears crawl out of the dark places in my mind, I think of the dread on her face when she realized who I was. I think of her disgust when I tried to protect her from the Commandant. She must hate me for subjecting her to something so demeaning. But it was the only way I could think of to keep her safe.

So many times in the past week, I've nearly walked to her quarters to see how she is. But showing kindness to a slave will only bring the Black Guard down on me.

Laia and Helene: they're so different. I like that Laia says things I don't expect, that she speaks almost formally, as if she's telling a story. I like that she defied my mother to go to the Moon Festival, whereas Helene always obeys the Commandant. Laia is the wild dance of a Tribal campfire, while Helene is the cold blue of an alchemist's flame.

But why am I even comparing them? I've known Laia a few weeks and Helene all my life. Helene's no passing attraction. She's family. More than that. She's part of me.

Yet she won't speak to me, won't look at me. The Third Trial is days away, and all I've got from her are glares and muttered insults.

Which brings another worry to the forefront of my mind. I'd been counting on Helene winning the Trials, naming me Blood Shrike, and then releasing me from my duty. I can't see her doing that if she loathes me. Which means that *if* I win the next Trial and *if* she wins the final Trial, she could force me to remain Blood Shrike against my will. And if that happens, I'll have to run, and then honour will demand that she have me hunted down and killed.

On top of that, I've heard students whispering that the Emperor is days away from Serra and planning vengeance against the Aspirants and anyone associated with them. The Cadets and Skulls pretend to shake off the rumours, but the Yearlings aren't so skilled at hiding their fear. You'd think the Commandant would be taking precautionary measures against an attack on Blackcliff, but she seems unconcerned. Probably because she wants us all dead. Or me, anyway.

You're screwed, Elias, a wry voice tells me. *Just accept it. Should have run when you had the chance*

My spectacular losing streak doesn't go unnoticed. My friends are worried about me, and Marcus makes a point of challenging me on the combat field every chance he gets. Grandfather sends a two-word note, inked with such force that the parchment is torn. *Always victorious.*

All the while, Helene watches, growing more infuriated every time she beats me in combat – or witnesses someone else beat me. She's itching to say something, but her stubbornness won't let her.

Until, that is, she finds Dex and Tristas tailing her to the barracks two nights before the Third Trial. After interrogating them, she finds me.

'What the hell is wrong with you, Veturius?' She grabs my arm outside the Skulls' barracks, where I was heading for a bit of rest before a graveyard shift on the wall. 'You think I can't defend myself? You think I need *bodyguards*?'

'No, I just—'

'You're the one who needs protection. You're the one who's been losing every battle. Skies, a dead dog could best you in a fight. Why don't you just hand the Empire over to Marcus right now?'

A group of Yearlings watches us with interest, scurrying away only when Helene snarls at them.

'I've been distracted,' I say. 'Worrying about you.'

'You don't need to worry about me. I can take care of myself. And I don't need your . . . your henchmen following me.'

'They're your friends, Helene. They're not going to stop being your friends just because you're mad at me.'

'I don't need them. I don't need any of you.'

'I didn't want Marcus to—'

'Screw Marcus. I could beat Marcus to a pulp with my eyes closed. And I could beat you too. Tell them to leave me alone.'

'No.'

She gets in my face, anger radiating off her in waves. 'Call them off.'

'Not gonna do it.'

She crosses her arms and stands inches from my face. 'I challenge you. Single combat, three battles. You win, I keep the bodyguards. You lose, you call them off.'

'Fine,' I say, knowing I can beat her. I've done it a thousand times before. 'When?'

'Now. I want this done with.' She makes for the closest training building, and I take my time following, watching the way she moves: *angry, favouring her right leg, must have bruised the left in practice, keeps clenching that right fist – probably because she wants to punch me with it.*

Rage colours her every movement. Rage that has nothing to do with her so-called bodyguards and everything to do with me and her and the confusion rolling around inside both of us.

This should be interesting.

Helene heads for the largest of the empty training rooms, launching an attack the second I'm through the door. As I expected, she comes at me with a right hook, hissing when I duck it. She's fast and vengeful, and for a few minutes, I think my losing streak might continue. But an image of Marcus gloating, of Marcus ambushing Helene, sets my blood boiling, and I unleash a vicious offence.

I win the first battle, but Helene rebounds in the second, nearly taking my head off with the swiftness of her attack. Twenty minutes later, when I yield, she doesn't bother to relish the victory.

'Again,' she says. 'Try and show up this time.'

We circle each other like wary cats until I fly towards her, my scim high. She is undaunted, and our weapons crash together in a starburst of sparks.

Battle rage takes me. There is perfection in a fight like this. My scim is an extension of my body, moving so swiftly that it might be its own master. The battle is a dance, one I know so well I barely have to think. And though the sweat floods off me and my muscles burn, desperate for rest, I feel alive, obscenely alive.

We match each other stroke for stroke until I get a hit on her right arm. She tries to switch sword arms, but I jab my scim at her wrist faster than she can parry. Her scim goes flying, and I tackle her. Her white-blonde hair tumbles free of her bun.

'Surrender!' I pin her down at the wrists, but she thrashes and rips one arm free, scrabbling for a dagger at her waist. Steel stabs at my ribs, and seconds later, I am on my back with a blade at my throat.

'Ha!' She leans down, her hair falling around us like a shimmering silver curtain. Her chest heaves, she's covered in sweat, hurt darkens her eyes – and she is still so beautiful that my throat tightens, and I want so badly to kiss her.

She must see it in my eyes, because the hurt turns to confusion as we gaze at each other. I know then that there is a choice to be made. A choice that might change everything.

Kiss her and she'll be yours. You can explain everything and she'll understand, because she'll love you. She'll win the Trials, you'll be Blood Shrike, and when you ask for freedom, she'll give it to you.

But will she? If I'm entangled with her, won't that make it worse? Do I want to kiss her because I love her or because I need something from her? Or both?

All this passes through my head in a second. *Do it*, my instincts scream. *Kiss her.*

I wrap her silk-smooth hair around my hand. Her breath catches, and she melts into me, her body suddenly, intoxicatingly pliant.

And then, as I pull her face towards me, as our eyes are closing, we hear the scream.

CHAPTER THIRTY-THREE

Laia

The school is mostly quiet when Izzi and I emerge from the slaves' quarters. A few students still out head to the barracks in small groups, their shoulders slumped with tiredness.

'Did you see the Farrars go in?' I ask Izzi on the way to the training building.

She shakes her head. 'I was sitting there staring at those pillars, bored as a stone, when I noticed one of the bricks was different – shiny, like it had been touched more than the others. And then – well, come on, I'll show you.'

We enter the building and are greeted by the almost musical ring of clashing scims. Ahead of us, a training-room door stands open, and gold torchlight pours into the hallway. A pair of Masks battles within, each brandishing two slender scims.

'It's Veturius,' Izzi says. 'And Aquilla. They've been at it for ages.'

As I watch them fight, I find that I'm holding my breath. They move like dancers, whirling back and forth across the room, graceful, liquid, deadly. And so swift, like shadows on the surface of a river. If I wasn't watching it with my own eyes, I would never believe anyone could move that fast.

Veturius knocks the scim from Aquilla's hand, and he is on her, their bodies entangled as they wrestle across the floor with a strange, intimate violence. He is all muscle and force, and yet I can see in the way he fights that he is holding himself back. He is refusing to unleash his whole strength on her. Even still, there is an animal freedom to how he moves, a controlled chaos that makes the air around him blaze. So different from Keenan, with his restrained solemnity and cool interest.

Why are you comparing them, anyway?

I turn from the Aspirants. 'Izzi, come on.'

The building seems empty other than Veturius and Aquilla, but Izzi and I edge along the walls carefully in case there's a student or Centurion lurking. We turn the corner, and I recognize the doors the Farrars used when I saw them enter here the first time, nearly a week ago.

'Here, Laia.' Izzi slips behind one of the pillars and raises her hand to a brick that, at first glance, looks like all the others. She taps it. With a quiet groan, a section of stone swings away into darkness. Lamplight illuminates a narrow, descending staircase. I look down, barely daring to believe what I'm seeing, then envelop Izzi in a grateful hug.

'Izzi, you did it!'

I don't understand why she's not smiling back until her face goes rigid and she grabs me.

'Shhh,' she says. 'Listen.'

The flat tones of a Mask's voice echo from the tunnel, and the stairwell glows with approaching torchlight.

'Close it!' Izzi says. 'Quickly, before they see!'

I put my hand to the brick, tapping it frantically.

Nothing happens.

'—pretend you don't see it, but you do.' A vaguely familiar voice rises from the stairwell as I paw at the brick. 'You've always known how I feel about her. Why do you torment her? Why do you hate her so much?'

'She's an Illustrian snob. She'd never have you anyway.'

'Maybe if you'd left her alone, I'd have had a chance.'

'She's our enemy, Zak. She's going to die. Get over it.'

'Then why did you tell her that you two are meant to be? Why do I get the feeling that you want her to be your Blood Shrike instead of me?'

'I'm messing with her head, you bleeding idiot. And apparently it's working so well that even you're affected.'

I recognize the voices now – Marcus and Zak. Izzi pushes me aside and punches at the brick. The entrance remains stubbornly open.

'Forget it!' Izzi says. 'Come on!'

She grabs me, but Marcus's face emerges at the bottom of the stairwell, and, spotting me, he bounds up, reaching me in two strides.

'Run!' I shout at Izzi.

Marcus grabs for Izzi, but I shove her out of the way, and his arm wraps around my neck instead, choking off my air. He wrenches my head back, and I stare into his pale yellow eyes.

'What's this? Spying, wench? Trying to find a way to sneak out of the school?'

Izzi stands unmoving in the hallway, right eye wide in terror. I can't let her get caught. Not after all she's done for me.

'Go, Iz!' I scream. 'Run!'

'Get her, you twit,' Marcus roars at his brother, who has just emerged from the tunnel. Zak makes a half-hearted effort to grab

Izzi, but she wrenches out of his grasp and runs back the way we came.

'Marcus, come on.' Zak sounds exhausted and looks longingly towards the heavy oak doors that lead outside. 'Leave her be. We have to be up early.'

'Don't you remember her, Zak?' Marcus says. I struggle and try to kick the soft place between his foot and ankle, but he yanks me off my feet. 'She's the Commandant's girl.'

'She's expecting me,' I choke out.

'She won't mind if you're late.' Marcus smiles, a jackal's grin. 'I made you a promise that day, outside her office, remember? I told you that one night, you'd be alone in a dark hallway and I'd find you. I always keep my promises.'

Zak groans. 'Marcus—'

'If you want to be such a eunuch, little brother,' Marcus says, 'then piss off and leave me to my entertainment.'

Zak regards his twin for a moment. Then he sighs and walks away.

No! Come back!

'Just you and me, beautiful,' Marcus whispers in my ear. I bite viciously at his arm and try to wriggle away, but he spins me around by my neck and shoves me against the pillar.

'Shouldn't have fought,' he says. 'I would have gone easy on you. But then, I like a little spirit in my women.' His fist comes whistling towards my face. An infinite, explosive moment later, my head hits the stone behind me with a sickening smack, and I'm seeing double.

Fight back, Laia. For Darin. For Izzi. For every Scholar this beast has abused. Fight. A scream bursts from me, and I claw at Marcus's face, but a punch to my stomach takes the wind out of my lungs. I double over, retching, and his knee comes up into my forehead. The hallway spins, and I drop to my knees. Then I hear him laughing, a sadistic chuckle that stokes my defiance. Sluggishly, I throw myself at his legs. It won't be like before, like during the raid when I let that Mask drag me about my own house like some dead thing. This time, I'll fight. Tooth and nail, I'll fight.

Marcus grunts in surprise, losing his footing, and I untangle myself and try to scramble to my feet. But he catches my arm and backhands me. My head strikes the floor, and then he's kicking me until my flesh is minced. When I stop resisting, he straddles me and pins my arms down.

I release one last scream, but it turns to a whimper as he lays a finger against my mouth. My eyes are closing, swelling shut. I can't see. I can't think. Far away, the bells of the clock tower toll eleven.

CHAPTER THIRTY-FOUR

Elias

At the sound of the scream, I roll out from under Helene and onto my feet, the kiss forgotten. She falls unceremoniously to her back.

The scream echoes again, and I snatch up my scim. A second later, she grabs hers and follows me into the hallway. Outside, the belltower tolls eleven.

A blonde slave-girl is running towards us: Izzi.

'Help!' she shouts. 'Please – Marcus is – he's—'

I'm already running up the darkened corridor, Izzi and Helene behind me. We don't have to go far. As we turn a corner, we find Marcus hunched atop a prone form, his face stretched into a savage leer. I can't see who it is, but it's obvious what he's planning to do.

He's not expecting company, which is why we're able to get him off the slave so quickly. I tackle him and rain down punches, growling in satisfaction at the snap of bone beneath my fist, revelling in the blood that sprays across the wall. As his head whips back, I stand and draw my scim, resting the point on his rib cage between the plates of his armour.

Marcus scrambles to his feet, his arms in the air. 'Are you going to kill me, Veturius?' he asks, still grinning despite the blood dripping down his face. 'With a training scim?'

'Might take longer.' I drive it harder into his ribs. 'But it'll do the job.'

'You're on watch tonight, Snake,' Helene says. 'What the hell are you doing in a dark hallway with a slave?'

'Practising for you, Aquilla.' Marcus licks a little of the blood off his lip before turning to me. 'The slave puts up more of a fight than you do, bastard—'

'Shut it, Marcus,' I say. 'Hel, check her.'

Helene leans down to see if the slave is breathing – it won't be the first time Marcus has killed a slave. I hear her groan.

'Elias . . .'

'What?' I'm getting angrier by the second, almost hoping Marcus will try something. An old-fashioned fistfight to the death will do me good. From the shadows, Izzi watches us, too frightened to move.

'Let him go,' Helene says. I stare at her in shock, but her face is unreadable. 'Go,' she says tersely to Marcus, pulling my sword arm down. 'Get out of here.'

Marcus smiles at Helene, that grating smirk that makes me want to beat the life from him. 'You and me, Aquilla,' he says as he backs away, eyes smouldering. 'I knew you'd start to see it.'

'Leave, damn it.' Helene hurls a knife at him, missing his ear by inches. 'Go!'

When the Snake disappears out the door, I turn on Helene. 'Tell me there was a reason for that.'

'It's the Commandant's slave. Your . . . friend. Laia.'

I see then the cloud of dark hair, the gold skin, which had been obscured by Marcus's body before. A sick feeling fills me as

I crouch down beside her and turn her over. Her wrist is broken, the bone jutting out against the skin. Bruises darken her arms and neck. She moans and tries to move. Her hair is a tangled mess, and both of her eyes are blackened and swollen shut.

'I'll kill Marcus for this,' I say, my voice flat and calm, a calm I don't feel. 'We have to get her to the infirmary.'

'Slaves are forbidden from seeking treatment in the infirmary,' Izzi whispers from behind us. I'd forgotten she was there. 'The Commandant will punish her for it. And you. And the physician.'

'We'll take her to the Commandant,' Helene says. 'The girl's her property. She has to decide what to do with her.'

'Cook can help her,' Izzi adds.

They're both right, but that doesn't mean I have to like it. I pick Laia up gently, mindful of her wounds. She is light, and I pull her head to my shoulder.

'You'll be fine,' I murmur to her. 'All right? You're going to be just fine.'

I stride out of the hall, not waiting to see if Helene and Izzi follow. What would have happened if Helene and I hadn't been nearby? Marcus would have raped Laia and she'd have bled out whatever life she had left on that cold stone floor. The knowledge fans the rage burning within me.

Laia shifts her head and moans. 'Damn – him—'

'To the lowest pit of hell,' I mutter. I wonder if she still has the bloodroot I gave her. *This is too much for bloodroot, Elias.*

'Tunnel,' she says. 'Darin – Maz—'

'Shhh,' I say. 'Don't talk now.'

'All evil here,' she whispers. 'Monsters. Little monsters and then big ones.'

We reach the Commandant's house, and Izzi holds open the gate to the servants' corridor. Upon seeing us through the propped kitchen door, Cook drops a bag of spice she's holding, staring at Laia in horror.

'Get the Commandant,' I order her. 'Tell her that her slave is injured.'

'In here.' Izzi gestures to a low door with a curtain strung across it. I lay Laia down on the pallet inside with aching slowness, one limb at a time. Helene hands me a threadbare blanket, and I pull it over the girl, knowing how futile it is. A blanket won't help her.

'What happened?' The Commandant speaks from behind me. Helene and I duck out into the servants' corridor, now crowded with, Izzi, Cook, and the Commandant.

'Marcus attacked her,' I say. 'He nearly killed her—'

'She shouldn't have been out at this hour. I dismissed her for the evening. Any injuries she's sustained are the result of her own foolhardiness. Leave her. You're on the east wall for watch tonight, as I recall.'

'Will you send for the physician? Shall I get him?'

The Commandant stares at me as if I'm off my head.

'Cook will tend to her,' she says. 'If she lives, she lives. If she dies . . .' My mother shrugs. 'Not that it's any business of yours. You slept with the girl, Veturius. That doesn't mean you own her. Get to watch.' She puts a hand on her whip. 'If you're late, I'll take every minute out of your hide. Or' – she tilts her head thoughtfully – 'the slave's, if you prefer.'

'But—'

Helene grabs me by the arm and pulls me down the corridor. 'Let go of me!'

'Didn't you hear her?' Helene says as she hauls me away from the Commandant's house and across the sand training fields. 'If you're late to watch, she'll whip you. The Third Trial's two days away. How will you survive it if you can't even put on your armour?'

'I thought you didn't care what happened to me anymore,' I say. 'I thought you were done with me.'

'What did she mean,' Helene asks quietly, 'when she said you'd slept with the girl?'

'She doesn't know what she's talking about,' I say. 'I'm not like that, Helene, you should know better. Look, I've got to find some way to help Laia. For one second, put aside the fact that you hate me and want me to suffer and die. Can you think of anyone I can take her to? Even someone down in the city—'

'The Commandant won't allow it.'

'She won't know—'

'She'll find out. What's wrong with you? The girl isn't even a Martial. And she has one of her own to help her. That cook's been around for ages. She'll know what to do.'

Laia's words echo in my mind. *All evil here. Monsters. Little monsters and then big ones.* She's right. What is Marcus if not the worst kind of monster? He beat Laia with the intent of killing her, and he won't even get punished for it. What is Helene when she so casually shrugs off the idea of helping the girl? And what am I? Laia's going to die in that dark little room. And I'm doing nothing to stop it.

What can you do? a pragmatic voice asks. *If you try to help, the Commandant will only punish you both, and that will kill the girl for sure.*

'You can heal her.' I realize it suddenly, stunned that I didn't think of it before. 'The way you healed me.'

'No.' Helene walks away from me, her entire body suddenly stiff. 'Absolutely not.'

I chase after her. 'You can,' I insist. 'Just wait half an hour. The Commandant will never know. Get into Laia's room and—'

'I won't do it.'

'Please, Helene.'

'What's it to you, anyway?' Helene says. 'Do you – are the two of you—'

'Forget that. Do it for me. I don't want her to die, all right? Help her. I know you can.'

'No you don't. *I* don't even know if I can. What happened with you after the Trial of Cunning was – bizarre – freakish. I'd never done it before. And it took something out of me. Not my strength exactly but . . . forget it. I'm not going to try it again. Not ever.'

'She'll die if you don't.'

'She's a slave, Elias. Slaves die all the time.'

I back away from her. *All evil here. Monsters . . .* 'This is wrong, Helene.'

'Marcus has killed before—'

'Not just the girl. This.' I look around. 'All of this.'

The walls of Blackcliff rise around us like impassive sentinels. There is no sound other than the rhythmic clink of armour as the legionnaires patrol the ramparts. The silence of the place, its brooding oppression, makes me want to scream. 'This school. The students that come out of it. The things we do. It's all wrong.'

'You're tired. You're angry. Elias, you need rest. The Trials—' She tries to put her hand on my shoulder, but I shake her off, sick at her touch.

'Damn the Trials,' I say to her. 'Damn Blackcliff. And damn you too.'

Then I turn my back on her and head to watch.

CHAPTER THIRTY-FIVE

Laia

Everything hurts – my skin, my bones, my fingernails, even the roots of my hair. My body doesn't feel like my own anymore. I want to scream. All I can manage is a moan.

Where am I? What happened to me?

Flashes of it come back. The secret entrance. Marcus's fists. Then shouts and gentle arms. A clean smell, like rain in the desert, and a kind voice. Aspirant Veturius, delivering me from my murderer so I can die on a slave's pallet instead of a stone floor.

Voices rise and fall around me – Izzi's anxious murmur and Cook's rasp. I think I hear the cackle of a ghul. It fades when cool hands coax my mouth open and pour liquid down. For a few minutes, my pain dulls. But it's still near, an enemy pacing impatiently outside the gates. And eventually, it bursts through, burning and reaving.

I watched Pop work for years. I know what injuries like this mean. I'm bleeding on the inside. No healer, no matter how skilled, can save me. I'm going to die.

The knowledge is more painful than my wounds, for if I die, Darin dies. Izzi remains in Blackcliff forever. Nothing in the Empire changes. Just a few more Scholars sent to their graves.

The shred of my mind that still clings to life rages. *Need a tunnel for Mazen. Keenan will be waiting for a report. Need something to tell him.*

My brother is counting on me. I see him in my mind's eye, huddled in a dark prison cell, his face hollow, his body shaking. *Live, Laia.* I hear him. *Live, for me.*

I can't, Darin. The pain is a beast that's taken over. A sudden chill penetrates my bones, and I hear laughter again. *Ghuls. Fight them, Laia.*

Exhaustion sweeps over me. I'm too tired to fight. And at least my family will be together now. Once I die, Darin will eventually join me, and we'll see Mother and Father, Lis, Nan and Pop. Zara might be there. And later, Izzi.

My pain fades as a great, warm tiredness descends. It's so enticing, like I've been working in the sun and have come home to sink into a feather bed, knowing nothing will disturb me. I welcome it. I want it.

'I'm not going to hurt her.'

The whisper is hard as glass, and it cuts into my sleep, yanking me back to the world, back to the pain. 'But I will hurt you, if you don't clear out.'

A familiar voice. The Commandant? No. Younger.

'If either of you say a word about this to anyone, you're dead. I swear it.'

A second later, cool night air pours into my room, and I drag my eyes open to see Aspirant Aquilla silhouetted in the door. Her silver-white hair is pulled back in a messy bun, and instead of armour, she wears black fatigues. Bruises mar the pale skin of her arms. She ducks into the room, her masked face blank, her body betraying a nervous energy.

'Aspirant – Aquilla—' I choke out. She looks at me as if I smell of rotting cabbage. She doesn't like me, that much is plain. Why is she here?

'Don't talk.' I expect venom, but her voice shakes. She kneels beside my pallet. 'Just keep quiet and . . . and let me think.'

About what?

My ragged breathing is the only sound in the room. Aquilla is so silent that it seems as if she's fallen asleep sitting up. She stares at her palms. Every few minutes, she opens her mouth, as if to speak. Then she clamps it shut again and wrings her hands.

A wave of pain washes over me, and I cough. The briny taste of blood fills my mouth, and I spit it out on the floor, in too much pain to care what Aquilla thinks.

She takes my wrist, her fingers cool against my skin. I flinch, thinking she means me harm. But she just holds my hand limply, the way you would if you were at the deathbed of a relative you barely knew and liked even less.

She starts to hum.

At first, nothing happens. She feels out the melody the way a blind man feels his way forward in an unfamiliar room. Her hum crests and falls, explores, repeats. Then something changes, and the hum rises into a song that wraps around me with the sweetness of a mother's arms.

My eyes close, and I drift into the strain. My mother's face appears, then my father's. They walk with me at the edge of a great sea, swinging me between them. Above us, the night sky gleams like polished glass, its wealth of stars reflected in the oddly still surface of the water. My toes skim the fine sand below my feet, and I feel as though I'm flying.

I understand now. Aquilla is singing me into death. She's a Mask, after all. And it's a sweet death. If I'd known it was this kind, I'd never have been so afraid.

The intensity of the song swells, though Aquilla keeps her voice low, as if she doesn't want to be heard. A flash of pure fire burns into me from crown to heel, snatching me from the peace of the seashore. I open my eyes wide, gasping. *Death is here*, I think. *This is the final pain before the end.*

Aquilla strokes my hair, and warmth flows from her fingers into my body, like spiced cider on a freezing morning. My eyes grow heavy, and I close them again as the fire recedes.

I return to the beach, and this time Lis races ahead of me, her hair a blue-black banner glowing in the night. I stare at her willow-fine limbs and dark blue eyes, and I've never seen anything so gorgeously alive. *You don't know how I've missed you, Lis.* She looks back at me, and her mouth moves – one word, sung over and over. I can't make it out.

Realization comes slowly. I'm seeing Lis. But it's Aquilla who's singing, Aquilla who is commanding me, with just one word repeated in an infinitely complex melody.

Live live live live live live live.

My parents fade – no! Mother! Father! Lis! I want to go back to them, see them, touch them. I want to walk the night shores, hear their voices, marvel at their closeness. I reach for them, but they're gone, and there's only me and Aquilla and the stifling walls of my quarters. And that's when I understand that Aquilla isn't singing me to a sweet death.

She's bringing me back to life.

CHAPTER THIRTY-SIX

Elias

The next morning at breakfast, I sit apart and speak to no one. A chill, dark fog has rolled in off the dunes, settling heavily over the city.

It matches the blackness of my mood nicely.

I've forgotten about the Third Trial, about the Augurs, about Helene. All I can think of is Laia. The memory of her bruised face, her broken body. I try to devise some way to help her. Bribing the head physician? No, he doesn't have the guts to defy the Commandant. Sneaking a healer in? Who would risk the Commandant's wrath to save a slave's life, even for a fat purse?

Does she still live? Maybe her injuries weren't as bad as I thought. Maybe Cook can heal her.

Maybe cats can fly, Elias.

I'm mashing my food to a pulp when Helene walks into the crowded mess hall. I'm startled at the sloppiness of her hair and the pink shadows beneath her eyes. She spots me and approaches. I stiffen and shove a spoonful of food into my mouth, refusing to look at her.

'The slave is feeling better.' She lowers her voice so the students around us can't hear. 'I . . . stopped by there. She got through the night. I . . . um . . . well . . . I . . .'

Is she going to apologize? After refusing to help an innocent girl who hadn't done anything wrong except be born a Scholar instead of a Martial?

'Better, is she?' I say. 'I'm sure you're thrilled.' I get up and walk away. Helene is stone-still behind me, as stunned as if I've punched her, and I feel a savage flood of satisfaction. *That's right, Aquilla. I'm not like you. I'm not going to forget her just because she's a slave.*

I send a silent thanks to Cook. If Laia survived, it's no doubt due to the older woman's ministrations. Should I visit the girl? What will I say? 'Sorry Marcus nearly raped and killed you. Heard you're feeling better, though.'

I can't visit her. She won't want to see me anyway. I'm a Mask. If she hates me for that alone, it's reason enough.

But maybe I can stop by the house. Cook can tell me how Laia's doing. I can take something for her, something small. Flowers? I look around the school grounds. Blackcliff doesn't have flowers. Maybe I'll give her a dagger. There are plenty of those around, and skies know she needs one.

'Elias!' Helene has followed me out of the mess hall, but the fog helps me evade her. I duck into a training building, watching from a window until she gives up and goes on her way. *See how she likes the silent treatment.*

A few minutes later, I find myself heading to the Commandant's house. *Just a quick visit. Just to see if she's all right.*

'Your mother hears about this, she'll skin you alive,' Cook says from the kitchen door when I slip into the servants' corridor. 'And the rest of us too, for letting you in here.'

'Is she all right?'

'She's not dead. Go on, Aspirant. Leave. I'm not joking about the Commandant.'

If a slave spoke like that to Demetrius or Dex, they'd backhand her. But Cook is only doing what she thinks is best for Laia. I do as she asks.

The rest of the day is a blur of failed combat battles, curt conversations, and narrow escapes from Helene. The mist gets so thick I can barely see my hand in front of my face, making training more gruelling than usual. When the curfew drums beat, all I want is sleep. I head to the barracks, dead on my feet, when Hel catches up to me.

'How was training?' She appears out of the mist silently as a wraith, and despite myself, I jump.

'Splendid,' I say darkly. Of course, it wasn't splendid, and Helene knows it. I haven't fought so poorly in years. What little focus I recovered during last night's battles with Hel is gone.

'Faris said you missed scim practice this morning. Said he saw you walking to the Commandant's house.'

'You and Faris gossip like schoolgirls.'

'Did you see the girl?'

'Cook didn't let me in. And the girl has a name. It's Laia.'

'Elias . . . it could never work out between you two.'

My answering laugh echoes weirdly in the mist. 'What kind of idiot do you take me for? Of course it couldn't work. I only wanted to find out if she was all right. So what?'

'So what?' Helene grabs my arm and yanks me to a halt. 'You're an Aspirant. You have a Trial to take tomorrow. Your life will be on the line, and instead you're mooning over some Scholar.' My hackles rise. She senses it and takes a breath.

'All I'm saying is that there are more important things to think about. The Emperor will be here in days, and he wants us all dead. The Commandant doesn't seem to know – or care. And I have a bad feeling about the Third Trial, Elias. We have to hope that Marcus gets eliminated. He can't win, Elias. He can't. If he does—'

'I know, Helene.' *I've staked every hope I have on these damned Trials.* 'Trust me, I know.' Ten hells. I liked her better when she wasn't speaking to me.

'If you know, then why are you letting yourself get destroyed in combat? How can you win the Trial if you don't have the confidence to defeat someone like Zak? Don't you understand what's at stake?'

'Of course I do.'

'But you don't! Look at you! You're too befuddled by that slave-girl—'

'It's not her that's befuddling me, all right? It's a million other things. It's – this place. And what we do here. It's you—'

'Me?' She looks bewildered, and that makes me angrier. 'What did I do—'

'You're in love with me!' I shout at her now because I'm so angry at her for loving me, even though the logical part of me knows that I'm being cruelly unfair. 'But I'm not in love with you, and you hate me for it. You've let that ruin our friendship.'

She just stares, the wound in her eyes raw and growing. Why did she have to fall for me? If she had controlled her emotions, we never would have fought the night of the Moon Festival. We would have spent the last ten days planning for the Third Trial instead of avoiding each other.

'You're in love with me,' I say again. 'But I could never be in love with you, Helene. Never. You're just like every other Mask. You were willing to let Laia die just because she's a slave—'

'I didn't let her die.' Helene's voice is quiet. 'I went to her last night, and I healed her. That's why she's alive. I sang to her, sang until my voice was gone and I felt like I'd had the life sucked out of me. Sang until she was well again.'

'*You* healed her? But—'

'What, you don't believe I could do something kind for another human? I'm not evil, Elias, no matter what you say.'

'I never said—'

'But you did.' Her voice rises. 'You just said I'm like every other Mask. You just said you could never – never love—' She spins away from me, but after only a few steps, turns back. Trails of mist sweep out behind her like a ghostly dress.

'You think I want to feel this way about you? I *hate* it, Elias. Watching you flirt with Illustrian girls and sleep with Scholar slaves and find the good in everyone – *everyone* – but me.' A sob escapes her – the only time I've ever heard her cry. She chokes it back. 'Loving you is the worst thing that has ever happened to me – worse than the Commandant's whippings, worse than the Trials. It's torture, Elias.' She digs a shaking hand into her hair. 'You don't know what it's like. You have no idea what I've given up for you, the deal I made—'

'What do you mean?' I say. 'What deal? With who? For what?'

She doesn't answer. She's walking – running – away from me. 'Helene!' I chase after her, my fingers brushing the wetness of her face for one tantalizing second. Then the mist swallows her up, and she's gone.

CHAPTER THIRTY-SEVEN

Laia

'Get her up, damn you.' The Commandant's orders cut through the fog of my brain, startling me from sleep. 'I didn't pay two hundred marks so she could sleep all day.'

My mind is like tar, my body racked with dull pain, but I'm aware enough to know that if I don't rise from this pallet, I really am dead. As I grab a cloak, Izzi pushes the curtain to my room aside.

'You're awake.' She's obviously relieved. 'Commandant's on the warpath.'

'What . . . what day is it?' I shiver – it's cold – far colder than is normal for summer. I have a sudden fear that I've been unconscious for weeks, that the Trials are over, that Darin is dead.

'Marcus attacked you last night,' Izzi says. 'Aspirant Aquilla—' Her eye is wide, and I know then that I didn't dream the Aspirant's presence – or the fact that she healed me. *Magic.* I find myself smiling at the thought. Darin would laugh, but there's no other explanation. And, after all, if ghuls and jinn walk our world, then why not forces of good too? Why not a girl who can heal with a song?

'Can you stand?' Izzi says. 'It's past noon. I took care of your morning chores and I'd do the others, but the Commandant's quite insistent that you—'

'Past noon?' The smile drops from my face. 'Skies – Izzi, I had a meeting with the Resistance two hours ago. I have to tell them about the tunnel. Keenan might still be waiting—'

'Laia, the Commandant sealed up the tunnel.'

No. No. That tunnel is the only thing that stands between Darin and death.

'She questioned Marcus last night after Veturius brought you in,' Izzi says miserably. 'He must have told her about the tunnel, because when I went by it this morning, the legionnaires were bricking it closed.'

'Did she question you?'

Izzi nods. 'And Cook too. Marcus told the Commandant that you and I were spying on him, but I, well . . .' She fidgets and looks over her shoulder. 'I lied.'

'You . . . you lied? For me?' Skies, when the Commandant finds out, she'll kill Izzi.

No, *Laia,* I tell myself. *Izzi won't die, because you'll find a way to get her out of here before it comes to that.*

'What did you say to her?' I ask.

'Told her that Cook sent us to get crowleaf from the storage room by the barracks and that Marcus waylaid us on the way back.'

'And she believed you? Over a Mask?'

Izzi shrugs. 'I've never lied to her before,' she says. 'And Cook backed up my story – said she was having horrible back pain and that crowleaf was the only thing that would help. Marcus called me a liar, but then the Commandant sent for Zak, and he admitted there was a chance that he'd left the tunnel entrance open and that we just happened to pass by. Commandant let me go after that.' Izzi looks at me worriedly. 'Laia, what are you going to tell Mazen?'

I shake my head. I have no idea.

* * *

Cook sends me into the city with a stack of letters for the courier without so much as a mention of the beating I took.

'Be quick about it,' the old woman says when I appear in the kitchen to resume my duties. 'There's a nasty storm coming, and I need you and Kitchen-Girl to board up the windows before they're blown out.'

The city is strangely quiet, its cobbled lanes emptier than usual, its spires shrouded in unseasonable fog. The smells of bread and beast, smoke and steel are dulled, as if the mist has weakened their potency.

Conscious of my freshly healed limbs, I move gingerly. But even after a half hour of walking, all that remains of the beating I took are ugly bruises and a dull soreness. I head first to the couriers' office in Execution Square, hoping that the Resistance is still waiting for me. The rebels don't disappoint. Within seconds of entering the square, I smell cedarwood. Moments later, Keenan materializes out of the fog.

'This way.' He says nothing of my injuries, and I'm stung by his lack of concern. Just as I'm willing myself not to care, he takes my hand as if it's the most natural thing in the world and leads me to the back room of a cramped, abandoned shoe shop.

Keenan sets a spark to a lamp hanging on the wall, and as the light flares, he turns and looks me full in the face. The aloofness drops. For a second, he's unveiled, and I know with lightning certainty that behind that coolness he feels something for me. His eyes are almost black as he takes in every bruise.

'Who did this?' he asks.

'An Aspirant. It's why I missed the meeting. I'm sorry.'

'Why are you apologizing?' He is incredulous. 'Look at you – look what they've done to you. Skies. If your father was alive and knew I let this happen—'

'You didn't let it happen.' I put a hand on his arm, surprised at the tautness of his body, like a wolf raring for a fight. 'It's no one's fault but the Mask who did it. And I'm better now.'

'You don't have to be brave, Laia.' His words are spoken with a quiet fierceness, and I suddenly feel shy of him. He raises his hand, slowly tracing my eyes, my lips, the curve of my neck with the tip of his finger.

'I've been thinking about you for days.' He puts his warm hand against my face, and I want so much to lean into it. 'Hoping I'd see you in the square wearing a grey scarf so this can all be over. So that you can get your brother back. And after, we could . . . you and I could . . .'

He trails off. My breath comes in short, shallow bursts, and my skin tingles in wild impatience. He moves closer, drawing up my gaze, pinning me with his eyes. *Oh skies, he's going to kiss me. . . .*

Then, bizarrely, he steps away from me. His eyes are guarded again, his face empty of any emotion but a sort of professional detachment. My skin burns in embarrassment at the rejection. A second later, I understand.

'There she is,' a gruff voice sounds from the door, and Mazen enters the room. I look to Keenan, but he appears almost bored, and I'm shaken at how his eyes can go cold as quickly as a candle being blown out.

He's a fighter, a practical voice chides me. *He knows what's important. As should you. Focus on Darin.*

'We missed you this morning, Laia.' Mazen takes in my injuries. 'Now I see why. Well, girl. Do you have what I want? Do you have an entrance?'

'I have something.' The lie takes me by surprise, as does the smoothness with which I tell it. 'But I need more time.' Surprise flashes across Mazen's face for a brief, naked second. Is it my lie that's caught him off guard? My request for more time? *Neither,* my instinct tells me. *Something else.* I fidget as I remember what Cook said days ago. *You ask him where, exactly, your brother is in Central Prison. What cell?*

I muster my courage. 'I . . . have a question for you. You know where Darin is, right? Which prison? Which cell?'

'Of course I know where he is. If I didn't, I wouldn't be spending all my time and energy figuring out how to free him, now would I?'

'But . . . well, Central is so heavily guarded. How will you—'

'Do you have a way into Blackcliff or not?'

'Why do you need one?' I burst out. He's not answering my questions, and some stubborn part of me wants to shake the answers loose from him. 'How will a secret entrance to Blackcliff help you free my brother from the most fortified prison in the south?'

Mazen's gaze hardens from wariness to something close to anger. 'Darin's not in Central,' he says. 'Before the Moon Festival, the Martials moved him to the death cells in Bekkar Prison. Bekkar provides backup guard to Blackcliff. So when we launch a surprise attack on Blackcliff with half of our forces, the soldiers will pour out of Bekkar to Blackcliff, leaving the prison open for our other forces to take.'

'Oh.' I fall silent. Bekkar is a small prison in the Illustrian

331

Quarter, not too far from Blackcliff, but that's all I know about it. Mazen's plan makes sense now. Perfect sense. I feel like an idiot.

'I didn't mention anything to you, or anyone else' – he looks pointedly at Keenan – 'because the more people who know about a plan, the more likely it is to be compromised. So, for the last time: do you have something for me?'

'There's a tunnel.' *Buy time. Say anything.* 'But I have to figure out where it lets out.'

'That's not enough,' Mazen says. 'If you have nothing, then this mission is a failure—'

'Sir.' The door pounds open, and Sana tumbles in. She looks as if she hasn't slept in days, and she doesn't share the smug smiles of the two men behind her. When she sees me, she does a double take. 'Laia – your face.' Her eyes drop to my scar. 'What happened—'

'Sana,' Mazen barks. 'Report.'

Sana snaps her attention to the Resistance leader. 'It's time,' she says. 'If we're going to do it, then we need to leave. Now.'

Time for what? I look at Mazen, thinking he'll tell them to wait a moment, that he'll finish with me. But instead he limps to the door as if I've ceased to exist.

Sana and Keenan exchange a glance, and Sana shakes her head, as if in warning. Keenan ignores her. 'Mazen,' he says. 'What about Laia?'

Mazen stops to consider me, the annoyance on his face ill-concealed. 'You need more time,' he says. 'You have it. Get me something by midnight, day after tomorrow. Then we'll get your brother out, and this whole thing will be over.'

He walks out, engaged in low conversation with his men, snapping at Sana to follow. The older woman gives Keenan an unreadable look before hurrying out.

'I don't understand,' I say. 'A minute ago, he said we were done.'

'Something's not right.' Keenan stares hard at the door. 'And I need to find out what it is.'

'Will he keep his promise, Keenan? To free Darin?'

'Sana's faction's been pushing him. They think he should have broken Darin out already. They won't let him back away from this. But . . .' He shakes his head. 'I have to go. Be safe, Laia.'

Outside, the fog is so heavy that I have to put my hands in front of me to keep from running into anything. It's the middle of the afternoon, but the sky grows darker by the second. A thick bank of clouds roils above Serra as if gathering strength for an assault.

As I head back to Blackcliff, I try to make sense of what just happened. I want to believe that I can trust Mazen, that he'll hold to his end of the bargain. But something is off. I've struggled for days to eke out extra time from him. It makes no sense for him to suddenly give it away so easily.

And something else sets my nerves on edge. It's how quickly Mazen forgot about me when Sana showed up. And it's how, when he promised to save my brother, he didn't quite look me in the eyes.

CHAPTER THIRTY-EIGHT

Elias

On the morning of the Trial of Strength, a bone-shaking rumble of thunder jerks me from sleep, and I lay in the darkness of my quarters for a long time, listening to the rain drub the barracks roof. Someone slips a parchment marked with the Augurs' diamond seal beneath my door. I rip it open.

Fatigues only. Battle armour is forbidden. Remain in your room. I will come for you.

—*Cain*

A quiet scratching comes at the door as I crumple the note. A terrified-looking slave-boy stands outside, offering a tray of lumpy gruel and hard flatbread. I force myself to shovel down every bite. As disgusting as it is, I need all the fuel I can get if I'm going to win in combat.

I strap on my weapons: both Teluman scims across my back, a brace of daggers across my chest, and one knife tucked into each boot. Then I wait.

The hours inch by, slower than a graveyard shift on the watchtowers. Outside, the wind rages, sending branches and leaves tumbling past my window. I wonder if Helene is in her room. Has Cain come for her already?

Finally, in the late afternoon, a knock comes at my door. I'm so charged I want to rip down the walls with my bare hands.

'Aspirant Veturius,' Cain says when I open the door. 'It is time.'

Outside, the cold takes my breath away, cutting through my thin clothes like an icy scythe. It feels as if I'm wearing nothing at all. Serra is never this cold in the summer. It's hardly ever this cold in the winter. I look sideways at Cain. The weather must be his doing – his and his ilk. The thought darkens my mood. Is there anything they can't do?

'Yes, Elias,' Cain answers my question. 'We cannot die.'

The hilts of my scims knock against my neck, cold as ice, and despite the all-weather boots, my feet are numb. I follow Cain closely, unable to make heads or tails of our direction until the high, arched walls of the amphitheatre rise up in front of us.

We duck into the amphitheatre's armoury, which is packed with men in red leather practice armour.

I wipe the rain from my eyes and stare in disbelief. 'Red Platoon?' Dex and Faris are there, along with the other twenty-seven men in my battle platoon, including Cyril, a barrel-shaped boy who hates taking orders but accepts mine readily, and Darien, who has fists like hammers. I should find comfort in knowing these men will back me up in the Trial, but instead, I'm jumpy. What does Cain have planned for us?

Cyril holds out my practice armour.

'All present and accounted for, Commander,' Dex says. He looks straight ahead, but his voice betrays his nerves. As I buckle on the armour, I take in the mood of the platoon. Tension radiates off them, but that's understandable. They know the details of the first two Trials. They must be wondering what Augur-conjured horror they'll have to face.

'In a few moments,' Cain says, 'you will exit this armoury and find yourself on the amphitheatre field. There, you will engage in a battle to the death. Battle armour is forbidden and has already been taken from you. Your goal is simple: you are to kill as many of the enemy as you can. The battle will end when you, Aspirant Veturius, defeat – or are defeated by – the leader of the enemy. I warn you now, if you show mercy, if you hesitate to kill, there will be consequences.'

Right. Like having our throats ripped open by whatever is waiting for us out there.

'Are you ready?' Cain asks.

A battle to the death. That means some of my men – my friends – might die today. Dex meets my eyes briefly. He has the look of a trapped man, a man with a gnawing secret. He flicks a fearful glance at Cain and lowers his gaze.

That's when I notice Faris's hands trembling. Beside him, Cyril toys anxiously with a dagger, rubbing its edge against his finger. Darien stares at me strangely. What is that in his eyes? Sadness? Fear?

Some dark knowledge haunts my men, something they aren't willing to tell me.

Has Cain given them cause to doubt victory? I glare at the Augur. Doubt and fear are treacherous emotions before a fight. Together, they can infiltrate the minds of good men and decide a battle before it's begun.

I eye the door to the theatre's field. Whatever's waiting for us out there, we'll have to be equal to it, or we'll die.

'We're ready.'

The door opens, and at Cain's nod, I lead the platoon out. The rain is mixed with sleet, and my hands tingle and grow stiff. The bellow of thunder and slap of rain on mud muffles the sound of our passage. The enemy won't hear us coming – but we won't hear them either.

'Split!' I shout to Dex, knowing he'll barely be able to make out my words over the storm. 'You cover left flank. If you find the enemy, report back to me. Do not engage.'

But for the first time since he became my lieutenant, Dex doesn't acknowledge my orders. He doesn't move. He stares over my shoulder into the mist obscuring the battlefield.

I follow his gaze, and movement catches my eye.

Leather armour. The flash of a scim.

Has one of my men slipped ahead for recon? No – I do a quick head count, and they are all arrayed behind me, awaiting orders.

Lightning splits the sky, illuminating the battlefield for a tantalizing moment.

Then the mist descends, thick as a blanket. But not before I see whom we're fighting. Not before shock turns my blood to ice and my body to stone.

I find Dex's eyes. The truth is there, in his pale, haunted gaze. And in Faris's and Cyril's. In every man's. They know.

At that moment, a blue-clad figure flies with familiar grace out of the mists, silver braid shining, descending upon Red Platoon like a falling star.

Then she sees me and falters, eyes widening.

'Elias?'

Strength of arms and mind and heart. For this? To kill my best friend? To kill her platoon?

'Commander.' Dex grabs me. 'Orders?'

Helene's men emerge from the mist, scims out and ready. *Demetrius. Leander. Tristas. Ennis.* I know these men. I grew to adulthood with them, suffered with them, sweated with them. I won't give the order to kill them.

Dex shakes me. 'Orders, Veturius. We need orders.'

Orders. Of course. I'm Red Platoon's commander. It's up to me to decide.

If you show mercy, if you do not kill your enemy, there will be consequences.

'Strike to injure only!' I shout. Damn the consequences. 'Do not kill. Do *not* kill.'

I barely have time to give the order before Blue Platoon is on us, fighting as viciously as if we're a tribe of border raiders. I hear Helene scream something, but I can't make it out in the cacophony of pounding rain and clashing swords. She disappears, lost in the chaos.

I turn to look for her and spot Tristas cutting through the mêlée, coming straight for me. He flings a saw-toothed dagger at my chest, and I only just deflect it with my scim. He reaches for his own scim and rushes me. I drop, letting him roll over me before bringing the blunt end of my blade to the back of his legs. He loses his footing and slips in the thickening mud, landing on his back with throat exposed.

Open for the kill.

I turn away, waiting to disarm my next foe. But as I do, Faris, who has gained the upper hand in a fight with another of Helene's men, starts to shake. His eyes bulge, the spear he holds falls from his nerveless fingers, and his face turns blue. His opponent, a quiet boy named Fortis, wipes sleet from his eyes and stares, open-mouthed, as Faris collapses to his knees, clawing at an enemy no one else can see.

What is happening to him? I rush forward, my mind screaming at me to do something. But as soon as I get within a foot of him, my body is flung back as if by an unseen hand. My vision goes black for a moment, but I scrabble to my feet anyway, hoping none of my foes will choose this moment to attack. *What is this? What's happening to Faris?*

Tristas staggers up from where I left him, his face lit with frightening intensity as he finds me. He means to end my life.

Faris's chokes fade. He's dying.

Consequences. There will be consequences.

Time shifts. The seconds stretch, each as long as an hour as I gaze at the mayhem of the battlefield. Red Platoon follows my orders to injure only – and we are suffering for it. Cyril is down. So is Darien. Every time one of my men shows mercy to the enemy, one of their comrades falls, their life wrung out of them by Augur devilry.

Consequences.

I look between Faris and Tristas. They came to Blackcliff when Helene and I did. Tristas, dark-haired and wide-eyed, covered in bruises from the brutality of initiation. Faris, starved and peaked, no hint of the humour and brawn he'd possess later in life. Helene and I befriended them in our first week, all of us defending each other as best as we could against our predatory classmates.

And now one of them will die. No matter what I do.

Tristas comes for me, tears streaking his mask. His black hair is covered in mud, and his eyes burn with the panic of a cornered animal as he looks between Faris and me.

'I'm sorry, Elias.'

He takes a step towards me, and suddenly, his body stiffens. The scim in his hand tips into the mud as he peers down at the blade emerging from his chest. Then he slides to the wet ground, his gaze fixed on me.

Dex stands behind him, revulsion bursting from his eyes as he watches one of his best friends die by his hand.

No. Not Tristas. Tristas, who's been engaged to his childhood sweetheart since he was seventeen, who helped me understand Helene, who has four sisters who adore him. I stare at his body, at the tattoo on his arm. *Aelia.*

Tristas, dead. *Dead.*

Faris stops struggling. He coughs and stands shakily, then looks down at Tristas's body with dawning shock. But he has as little time to grieve as I do. One of Helene's men sends a mace whistling towards his head, and he is soon locked in another battle, jabbing and lunging as if he hadn't been perched on the edge of the abyss a minute before.

Dex is in my face then, his eyes wild. 'We have to kill them! Give the order!'

My mind won't think the words. My lips won't speak them. I know these men. And Helene – I can't let them kill Helene. I think of the nightmare battlefield – Demetrius and Leander and Ennis. *No. No. No.*

Around me, my men drop, suffocating as they refuse to kill their friends, or falling beneath the merciless blades of Blue Platoon.

'Darien's dead, Elias!' Dex shakes me again. 'Cyril too. Aquilla gave the order already. You have to give it too, or we're done for.'

'Elias.' He forces me to meet his eyes. 'Please.'

Unable to speak, I raise my hands and give the signal, my skin crawling as word passes down the battlefield from soldier to soldier.

Red Commander's orders. Fight to kill. No quarter.

*   *   *

There is no cursing, no yelling, no bluffing. We are, all of us, trapped in a pocket of unending violence. Swords grinding and friends dying and the sleet knifing down on us.

I've given the order, and so I take the lead. I show no hesitation, because if I do, my men will falter. And if they falter, we all die.

So I kill. Blood taints everything. My armour, my skin, my mask, my hair. The hilt of my scim drips with it, making it slippery beneath my hand. I'm Death himself, presiding over this butchery. Some of my victims die with merciful swiftness, gone before their bodies touch the ground.

Others take longer.

A wretched part of me wants to do it stealthily. Just slip up behind them and slide my scim in so I don't have to see their eyes. But the battle is uglier than that. Harder. Crueller. I stare into the faces of the men I kill, and though the storm muffles the groans, every death carves its way into my memory, each one a wound that will never heal.

Death supplants everything. Friendship, love, loyalty. The good memories I have of these men – of helpless laughter, of bets won and pranks hatched – they are stolen away. All I can remember are the worst things, the darkest things.

Ennis, sobbing like a child in Helene's arms when his mother died six months back. His neck snaps in my hands like a twig.

Leander and his never-to-be-requited love for Helene. My scim slides into his neck like a bird through a clear sky. Easily. Effortlessly.

Demetrius, who screamed in futile rage after he watched his ten-year-old brother whipped to death by the Commandant for desertion. He smiles when he sees me coming, drops his weapon and waits as if the edge of my blade is a gift. What does Demetrius see as the light leaves his eyes? His little brother waiting for him? An infinity of darkness?

On goes the slaughter, and all the while, lurking in the back of my head is Cain's ultimatum. *The battle will end when you, Aspirant Veturius, defeat – or are defeated by – the leader of the enemy.*

I've tried to seek out Helene and end this quickly, but she's elusive. When she finally finds me, I feel as if I've been battling for days, though in truth, it has been no more than half an hour.

'Elias.' She shouts my name, but her voice is weak with reluctance. The battle slows to a halt as our men stop attacking each other, as the mist clears enough for them to turn and watch Helene and me. Slowly, they gather around us, forming a half circle pocked by empty spaces where living men should stand.

Hel and I face each other, and I wish for the Augurs' power to know her mind. Her blonde hair is a tangle of blood, mud, and ice, her braid unpinned and hanging limply down her back. Her chest rises and falls heavily.

I wonder how many of my men she's killed.

Her fist tightens around the hilt of her scim – a warning she knows I won't miss.

Then she attacks. Though I pivot and bring up my scim to parry, my insides are paralysed. I am staggered at her vehemence. Another part of me understands. She wants this madness done.

At first, I try to deflect her, unwilling to go on the offensive. But a decade of ruthlessly honed instinct rebels at such passivity. Soon, I'm fighting in earnest, using every trick I know to survive her onslaught.

My mind flickers to the attack poses Grandfather taught me, the ones the Blackcliff Centurions don't know. The ones Helene won't be able to defend against.

You can't kill Hel. You can't.

But what choice is there? One of us has to kill the other, or the Trial won't end.

Let her kill you. Let her win.

As if she senses my weakness, Helene grits her teeth and drives me back, her pale eyes glacial, daring me to challenge her. *Let her, let her, let her.* Her scim cuts into my neck, and I counter with a quick thrust just as she's about to take my head off.

My battle rage rushes through me, shoving all other thoughts aside. Suddenly, she isn't Helene. She is an enemy who wants me dead. An enemy I must survive.

I fling my scim to the sky, watching with mercenary satisfaction as Helene's eyes flick up to follow the weapon's path. Then I strike, coming down on her like an executioner. My knee drives into her chest, and even through the storm, I hear the crack of a rib and the surprised whoosh of her breath leaving her.

She is beneath me, her ocean eyes terrified as I pin her scim arm down. Our bodies are entangled, entwined, but Helene is foreign to me suddenly, unknowable as the heavens. I tear a dagger from my chest, and my blood roars as my fingers touch the cold hilt. She knees me and grabs her scim, determined to finish me before I can finish her. I'm too fast. I lift the dagger high, my rage peaking, holding like the highest note of a mountain storm.

And then I bring the blade down.

CHAPTER THIRTY-NINE

Laia

In the predawn darkness, the storm churning above Serra strikes with the wrath of a conquering army. The servants' corridor swims in a half foot of rain, and Cook and I sweep out the water with rush brooms while Izzi tirelessly stacks sandbags. Rain lashes my face like the icy fingers of a ghost.

'Nasty day for a Trial!' Izzi calls to me over the downpour.

I don't know what the Third Trial will be, and I don't care, except to hope that it serves as a distraction for the rest of the school while I look for a secret entrance into Blackcliff.

No one else seems to share my indifference. In Serra, bets over who will win border on the obscene. The odds, Izzi tells me, have shifted to favour Marcus instead of Veturius.

Elias. I whisper his name to myself. I think of his face without the mask and the low, thrilling timbre of his voice when he whispered in my ear at the Moon Festival. I think of how he moved when he fought with Aquilla, that sensual beauty that took my breath away. I think of his implacable anger when Marcus nearly killed me.

Stop, Laia. Stop. He's a Mask and I'm a slave, and thinking of him in this way is so wrong that I wonder for a second if the beating Marcus gave me has muddled my brain.

'Inside, Slave-Girl.' Cook takes my broom, her hair a wild halo in the storm. 'Commandant's calling.'

I rush upstairs, soaked through and shivering, to find the Commandant pacing her room with a violent energy, her blonde tresses unbound.

'My hair,' the woman says when I dart into her chambers. 'Quickly, girl, or I'll have it out of your hide.'

The second I finish, she leaves the room, snatching her weapons from the wall, not bothering to give me her usual litany of orders.

'Shot out of here like a wolf on the hunt,' Izzi says when I enter the kitchen. 'Went straight for the amphitheatre. That must be where the Trial is. I wonder—'

'You and the rest of the school, girl,' Cook says. 'We'll find out soon enough. We're stuck inside today. Commandant said any slave out on the grounds will be killed on sight.'

Izzi and I exchange a glance. Cook kept us up preparing for the storm until past midnight last night, and I'd been planning to look for a secret entrance today.

'It's not worth the risk, Laia,' Izzi warns me when Cook turns away. 'You still have tomorrow. Rest your mind for a day, and a solution might present itself.' A rumble of thunder greets her comment. I sigh and nod. I hope she's right.

'Get to work, you two.' Cook shoves a rag in Izzi's hand. 'Kitchen-Girl, you finish the silver, polish the banister, scrub the—'

Izzi rolls her eye and throws down the cloth. 'Dust the furniture, hang the laundry, I know. Let it wait, Cook. The Commandant's gone for an entire day. Can't we appreciate that, even for a minute?' Cook presses her lips together in disapproval, but Izzi assumes a wheedling tone. 'Tell us a story. Something scary.' She shivers in anticipation, and Cook makes a strange sound that could be a laugh or a groan.

'Life isn't scary enough for you, girl?'

Quietly, I slip to the back of the kitchen worktable to press the seemingly endless stack of the Commandant's uniforms. It's been ages since I've heard a good tale, and I long to get lost in one. But if Cook knows that, she'll probably keep silent on principle.

The old woman appears to ignore us. Her hands, small and fine, sift through jars of spices as she prepares lunch.

'You won't give up, will you?' I think at first that Cook is speaking to Izzi, only to look up and find her regarding me. 'You mean to see this mission to save your brother through to the end. No matter what the cost.'

'I have to.' I wait for her to launch into another of her rants against the Resistance. But instead, she nods, unsurprised. 'I have a story for you, then,' she says. 'It has no hero or heroine. It has no happy ending. But it's a story you need to hear.'

Izzi raises an eyebrow and takes up her polishing cloth. Cook shuts one spice jar and opens another. Then she begins.

'Long ago,' she says, 'when man knew not greed, malice, tribe, nor clan, jinn walked the earth.'

Cook's voice is nothing like a Tribal *Kehanni*'s: it is stern where a tale-spinner's would be gentle, all edges where a tale-spinner's would be mellow and curved. But the old woman's cadence reminds me of the Tribespeople anyway, and I'm pulled into the tale.

'Immortal the jinn were.' Cook's eyes are quiet, as if she's lost in an inner musing. 'Created of sinless, smokeless fire. They rode the winds and read the stars, and their beauty was the beauty of the wild places.

'Though the jinn could manipulate the minds of lesser creatures, they were honourable and occupied themselves with the raising of their young and the protection of their mysteries. Some were fascinated by the untempered race of man. But the leader of the jinn, the King-of-No-Name, who was oldest and wisest of them, counselled his people to avoid men. So they did.

'As centuries passed, men grew strong. They befriended the race of wild elementals, the efrits. In their innocence, the efrits showed men the paths to greatness, granting them powers of healing and fighting, of swiftness and fortune-telling. Villages became cities. Cities rose into kingdoms. Kingdoms fell and were melded into empires.

'From this ever-changing world arose the Empire of the Scholars, strongest among men, dedicated to their creed: *Through knowledge, transcendence.* And who had more knowledge than the jinn, the oldest creatures of the earth?

'In an attempt to learn the secrets of the jinn, the Scholars sent delegations to negotiate with the King-of-No-Name. They received a gentle but firm response.

'We are jinn. We are apart.

'But the Scholars hadn't created an empire by giving up at the first rejection. They sent cunning messengers, raised to oration the way Masks are raised to war. When that failed, they sent wise men and artists, spellcasters and politicians, teachers and healers, royalty and commoners.

'The response was the same. *We are jinn. We are apart.*

'Soon, hard times struck the Scholar Empire. Famine and plague took whole cities. Scholar ambition turned to bitterness The Scholar Emperor grew angry, believing that if only his people had the knowledge of the jinn, they could rise again. He gathered the finest Scholar minds into a Coven and set them to one task: mastery of the jinn.

'The Coven found dark allies among the fey – cave efrits, ghuls, wraiths. From these twisted creatures, the Scholars learned to trap the jinn with salt and steel and summer rain still warm from the heavens. They tormented the old creatures, seeking the source of their power. But the jinn kept their secrets.

'Enraged at the evasion of the jinn, the Coven no longer cared for fey secrets. They sought now only to destroy the jinn. Efrits, ghuls, and wraiths abandoned the Scholars, understanding the full extent of man's thirst for power. Too late. The fey had given their knowledge freely and in trust, and the Coven used that knowledge to create a weapon that would conquer the jinn forever. They called it the Star.

'The fey watched in horror, desperate to stop the doom they helped unleash. But the Star gave the humans unnatural power, and so the lesser creatures fled, disappearing into the deep places to wait out the war. The jinn stood fast, but they were too few. The Coven cornered them and used the Star to lock them forever in a grove of trees, a living, growing prison, the only place powerful enough to bind such creatures.

'The power unleashed by the jailing destroyed the Star – and the Coven. But the Scholars rejoiced, for the jinn were defeated. All but the greatest of them.'

'The king,' Izzi says.

'Yes. The King-of-No-Name escaped imprisonment. But he had failed to save his people, and his failure drove him mad. It was a madness he carried with him like a cloud of ruin. Wherever he went, darkness fell, deeper than a midnight ocean. The king was at long last given a name: the Nightbringer.'

My head snaps up.

My Lord Nightbringer . . .

'For hundreds of years,' Cook says, 'the Nightbringer plagued mankind however he could. But it was never enough. Like rats, men scurried into their hiding places when he came. And like rats, they emerged as soon as he was gone. So he began to plan. He allied himself with the Scholars' ancient enemy, the Martials, a cruel people exiled to the northern reaches of the continent. He whispered to them the secrets of steelcraft and statecraft. He taught them to rise above their brutish roots. Then he waited. Within a few generations, the Martials were ready. They unleashed the invasion.

'The Scholar Empire fell quickly, its people enslaved, broken. But still alive. And so the Nightbringer's thirst for revenge remains unquenched. He lives now in the shadows, where he lures and enslaves the lesser of his brethren – the ghuls, the wraiths, the cave efrits – to punish them for their betrayal so long ago. He watches, he waits, until the time is right, until he can exact his full revenge.'

As Cook's words die away, I realize I'm holding the press midair. Izzi gapes, her polishing forgotten. Lightning flashes outside, and a gust of wind rattles the windows and doors.

'Why do I need to know this story?' I ask.

'You tell me, girl.'

I take a deep breath. 'Because it's true, isn't it?'

Cook smiles her twisted smile. 'You've seen the Commandant's nighttime visitor, I take it.'

Izzi looks between us. 'What visitor?'

'He – he called himself the Nightbringer,' I say. 'But it can't be '

'He's exactly what he says he is,' Cook says. 'Scholars want to close their eyes to the truth. Ghuls, wraiths, wights, jinn – they're just stories. Tribal myths. Campfire tales. Such arrogance.' She sneers. 'Such pride. Don't you make that mistake, girl. Open your eyes to it, or you'll end up like your mother. Nightbringer was right in front of her, and she never even knew it.'

I set the press down. 'What do you mean?'

Cook speaks quietly, as if she's afraid of her own words. 'He infiltrated the Resistance,' she says. 'Took human form and p-posed as – as a fighter.' She clenches her jaw and huffs before going on. 'Got close to your mother. Manipulated and used her.' Cook pauses again, her face growing pinched and pale. 'Y-your fath-father caught on. N-Nightbringer – had – help. A tr-trai-traitor. Out-outwitted Jahan and – and sold your parents to Keris – no – I—'

'Cook?' Izzi jumps up as the old woman grabs her head with one hand and staggers back into the wall with a moan. 'Cook!'

'Away—' The older woman shoves Izzi in the chest, nearly knocking her to the floor. 'Get away!'

Izzi raises her hands, her voice pitched low as if she's speaking to a frightened animal. 'Cook, it's all right—'

'Get to work!' Cook draws herself upright, the brief quiet in her eyes shattered, replaced with something close to madness. 'Leave me be!'

Izzi pulls me from the kitchen hurriedly. 'She gets like that sometimes,' she says once we're out of earshot. 'When she talks about the past.'

'What's her name, Izzi?'

'She's never told me. I don't think she wants to remember it. Do you think it's true? What she said about the Nightbringer? And about your mother?'

'I don't know. Why would the Nightbringer go after my parents? What did they ever do to him?' But even as I ask the question, I know the answer. If the Nightbringer hates the Scholars as much as Cook says, then it's no wonder he sought to destroy the Lioness and her lieutenant. Their movement was the only hope the Scholars ever had.

Izzi and I return to our work, each of us silent, our heads filled with thoughts of ghuls and wraiths and smokeless fire. I find that I can't stop wondering about Cook. Who is she? How well did she know my parents? How did a woman who crafted explosives for the Resistance end up a slave? Why not just blow the Commandant to the tenth ring of hell?

Something occurs to me suddenly, something that makes my blood run cold.

What if Cook is the traitor?

Everyone caught with my parents was killed – everyone who would know anything about the betrayal. And yet Cook's told me things about that time that I've never heard before. How would she know, unless she was there?

But why would she be a slave in the Commandant's house if she'd handed over Keris's biggest catch?

'Perhaps someone in the Resistance will know who Cook is,' I say that evening as Izzi and I trudge to the Commandant's bedroom with buckets and dusters. 'Perhaps they'll remember her.'

'You should ask your red-haired fighter,' Izzi says. 'He seems like a sharp one.'

'Keenan? Maybe . . .'

'I knew it,' Izzi crows. 'You like him. I can tell by how you say his name. *Keenan.*' She grins at me, and a blush races up my neck. 'He's a looker,' she comments. 'Which you've noticed, I take it.'

'Don't have time for that. I've got other things on my mind.'

'Oh, stop,' Izzi says. 'You're human, Laia. You're allowed to like a boy. Even Masks have crushes. Even I—'

We both freeze as the front door rattles downstairs. The latch clicks open, and wind gusts through the house with a bone-chilling shriek.

'Slave-Girl!' The Commandant's voice cracks up the stairwell. 'Come here.'

'Go.' Izzi shoves me to my feet. 'Quick!'

Duster in hand, I hurry down the stairs, where the Commandant is waiting for me, flanked by two legionnaires. Instead of her usual disgust, her silver face is almost thoughtful as she regards me, as if I've transformed into something unexpectedly fascinating.

I notice a fourth figure then, lurking in the shadows behind the legionnaires, his skin and hair as white as bones bleached in the sun. An Augur.

'Well' – the Commandant throws a wary look at the Augur – 'is she the one?'

The Augur gazes at me with black eyes that swim in a sea of blood red. Rumour says the Augurs can read minds, and the things in my head are enough to take me straight to the gallows for treason. I force myself to think of Pop and Nan and Darin. A great, familiar grief fills my senses. *Read my mind then.* I meet the Augur's gaze. *Read the pain your Masks have caused me.*

'She's the one.' The Augur doesn't break eye contact, seemingly mesmerized by my anger. 'Bring her.'

'Where are you taking me?' The legionnaires bind my hands. 'What's going on?' *They've learned about the spying. They must have.*

'Quiet.' The Augur draws up his hood, and we follow him into the storm. When I scream and try to tear free, one of the soldiers gags and blindfolds me. I expect the Commandant to accompany us, but instead she slams the door behind me. At least they haven't taken Izzi. She's safe. But for how long?

Within seconds, I'm soaked to the skin. I struggle against the legionnaires, but all I succeed in doing is ripping my dress so that it's barely decent. Where are they taking me? *The dungeons, Laia. Where else?*

I hear Cook's voice, telling the story of the Resistance spy who came before me. *Commandant caught him. Tortured him in the school's dungeon for days. Some nights we could hear him. Screaming.*

What will they do to me? Will they take Izzi too? Tears leak from my eyes. I was supposed to save her. I was supposed to get her out of Blackcliff.

After endless minutes of trudging through the storm, we stop. A door opens, and a moment later, I'm airborne. I land hard on a chilly stone floor.

I try to stand and scream through the gag, straining at the bonds around my wrists. I try to work off my blindfold so I can at least see where I am.

To no avail. The lock clicks, footsteps retreat, and I'm left alone to await my fate.

CHAPTER FORTY

Elias

My blade cuts through Helene's leather armour, and part of me screams, *Elias, what have you done? What have you done?*

Then the dagger shatters, and while I'm still staring at it in disbelief, a powerful hand grabs my shoulder and pulls me off Helene.

'Aspirant Aquilla.' Cain's voice is cold as he flicks open the top of Helene's tunic. Glimmering beneath is the Augur-forged shirt Hel won in the Trial of Cunning. Except, like the mask, it's no longer separate from her. It's melded to her, a second, scim-proof skin. 'Do you not recall the rules of the Trial? Battle armour is forbidden. You are disqualified.'

My battle rage fades, leaving me feeling like my insides have been whittled away. I know that this image will haunt me forever, staring down at Helene's frozen face, the sleet thick around us, the screaming wind that can't drown out the sound of death.

You nearly killed her, Elias. You nearly killed your best friend.

Helene doesn't speak. She stares at me and puts her hand to her heart, as if she can still feel that dagger coming down.

'She didn't think to remove it,' a voice speaks from behind me. A slight shadow emerges from the mist: a female Augur. Other shadows follow, creating a circle around Hel and me.

'She didn't think of it at all,' the female Augur says. 'She's worn it since the day we gave it to her. It's joined with her. Like the mask. An honest error, Cain.'

'But an error nonetheless. She has forfeited the victory. And even if she had not . . .'

I would have won anyway. Because I would have killed her.

The sleet slows to a drizzle, and the mist on the battlefield clears, revealing the carnage. The amphitheatre is strangely quiet, and I notice then that the stands are filled with students and Centurions, generals and politicians. My mother watches from the front row, unreadable as ever. Grandfather stands a few rows behind her, his hand tight on his scim. The faces of my platoon are a blur. Who survived? Who died?

Tristas, Demetrius, Leander: dead. Cyril, Darien, Fortis: dead.

I drop to the ground beside Helene. I say her name.

I'm sorry I tried to kill you. I'm sorry I gave the order to kill your platoon. I'm sorry. I'm sorry. The words don't come. Only her name, whispered over and over in the hopes that she will hear, that she will understand. She looks past my face into the roiling sky as if I'm not there.

'Aspirant Veturius,' Cain says. 'Rise.'

Monster, murderer, devil. Dark, vile creature. I hate you. I hate you. Am I speaking to the Augur? To myself? I don't know. But I do know that freedom isn't worth this. Nothing is worth this.

I should have let Helene kill me.

Cain says nothing of the bedlam in my mind. Maybe, in a battlefield choked with the tormented thoughts of broken men, he cannot hear mine.

355

'Aspirant Veturius,' he says, 'as Aquilla has forfeited, and you, of all Aspirants, have the most men left alive, we, the Augurs, name you victor in the Trial of Strength. Congratulations.'

Victor.

The word thuds to the ground like a scim falling from a dead hand.

* * *

Twelve men from my platoon survive. The other eighteen lie in the back room of the infirmary, cold beneath thin white sheets. Helene's platoon fared worse, with only ten survivors. Earlier, Marcus and Zak fought each other, but no one seems to know much about that battle.

The men of the platoons knew who their enemy would be. Everyone knew what this Trial would be – everyone but the Aspirants. Faris tells me this. Or maybe Dex.

I don't remember how I arrive at the infirmary. The place is chaos, the head physician and his apprentices overwhelmed as they try to save wounded men. They shouldn't bother. The blows we dealt were killing blows.

The healers realize the truth soon enough. By the time night falls, the infirmary is quiet, occupied by bodies and ghosts.

Most of the survivors have left, half ghost themselves. Helene is spirited away to a private room. I wait outside her door, throwing black looks at the apprentices trying to get me to leave. I have to speak to her. I have to know if she's all right.

'You didn't kill her.'

Marcus. I don't draw a weapon at the sound of his voice, though I have a dozen at hand. If Marcus decides to kill me in this moment, I won't lift a finger to stop him. But for once, there's no venom in him. His armour is spattered with blood and mud, like mine, but he seems different. Diminished, like something vital has been torn out of him.

'No,' I say. 'I didn't kill her.'

'She was your enemy on the battlefield. It's not a victory until you defeat your enemy. That's what the Augurs said. That's what they told me. You were supposed to kill her.'

'Well, I didn't.'

'He died so easily.' Marcus's yellow eyes are troubled, his lack of malice so profound that I barely recognize him. I wonder if he actually sees me or if he just sees a body – someone alive, someone listening.

'The scim – it tore through him,' Marcus says. 'I wanted to stop it. I tried, but it was too fast. My name was his first word, did you know? And – and his last. Just before the end, he said it. *Marcus*, he said.'

It dawns on me then. I haven't seen Zak among the survivors. I haven't heard anyone speak his name.

'You killed him,' I say softly. 'You killed your brother.'

'They said I had to defeat the enemy commander.' Marcus raises his eyes to mine. He seems confused. 'Everyone was dying. Our friends. He asked me to end it. To make it stop. He begged me. My brother. My little brother.'

Revulsion rises inside me like bile. I've spent years loathing Marcus, thinking of him as nothing more than a snake. Now I can only pity him, though neither of us deserves pity. We are murderers of our own men – of our own blood. I'm no better than he is. I watched and did nothing as Tristas died. I killed Demetrius, Ennis, Leander, and so many others. If Helene hadn't unwittingly broken the rules of the Trial, I'd have killed her too.

The door to Helene's room opens, and I rise, but the physician shakes his head.

'No, Veturius.' He's pale and subdued, all his bluster gone. 'She's not ready for visitors. Go, lad. Go and get some rest.'

I almost laugh. Rest.

When I turn back to Marcus, he is gone. I should find my men. Check on them. But I can't face them. And they, I know, won't want to see me. We will never forgive ourselves for what we did today.

'I *will* see Aspirant Veturius,' a quarrelsome voice says from the hallway outside the infirmary. 'That's my grandson, and I damn well want to make sure he's— Elias!'

Grandfather shoves past a frightened apprentice as I walk out the infirmary door, pulling me to him, his arms strong around me. 'Thought you were dead, my boy,' he says into my hair. 'Aquilla's got more spit than I gave her credit for.'

'I nearly killed her. And the others. I killed them. So many. I didn't want to. I—'

I'm going to be sick. I turn from him and retch right there, at the door of the infirmary, not stopping until there's nothing left to get out.

Grandfather calls for a glass of water, waiting quietly as I drink it down, his hand never leaving my shoulder.

'Grandfather,' I say. 'I wish . . .'

'The dead are dead, my boy, and at your hand.' I don't want to hear the words, but I need them, for they are the truth. Anything less would be an insult to the men I killed. 'No amount of wishing will change it. You'll be trailing ghosts now. Like the rest of us.'

I sigh and look down at my hands. I can't stop them from shaking. 'I have to go to my quarters. I have to get – get cleaned up.'

'I can walk you—'

'That won't be necessary.' Cain appears from the shadows, as welcome as a plague. 'Come, Aspirant. I would speak to you.'

I follow the Augur with heavy steps. What do I do? What do I say to a creature who cares nothing for loyalty or friendship or life?

'I find it hard to believe,' I say quietly, 'that you didn't realize Helene was wearing scim-proof armour.'

'Of course we realized it. Why do you think we gave it to her? The Trials are not always about action. Sometimes, they are about intent. You weren't meant to kill Aspirant Aquilla. We only wanted to know if you would.' He glances at my hand, which I didn't even realize was inching towards my scim. 'I've told you before, Aspirant. We cannot die. Besides, haven't you had enough of death?'

'Zak. And Marcus.' I can barely speak. 'You made him kill his own brother.'

'Ah. Zacharias.' Sadness flits across Cain's face, infuriating me further. 'Zacharias was different, Elias. Zacharias had to die.'

'You could have picked anyone – anything for us to fight.' I don't look at him. I don't want to retch again. 'Efrits or wights. Barbarians. But you made us fight each other. Why?'

'We had no choice, Aspirant Veturius.'

'No choice.' A terrible anger consumes me, virulent as a sickness. And though he is right, though I have had enough of death, in this moment all I want is to plunge my scim through Cain's black heart. 'You created these Trials. Of course you had a choice.'

Cain's eyes flash. 'Do not speak of things you do not understand, child. What we do, we do for reasons beyond your comprehension.'

'You made me kill my friends. I almost killed Helene. And Marcus – he killed his brother – his twin – because of *you*.'

'You'll be doing far worse before this is over.'

'Worse? How much worse can this get? What will I have to do in the Fourth Trial? Murder children?'

'I'm not talking about the Trials,' Cain says. 'I'm talking about the war.'

I stop mid-stride. 'What war?'

'The one that haunts our dreams.' Cain keeps walking, gesturing for me to follow. 'Shadows gather, Elias, and their gathering cannot be stopped. Darkness grows in the heart of the Empire, and it will grow more still, until it covers this land. War comes. And it must come. For a great wrong must be righted, a wrong that grows greater with every life destroyed. The war is the only way. And you must be ready.'

Riddles, always riddles with the Augurs. 'A wrong,' I say through gritted teeth. 'What wrong? When? How can a war fix it?'

'One day, Elias Veturius, these mysteries will be made clear. But not this day.'

He slows as we enter the barracks. Every door is closed. I hear no curses, no sobs, no snores, nothing. Where are my men?

'They sleep,' Cain says. 'For this night, they will not dream. Their sleep will not be haunted by the dead. A reward for their valour.'

A paltry gesture. They still have tomorrow night to wake up screaming. And all the nights after.

'You have not asked about your prize,' Cain says, 'for winning the Trial.'

'I don't want a prize. Not for this.'

'Nonetheless,' the Augur says as we arrive at my room, 'you will have it. Your door will be sealed until dawn. No one will disturb you. Not even the Commandant.' He drifts out of the barracks doors, and I watch him go, wondering uneasily about his talk of war and shadows and darkness.

I'm too exhausted to think long on it. My whole body aches. I just want to sleep and forget this ever happened, even if it's just for a few hours. I push the questions out of my head, unlock the door, and enter my quarters.

CHAPTER FORTY-ONE

Laia

When the door to my cell opens, I bolt towards the sound, determined to escape into the hallway beyond. But the chill in the room has penetrated my bones. My limbs are too heavy, and a hand catches me easily about the waist.

'Door's sealed by an Augur.' The hand releases me. 'You'll hurt yourself.'

My blindfold is pulled off, and a Mask stands before me. I know him instantly. Veturius. His fingers brush my wrists and neck as he unbinds my hands and pulls off my gag. For a second, I'm bewildered. He saved my life all those times so he could interrogate me now? I realize that some naïve sliver of me hoped that he was better than this. Not good, necessarily. Just not evil. *You knew this, Laia,* a voice chides me. *You knew he was playing a sick game.*

Veturius kneads his neck awkwardly, and that's when I notice that his leather armour is covered in blood and muck. He has bruises and cuts all over, and his fatigues hang in dull, tattered strips. He looks down at me, and his eyes glint in brief, hot rage before cooling into something else – shock? Sadness?

'I won't tell you anything.' My voice is high and thin, and I grit my teeth. *Be like Mother. Don't show fear.* I grab my armlet with one hand. 'I didn't do anything wrong. So you can torture me all you want, but it won't do you any good.'

Veturius clears his throat. 'That's not why you're here.' He is rooted to the stone floor, regarding me as if I am a puzzle.

I glare back at him. 'Why did that – that red-eyed *thing* bring me to this cell, if I'm not to be interrogated?'

'Red-eyed thing.' He nods. 'Good description.' He looks around the chamber as if seeing it for the first time. 'This isn't a cell. It's my room.'

I eye the narrow cot, the chair, the cold hearth, the ominous black bureau, the hooks on the wall – for torture, I assumed. It's bigger than my quarters, though just as spare. 'Why am I in your room?'

The Mask goes to the bureau and rifles through it. I tense – what's in there?

'You're a prize,' he says. 'My victory prize for winning the Third Trial.'

'A prize?' I say. 'Why would I be—'

The knowledge sweeps through me suddenly, and I shake my head – as if that will make a difference. I'm keenly aware of the amount of skin showing through my ripped dress, and I try to draw the remnants of cloth together. I take a step back, straight into the chill, rough stone of the wall. It's as far away as I can get, but it won't be far enough. I've seen Veturius fight. He is too fast, too big, too strong.

'I'm not going to hurt you.' He turns from the bureau, looking at me with an odd sympathy in his eyes. 'That's not how I am.' He holds out a clean, black cloak. 'Take this – it's freezing.'

I eye the cloak. I'm so cold. I've been cold since the Augur threw me in here hours ago. But I can't take what Veturius offers. There's a trick in this. There must be. Why would I have been chosen as his prize if not for *that*? After a moment, he sets the cloak on the cot. I can smell the rain on him, and something darker. Death.

Silently, he starts a fire in the hearth. His hands tremble.

'You're shaking,' I observe.

'I'm cold.'

The wood catches, and he feeds the fire patiently, absorbed in the task. There are two scims strapped to his back, only a few feet away. I can grab one if I'm fast enough.

Do it! Now, while he's distracted! I lean forward, but just as I'm about to lunge, he turns. I freeze, teetering ridiculously.

'Take this instead.' Veturius takes a dagger from his boot and tosses it to me before turning back to the flames. 'It's clean, at least.'

The dagger's warm heft is comforting in my hand, and I test the edge on my thumb. Sharp. I sink back against the wall and eye him warily.

The fire eats away at the cold in the room. When it is burning brightly, Veturius unstraps his scims and leans them against the wall, well within my reach.

'I'll be in there.' He nods to a closed door in the corner of the room, one I'd assumed led to a torture chamber. 'That cloak won't bite, you know. You're stuck here until dawn. Might as well make yourself comfortable.'

He opens the door and disappears into the bathing chamber beyond. A moment later, I hear water pour into a tub.

The silk of my dress steams in the heat of the fire, and with one eye on the bath door, I let its warmth seep into me. Then I consider Veturius's cloak. My skirt is ripped to my thigh, and a sleeve of my shirt hangs by a few threads. The laces of my bodice are torn, revealing far too much of me. I look uneasily towards the bath. He'll finish soon.

Eventually, I pick up the cloak and wrap it around myself. It is made of thick, finely woven cloth that is softer to the touch than I expect. I recognize the smell – his smell – spice and rain. I inhale deeply before jerking my nose away as the door rattles and Veturius emerges with his bloodied armour and weapons.

He's scrubbed the mud from his skin and changed into clean fatigues.

'You'll get tired standing all night,' he says. 'You can sit on the bed. Or take the chair.' When I don't move, he sighs. 'You don't trust me – I get it. But if I wanted to hurt you, I'd already have done it. Please, sit down.'

'I'm keeping the knife.'

'You can have a scim too. I have a pile of weapons I never want to see again. Take them all.'

He drops into the chair and begins cleaning his greaves. I sit stiffly on his bed, ready to bring up the knife if I have to. He is close enough to touch.

He says nothing for a long time, his movements heavy and tired. Beneath the shadow of his mask, his full mouth seems harsh, his jaw unyielding. But I remember his face from the festival. It's a handsome face, and even the mask can't hide that. His diamond-shaped Blackcliff tattoo is a dark shadow on the back of his neck, parts of it tinged silver where the metal of his mask cleaves to his skin.

He looks up, sensing my gaze, and then glances quickly away. But not before I see telltale redness in his eyes.

I loosen my white-knuckled grip on the knife. What could upset a Mask, an Aspirant, enough to bring him to tears?

'What you told me about living in the Scholars' Quarter,' he says, breaking the quiet of the room, 'with your grandparents and your brother. That was true, once.'

'Until a few weeks ago. The Empire raided us. A Mask came. Killed my grandparents. Took my brother.'

'And your parents?'

'Dead. A long time ago now. My brother's the only one left. But he's in the death cells in Bekkar Prison.'

Veturius glances up at me. 'Bekkar doesn't have death cells.'

His comment is offhand and so unexpected that it takes a moment to sink in. He looks back down at his work, blind to the impact his words have had on me. 'Who told you he was in a death cell? And who told you he was in Bekkar?'

'I . . . heard a rumour.' *Idiot, Laia. You walked into this.* 'From . . . a friend.'

'Your friend's wrong. Or confused. Serra's only death cells are in Central. Bekkar's much smaller and usually filled with swindling Mercators and Plebeian drunks. It's no Kauf, that's for sure. I would know. I've done guard duty at both.'

'But if Blackcliff, say, got attacked . . .' My mind races as I think of what Mazen told me. 'Isn't it Bekkar that provides your . . . security?'

Veturius chuckles without smiling. 'Bekkar, protecting Blackcliff? Don't let my mother hear. Blackcliff has three thousand students bred for war, Laia. Some are young, but unless they're green, they're dangerous. The school doesn't need backup, least of all from a pack of bored auxes who spend their days taking bribes and racing roaches.'

Could I have misheard Mazen? No, he said Darin was in the death cells in Bekkar and that the prison provided Blackcliff's security backup, all of which Veturius has just refuted. Is Mazen's information bad, or is he lying to me? Once, I'd have given him the benefit of the doubt, but Cook's suspicions . . . and Keenan's . . . and my own weigh heavy on me. Why would Mazen lie? Where is Darin, really? Is he even alive?

He is alive. He must be. I'd know if my brother was dead. I'd feel it.

'I've upset you,' Veturius says. 'I'm sorry. But if your brother's in Bekkar, he'll be out soon. No one stays in there more than a few weeks.'

'Of course.' I clear my throat and try to wipe the confusion from my face. Masks can smell a lie. They can sense deceit. I have to act as normal as I can. 'It was just a rumour.'

He gives me a swift look, and I hold my breath, thinking he is about to question me further. But he just nods and raises his leather greaves, now clean, to the firelight before hanging them from the hooks embedded into the wall.

So that's what those hooks are for.

Is it possible Veturius won't hurt me? He's pulled me from death so many times. Why do that if he wishes violence upon me?

'Why did you help me?' I blurt out. 'Down in the dunes after the Commandant marked me, and at the Moon Festival, and when Marcus attacked me – every time, you could have turned away. Why didn't you?'

He looks up, thoughtful. 'The first time, I felt bad. I let Marcus hurt you the day I met you, outside the Commandant's office. I wanted to make up for it.'

I make a small noise of surprise. I didn't even think he noticed me that day.

'And then later – at the Moon Festival and with Marcus—' He shrugs. 'My mother would have killed you. Marcus too. I couldn't just let you die.'

367

'Plenty of Masks have stood and watched as Scholars died. You didn't.'

'I don't enjoy others' pain,' he says. 'Maybe that's why I've always hated Blackcliff. I was going to desert, you know.' His smile is sharp as a scim and as joyless.

'I had it all planned out. I dug a path from that hearth' – he points – 'to the entrance of the West Branch tunnel. The only secret entrance in the whole of Blackcliff. Then I mapped my way out of here. I was going to use tunnels the Empire thinks are caved in or flooded. I stole food, clothing, supplies. I drained my inheritance so I could buy what I needed on the way. I planned to escape through the Tribal lands and take a ship south from Sadh. I was going to be free – from the Commandant, Blackcliff, the Empire. So stupid. As if I could ever be free of this place.'

I almost stop breathing as his words sink in. *The only secret entrance in the whole of Blackcliff.*

Elias Veturius has just given me Darin's freedom.

That is, if Mazen is telling the truth. I'm not so sure anymore. I want to laugh at the absurdity of it – Veturius giving me the key to my brother's freedom, just as I realize that such information might not mean anything.

I've been silent too long. *Say something.*

'I thought being chosen for Blackcliff was an honour.'

'Not for me,' he says. 'Coming to Blackcliff wasn't a choice. The Augurs brought me here when I was six.' He picks up his scim and slowly wipes it clean. I recognize the intricate etchings on it – it's a Teluman blade. 'I lived with the Tribes back then. I'd never met my mother. I'd never even heard the name Veturius.'

'But how . . .' Veturius as a child. I've never considered it. I've never wondered if he knew his father, or if the Commandant raised him and loved him. I've never wondered, because he's never been anything more than a Mask.

'I'm bastard-born,' Veturius says. 'The only mistake Keris Veturia has ever made. She bore me and then exposed me in the Tribal desert. It's where she was stationed. That would have been the end of me, but a Tribal scouting party happened along. Tribesmen think baby boys are good luck, even abandoned ones. Tribe Saif adopted me, raised me as one of their own. Taught me their language and stories, dressed me in their clothes. They even gave me my name. Ilyaas. My grandfather changed it when I came to Blackcliff. Turned it into something more appropriate for a son of Gens Veturia.'

The tension between Veturius and his mother is suddenly clear. The woman never even wanted him. Her ruthlessness astounds me. I'd helped Pop bring dozens of newborns into the world. What kind of person could leave something so small, so precious, to die of heat and starvation?

The same person who could carve a K into a girl for opening a letter. The same person who would dash out a five-year-old's eye with a poker.

'What do you remember from that time?' I ask. 'From when you were a child? From before Blackcliff?'

Veturius frowns and puts a hand to his temple. The mask shimmers strangely at his touch, like a pool rippling beneath a drop of rain.

'I remember everything. The caravan was like a small city – Tribe Saif is dozens of families strong. I was fostered by the tribe's *Kehanni*, Mamie Rila.'

He speaks for a long time, and his words weave a life before my eyes, the life of a dark-haired, curious-eyed child who sneaked out from lessons so he could go adventuring, who waited eagerly at the edge of camp for the men of the Tribe to return from their merchant forays. A boy who scrapped with his foster brother one minute and laughed with him the next. A child without fear, until the Augurs came for him and plunged him into a world ruled by it. But for the Augurs, it could be Darin he is speaking of. It could be me.

When he falls silent, it's as if a warm, gold haze has been lifted from the room. He has a *Kehanni*'s skill at storytelling. I look up at him, surprised to see not the boy but the man he has become. Mask. Aspirant. Enemy.

'I've bored you,' he says.

'No. Not at all. You – you were like me. You were a child. A normal child. And that was taken from you.'

'Does that bother you?'

'Well, it certainly makes you harder to hate.'

'Seeing the enemy as a human. A general's ultimate nightmare.'

'The Augurs brought you to Blackcliff. How did it happen?'

This time, his pause is longer, heavy with the taint of a memory better forgotten.

'It was autumn – the Augurs always bring a new crop of Yearlings in when the desert winds are at their worst. The night they came to the Saif encampment, the Tribe was happy. Our chief had just returned from a successful trade, and we had new clothes and shoes – even books. The cooks slaughtered two goats and spit-roasted them. The drums beat, the girls sang, and stories poured from Mamie Rila for hours.

'We celebrated into the night, but finally, everyone slept. Everyone but me. I'd had this strange sense for hours – that some darkness was closing in. I saw shadows outside the wagon, shadows circling the camp. I looked out of the wagon, where I was sleeping, and saw this . . . this man. Black clothing and red eyes and skin without any colour at all. An Augur. He said my name. I remember thinking he must be part reptile, because his voice came out of him like a hiss. And that was it. I was chained to the Empire. I was chosen.'

'Were you afraid?'

'Terrified. I knew he was there to take me away. And I didn't know where, or why. They brought me to Blackcliff. Cut off my hair, took my clothes, and put me in a pen outside with the others for a culling. Soldiers threw us mouldy bread and jerky once a day, but back then, I wasn't very big, so I never got much. Midway through the third day, I was sure I would die. So I sneaked out of the pen and stole food from the guards. I shared it with my lookout. Well . . .' He looks up, considering. 'I say *share*, but really, she ate most of it. Anyway, after seven days, the Augurs opened the pen, and those of us still alive were told that if we fought hard, we would be the guardians of the Empire, and if we didn't, we'd be dead.'

I can see it. The small bodies of those left behind. The fear in the eyes of those who lived. Veturius as a boy, afraid and starved, determined not to die.

'You survived.'

'I wish I hadn't. If you'd seen the Third Trial – if you knew what I did . . .' He polishes the same spot on one of the scims over and over.

'What happened?' I ask softly. He is silent for so long that I think I've angered him, that I've crossed a line. Then he tells me. He pauses frequently, and his voice goes from broken to flat. He keeps working on the scim, shining it, then sharpening it with a whetstone until it gleams.

When he is done speaking, he hangs the scim up. The streaks running down his mask catch the firelight, and I understand, now, why he was shaking when he walked in, why his eyes are so haunted.

'So you see,' he says, 'I'm just like the Mask who killed your grandparents. I'm just like Marcus. Worse, actually, because such men consider it their duty to kill. I know better. And I did it anyway.'

'The Augurs didn't give you a choice. You couldn't find Aquilla to end the Trial, and if you hadn't fought, you'd have died.'

'Then I should have died.'

'Nan always said that as long as there is life, there is hope. If you'd refused to give the order, your men would be dead right now – either at the hands of the Augurs or on the blades of Aquilla's platoon. Don't forget: she chose life for herself and her men. Either way, you'd have blamed yourself. Either way, people you cared about would have suffered.'

'Doesn't matter.'

'But it *does* matter. Of course it matters. Because you're not evil.' The knowledge is a revelation and one so staggering that I badly want him to see it too. 'You're not like the others. You killed to save. You put others first. Not – not like me.'

I can't bring myself to look at Veturius. 'When the Mask came, I ran.' The words spill out of me, a tumbling river I've dammed up for too long. 'My grandparents were dead. The Mask had Darin, my brother. Darin told me to run, even though he needed me. I should have helped him, but I couldn't. No.' I dig my fists into my thighs. 'I *didn't*. I *chose* not to stay. I chose to run, like a coward. I still don't understand it. I should have stayed, even if that meant dying.'

My eyes seek the floor in shame. But then his hand is on my chin, tipping my face up. His clean scent washes over me.

'As you say, Laia' – he forces me to meet his eyes – 'there's hope in life. If you hadn't run, you'd be dead. And Darin too.' He lets me go and sits back. 'Masks don't like defiance. He'd have made you pay for it.'

'Doesn't matter.'

Veturius smiles that knife's-edge smile. 'Look at us,' he says. 'Scholar slave and Mask, each trying to persuade the other that they're not evil. The Augurs do have a sense of humour, don't they?'

My fingers are clenched around the hilt of the dagger Veturius gave me, and a hot anger rises inside me – at the Augurs for letting me think I was to be interrogated. At the Commandant for leaving her own child to die a torturous death, and at Blackcliff for training that child to be a killer. At my parents for dying and my brother for apprenticing himself to a Martial. At Mazen for his demands and secrets. At the Empire and its iron-fisted control over every aspect of our lives.

I want to defy all of them – the Empire, the Commandant, the Resistance. I wonder where such defiance comes from, and my armlet feels hot suddenly. Perhaps there's more of my mother in me than I thought.

'Maybe we don't have to be Scholar slave and Mask.' I drop the dagger. 'For tonight, maybe we can just be Laia and Elias.'

Emboldened, I reach out and pull at the edge of his mask, which has never seemed like a part of him. It resists, but now I want it off. I want to see the face of the boy I've been speaking to all night, not the Mask I always thought he was. So I pull harder, and the mask falls into my hands with a hiss. The back is bent into sharp spikes wet with blood. The tattoo on his neck glistens with a dozen small wounds.

'I'm so sorry,' I say. 'I didn't realize . . .'

He looks into my eyes, and something undefined burns in his

gaze, a flash of emotion that brings a different sort of fire to my skin.

'I'm glad you took it off.'

I should look away. I cannot. His eyes are nothing like his mother's. Hers are the brittle grey of broken glass, but Elias's, with their ring of dark lashes, are a deeper hue, like the thick heart of a storm cloud. They draw me in, mesmerize me, refuse to release me. I lift tentative fingers to his skin. The stubble of his cheek is rough beneath my palm.

Keenan's face flashes through my mind and fades as quickly. He is far away, distant, dedicated utterly to the Resistance. Elias is here, before me, warm and beautiful and broken.

He's a Martial. A Mask.

But not here. Not tonight, in this room. Here, now, he is just Elias and I am just Laia, and we are, both of us, drowning.

'Laia . . .'

There is a plea in his voice, in his eyes. What does it mean? Does he want me to back away? Does he want me to come closer?

I lift myself up on my toes, and his face comes down at the same time. His lips are soft, softer than I could have imagined, but there is a hard desperation behind them, a need. The kiss speaks. It begs. *Let me forget, forget, forget.*

His cloak falls away from me, and my body is against his. He pulls me to his chest, his hands running down my back, clasping my thigh, drawing me closer, closer. I arch into him, revelling in his strength, his fire, the alchemy between us twisting and burning and melding until it feels like gold.

Then he breaks away, his hands held out before him.

'I'm sorry,' he says. 'I'm so sorry. I didn't mean to. I'm a Mask and you're a slave, and I shouldn't have—'

'It's all right.' My lips burn. 'I'm the one who . . . started it.'

We stare at each other, and he looks so confused, so angry at himself that I smile, sadness and embarrassment and desire coursing through me. He picks his cloak up from the floor and holds it out to me, averting his eyes.

'Will you sit?' I ask tentatively, covering myself once more. 'Tomorrow I'll be a slave and you'll be a Mask, and we can hate each other like we're supposed to. But for now . . .'

He eases down next to me, keeping a careful distance between us. That alchemy lures, beckons, burns. But his jaw is clenched, and his hands are fisted together like each is a lifeline for the other. Reluctantly, I put a few more inches between us.

'Tell me more,' I say. 'What was it like as a Fiver? Were you happy to leave Blackcliff?'

He relaxes a little, and I coax the memories from him like Pop used to with frightened patients. The night passes, filled with his stories of Blackcliff and the Tribes, and my tales of patients and the Quarter. We do not speak again of the raid or the Trials. We do not speak of the kiss or the sparks still dancing between us.

Before I know it, the sky begins to lighten.

'Dawn,' he says. 'Time to start hating each other again.'

He puts on his mask, his face going still as it digs into him, and then pulls me to my feet. I stare at our hands, at my slim fingers entwined in his larger ones, at the veined muscles of his forearm, the slight bones of my wrist, the warmth of our skin meeting. It seems somehow significant, my hand in his. I look up into his face, surprised at how near he is to me, at the fire in his gaze, the life, and my pulse quickens. But then he drops my hand and steps away.

I offer him back his cloak, along with the dagger, but he shakes his head.

'Keep them. You still have to walk back through the school

and—' His eyes drop to my ripped dress, my bare skin, and he jerks them up again. 'Keep the knife too. A Scholar girl should always carry a weapon, no matter what the rules say.' He pulls a leather strap from his bureau. 'Thigh sheath. It'll keep the blade safe and out of sight.'

I regard him anew, at last seeing him for what he is. 'If you could just be who you are in here' – I place my palm over his heart – 'instead of who they made you, then you would be a great Emperor.' I feel his pulse thud against my fingers. 'But they won't let you, will they? They won't let you have compassion or kindness. They won't let you keep your soul.'

'My soul's gone.' He looks away. 'I killed it dead on that battlefield yesterday.'

I think of Spiro Teluman then. Of what he said to me the last time I saw him. 'There are two kinds of guilt,' I say softly. 'The kind that's a burden and the kind that gives you purpose. Let your guilt be your fuel. Let it remind you of who you want to be. Draw a line in your mind. Never cross it again. You have a soul. It's damaged, but it's there. Don't let them take it from you, Elias.'

His eyes meet mine when I say his name, and I reach up a hand to touch his mask. It is smooth and warm, like rock polished by water and then left to heat in the sun.

I let my arm fall. Then I leave his room and walk to the doors of the barracks and out into the rising sun.

CHAPTER FORTY-TWO

Elias

After the barracks door shuts behind Laia, I still feel the feather-light touch of her fingertips on my face. I see the expression in her eyes as she reached up to me: a careful, curious look that caught my breath.

And that kiss. Burning skies, the feel of her, how she'd arched into me, wanted me. A few precious moments of freedom from who I am, what I am. I close my eyes, remembering, but other memories shove their way in. Darker memories. She'd kept them at bay. For hours, she'd fought them off, and she hadn't even known it. But they are here now, and they won't be ignored.

I led my men to slaughter.

I murdered my friends.

I nearly killed Helene.

Helene. I have to go to her. I have to make things right with her. Our anger's stood too long. Maybe, after this nightmare we've wrought, we can find a way forward together. She must be as horrified as I am at what happened. As sickened.

I snatch my scims from the wall. The thought of what I'd done

377

with them makes me want to toss them to the dunes, Teluman blades or not. But I'm too used to having weapons across my back. I feel naked without them.

The sun shines as I emerge from the barracks, unfeeling in a cloudless sky. It seems profane somehow – the world clean, the air warm – when scores of young men lay cold in their coffins, waiting to return to the earth.

The dawn drums thunder out and begin listing the names of the dead. Each name summons an image in my head – a face, a voice, a form – until it feels as if my fallen comrades are rising up around me, a phalanx of ghosts.

Cyril Antonius. Silas Eburian. Tristas Equitius. Demetrius Galerius. Ennis Medalus. Darien Titius. Leander Vissan.

The drumming goes on. The families will have collected the bodies by now. Blackcliff has no graveyard. Among these walls, all that remains of the fallen is the emptiness of where they walked, the silence where their voices rang.

In the belltower courtyard, Cadets lunge and parry with staffs as a Centurion circles them. I should have known the Commandant wouldn't cancel classes, not even to honour the deaths of dozens of her students.

The Centurion nods as I pass, and I'm confused by his lack of disgust. Doesn't he know I'm a murderer? Wasn't he watching yesterday?

How can you ignore it? I want to shout. *How can you pretend it didn't happen?*

I head for the cliffs. Helene will be down in the dunes, where we have always mourned our dead. On my way there, I see Faris and Dex. Without Tristas, Demetrius, and Leander by their sides, they look bizarre, like an animal missing its legs.

I think they will pass me by. Or attack me for giving the order that took their souls. Instead, they stop before me, quiet, despondent. Their eyes are as red as mine.

Dex massages his neck, his thumb moving in ceaseless circles over the Blackcliff tattoo. 'I keep seeing their faces,' he says. 'Hearing them.'

For long moments, we stand together in silence. But it is selfish of me to share such grief, to take comfort in knowing that they feel the same self-hatred that I do. I'm the reason they are haunted.

'You followed orders,' I say. This burden, at least, I can take. 'Orders I gave. Their deaths aren't on you. They're on me.'

Faris meets my eyes, a ghost of the big, joyful boy he had once been. 'They're free now,' he says. 'Free of the Augurs. Of Blackcliff. Not like us.'

When Dex and Faris walk away, I rappel to the desert floor, where Helene sits cross-legged in the shade of the cliffs, her feet buried to the ankles in the hot sand. Her hair ripples in the wind, glowing gold-white like the curve of a sunlit dune. I approach her as one would an angry horse.

'You don't need to be so cat-footed,' she says when I'm a few feet away. 'I'm not armed.'

I sit beside her. 'Are you all right?'

'I'm alive.'

'I'm sorry, Helene. I know you can't forgive me, but—'

'Stop. We didn't have a choice, Elias. If I'd got the upper hand, I'd have done the same thing to you. I killed Cyril. I killed Silas and Lyris. I nearly killed Dex, but he backed off, and I couldn't find him again.' Her silver face could be carved of marble, it's so emotionless. *Who is this person?* 'If we'd refused to fight,' she says, 'our friends would have died. What were we supposed to do?'

'I killed Demetrius.' I search her face for anger. She and

Demetrius grew close after his brother died – she was the only one who ever knew what to say to him. 'And – and Leander.'

'You did what you had to. Just as I did what I had to. Just as Faris and Dex and all the others who survived did what they had to.'

'I know they did what they had to do, but they followed an order *I* gave. An order I should have been strong enough *not* to give.'

'You'd have died, Elias.' She doesn't look at me. She's working so hard to convince herself that it's all right. That what we did was necessary. 'Your men would have died.'

'The battle will end when you defeat or are defeated by the leader of the enemy. If I'd been willing to die first, Tristas would still be alive. Leander. Demetrius. All of them, Helene. Zak knew it – he begged Marcus to kill him. I should have done the same. You'd be named Empress—'

'Or the Augurs would name Marcus, and I'd be his – his *slave*—'

'*We* told our men to kill.' Why doesn't she understand? Why isn't she willing to face it? '*We* gave the order. We followed it ourselves. It's unforgivable.'

'What did you think was going to happen?' Helene pushes herself to her feet, and I stand too. 'Did you think the Trials would get easier? Didn't you know this would come? They've made us live our deepest fears. They've thrown us at the mercy of creatures that shouldn't exist. Then they turned us against each other. *Strength of arms and mind and heart.* You're surprised? You're naïve, is what you are. You're a fool.'

'Hel, you don't know what you're saying. I almost killed you—'

'Thank the skies for it!' She's in front of me, so close that strands of her long hair blow into my face. 'You fought back. After losing so many training battles, I wasn't sure you would. I was so scared – I thought you'd be dead out there—'

'You're sick.' I back away from her. 'Don't you have any regret? Any remorse? Those were our friends we killed.'

'They were soldiers,' Helene says. 'Empire soldiers who died in battle, who died with honour. I'll celebrate them. I'll mourn them. But I won't regret what I did. I did it for the Empire. I did it for my people.' She paces back and forth. 'Don't you see, Elias? The Trials are bigger than you or me, bigger than our guilt, our shame. We're the answer to a five-hundred-year-old question. When Taius's line fails, who will lead the Empire? Who will ride at the head of a half-million-strong army? Who will control the destinies of forty million souls?'

'What about our destinies? Our souls?'

'They took our souls a long time ago, Elias.'

'No, Hel.' Laia's words ring in my head, words I want to believe. Words I need to believe. *You have a soul. Don't let them take it from you.* 'You're wrong. I can never fix what I did yesterday, but when the Fourth Trial comes, I won't—'

'Don't, Elias.' Helene puts her fingers over my mouth, her anger replaced with something like despair. 'Don't make vows when you can't know their cost.'

'I crossed a line yesterday, Helene. I won't cross it again.'

'Don't say that.' Her hair flies about, and her eyes are wild. 'How can you become Emperor if that's the way you think? How can you win the Trials if—'

'I don't want to win the Trials,' I say. 'I've never wanted to win them. I didn't even want to take them. I was going to desert, Helene. Right after graduation, when everyone else would be celebrating, I was going to run.'

She shakes her head, holding up her hands as if to ward off

my words. But I don't stop. She needs to hear this. She needs to know the truth of who I am.

'I didn't run, because Cain told me the only chance I had to be truly free was to take the Trials. I want *you* to win the Trials, Hel. I want to be named Blood Shrike. And then I want you to set me free.'

'Set you free? *Set you free?* This *is* freedom, Elias! When will you understand that? We're Masks. Our destiny is power and death and violence. It's what we are. If you don't own that, then how can you ever be free?'

She's delusional. I'm trying to comprehend this dreadful truth when I hear the sound of approaching bootsteps. Hel hears it too, and we whirl to find Cain rounding a curve in the cliffs. A squadron of eight legionnaires accompanies him. He says nothing of the fight Helene and I are having, though he must have heard at least part of it. 'You will come with us.'

The legionnaires split, four taking hold of me and the other four grabbing Helene.

'What's going on?' I try to shake them off, but they're big brutes, bigger than me, and they don't budge. 'What is this?'

'This, Aspirant Veturius, is the Trial of Loyalty.'

CHAPTER FORTY-THREE

Laia

When I enter the Commandant's kitchen, Izzi rushes me. Her eye is shadowed, and her blonde hair is a bird's nest, as if she hasn't slept all night.

'You're alive! You're . . . you're *here*! We thought . . .'

'Did they harm you, girl?' Cook comes up behind Izzi, and I'm shocked to see that she too is dishevelled, her eyes red-rimmed. She takes my cloak, and when she sees my dress, she tells Izzi to bring me another. 'Are you all right?'

'I'm fine.' What else can I say? I am still trying to make sense of what has just transpired. At the same time, I'm remembering what Elias said about Bekkar Prison, and one thing becomes clear: I have to get out of here and find the Resistance. I have to figure out where Darin is and what's really going on.

'Where did they take you, Laia?' Izzi is back with the dress, and I change into it quickly, hiding the dagger at my thigh as best as I can. I'm reluctant to tell them what's happened, but I won't lie to them, not when it's clear that they've spent the entire night fearing for my life.

383

'They gave me to Veturius as a prize for winning the Third Trial.' At the twin looks of horror on their faces, I add, in a rush, 'But he didn't hurt me. Nothing happened.'

'Indeed?' The Commandant's voice chills my blood, and as one, Izzi, Cook, and I turn to the kitchen door.

'Nothing happened, you say.' She cocks her head. 'How very interesting. Come with me.'

I follow her to her study, my feet leaden. Once inside, my eyes dart to the wall of dead fighters. It's like being in a room of ghosts.

The Commandant closes the study door and circles me.

'You spent the night with Aspirant Veturius,' she says.

'Yes, sir.'

'Did he rape you?'

So easily she asks such an abhorrent question. As if asking my age or my name.

'No, sir.'

'Why would that be, when the other night he seemed so very interested in you? He couldn't keep his hands off you.'

She is, I realize, talking about the night of the Moon Festival. As if she can smell my fear, she steps towards me.

'I – I don't know.'

'Could it be that the boy actually *cares* about you? I know he's aided you – the day he carried you up from the dunes, and a few nights ago with Marcus.' She takes another step. 'But the night I found you two in the servants' corridor – that's the night I've been wondering about. What were you doing together? Is he in league with you? Has he turned?'

'I – I'm not sure what you—'

'Did you think you could fool me? Did you think I didn't know?'

Oh skies. It can't be.

'I have spies too, slave. Among the Mariners, the Tribesmen.' Now she's inches away, and her smile is like a thin garrotte around my throat. 'Even in the Resistance. You'd be surprised where I have eyes. Those Scholar rats know only what I want them to know. What were they up to the last time you met them? Were they planning something significant? Something involving a great many men? Perhaps you're wondering what it was. You'll find out soon enough.'

Her hand is around my neck before I can think to dodge her. I kick out, and she tightens her grip. The muscles of her arms bulge, but her eyes are as flat and dead as ever.

'Do you know what I do to spies?'

'I – not – don't—' I can't breathe. I can't think.

'I teach them a lesson. Them and anyone in league with them. Kitchen-Girl, for instance.' *No, not Izzi, not Izzi.* Just as spots begin exploding at the edge of my vision, a knock comes at the door. She releases me, letting me fall to the floor in a heap. Casually, as if she hadn't just nearly murdered a slave, she opens the door.

'Commandant.' An Augur waits outside – a woman this time – small and ethereal. I expect to see legionnaires behind her like before, but she is alone. 'I'm here for the girl.'

'You can't have her,' the Commandant says. 'She is a criminal and—'

'I'm here for the girl.' The Augur's face hardens, and she and the Commandant lock eyes, a silent and fierce battle of wills. 'Give her to me and come. We are needed in the amphitheatre.'

'She's a spy—'

'And she will be appropriately punished.' The Augur turns to me, and I can't look away from her. For an instant, I see myself in the dark pool of her eyes – my heart stopped, my face lifeless.

As if the knowledge has been planted in my head, I realize that the Augur is taking me to the Reaper, that my death is close – closer than during the raid, closer than when Marcus beat me.

'Don't give me to her,' I find myself begging the Commandant. 'Please, don't—'

The Augur doesn't let me finish. 'Do not set your will against the Augurs, Keris Veturia. You will fail. You can come willingly to the amphitheatre, or I can compel you. Which shall it be?'

The Commandant hesitates, and the Augur waits like a rock in a river, patient, unmovable. Finally, the Commandant nods and sweeps out the door. For the second time in a day, I'm gagged and bound. Then the Augur follows in the Commandant's wake, dragging me after.

CHAPTER FORTY-FOUR

Elias

'I'll go quietly,' I say as the soldiers restrain and blindfold Helene and me. 'But get your damned hands off me.' In response, one of them shoves a gag in my mouth and takes my scims.

The legionnaires haul us up the cliffs and through the school. Bootsteps shuffle and thump around me, Centurions shout orders, and I hear *amphitheatre* and *Fourth Trial*. My whole body tenses. I don't want to go back to the place where I killed my friends. I never want to set foot there again.

Cain is a pocket of silence ahead of me. Is he reading me right now? Is he reading Helene? *Doesn't matter.* I try to forget him, to think as I would if he wasn't here.

Loyalty to break the soul. The words are too close to what Laia said. *You have a soul. Don't let them take it from you.* That, I sense, is exactly what the Augurs will try to do. So I draw that line Laia spoke of, a deep runnel in the earth of my mind. *I won't cross it. No matter the cost. I won't.*

I feel Helene beside me, fear radiating off her, chilling the air around us and setting my nerves on edge.

'Elias.' The legionnaires didn't gag her, probably because she had the sense not to be mouthy. 'Listen to me. Whatever the Augurs ask you to do, you must do it, understand? Whoever wins this Trial is Emperor – the Augurs said there would be no tie. Be strong, Elias. If you don't win this, everything is lost.'

There is an urgency to her that unsettles me, a warning in her words beyond the obvious. I wait for her to say something else, but either she's been gagged or Cain has silenced her. Moments later, hundreds of voices reverberate around me, filling me crown to toe. We've reached the amphitheatre.

The legionnaires pull me up a set of steps before forcing me to my knees. Helene comes down beside me, and the bindings, blindfolds, and gag come off.

'I see they muzzled you, bastard. Pity they didn't make it permanent.'

Marcus, kneeling on the other side of Helene, glares at me, hatred spilling from every pore. His body is bunched, a snake ready to strike. He wears no weapon save a dagger at his belt. All his gravitas from the Third Trial has morphed into a poisonous vitriol. Zak always seemed like the weaker twin, but at least he tried to check the Snake. Without his quiet-voiced brother at his back, Marcus seems almost feral.

I ignore him and attempt to steel myself for whatever is coming next. The legionnaires have left us on a raised dais behind Cain, who stares fixedly at the amphitheatre's entrance as if awaiting something. A dozen other Augurs are arrayed around the dais, tattered shadows who darken the stadium with their very presence. I count them again – thirteen, including Cain. Which means one is missing.

The rest of the amphitheatre is packed. I spot the governor, the rest of the city councillors. Grandfather sits a few rows behind the Commandant's pavilion with a group of his personal guard, his eyes on me.

'The Commandant's late.' Hel nods to my mother's empty seat.

'Wrong, Aquilla,' Marcus says. 'She's right on time.' As he speaks, my mother walks through the gates of the amphitheatre. The fourteenth Augur follows her, managing, despite her seeming frailty, to pull a bound and gagged girl behind her. I see a mane of heavy black hair come loose, and my heart seizes – it's Laia. What's she doing here? Why is she tied up?

The Commandant takes her seat while the Augur deposits Laia on the dais beside Cain. The slave-girl tries to speak through her gag, but it's knotted too tightly.

'Aspirants.' As soon as Cain speaks, the stadium falls silent. A flock of seabirds wheels overhead, screeching. Down in the city, a merchant peddles his wares, the singsong strains of his voice reaching even here.

'The final Trial is the Trial of Loyalty. The Empire has decreed that this slave-girl is to die.' Cain gestures to Laia, and my stomach drops as if I've jumped from a great height. *No. She's innocent. She's done nothing wrong.*

Laia's eyes go wide. She tries to back away on her knees. The same Augur who delivered her to the dais kneels behind her and holds her still with an iron grip, like a butcher holding a lamb for slaughter.

'When I tell you to proceed,' Cain goes on calmly, as if he's not talking about the death of a seventeen-year-old girl, 'you will all simultaneously attempt to execute her. Whoever carries out the order will be declared victor of the Trial.'

'This is wrong, Cain,' I burst out. 'The Empire has no reason to kill her.'

'Reason does not matter, Aspirant Veturius. Only loyalty. If you

389

defy the order, you fail the Trial. The punishment for failure is death.'

I think of the nightmare battlefield, and my blood goes leaden at the memory. Leander, Demetrius, Ennis – they had all been on that field. I'd killed them all.

Laia had been there too, throat cut, eyes dim, hair a sodden cloud around her head.

But I haven't done it yet, I think desperately. *I haven't killed her.*

The Augur looks at each of us in turn before taking a scim from the legionnaires – one of mine – and laying it on the dais equidistant from Marcus, Helene, and me.

'Proceed.'

My body knows what to do before my mind, and I dive in front of Laia. If I can place myself between her and the others, she might have a chance.

Because I don't care what I saw on that nightmare battlefield. I won't kill her. And I won't let anyone else kill her either.

I get to her before Helene or Marcus and spin into a crouch, expecting an attack from one or both of them. But instead of coming for Laia, Helene leaps for Marcus, knocking her fist against his temple. He drops like a stone, clearly not expecting her attack, and she shoves him off the dais, then kicks my scim towards me.

'Do it, Elias!' she says. 'Before Marcus comes to!'

Then she sees that I'm guarding the girl instead of killing her, and she makes a strange, choked sound. The crowd is silent, holding its breath.

'Don't do this, Elias,' she says. 'Not now. We're almost there. You'll be Emperor. Foretold. Please, Elias, think of what you could do for – for the Empire—'

'I told you there's a line I'm not crossing.' I feel strangely calm as I say it, calmer than I've felt in weeks. Laia's eyes shift from Helene to me rapidly. 'This is that line. I won't kill her.'

Helene picks up the scim. 'Then step aside,' she says. 'I'll do it. I'll make it quick.' She moves towards me slowly, her eyes never leaving my face.

'Elias,' she says. 'She's going to die no matter what you do. The Empire's decreed it. If you or I don't do it, Marcus will – he'll wake up eventually. We can end this before he does. If she has to die, at least something good will come of it. I'll be Empress. You'll be Blood Shrike.' She takes another step.

'I know you don't want rulership,' she says softly. 'Or lordship over the Black Guard. I didn't understand before. But I – I do now. So if you let me take care of this, I vow, by blood and by bone, that the second I'm named Empress, I'll release you from your oaths to the Empire. You can go wherever you want. Do whatever you want. You'll be beholden to no one. You'll be free.'

I've been watching her body, waiting for her muscles to tense in preparation for the attack, but now my eyes snap to hers. *You'll be free.* The only thing I've ever wanted and she's handing it to me on a silver platter with a vow I know she'd never break.

For a brief, terrible moment, I consider it. I want it more than anything I've wanted in my life. I see myself sailing out of port at Navium, leaving for the southern kingdoms, where no one and nothing have a claim over my body or my soul.

Well, my body, anyway. Because if I allow Helene to kill Laia, I won't have a soul.

'If you want to kill her,' I say to Helene, 'you'll have to kill me first.'

A tear snakes down her face, and for a second, I see through her eyes. She wants this so badly, and it's no enemy keeping it from her. It's me.

We are everything to each other. And I'm betraying her. Again.

Then I hear a thud – the unmistakable sound of steel sinking into flesh. Behind me, Laia pitches forward so suddenly that the Augur falls with her, her hands still pinning the girl's limp arms. Laia's hair is a storm around her, but I can't see her face, her eyes.

'No! Laia!' I'm down beside her, shaking her, trying to turn her over. But I can't get the damned Augur off her, because the woman is shaking in terror, her robes tangled with Laia's skirts. Laia is silent, her body limp as a rag doll's.

I spot the hilt of a dagger that's fallen to the dais, the rapidly widening pool of blood spilling out of her. No one can lose that much blood and live.

Marcus.

Too late I see him standing at the back of the stage. Too late I realize that Helene and I should have killed him, that we shouldn't have risked him waking up.

The explosion of sound that follows Laia's death staggers me. Thousands of voices yell at once. Grandfather bellows louder than a gored bull.

Marcus jumps onto the dais, and I know he's coming for me. I want him to come. I want to crush the life out of him for what he's done.

I feel Cain's hand on my arm, restraining me. Then the gates to the amphitheatre burst open. Marcus jerks his head around, shocked into stillness as a foam-coated stallion gallops through the doors of the stadium. The legionnaire riding him slides to the ground, landing on his feet as the beast rears beside him.

'The Emperor,' the legionnaire says. 'The Emperor is dead! Gens Taia has fallen!'

'When?' The Commandant cuts in. There's not an ounce of shock on her face. 'How?'

'A Resistance attack, sir. He was killed en route to Serra, only a day from the city. He and all who were with him. Even – even children.'

Waiting vines circle and strangle the oak. The way is made clear, just before the end. That was the foretelling the Commandant spoke of in her office weeks ago, and now it suddenly makes sense. The vines are the Resistance. The oak is the Emperor.

'Bear witness, men and women of the Empire, students of Blackcliff, Aspirants.' Cain releases my arm and his voice booms out, shaking the foundations of the amphitheatre and silencing the panic setting in. 'Thus do the Augurs' visions bear fruit. The Emperor is dead, and a new power must rise, lest the Empire be destroyed.

'Aspirant Veturius,' Cain says. 'You were given the chance to prove your loyalty. But instead of killing the girl, you defended her. Instead of following my order, you defied it.'

'Of course I defied it!' This isn't happening. 'This wasn't a Trial of Loyalty for anyone but me. I'm the only one who cared about her. This Trial was a joke—'

'This Trial told us what we needed to know: You are not fit to be Emperor. You are stripped of name and rank. You will die tomorrow at dawn by beheading before the Blackcliff belltower. Those who were your peers will bear witness to your shame.'

Two Augurs fasten chains around my hands and wrists. I hadn't noticed the chains before. Did they conjure them from thin air? I'm too dazed to fight. The Augur who restrained Laia lifts the girl's body with difficulty and staggers off the dais.

'Aspirant Aquilla,' Cain says. 'You were prepared to strike down the enemy. But you faltered when faced with Veturius, deferring to his wishes. Such loyalty to a peer is admirable. But not in an Emperor. Out of all three Aspirants, only Aspirant Farrar attempted to carry out my order without question, with unflinching loyalty to the Empire. Thus, I name him victor of the Fourth Trial.'

Helene's face is white as bone, her mind, like mine, unable to take in the travesty occurring in front of our eyes.

'Aspirant Aquilla.' Cain pulls Hel's scim from his robes. 'Do you remember your vow?'

'But you can't mean—'

'I will keep my vows, Aspirant Aquilla. Will you keep yours?'

She eyes the Augur as one would a traitorous lover, taking the scim when he offers it. 'I will.'

'Then kneel now and swear fealty, for we, the Augurs, name Marcus Antonius Farrar Emperor, he who was Foretold, High Commander of the Martial Army, Imperator Invictus, Overlord of the Realm. And you, Aspirant Aquilla, are named his Blood Shrike, his second-in-command, and the sword that executes his will. Your allegiance cannot be broken, unless by death. Swear it.'

'No!' I roar. 'Helene, don't do it!'

She turns to me, and the look in her eyes is a knife twisting inside me. *You chose, Elias*, her pale eyes say. *You chose her.*

'Tomorrow,' Cain says, 'after Veturius's execution, we will crown the Foretold.' He looks at the Snake. 'The Empire is yours, Marcus.'

Marcus glances over his shoulder with a smile, and I realize with a jolt that it's something I've seen him do hundreds of times. It's the look he would throw his brother when he'd insulted an enemy, or won a battle, or otherwise wished to gloat. But his smile fades. Because Zak's not there.

His face goes blank, and he looks down at Helene without conceit or triumph. His utter lack of feeling chills my blood.

'Your fealty, Aquilla,' he says flatly. 'I'm waiting.'

'Cain,' I say. 'He's not fit. You know he's not. He's mad. He'll destroy the Empire.'

No one hears me. Not Cain. Not Helene. Not even Marcus.

When Helene speaks, she is everything a Mask should be: calm, collected, impassive.

'I swear fealty to Marcus Antonius Farrar,' she says. 'Emperor, he who was Foretold, High Commander of the Martial Army, Imperator Invictus, Overlord of the Realm. I will be his Blood Shrike, his second-in-command, the sword that executes his will, until death. I swear it.'

Then she bows her head and offers the Snake her sword.

PART THREE

BODY AND SOUL

CHAPTER FORTY-FIVE

Laia

'If you wish to live, girl, then let them think you dead.'

Above the sudden din of the crowd, I barely hear the Augur's panting whisper. Mystified by the fact that a Martial holy woman wants, for some reason, to help me, I'm stunned into silence. As her weight crushes me to the dais, the dagger Marcus has flung into her side is jarred loose. Blood seeps across the platform, and I shudder, chillingly reminded of how Nan died, in a pool of blood just like this one.

'Don't move,' the Augur says. 'No matter what happens.'

I do what she says, even as Elias shouts my name and tries to pull her off me. The messenger announces the Emperor's assassination; Elias is sentenced to death and chained. Throughout, I remain still. But when the Augur named Cain announces the coronation, I stifle a gasp. After the coronation, the death cell prisoners will be executed – which means that unless the Resistance gets him out of prison, Darin will die tomorrow.

Or will he? Mazen says Darin's in Bekkar's death cells. Elias says Bekkar doesn't have death cells.

I want to scream with frustration. I need clarity. The only one who can give it to me is Mazen, and the only way I'm going to find him is if I get out of here. But I can't exactly stand up and stroll out. Everyone thinks I'm dead. Even if I could leave, Elias just sacrificed his life for mine. I can't abandon him.

I lay uselessly, unsure of what to do, when the Augur decides for me. 'You move now, you die,' she warns, pulling herself off me. When all eyes are on the tableaux beside us, she lifts me up and staggers towards the amphitheatre door.

Dead. Dead. I can practically hear the woman in my head. *Pretend you're dead.* My limbs flop, and my head lolls. I keep my eyes closed, but when the Augur misses a step and nearly falls, they fly open of their own accord. No one notices, but for a brief moment, as Aquilla swears her fealty, I catch a glimpse of Elias's face. And though I've seen my brother taken and my grandparents killed, though I've suffered beatings and scarrings and visited the night shores of Death's realm, I know I've never felt the type of desolation and hopelessness I see in Elias's eyes at that moment.

The Augur rights herself. Two of her fellows close around her, the way brothers flank a little sister in a rough crowd. Her blood soaks my clothes, blending into the black silk. She's lost so much that I don't understand how she can muster the strength to walk.

'Augurs cannot die,' she says through gritted teeth. 'But we can bleed.'

We reach the amphitheatre gates, and once through, the woman sets me on my feet in an alcove. I expect her to explain why she chose to take that dagger for me, but she just limps away, her brethren supporting her.

I look back through the amphitheatre gates to where Elias kneels, chained. My head tells me I can do nothing for him, that if I try to help him, I'll die. But I can't bring myself to walk away.

'You are unhurt.' Cain has slipped away from the still-packed amphitheatre, unnoticed by the jabbering crowd. 'Good. Follow me.' He catches the look I cast at Elias and shakes his head.

'He is beyond your aid right now,' Cain says. 'He has sealed his fate.'

'So that's it for him?' I'm appalled at Cain's callousness. 'Elias refuses to kill me, and he dies for it? You're going to punish him for showing mercy?'

'The Trials have rules,' Cain says. 'Aspirant Veturius broke them.'

'Your rules are twisted. Besides, Elias wasn't the only one who violated your instructions. Marcus was supposed to kill me, and he didn't. You still made him Emperor.'

'He *thinks* he killed you,' Cain says. 'And he revels in the knowledge. That is what matters. Come, you must leave the school. If the Commandant knows you survived, your life is forfeit.'

I tell myself the Augur is right, that I can't do anything for Elias. But I'm uneasy. I've done this before. I've left someone behind and lived to regret it every moment after.

'If you do not come with me, your brother *will* die.' The Augur senses my conflict and presses. 'Is that what you want?'

He heads towards the gates, and after a dreadful few moments of indecision, I turn away from Veturius and follow him. Elias is resourceful – he might still find a way to avoid death. *But I won't, Laia.* I hear Darin. *Not unless you help me.*

The legionnaires manning Blackcliff's gates seem not to see us as we pass out of the school, and I wonder if Cain has used Augur sorcery on them. Why is he helping me? What does he want in exchange?

If he can read my suspicions, he doesn't let on, instead leading me rapidly through the Illustrian Quarter and deep into the sweltering streets of Serra. His route is so convoluted that it seems for a time as if he has no destination in mind. No one looks twice at us, and no one speaks of the Emperor's death or of Marcus's coronation. The news hasn't yet leaked out.

The silence between Cain and me stretches until I think it will fall and shatter on the ground. How will I get away from him and find the Resistance? I dash the thought from my head, lest the Augur pick it out – but then, I've already thought it, so it must be too late. I look askance at him. Is he reading all of this? Can he hear every thought?

'It's not really mind-reading,' Cain murmurs, and I wrap my arms around myself and lean away, though I know doing so won't shield my thoughts any better.

'Thoughts are complex,' he explains. 'Messy. They are tangled as a jungle of vines, layered like the sediment in a canyon. We must weave through the vines, trace the sediment. We must translate and decipher.'

Ten hells. What does he know about me? Everything? Nothing?

'Where to begin, Laia? I know your every sinew is turned towards finding and saving your brother. I know your parents were the most powerful leaders the Resistance ever had. I know you're falling for a Resistance fighter named Keenan but that you don't trust him to love you back. I know you're a Resistance spy.'

'But if you know I'm a spy—'

'I know,' Cain says, 'but it matters not.' Ancient sadness flares in his eyes, as if he's remembering someone long dead. 'Other thoughts speak more clearly of who you are, what you are, in your deepest heart. In the night, your loneliness crushes you, as if the sky itself has swooped down to smother you in its cold arms—'

'That's not – I—'

But Cain ignores me, his red eyes unfocused, his voice jagged, as if he is speaking his own innermost secrets instead of mine.

'You fear you will never have your mother's courage. You fear your cowardice will spell the doom of your brother. You yearn to understand why your parents chose the Resistance over their children. Your heart wants Keenan, and yet your body is alight when Elias Veturius is near. You—'

'Stop.' It's unbearable, this knowledge of me from someone who isn't me.

'You are full, Laia. Full of life and dark and strength and spirit. You are in our dreams. You will burn, for you are an ember in the ashes. That is your destiny. Being a Resistance spy – that is the smallest part of you. That is nothing.'

I scramble for words but find none. It is wrong that he knows so much of me and I know nothing of him in return.

'There's nothing to me that is worth anything, Laia,' the Augur says. 'I am an error, a mistake. I am failure and malice, greed and hatred. I am guilty. We are, all of us Augurs, guilty.' At my confusion, he sighs. His black eyes meet mine, and his description of himself and his kindred fades from my mind like a dream upon waking.

'We are here,' he says.

I look around uncertainly. A quiet street stretches in front of me with a row of identical houses on each side. The Mercator Quarter? Or perhaps the Foreign Quarter? I can't tell. The few people on the streets are too far away to recognize.

'What – what are we doing here?'

'If you wish to save your brother, you need to speak with the Resistance,' he says. 'I have brought you to them.' He nods to the street before me. 'Seventh house on the right. In the basement. The door's unlocked.'

'Why are you helping me?' I ask him. 'What trick—'

'No trick, Laia. I cannot answer your questions except to say that for now, our interests align. I vow to you by blood and by bone that I do not deceive you in this. Go now, quickly. Time will not wait, and I fear you have little enough as it is.'

Despite his calm expression, there's no mistaking the urgency in his voice. It fans my own unease. I nod my thanks, wondering at the strangeness of the last few minutes, and go.

* * *

As the Augur predicted, the back door to the house's basement is unlocked. I take two steps down the stairs before a scimpoint meets my neck.

'Laia?' The scim drops, and Keenan moves into the light. His red hair sticks up at odd angles, and a bandage wrapped haphazardly around his bicep is stained with blood. His freckles stand out jarringly against the sick paleness of his skin. 'How did you find us? You shouldn't be here. It's not safe for you. Quick' – he glances over his shoulder – 'before Mazen sees – go!'

'I discovered an entrance to Blackcliff. I have to tell him. And there's something else – a spy—'

'No, Laia,' Keenan says. 'You can't—'

'Who's there, Keenan?' Footsteps clump toward us, and a second later, Mazen sticks his head in the stairwell.

'Ah. Laia. You tracked us down.' The older man shoots a look at Keenan, as if he must be responsible for this development. 'Bring her.'

The tone of his voice raises the hair on my neck, and I reach through the slit in my skirt pocket for the dagger Elias gave me.

'Laia, listen to me,' Keenan whispers as he ushers me down the stairs. 'No matter what he says, I—'

'Come now,' Mazen cuts Keenan off as we enter the basement. 'I haven't got all day.' The basement is small, with crates of goods in one corner and a round table in the centre. Two men sit at the table, unsmiling and cold-eyed – Eran and Haider.

I wonder if one of them is the Commandant's spy.

Mazen kicks a rickety chair in my direction, the invitation to sit obvious. Keenan stands just behind me, shifting from foot to foot, an animal ill at ease. I try not to look at him.

'Well now, Laia,' Mazen says as I take a seat. 'Any information for us? Other than the fact that the Emperor is dead.'

'How did you—'

'Because I'm the one who killed him. Tell me, have they named a new Emperor yet?'

'Yes.' *Mazen killed the Emperor?* I want him to tell me more, but I sense his impatience. 'They named Marcus. The coronation is tomorrow.'

Mazen exchanges glances with his men and stands. 'Eran, send out the runners. Haider, get the men ready. Keenan, deal with the girl.'

'Wait!' I stand as they do. 'I have more – an entrance into Blackcliff. That's the reason I came. So that you can get Darin out. And there's something else you should know—' I mean to tell him about the spy, but he doesn't let me.

'There's no secret entrance into Blackcliff, Laia. Even if there was, I wouldn't be stupid enough to try to attack a school of Masks.'

'Then how—'

'How?' he muses. 'A good question. How do you get rid of a girl who blunders into your hideout at the most inopportune moment, claiming to be the long-lost daughter of the Lioness? How do you appease an essential faction in the Resistance when they stupidly insist you help her save her brother? How do you make it look like you're helping her when in fact you don't have the time or the men to do so?'

My mouth goes dry.

'I'll tell you how,' Mazen says. 'You give the girl a mission she won't come back from. You send her to Blackcliff, home of her parents' killer. You give her impossible tasks, like spying on the most dangerous woman in the Empire, like learning about the Trials before they even occur.'

'You – you knew that the Commandant killed—'

'It's nothing personal, girl. Sana threatened to pull her men from the Resistance over you. She'd been looking for an excuse, and when you walked in, she had it. But I needed her and her men more than ever. I've spent years building up what the Empire destroyed when they killed your mother. I couldn't let you ruin all of that.

'I expected that the Commandant would be rid of you in days, if not hours. But you survived. When you brought me information – real information – at the Moon Festival, my men warned me that Sana and her faction would consider the bargain met. She'd demand your brother be broken out of Central. Only problem was, you'd just told me the very thing that made it impossible for me to put up the men to do so.'

I think back. 'The Emperor's arrival in Serra.'

'When you told me of it, I knew we'd need every last Resistance fighter we had if we wanted to assassinate him. A much worthier cause than rescuing your brother, don't you think?'

I remember then what the Commandant told me. *Those Scholar rats know only what I want them to know. What were they up to the last time you met them? Were they planning something significant?*

Realization strikes me like a blow. The Resistance doesn't even know they've played into the Commandant's hands. Keris Veturia *wanted* the Emperor dead. The Resistance killed the Emperor and the most important members of his house, Marcus stepped into his place, and now there will be no civil war, no struggle between Gens Taia and Blackcliff.

You fool! I want to scream. *You walked right into her trap!*

'I needed to keep Sana's faction happy,' Mazen says. 'And I needed to keep you away from them. So I sent you to Blackcliff with an even more impossible task: find me a secret entrance into the most well-guarded, heavily fortified Martial fort outside of Kauf Prison. I told Sana that your brother's escape depended on it – and that giving any more details could imperil the jailbreak. Then I gave her and every other fighter a mission greater than one foolish girl and her brother: a revolution.'

He leans forward, his eyes glowing with fervour. 'It's only a matter of time before word gets out that Taius is dead. When it does – chaos, unrest. It's what we've been waiting for. I only wish your mother was here to see it.'

'Don't you talk about my mother.' In my rage, I forget to tell him of the spy. I forget to tell him that the Commandant will know of his grand plan. 'She *lived* by Izzat. And you're selling out her children, you bastard. Did you sell her out too?'

Mazen rounds the table, a vein pulsing in his neck. 'I'd have followed the Lioness into a fire. I'd have followed her into hell. But you're not like your mother, Laia. You're more like your father. And your father was weak. As for *Izzat* – you're a child. You have no idea what it means.'

My breathing stutters, and I reach out a shaking hand to the table to steady myself. I look back at Keenan, who refuses to meet my eyes. *Traitor.* Had he always known that Mazen didn't mean to help? Had he watched and laughed as the foolish little girl went off on impossible missions?

Cook was right the whole time. I never should have trusted Mazen. I never should have trusted any of them. Darin knew better. He wanted to change things, but he'd figured out it couldn't be with the rebels. He'd realized they weren't worthy of his trust.

'My brother,' I say to Mazen. 'He's not in Bekkar, is he? Is he alive?'

Mazen sighs. 'Where the Martials took your brother, no one can follow. Give it up, girl. You can't save him.'

Tears threaten to spill down my cheeks, but I fight them back. 'Just tell me where he is.' I try to keep my voice reasonable. 'Is he in the city? In Central? You know. Tell me.'

'Keenan. Get rid of her,' Mazen commands. 'Elsewhere,' he adds as an afterthought. 'A body won't go unnoticed in this neighbourhood.'

I feel as Elias must have felt only a short time ago. Betrayed. Desolate. Fear and panic threaten to strangle me; I knot them up and shove them away.

Keenan tries to take my arm, but I dodge him, pulling out Elias's dagger. Mazen's men rush forward, but I'm closer than they are, and they aren't fast enough. In an instant, I have the blade at the Resistance leader's throat.

'Back!' I say to the fighters. They lower their weapons reluctantly. My pulse pounds in my ears, and I have no fear in this moment, only rage for everything Mazen has put me through.

'You tell me where my brother is, you lying son of a whore.' When Mazen says nothing, I dig the blade in deeper, drawing out a thin line of blood. 'Tell me,' I say. 'Or I'll slit your throat here and now.'

'I'll tell you,' he rasps. 'For all the good it will do. He's in Kauf, girl. They shipped him there the day after the Moon Festival.'

Kauf. Kauf. Kauf. I force myself to believe it. To face it. Kauf, where my parents and sister were tortured and executed. Kauf, where only the foulest criminals are sent. To suffer. To rot. To die.

It's over, I realize. Nothing I've endured – the whippings, the scarring, the beatings – none of it matters. The Resistance will kill me. Darin will die in prison. There's nothing I can do to change it.

My knife is still at Mazen's throat. 'You'll pay for this,' I say to him. 'I swear it to the skies, to the stars. You'll pay.'

'I very much doubt it, Laia.' His eyes dart over my shoulder and I turn – too late. I catch a flash of red hair and brown eyes before pain bursts in my temple and I fall into darkness.

* * *

When I come to, my first feeling is that of relief that I'm not dead. My next is of blunt, consuming rage as Keenan's face swims into focus. *Traitor! Deceiver! Liar!*

'Thank the skies,' he says. 'I thought I'd hit you too hard. No – wait –' I fumble for my knife, every second I'm conscious making me more lucid and, thus, more murderous. 'I'm not going to hurt you, Laia. Please – listen.'

My knife is gone, and I look around wildly. He's going to kill me now. We're in some sort of large shed; sunlight seeps through the cracks between the warped wooden boards, and there's a jungle of gardening implements leaning against the walls.

If I can escape him, I can hide out in the city. The Commandant thinks I'm dead, so if I can get the slaves' cuffs off, I might be

able to leave Serra. But then what? Do I go back to Blackcliff for
Izzi, lest she be taken by the Commandant and tortured? Do I
try to help Elias? Do I try to make my way to Kauf and break
Darin out? The prison's more than a thousand miles away. I have
no idea how to get there. No skills to survive a country swarming
with Martial patrols. If, by some miracle, I do make it there, how
will I get in? How will I get out? Darin might be dead by then.
He might be dead now.

He's not dead. If he was dead, I'd know.

All this passes through my mind in an instant. I jump to my
feet and lunge for a rake: right now, what matters most is getting
away from Keenan.

'Laia, no.' He grabs my arms and forces them to my sides. 'I'm
not going to kill you,' he says. 'I swear it. Just listen.'

I stare into his dark eyes, hating myself for how weak and stupid
I feel. 'You knew, Keenan. You knew Mazen never wanted to help
me. And you told me my brother was in the death cells. You used
me—'

'I didn't know—'

'If you didn't know, then why did you knock me out in that
basement? Why did you just stand there while Mazen ordered
you to kill me?'

'If I hadn't gone along with it, he'd have murdered you himself.'
It's the anguish in Keenan's eyes that makes me listen. For once,
he's holding nothing back. 'Mazen locked up everyone he thinks
is against him. "Confining them," he says, for their own good.
Sana's under full guard. I couldn't let him do the same to me –
not if I wanted to help you.'

'Did you know Darin had been sent to Kauf?'

'None of us knew. Mazen played the whole thing too close.
He never let us hear the reports from his spies in the prison. He

never gave us details of his plan to get Darin out. He ordered me to tell you your brother was in the death cells – maybe he was hoping to goad you into taking a risk that would get you killed.' Keenan lets me go. 'I trusted him, Laia. He's led the Resistance for a decade. His vision, his dedication – those are the only things that kept us together.'

'Just because he's a good leader doesn't mean he's a good person. He lied to you.'

'And I'm a fool for not seeing it. Sana suspected he wasn't being truthful. When she realized that you and I were . . . friends, she told me her suspicions. I was sure she was wrong. But then, at that last meeting, Mazen said your brother was in Bekkar. And it didn't make any sense because Bekkar's a tiny prison. If your brother was there, we'd have bribed someone to get him out ages ago. I don't know why he said it. Maybe he thought I wouldn't notice. Maybe he panicked when he realized you wouldn't just take him at his word.'

Keenan wipes a tear from my face. 'I told Sana what Mazen said about Bekkar, but we rode to attack the Emperor that night. She didn't confront Mazen until afterwards, and she made me stay out of it. A good thing, too. She thought her faction would get behind her, but they abandoned her when Mazen persuaded them that she was an obstacle to his revolution.'

'The revolution won't work. The Commandant's known from the beginning that I'm a spy. She knew the Resistance was going to attack the Emperor. Someone in the Resistance is reporting to her.'

Keenan's face goes pale. 'I knew the attack on the Emperor was too easy. I tried to tell Mazen, but he wouldn't have it. And all the time, the Commandant wanted us to attack. She wanted Taius out of the way.'

411

'She'll be ready for Mazen's revolution, Keenan. She'll crush the Resistance.'

Keenan digs around in his pockets for something. 'I have to get Sana out. I have to tell her about the spy. If she can get to Tariq and the other leaders in her faction, she might be able to stop them before they walk into a trap. But first—' He pulls out a small paper packet and a square of leather and hands them to me. 'Acid, to break off your cuffs.' He explains how I'm to use them, making me repeat the directions twice. 'No mistakes on this – there's barely enough. It's very hard to find.

'Lay low tonight. Tomorrow morning at fourth bell, get to the river docks. Find a galley called the *Badcat*. Tell them you have a shipment of gems for the jewellers of Silas. Not your name, not my name, nothing else. They'll hide you in the hold. You'll go upriver to Silas, about a three-week trip. I'll meet you there. And we'll figure out what to do about Darin.'

'He'll die in Kauf, Keenan. He might not even survive the journey there.'

'He'll survive. The Martials know how to keep people alive when it suits them. And prisoners are taken to Kauf to suffer, not to die. Most prisoners hold out for a few months; some hold out for years.'

Where there is life, Nan used to say, *there is hope*. My own hope flares, a candle in the dark. Keenan's getting me out. He's saving me from Blackcliff. He'll help me save Darin.

'My friend Izzi. She's helped me. But the Commandant knows we talk. I have to save her. I swore to myself that I would.'

'I'm sorry, Laia. I can get you out – no one else.'

'Thank you,' I whisper. 'Please, consider your debt to my father paid—'

'You think I'm doing this for him? For his memory?' Keenan

leans forward, his eyes nearly black with intensity, his face so close that I can feel his breath against my cheek. 'Maybe it started that way. But not now. Not anymore. You and I, Laia. We're the same. For the first time since I can remember, I don't feel alone. Because of you. I can't – I can't stop thinking about you. I've tried not to. I've tried to push you out—'

Keenan's hand travels ever so slowly up my arms and to my face. His other hand follows the curve of my hip. He pushes my hair back, searching my face as if for something he has lost.

And then he is pressing me against the wall, his hand at the small of my back. He kisses me – a hungry kiss, unyielding in its desire. A kiss that has been stored up for days, a kiss that has been stalking me impatiently, waiting to be released.

For a moment, I stand frozen, Elias's face and the Augur's voice swirling in my head. *Your heart wants Keenan, and yet your body is alight when Elias Veturius is near.* I push the words away. *I want this. I want Keenan. And he wants me back.* I try to lose myself in the feel of his hand tangled with mine, in the silk of his hair between my fingers. But I keep seeing Elias in my mind, and when Keenan pulls away, I can't meet his gaze.

'You'll need this.' He hands me Elias's dagger. 'I'll find you in Silas. I'll find a way to Darin. I'll take care of everything. I promise.'

I force myself to nod, wondering why the words bother me so. Seconds later he's out the shed's door, and I'm staring at the packet of acid he gave me.

My future, my freedom, all here in a little packet that will break me from these bonds.

What had this envelope cost Keenan? What had passage on the ship cost? And once Mazen realizes he's been betrayed by his former lieutenant? What will *that* cost Keenan?

He only wants to help me. Yet I take no comfort in what he

said: *I'll find you in Silas. I'll find a way to Darin. I'll take care of everything. I promise.*

Once, I'd have wanted that. I'd have wanted someone to tell me what to do, to fix everything. Once, I'd have wanted to be saved.

But what has that got me? Betrayal. Failure. It's not enough to expect Keenan to have all the answers. Not when I think of Izzi, who even now might be suffering at the Commandant's hands because she chose friendship over self-preservation. Not when I think of Elias, who gave up his own life for mine.

The shed is stifling suddenly, hot and close, and I'm across the floor and out the door. A plan forms in my head, tentative, outlandish, and mad enough that it just might work. I wind my way through the city, across Execution Square, past the docks, and down to the Weapons Quarter. To the forges.

I need to find Spiro Teluman.

CHAPTER FORTY-SIX

Elias

Hours pass. Or maybe days. I have no way to know. Blackcliff's bells don't penetrate the dungeon. I can't even hear the drums. The granite walls of my windowless cell are a foot thick, the iron bars two inches wide. There are no guards. There's no need for them.

Strange, to have survived the Great Wastes, to have fought supernatural creatures, to have sunk so low as to kill my own friends, only to die now – in chains, still masked, stripped of my name, branded a traitor. Disgraced – an unwanted bastard, a failure of a grandson, a murderer. A nobody. A man whose life means nothing.

Such foolish hope, to have thought that despite being raised to violence I might one day be free of it. After years of whippings and abuse and blood, I should have known better. I should never have listened to Cain. I should have deserted Blackcliff when I had the chance. Maybe I'd have been lost and hunted, but at least Laia would be alive. At least Demetrius and Leander and Tristas would be alive.

Now it's too late. Laia's dead. Marcus is Emperor. Helene's his Blood Shrike. And soon I'll be dead. *Lost as a leaf on the wind.*

The knowledge is a demon gnawing insatiably at my mind. How did this happen? How could Marcus – mad, depraved Marcus – be overlord of the Empire? I see Cain naming him Emperor, see Helene kneeling before him, swearing to honour him as her master, and I bang my head against the bars in a futile and painful attempt to get the images out of my mind.

He succeeded where you failed. He showed strength where you showed weakness.

Should I have killed Laia? I'd be Emperor if I had. She died anyway, in the end. I pace my prison cell. Five steps one way, six another. I wish I'd never carried Laia up the cliffs after my mother marked her. I wish I'd never danced with her or spoken with her or seen her. I wish I had never allowed my accursedly single-minded male brain to linger over every detail about her. That is what brought her to the Augurs' attention, what made them choose her as the prize for the Third Trial and the victim for the Fourth. She's dead, and it's because I singled her out.

So much for keeping my soul.

I laugh, and it echoes in the dungeon like shattered glass. What did I think was going to happen? Cain was clear enough: whoever killed the girl won the Trial. I just didn't want to believe that rulership of the Empire could come down to something so brutal. *You're naïve, Elias. You're a fool.* Helene's words from a few hours before come back to me.

I couldn't agree more, Hel.

I try to rest but instead fall into the dream of the killing field. Leander, Ennis, Demetrius, Laia – bodies everywhere, death everywhere. My victims' eyes are open and staring, and the dream is so real I can smell the blood. I think for a long time that I must be dead, that this is some ring of hell I'm walking.

Hours, or minutes later, I jerk awake. I know immediately that I'm not alone.

'Nightmare?'

My mother stands outside my cell, and I wonder how long she's been watching me.

'I have them too.' Her hand strays to the tattoo at her neck.

'Your tattoo.' I've been wanting to ask about those blue whorls for years, and, as I'm going to die anyway, I figure I have nothing to lose. 'What is it?' I don't expect her to answer, but to my surprise, she unbuttons her uniform jacket and pulls up the shirt beneath to reveal a stretch of pallid skin. The markings that I mistook as designs are actually letters that twine around her torso like a coil of nightshade: *ALWAYS VICTO*

I raise an eyebrow – I wouldn't expect Keris Veturia to wear her house's motto so proudly, especially considering her history with Grandfather. Some of the letters are newer than others. The first *A* is faded, as if it was inked years ago. The *T*, meanwhile, looks just days old.

'Run out of ink?' I ask her.

'Something like that.'

I don't ask her anything else about it – she's said all she's going to. She stares at me in silence. I wonder what she's thinking. Masks are supposed to be able to read people, to understand them by observing them. I can tell if strangers are nervous or fearful, honest or insincere, just by watching them for a few seconds But my own mother is a mystery to me, her face as dead and remote as a star.

Questions spring free in my mind, questions I thought I no longer cared about. *Who is my father? Why did you leave me to die? Why didn't you love me?* Too late to ask them now. Too late for the answers to mean anything.

'The moment I knew you existed' – her voice is soft – 'I hated you.'

Despite myself, I look up at her. I know nothing about my conception or birth. Mamie Rila only told me that if the Tribe Saif hadn't found me exposed in the desert, I'd have died. My mother wraps her fingers around the bars of my cell. Her hands are so small.

'I tried to get you out of me,' she says. 'I used lifesbane and nightswood and a dozen other herbs. Nothing worked. You thrived, eating away at my health. I was sick for months. But I managed to get my commander to send me on a solo mission hunting Tribal rebels. So no one knew. No one suspected.

'You grew and grew. Got so big I couldn't ride a horse, swing a sword. I couldn't sleep. I couldn't do anything but wait until you were born so I could kill you and be done with it.'

She leans her forehead against the bars, but her eyes don't leave mine. 'I found a Tribal midwife. After I'd attended a few dozen births with her and learned what I needed, I poisoned her.

'Then one winter morning, I felt the pains. Everything was prepared. A cave. A fire. Hot water and towels and cloths. I wasn't afraid. Suffering and blood I knew well. The loneliness was an old friend. The anger – I used it to carry me through.

'Hours later, when you emerged, I didn't want to touch you.' She releases the bars and paces outside my cell. 'I needed to tend to myself, to make sure there was no infection, no danger. I wasn't about to let the son kill me after the father had failed.

'But some weakness took me, some ancient beast's inclination. I found myself cleaning your face and mouth. I saw that your eyes were open. And they were my eyes.

'You didn't cry. If you had, it would have been easier. I'd have broken your neck the way I'd break a chicken's neck, or a Scholar's. Instead, I wrapped you, held you, fed you. I laid you in the crook of my arm and watched as you slept. It was deep night then, the time of night that doesn't feel quite real. The time of night that's like a dream.

'One dawn later, when I could walk, I got on my horse and carried you to the nearest Tribal camp. I watched them for a time and saw a woman I liked. She picked up children like sacks of grain and carried a large stick wherever she went. And though she was young, she didn't seem to have any children of her own.'

Mamie Rila.

'I waited until night. And left you in her tent, on her bed. Then I rode away. But after a few hours, I turned back. I had to find you and kill you. No one could know of you. You were a mistake, a symbol of my failure.

'By the time I got back, the caravan was gone. Worse, they'd split up. I was weak and exhausted and had no way to track you. So I let you go. I'd already made one mistake. Why not one more?

'And then six years later, the Augurs brought you to Blackcliff. My father ordered me back from the mission I was on. Ah, Elias —'

I start. She's never said my name before.

'You should have heard the things he said. *Whore. Slut. Streetwalker. What will our enemies say? Our allies?* As it turns out, they said nothing. He made sure of that.

'When you survived your first year at the school, when he saw his own strength in you, then you were all he could talk about. After years of disappointment, the great Quin Veturius had an heir he could be proud of. Did you know, *son*, that I was the best student this school had seen in a generation? The fastest? The strongest? After I left, I caught more Resistance scum alone than the rest of my class put together. I brought down the Lioness herself. None of that mattered to my father. Not before you were born. Even less so once you arrived. When it came time for him to name an heir, he didn't even consider choosing me. Instead, he named you. A bastard. A mistake.

'I hated him for it. And you, of course. But more than both of you, I hated myself. For being so *weak*. For not killing you when I had the chance. I vowed I'd never again make such a mistake. I'd never again show weakness.'

She comes back to the bars and pins me with her eyes.

'I know what's in your mind,' she says. 'Remorse. Anger. You go back in your head and imagine yourself killing the Scholar girl, the way I imagined killing you. Your regret weighs you down like lead in your blood – if you'd only done it! If only you'd had the strength! One mistake and you've given up your life. Is it not so? Is it not torture?'

I feel an odd mix of disgust and sympathy for her as I realize that this is the closest she'll ever come to relating to me. She takes my silence as assent. For the first and probably the only time in my life, I see something a little like sadness in her eyes.

'It's a hard truth, but there is no going back. Tomorrow, you'll die. Nothing can stop it. Not me, not you, not even my indomitable father, though he's tried. Take comfort in knowing that your death will give your mother peace. That the gnawing sense of wrong that has haunted me for twenty years will be set right. I'll be free.'

For a few seconds, I can't bring myself to say anything. That's it? I'm going to my death, and all she's willing to say is what I already know? That she hates me? That I'm the biggest mistake she ever made?

No, that's not true. She's told me that she'd been human once.

That she'd had mercy in her. She hadn't exposed me as I'd always been told. When she left me with Mamie Rila, she'd tried to give me life.

But when that brief mercy faded, when she regretted her humanity in favour of her own desires, she became what she is now. Unfeeling. Uncaring. A monster.

'If I feel regret,' I say, 'it's that I wasn't willing to die sooner. That I wasn't willing to cut my own throat in the Third Trial instead of killing men I'd known for years.' I stand and go towards her. 'I don't regret not killing Laia. I'll never regret that.'

I think of what Cain said to me that night we stood on the watchtower and looked out at the dunes. *You'll have a chance at true freedom – of body and of soul.*

And suddenly, I don't feel bewildered or defeated. This – *this* – was what Cain spoke of: the freedom to go to my death knowing it's for the right reason. The freedom to call my soul my own. The freedom to salvage some small goodness by refusing to become like my mother, by dying for something that is worth dying for.

'I don't know what happened to you,' I say. 'I don't know who my father was or why you hate him so much. But I know my death won't free you. It won't give you peace. You're not the one killing me. *I* chose to die. Because I'd rather die than become like you. I'd rather die than live with no mercy, no honour, no soul.'

I wrap my hands around the bars and look down into her eyes. For a second, confusion flashes there, an all-too-brief crack in her armour. Then her gaze turns to steel. It doesn't matter. All I feel for her in this moment is pity.

'Tomorrow, I'm the one who will be set free. Not you.'

I release the bars and move to the back of the cell. Then I

slide to the floor and close my eyes. I don't see her face as she leaves. I don't hear her. I don't care.

The killing blow is my release.

Death is coming for me. Death is nearly here.

I am ready for him.

CHAPTER FORTY-SEVEN

Laia

I watch Teluman working from his open door for long minutes before I summon up the courage to enter his shop. He hammers a strip of heated metal with careful, measured strokes, his brightly tattooed arms sweating from the strain.

'Darin's in Kauf.'

He stops mid-swing and turns. The alarm in his eyes at my words is strangely comforting. At least there is one other person who cares about my brother's fate as much as I do.

'He was sent there ten days ago,' I say. 'Just after the Moon Festival.' I raise my still-cuffed wrists. 'I have to go after him.'

I hold my breath as he considers. Teluman helping me is the first step in a plan that depends almost entirely on other people doing what I ask of them.

'Lock the door,' he says.

It takes him nearly three hours to break the cuffs off, and he says almost nothing the entire time, except to occasionally ask me if I need anything. When I'm free of the cuffs, he offers me a salve for my chafed wrists and then disappears into the back room. A moment later he emerges with a beautifully decorated scim – the same blade he used to scare the ghuls away the day I met him.

'This is the first true Teluman blade I made with Darin,' he says. 'Take it to him. When you free him, you tell him Spiro Teluman will be waiting in the Free Lands. You tell him we have work to do.'

'I'm afraid,' I whisper. 'Afraid I'll fail. Afraid he'll die.' The fear flares through me then, as if by speaking of it I've breathed life into it. Shadows gather and pool near the door. Ghuls.

Laia, they say. *Laia*.

'Fear is only your enemy if you allow it to be.' Teluman hands me Darin's blade and nods to the ghuls. I turn and, as Teluman speaks, advance upon them.

'Too much fear and you're paralysed,' he says. The ghuls aren't cowed yet. I raise the scim. 'Too little fear and you're arrogant.' I strike out at the closest ghul. It hisses and skitters under the door. Some of its fellows back away, but others lunge at me. I force myself to stand fast, to meet them with the edge of the blade. Moments later, the few that were brave enough to remain flee with wrathful hisses. I turn back to Teluman. He finds my eyes.

'Fear can be good, Laia. It can keep you alive. But don't let it control you. Don't let it sow doubts within you. When the fear takes over, use the only thing more powerful, more indestructible, to fight it: your spirit. Your heart.'

The sky is dark when I leave the smithy with Darin's scim hidden beneath my skirt. Martial squads patrol the streets in force, but I avoid them easily in my black dress, blending into the night like a wraith.

As I walk, I remember how Darin tried to defend me from the Mask during the raid, even when the man gave him the chance to run. I imagine Izzi, small and frightened yet determined to befriend me though she knew well what the cost could be. And I think of Elias, who could have been miles away from Blackcliff by now, free as he always wanted, if he'd only let Aquilla kill me.

Darin, Izzi, and Elias put me first. No one made them do it. They did it because they felt it was the right thing to do. Because whether they know what *Izzat* is or not, they live by it. Because they are brave.

My turn to do right, a voice says in my head. Not Darin's words anymore, but my own. That voice has always been my own. *My turn to live by Izzat*. Mazen said I didn't know what *Izzat* was. But I understand it better than he ever will.

By the time I navigate the treacherous hidden trail and scramble up to the Commandant's courtyard, the school is still and quiet. The lamps in the Commandant's study are lit, and voices drift out her open window, too faint to hear. That suits me fine — not even the Commandant can be in two places at once.

The slaves' quarters are dark but for one light. I hear muffled sobbing. Thank the skies. The Commandant hasn't taken her for interrogation yet. I peer through the curtain of her room. She isn't alone.

'Izzi. Cook.'

They sit on the cot together, Cook with her arm around Izzi. When I speak, their heads jerk up, faces blanching like they've been confronted with a ghost. Cook's eyes are red, her face wet, and when she sees me, she lets out a cry. Izzi throws herself at me, hugging me so tightly I think she'll break a rib.

'Why, girl?' Cook wipes her tears away almost angrily. 'Why come back? You could have run. Everyone thinks you're dead. There's nothing here for you.'

'But there *is* something here.' I tell Cook and Izzi all that has happened since this morning. I tell them the truth about Spiro Teluman and Darin and what the two of them were trying to do. I tell them of Mazen's betrayal. Then I tell them my plan.

After I finish, they sit silently. Izzi fiddles with her eyepatch. Part of me wants to take her by the shoulders and beg her for help, but I can't coerce her into doing this. This has to be her choice. Cook's choice.

'I don't know, Laia.' Izzi shakes her head. 'It's dangerous . . .'

'I know,' I say. 'I'm asking so much of you. If the Commandant catches us—'

'Contrary to what you might think, girl,' Cook says, 'the Commandant is not all-powerful. She underestimated you, for one. She misread Spiro Teluman — he is a man and so, in her mind, is only capable of a man's base appetites. She hasn't connected you to your parents. She makes mistakes, like anyone else. The only difference is that she doesn't make the same mistake twice. Keep that in mind and you just might be able to outwit her.'

The old woman considers for a moment. 'I can get what we need from the school's armoury. It's well stocked.' She stands up, and when Izzi and I stare at her, she lifts her eyebrows.

'Well, don't just sit there like lumps on a log.' She gives me a kick, and I yelp. 'Move.'

* * *

Hours later, I awake to Cook's hand on my shoulder. She bends down beside me, her face barely visible in the predawn gloom.

'Get up, girl.'

I think of another dawn, the one after my grandparents were killed and Darin was taken. That day, I thought my world was ending. In a way, I was right. Now it's time to remake my world. Time to redo my ending. I put my hand to my armlet. This time, I will not falter.

Cook slumps against the entry to my room, sliding a hand across her eyes. She's been up nearly all night, as I have. I didn't want to sleep at all, but in the end, she insisted on it.

'No rest, no wits,' she said when forcing me to my cot just an hour before. 'And you'll need all your wits if you want to get out of Serra alive.'

Hands shaking, I pull on the combat boots and fatigues Izzi filched from the school's supply closets. I buckle Darin's scim to a belt Cook rustled up and pull my skirt over it all. Elias's knife stays attached to the strap on my thigh. My mother's armlet is hidden beneath a loose, long-sleeved tunic. I think at first to wear a scarf, to cover the Commandant's mark, but in the end I decide against it. Though I once hated the sight of the scar, I view it with a sort of pride now. As Keenan said, it means I survived her.

Beneath the tunic, hanging diagonally across my chest, is a soft leather satchel filled with flatbread, nuts, and fruit sealed in oilskin, along with a canteen of water. Another package holds gauze, herbs, and oils for healing. I shove Elias's cloak on top of it all.

'Izzi?' I ask Cook, who watches me silently from the door.

'On her way.'

'You won't change your mind? You won't come?'

Her silence is her answer. I look into her blue eyes, distant and familiar all at once. I have so many questions for her. What's her name? What happened with the Resistance that was so horrible she can't speak of them without stuttering and convulsing? Why does she hate my mother so much? Who *is* this woman who is more closed, even, than the Commandant? Unless I ask her now, I will never know the answers. After this, I doubt I'll see her again.

'Cook—'

'Don't.'

The word, though quietly spoken, is like a door slamming in my face.

'Are you ready?' she asks.

The belltower tolls. In two hours, the dawn drums will beat.

'Doesn't matter if I'm ready,' I say. 'It's time.'

CHAPTER FORTY-EIGHT

Elias

When the dungeon door rattles, my skin prickles, and I know even before opening my eyes who will escort me to the gallows.

'Morning, Snake,' I greet him.

'Get up, bastard,' Marcus says. 'It's nearly dawn, and you have an appointment.'

Four unfamiliar Masks and a squad of legionnaires stand behind him. Marcus looks at me like I'm a roach, but strangely, I don't mind. My sleep was dreamless and deep, and I rise languidly, stretching as I meet the Snake's eyes.

'Chain him,' Marcus says.

'Doesn't the great Emperor have more important things to do than escort a mere criminal to the gallows?' I ask. The guards clamp an iron collar around my neck and hobble my legs. 'Shouldn't you be out scaring small children or killing your relatives?'

Marcus's face darkens, but he doesn't rise to the bait. 'I wouldn't miss this for anything.' His yellow eyes glitter. 'I'd have raised the axe myself, but the Commandant thought it unseemly. Besides, I'd much rather watch my Blood Shrike do it.'

It takes a moment before I realize that he means for Helene to kill me. He's watching me, waiting for my disgust, but it never comes. The thought of Helene taking my life is strangely comforting. I'd rather die by her hand than an unknown executioner's. She'll make it clean and quick.

'Still listening to what my old lady tells you, eh?' I say. 'Guess you'll always be her lapdog.'

Anger flashes across Marcus's face, and I grin. So, the trouble's already begun. Excellent.

'The Commandant is wise,' Marcus says. 'I keep her counsel and will do so as long as it suits me.' He drops the formal posturing and leans close, the smugness rolling off him so thickly that I think I'll choke on it. 'She helped me with the Trials from the beginning. Your own mother told me what was coming, and the Augurs never even knew.'

'So what you're saying is that you cheated and you still barely managed to win.' I applaud slowly, my chains clanking. 'Well done.'

Marcus seizes my collar and slams my head into the wall. I groan before I can help myself, feeling as if a great chunk of stone has been driven into my skull. The guards unleash a volley of punches to my stomach, and I drop to my knees. But when they back away, satisfied that I've been cowed, I dive forward and take Marcus out at the waist. He's still sputtering when I snatch a dagger from his belt and hold it to his throat.

Four scims whip out of their scabbards, eight bows notch, and all are pointed at me.

'I'm not going to kill you,' I say, nestling the blade into his neck. 'Just wanted you to know I could. Now take me to my execution, *Emperor*.'

I drop the knife. If I'm going to die, it will be because I refused to murder a girl. Not because I slit the Emperor's throat.

Marcus shoves me away, grinding his teeth in rage.

'Get him up, you idiots,' he roars at the guards. I can't help but laugh, and he strides out of my cell, seething. The Masks lower their scims and haul me to my feet. *Free, Elias. You're almost free.*

Outside, the stones of Blackcliff are gentled by the dawn, and the cool air warms quickly, promising a scorching day. A wild wind races through the dunes and breaks upon the granite of the school. I might not miss these walls as a dead man, but I will miss the wind and the scents it carries, of faraway places where freedom can be found in life instead of death.

Minutes later, we arrive at the belltower courtyard, where a platform has been erected for my beheading.

Blackcliff's students dominate the yard, but there are other faces here too. I see Cain beside the Commandant and Governor Tanalius. Behind them, the heads of Serra's Illustrian houses stand shoulder-to-shoulder with the city's top military brass. Grandfather isn't here, and I wonder if the Commandant's moved against him yet. She will at some point. She's spent years coveting rulership of Gens Veturia.

I straighten my shoulders and hold my head high. When the axe comes down, I will die the way Grandfather would want me to: proudly, like a Veturius. *Always victorious.*

I turn my attention to the platform, where death awaits me in the form of a polished axe held by my best friend. She glows in her ceremonials, looking more like an empress than a Blood Shrike.

Marcus breaks off, and the crowd shifts back as he moves to stand beside the Commandant. The four Masks march me up the platform stairs. I think I catch a flash of movement beneath the gallows, but before I can look again, I'm on the platform beside

Helene. The few people who had been speaking fall silent as Hel turns me to face the crowd.

'Look at me,' I whisper, needing, suddenly, to see her eyes. The Augurs made her swear fealty to Marcus. I understand that. It's a consequence of my failure. But now, preparing me for death, she is cold-eyed and hardhanded. Not a single tear. Did we never laugh together as Yearlings? Did we never fight our way out of a Barbarian camp, or fall into joyful hysterics after successfully robbing our first farmhouse, or carry each other when one of us was too weak to go on alone? Did we never love each other?

She ignores me, and I make myself look away from her and into the crowd. Marcus leans towards the governor, listening to something he says. It's strange not to see Zak at his back. I wonder if the new Emperor misses his twin. I wonder if he will think rulership is worth the death of the only human who ever understood him.

On the other side of the courtyard, Faris stands taller and wider than everyone else, his eyes bewildered as a lost child's. Dex is beside him, and I'm surprised at the streak of wetness that runs down his rigid jaw.

My mother, meanwhile, looks more relaxed than I've ever seen her. And why not? She's won.

Beside her, Cain watches me, his cowl thrown back. *Lost*, he said, just a few weeks ago, *like a leaf in the wind.* And so I am. I won't forgive him for the Third Trial. But I can thank him for helping me understand what true freedom is. He nods in acknowledgment, reading my thoughts one last time.

Helene removes the metal collar. 'Kneel,' she says.

My mind snaps back to the platform, and I submit to her order.

'Is this how it ends, Helene?' I'm surprised at how civil I sound, as if I'm asking her about a book she's read but that I have yet to finish.

Her eyes flicker, so I know she hears me. She says nothing, just checks the chains on my legs and arms and then nods to the Commandant. My mother reads the charges against me, which I don't pay much attention to, and pronounces the punishment, which I also ignore. Dead is dead, no matter how it happens.

Helene steps forward and lifts her axe. It will be one clean sweep, left to right. Air. Neck. Air. Elias dead.

Now it hits me. This is it. This is the end. Martial tradition says a soldier who dies well dances among the stars, battling foes for all eternity. Is that what awaits me? Or will I slip into endless darkness, unbroken and quiet?

Uneasiness latches onto me, like it's been waiting around a corner all this time and only now has the gall to emerge. Where do I fix my eyes? On the crowd? The sky? I want comfort. I know I won't find any.

I look at Helene again. Who else is there? She's only two feet away, her hands loose around the axe handle.

Look at me. Don't make me face this alone.

As if she's heard my thoughts, her eyes meet mine, that familiar pale blue offering me solace, even as she lifts the axe. I think of the first time I looked into those eyes, as a freezing six-year-old getting pummelled in the culling pen. *I'll watch your back,* she'd said, with all the gravitas of a Cadet. *If you watch mine. We can make it if we stick together.*

Does she remember that day? Does she remember all the days since?

I'll never know. As I stare into her eyes, she brings the axe down. I hear the whoosh as it cuts through the air and feel the burn of steel biting into my neck.

CHAPTER FORTY-NINE

Laia

The belltower courtyard fills up slowly, with groups of younger students arriving first, followed by the Cadets, and last, the Skulls. They form up in the centre of the courtyard directly in front of the stage, just as Cook said they would. A few of the Yearlings stare at the execution platform with a frightened sort of fascination. Most don't look, though. They keep their eyes on the ground or on the black walls looming over them.

I wonder, as the Illustrian city leaders file in, if the Augurs will attend.

'You best hope not,' Cook said when I'd voiced my worry in this very courtyard last night. 'They hear you thinking what you're thinking and you're dead.'

By the time the dawn drums beat out, the courtyard is full. Legionnaires line the walls, and a few archers patrol Blackcliff's rooftops, but other than that, security is light.

The Commandant arrives with Aquilla after nearly everyone else and stands at the front of the crowd beside the governor, her face harsh in the grey morning light. By now, I shouldn't be surprised at her utter lack of emotion, but I can't help but stare at her from where I crouch beneath the execution dais. Doesn't she care that it's her son who is going to die today?

Aquilla, standing on the stage, looks calm, almost serene – strange for a girl holding the axe that's to take off her best friend's head. I watch her through a crack in the wood at her feet. Had she ever cared about Veturius? Had their friendship, which seemed so precious to him, ever been real to her? Or had she betrayed him the way Mazen betrayed me?

The dawn drums fall silent, and boots march lockstep towards the courtyard, accompanied by the clank of chains. The crowd parts as four unfamiliar Masks escort Elias across the yard. Marcus leads them, veering off to stand beside the Commandant. I dig my nails into my palm at the satisfaction on his face. *You'll get yours, swine.*

Despite the manacles on his hands and ankles, Elias's shoulders are thrown back, and he holds his head proudly. I can't see his face. Is he frightened? Angry? Does he wish he had killed me? Somehow, I doubt it.

The Masks leave Elias on the stage and take up positions behind it. I eye them nervously – I didn't expect them to remain so close. One of them looks familiar.

Oddly familiar.

I look closer, and my stomach seizes. It's the Mask who raided my home, who burned it to the ground. The Mask who killed my grandparents.

I find myself taking a step towards him, reaching for the scim beneath my skirt, before stopping myself. *Darin. Izzi. Elias.* I have bigger things to worry about than revenge.

For the hundredth time, I look down at the candles burning behind a screen at my feet. Cook gave me four, along with tinder and flint.

'The flame can't go out,' she said. 'If it goes out, you're done.'

As I wait, I wonder if Izzi has reached the *Badcat*. Did the acid work on Izzi's cuffs? Did she remember what to say? Did the crew take her on without questions? And what will Keenan say when he goes to Silas and realizes I've given my chance at freedom away to my friend?

He'll understand. I know he will. If not, Izzi will explain it to him. I smile. Even if none of the rest of my plan works, this wasn't all for nothing. I got Izzi out. I saved my friend.

The Commandant reads out the charges against Veturius. I bend down, my hand hovering over the candles. *This is it.*

'The timing,' Cook said last night, 'has to be perfect. When the Commandant begins reading the charges, watch the clock tower. Don't take your eyes off it. No matter what happens, you have to wait for the signal. When you see it, move. Not a moment sooner. Not a moment later.'

When she gave me the order, it seemed like it would be easy enough to follow. But now the seconds are ticking away, the Commandant is droning on, and I'm getting antsy. I stare at the clock tower through a slim crack in the base of the dais, trying not to blink. What if one of the legionnaires catches Cook? What if she doesn't remember the formula? What if she makes a mistake? What if I make a mistake?

Then I see it. A flicker of light skittering across the clock face quicker than a hummingbird's wings. I grab a candle and light the fuse at the back of the stage.

It catches immediately and begins burning with more fury and sound than I expect. The Masks will see. They'll hear.

But no one moves. No one looks. And I remember something else Cook said.

Don't forget to take cover. Unless you want your head blown off.

I scurry to the end of the stage farthest from the fuse and crouch, covering my neck and head with my arms and hands, waiting. Everything hinges on this. If Cook remembers the formula wrong, if she doesn't get to her fuses on time, if my fuse is discovered or put out, it's all over. There is no backup plan.

Above me, the stage creaks. The fuse hisses as it burns.

And then.

BOOM. The stage explodes. Chunks of wood and scrap geyser into the air. A deeper boom rumbles and another and another. The courtyard is suddenly fogged with clouds of dust. The explosions are nowhere and everywhere, ripping through the air like a thousand screams, leaving me momentarily deaf.

They have to be harmless, I told Cook a dozen times. *Meant to distract and confuse. Strong enough to knock people down, but not strong enough to kill. I don't want anyone dead because of me.*

Leave it to me, she said. *I've no wish to murder children.*

I peer out from under the stage, but it's difficult to see through the dust. It seems as if the walls of the belltower have burst out, though in truth, the dust is from more than two hundred bags of sand Izzi and I spent all night filling and ferrying to the courtyard. Cook set each one with a charge and connected them together. The result is spectacular.

Behind me, the entire back of the stage is gone, the Masks beyond it unconscious on the ground, including the one who murdered my family. The legionnaires are in a panic, running, shouting, trying to escape. The students drain out of the courtyard, the older ones half dragging, half carrying the Yearlings. Deeper booms echo from further away. The mess hall, a few classrooms — all abandoned at this time and likely collapsing at this very moment. A gleeful grin spreads across my face. Cook hasn't forgotten a thing.

The drums beat in a frenetic tattoo, and I don't have to understand their strange language to know that it's a breach alarm. Blackcliff is pure havoc, worse than I could have imagined. More than I could have hoped for. It's perfect.

I do not doubt. I do not hesitate. I am the Lioness's daughter, and I have the Lioness's strength.

'I'm coming for you, Darin,' I say to the wind, hoping it will carry my message. 'You stay alive. I'm coming, and nothing's going to stop me.'

Then I swing out from my hiding place and hop onto the execution stage. It's time to free Elias Veturius.

CHAPTER FIFTY

Elias

Is this what happens to everyone when they die? One second, you're alive, the next, you're dead, and then *BOOM*, an explosion that tears apart the very air. A violent welcome to the afterlife, but at least there is one.

Screams fill my ears. I open my eyes and find that I'm not, in fact, lying on a fair netherworld plain. Instead, I'm flat on my back beneath the very same platform where I was supposed to have died. Smoke and dust choke the air. I touch my neck, which stings something fierce. My hands come away dark with blood. Does this mean I'll have a severed head in the afterlife, I wonder stupidly. Seems a bit unfair . . .

A pair of familiar gold eyes appears above my face.

'You're here too?' I ask. 'I thought Scholars had a different afterlife.'

'You're not dead. Not yet, anyway. And neither am I. I'm setting you free. Here, sit up.'

She puts her arms under me and helps me up. We're beneath the execution dais; she must have dragged me here. The entire back of the stage is gone, and through the dust, I can barely make out the prone forms of four Masks. As I take in what I see, I understand, slowly, that I'm still alive. There's been an explosion. Multiple explosions. The courtyard is in chaos.

'Did the Resistance attack?'

'*I* attacked,' Laia says. 'The Augurs tricked everyone into thinking I died yesterday. I'll explain later. What's important is that I'm setting you free – for a price.'

'What price?' I feel steel against my neck and glance down. She is holding the knife I gave her to my throat. She pulls two pins from her hair, keeping them just out of reach.

'These pins are yours. You can pick your locks. Use the confusion to get out of here. Leave Blackcliff forever, like you wanted. On one condition.'

'Which is . . .'

'You get me out of Blackcliff. You guide me to Kauf Prison. And you help me break my brother out of there.'

That's three conditions. 'I thought your brother was in—'

'He's not. He's in Kauf, and you're the only person I know who's ever been there. You have the skills to help me survive the trip north. That tunnel of yours – no one knows of it. We can use it to escape.'

Ten burning hells. Of course she won't just set me free for the hell of it. From the mayhem around us, it's clear that she's gone through considerable trouble to pull this off.

'Decide, Elias.' The clouds of dust shielding us from view are slowly starting to clear. 'There's no time.'

It takes me a moment. She offers me freedom, not realizing that even chained, even facing execution, my soul is already free. It was free when I rejected my mother's twisted way of thinking. It was free when I decided that dying for what I believed in was worth it.

True freedom – of body and of soul.

What happened in my prison cell was freedom of my soul. But this – this is freedom of my body. This is Cain keeping his promise.

'Fine,' I say. 'I'll help you.' I don't know how, but that's a minor detail right now. 'Hand them over.' I reach for the pins, but she holds them back.

'Swear it!'

'I swear on my blood, bones, honour, and name, I will help you escape Blackcliff, I will help you get to Kauf, and I will help you save your brother. Pins. Now.'

Seconds later, my manacles are off. The hobbles around my ankles are next. Behind the stage, the Masks stir. Helene still lies facedown, but she mutters as she shudders awake.

In the courtyard, my mother climbs to her feet, peering through the dust and smoke at the dais. Hag. Even when the world explodes around her, her main concern is that I'm dead. Soon enough she'll have the entire damn school after me.

'Come on.' I grab Laia's hand and pull her out from under the stage.

She stops, staring at the unmoving form of a Mask, one who escorted me to the courtyard. She brings up the dagger I gave her, and her hand shakes.

'He killed my grandparents,' she says. 'He burned my home.'

'I completely sympathize with your desire to stab your family's killer,' I say, glancing back towards my mother. 'But trust me, nothing you could do would begin to compare to the torment he'll face once the Commandant gets her hands on him. He was guarding me. He failed. My mother hates failure.'

Laia glares at the Mask for a second more before giving me a quick nod. As we duck through the arches at the base of the belltower, I look over my shoulder. My stomach sinks. Helene is staring straight at me. Our eyes lock for a moment.

Then I turn and push open the doors to a classroom building. Students rush through the corridors, but they're mostly Yearlings, and none of them look twice at us. The structure rumbles ominously.

'What the hell did you do to this place?'

'Set charges in sandbags all over the courtyard. And – and there might be some explosives in other places. Like the mess hall. And the amphitheatre. And the Commandant's house,' she says, quickly adding, 'All empty. Didn't want to kill anyone, just create a distraction. Also . . . I'm sorry I held a knife to you.' She looks embarrassed. 'I wanted to make sure you'd say yes.'

'Don't be sorry.' I look around for the clearest exit, but most are flooded with students. 'You'll be holding a knife to more than one throat before this is all over. You'll need to practise technique, though. I could have disarmed you—'

'Elias?'

It's Dex. Faris stands behind him open-mouthed, flummoxed at finding me alive, chain-free, and standing hand-in-hand with a Scholar girl. For a second, I think I'm going to have to fight them. But then Faris grabs Dex and uses sheer bulk to turn him around and shove him into the crowd, away from me. He looks over his shoulder once. I think I see him smile.

Laia and I burst from the building and skid down a grassy slope. I make for the doors of a training building, but she pulls me back.

'Another way.' Her chest heaves from the running. 'That building—'

She grabs my arm as the ground beneath us shakes. The building shudders and collapses. Flames explode from its innards, sending plumes of black smoke into the sky.

'I hope there isn't anyone inside,' I say.

'Not a soul.' Laia releases my arm. 'Doors were barred ahead of time.'

'Who's helping you?' She can't have done all this alone. That red-haired fellow at the Moon Festival, perhaps? He had the look of a rebel.

'Never mind that!' We sprint around the remains of the training building, and Laia begins to lag. I pull her along mercilessly. We can't slow down now. I don't let myself think about how close I am to freedom, or how close I came to death. I think only about the next step, the next turn, the next move.

The Skulls' barracks rise ahead of us, and we duck inside. I look back – no sign of Helene. 'In.' I push open the door to my room and lock it behind us.

'Pull up the centre hearthstone,' I say to Laia. 'The entrance is beneath. I just have to grab a few things.'

I don't have time for full armour, but I buckle on my chest plate and bracers. Then I find a cloak and strap on my knives. My Teluman blades are long gone, abandoned on the dais of the amphitheatre yesterday. I feel a pang of loss. The Commandant has probably claimed them by now.

From my bureau, I pull out the wooden token given to me by Afya Ara-Nur. It marks a favour owed, and Laia and I will need all the favours we can get in the days to come. As I pocket it, someone pounds on the door.

'Elias.' Helene's voice is pitched low. 'I know you're in there. Open up. I'm alone.'

I stare at the door. She swore fealty to Marcus. She nearly took my head off minutes ago. And from how quickly she caught up to us, it's clear she came after me like a hound after a fox. Why? Why do I matter so little to her, after everything we've been through?

Laia's got the hearthstone up. She looks between me and the door.

'Don't open it.' She sees my indecision. 'You didn't see her before your execution, Elias. She was calm. Like . . . like she wanted to do it.'

'I have to ask her why.' I know when I say the words that this will be the life or death of me, what happens now. 'She's my oldest friend. I have to understand.'

'Open up.' Helene bangs on the door again. 'In the name of the Emperor—'

'The Emperor?' I yank open the door, dagger in hand. 'You mean the lowborn, murdering rapist who's been trying to kill us for weeks?'

'That's the one,' Helene says. She slips under my arm, her scims still in their sheaths, and hands me, to my astonishment, the Teluman blades. 'You know, you sound just like your grandfather. Even when I was smuggling him out of the damn city, all he could talk about was the fact that Marcus was a Plebeian.'

She smuggled Grandfather out of the city? 'Where is he now? How did you get these?' I hold up the scims.

'Someone left them in my room last night. An Augur, I assume. As for your grandfather, he's safe. Probably making some innkeeper's life hell even as we speak. He wanted to lead an attack on Blackcliff to set you free, but I convinced him to lay low for a while. He's clever enough to keep a rein on Gens Veturia, even while in hiding. Forget about him, and listen. I need to explain—'

At that moment, Laia clears her throat pointedly, and Helene draws her scim.

'I thought she was dead.'

Laia grips her dagger tightly. '*She* is alive and well, thanks. *She* set him free. Which is more than I can say for you. Elias, we need to leave.'

'We're escaping.' I hold Helene's eyes. 'Together.'

'You have a few minutes,' Helene says. 'I sent the legionnaires the other way.'

'Come with us,' I say. 'Break your oath. We'll escape Marcus together.' Laia lets out a sound of protest – this isn't part of her plan. I continue on regardless. 'We can figure out how to bring him down together.'

'I want to,' Hel says. 'You don't know how much. But I can't. It's not the oath to Marcus that's the problem. I made another vow – a different vow – one I can't break.'

'Hel—'

'Listen to me. Right after graduation, Cain came to me. He told me death was coming for you, Elias, but that I could stop it. I could make sure you lived. All I had to do was swear fealty to whoever won the Trial – and hold to that fealty no matter what the cost. That meant that if you won, I'd swear myself to you. If not . . .'

'What if you'd won?'

'He knew I wouldn't win. Said it wasn't my fate. And Zak was never strong enough to stand up to his brother. It was always between you and Marcus.' She shudders. 'I've dreamt of Marcus, Elias. For months now. You think I just hate him, but I'm – I'm afraid of him. Afraid of what he'll make me do, now that I can never say no to him. Afraid of what he'll do to the Empire, the Scholars, the Tribes.

'It's why I tried to get Elias to kill you in the Trial of Loyalty.' Hel looks at Laia. 'Why I nearly killed you myself. You'd have been one life against the darkness of Marcus's reign.'

All Helene's actions of the past few weeks suddenly make sense.

She's been desperate for me to win because she knew what would happen if I didn't. Marcus would rise and release his madness on the world, and she would become his slave. I think of the Trial of Courage. *Can't die*, she'd said. *Have to live.* So she could save me. I think of the night before the Trial of Strength. *You have no idea what I've given up for you – the deal I made.*

'Why, Helene? Why didn't you tell me?'

'You think the Augurs would have let me? Besides, I know you, Elias. You wouldn't have killed her, even if you'd known.'

'You shouldn't have taken that vow,' I whisper. 'I'm not worth that much. Cain—'

'Cain kept his vow. He said if I swore fealty and held it, you'd live. Marcus ordered me to swear my loyalty, so I did. He ordered me to swing that axe at your head. So I did. And here you are. Still alive.'

I touch the wound at my neck – a few inches more, and I'd have been dead. She'd trusted the Augurs with everything – her life, my life. But then, that's who Helene is: her faith is steadfast. Her loyalty. Her strength. *They always underestimate me.* I'd underestimated her more than anyone.

Cain and the other Augurs saw it all. When he told me I had a chance at freedom of body and soul, he knew he'd force me to pick between keeping my soul and losing it. He saw what I would do, that Laia would free me, that we'd escape. And he knew that in the end, Helene would swear fealty to Marcus. The vastness of that knowledge staggers me. For the first time, I catch a tiny glimpse of the burden the Augurs must live with.

There is no time to wonder at such things now. The barracks doors creak open, and somebody barks orders. Legionnaires, tasked with sweeping the school.

'After I escape,' I say. 'Break the oath then.'

'No, Elias. Cain kept his promise. I'll keep mine.'

'Elias,' Laia warns softly.

'You forgot something.' Helene lifts her hands and pulls at my mask. It clings tenaciously, as if it knows that once it's off, it will never get a chance at me again. Slowly, Hel rips it free, rending the flesh of my neck as the metal releases. Blood pours down my back. I hardly notice it.

Footsteps echo in the hall. A mailed hand clanks against the door. I have so much left to say to her.

'Go.' She shoves me towards Laia. 'I'll cover you this last time. But after this, I belong to him. Remember, Elias. After this, we're enemies.'

Marcus will send her after me. Perhaps not right away, perhaps not until she's proved herself. But eventually, he will. We both know it.

Laia ducks into the tunnel, and I follow. When Helene reaches for the hearthstone to pull it over me, I grab her arm. I want to thank her, apologize to her, beg her forgiveness. I want to drag her down here with me.

'Let me go, Elias.' She puts soft fingers to my face and smiles a sad, sweet smile that's mine alone. 'Let me go.'

'Don't forget this, Helene,' I say. 'Don't forget us. Don't become like him.'

She nods once, and I pray that her nod is a promise. Then she takes hold of the stone and pulls the hearth closed.

Ahead of me, Laia inches forward, her hand outstretched as she feels her way through the dark. Seconds later, she drops from my tunnel into the catacombs with a startled yelp.

For now, Helene can cover for us. But when order is restored at Blackcliff, Serra's ports will shut down, the legionnaires will bar the city gates, and the streets and tunnels will be flooded with soldiers. The drums will beat from here to Antium, alerting every guardhouse and garrison that I've escaped. Rewards will be offered; hunting parties will form; ships, wagons, caravans will all be searched. I know Marcus and I know my mother. Neither will stop until they have my head.

'Elias?' Laia doesn't sound afraid, just wary.

The catacombs are tomb-black, but I know where we are: in a burial chamber that hasn't been patrolled in years. Ahead of us are three entrances, two that are blocked and one that just looks blocked.

'I'm with you, Laia.' I reach out and take her hand. She squeezes it.

I take a step, Laia close beside me. Then another. My mind ranges out, planning our next moves: escape Serra. Survive the road north. Break into Kauf. Save Laia's brother.

There will be so much more in between. So much uncertainty. I don't know if we'll survive the catacombs, let alone the rest of it.

But it doesn't matter. For now, these steps are enough. These first few precious steps into darkness. Into the unknown.

Into freedom.

Acknowledgements

My fervent thanks, first and always, to my parents: my mother, my north star, my safe place, for being the exact opposite of the Commandant; and my father, who taught me the meaning of perseverance and faith, and who never once doubted me.

My husband, Kashi, is my greatest defender and the most fearless man I know. Thank you for convincing me to climb this mountain and for carrying me when I fell. To my boys, my inspirations: here's hoping you grow up to have Elias's courage, Laia's determination, and Helene's capacity to love.

Haroon, trailblazer and purveyor of fine music, thank you for having my back like no one else, and for reminding me what it means to be family. Amer, personal Gandalf and perfect human, thank you for a thousand things, but most of all for teaching me to believe in myself.

My deepest appreciation to: Alexandra Machinist – ninja-agent, slayer of doubt, and answerer of 32,101 questions – I'm in awe of you. Thank you for your unshakeable belief in this book; Cathy Yardley, whose guidance has changed my life – I'm honoured to have you as a mentor and a friend; Stephanie Koven, my tireless international champion – thank you for helping me share my book with the world; and Kathleen Miller, whose friendship is a most precious gift.

I couldn't imagine a better publishing home than Penguin. My thanks to Don Weisberg, Ben Schrank, Gillian Levinson (who loves me, even when I send her fourteen emails in one day), Shanta Newlin, Erin Berger, Emily Romero, Felicia Frazier, Emily Osborne, Casey McIntyre, Jessica Shoffel, Lindsay Boggs, and the remarkable people in sales, marketing, and publicity who championed this book.

For their steadfast faith in me, I owe a debt of gratitude to my family: Uncle and Auntie Tahir; Heelah, Imaan, and Armaan Saleem; Tala Abbasi; and Lilly, Zoey, and Bobby.

My heartfelt thanks to Saul Jaeger, Stacey LaFreniere, Connor Nunley, and Jason Roldan for their service to their country and for showing me what it means to have the soul of a warrior.

The maps you see in this book are by Jonathan Roberts, cartographer extraordinaire. Thank you, Jonathan, for bringing Blackcliff and the Empire to life so beautifully.

For their encouragement and general awesomeness, great thanks to: Andrea Walker, Sarah Balkin, Elizabeth Ward, Mark Johnson, Holly Goldberg Sloan, Tom Williams, Sally Wilcox, Kathy Wenner, Jeff Miller, Shannon Casey, Abigail Wen, Stacey Lee, Kelly Loy Gilbert, Renee Ahdieh, and the Writer Unboxed community.

Sincere thanks to Angels and Airwaves for 'The Adventure', Sea Wolf for 'Wicked Blood', and M83 for 'Outro'. Without those songs, this book wouldn't exist.

Last (but only because I know He doesn't mind), I thank the one who has been with me from the beginning. I look for your 7s everywhere. Without you, I am nothing.